THE ISLE
of Whispers

Veda Raman

To my family.

Prologue

I t stands in the western ocean.

Its coasts, hidden by mist. Secrets intertwined into every leaf, every grain of sand. Whispers of forgotten knowledge echoing through the dense forests.

Only legends speak of its existence. Few outsiders have found their way to its shores, and almost nobody has come back.

Ancient forces are at work here, so powerful they cannot be controlled, so old that nobody knows what they are.

So it stands, untouched by civilization, mysterious and wondrous. It has stories to tell, if you are willing to listen.

The island sees all.

The island controls all.

Amidst the dark happenings, nobody notices the slight change on the island. The subtle shifts of cosmic energy. The power gathering, until it lets out a silent call that echoes across the isle, a call that makes Whispers turn their heads.

Three handprints, imprinted into rock, start to glow.

You, who are being called. You do not know what is about to happen. You do not know that your lives will change forever.

Many, many miles away, three young humans feel something strange. They are at a gala, clothed in silk, jewels, and despair, polite chatter in the air. They all turn their heads at the same time, looking off into the distance.

When the island calls, you cannot ignore it.

Chapter 1

T he sea was supposed to be their friend, not their foe.

The day had started out warm and sunny, the oceans calm. A few puffy clouds gathered overhead, and a larger gathering of clouds floated in the distance, on the line between the sky and the water.

Kiera slipped off her sandals and sat down on the edge of the boat, dragging her toes through the cool water. The gentle swish of the waves lapping at the boat was calming, the whispers of the sea steady and hypnotic.

"Why, Kiera, you're dressed too nicely for a journey out at sea," a voice teased behind her. She turned, smirking, as Aaron sat down next to her.

"Why, Aaron, if you're here, who's driving the boat?" she retorted, gently splashing his shoe with her foot.

"I let the sea drive," he explained grandly. "It's a tried and true method."

Kiera rolled her eyes. "Perfect. When we wreck, should I thank the sea personally, or write it a note?" She glanced over at Evannah. "And besides, I'm not dressed nearly as nicely as your sister." It was true, while Kiera had twisted her hair into the traditional court braid, Evannah had put on a long white dress that was definitely not appropriate for sailing. But it did sound like Aaron was giving her a compliment.

Anyway, Kiera had never fit in with the court like Evannah had. They had always had too much to say about her boundless energy. And that wouldn't work for a lady of the Neomerican court.

They would have much preferred a girl like Evannah, a girl who had had her once strong and bold personality beaten out of her until she was an obedient young lady. A polite, somewhat bland one, to Kiera's standards.

Evannah walked over to sit beside them, hands neatly folded in her lap. Best friends since childhood, Kiera and Evannah had been raised side by side in the glittering, suffocating halls of Neomerica's royal court.

Their parents were powerful advisors to the nation's leaders—wealthy, polished, and perfectly at home in a world of politics and power plays.

That was part of the reason that they were currently traveling through the ocean, just the three of them, far away from everything they knew. Just the three of them, and the freedom they weren't supposed to have.

Evannah stared off into the distance thoughtfully, unnaturally still. Evannah and Aaron were twins, and somehow managed to look really similar and completely different at the same time.

They had the same features, face, and structure, both taller than Kiera. Evannah looked like a typical North Neomerica, with her pale skin and long dark hair. Aaron, on the other hand, looked like his mother, dark hair and bronze skin. Kiera had never met the twins' mother; Aalliah, the former High Courtieress, had died when they were babies. But she had had Aaron's dark brown eyes tinted golden.

It was those eyes she looked into right now. She couldn't meet Evannah's ice blue ones.

Not knowing what she knew.

Evannah lifted a hand to point toward the distance. "Storm on the horizon," she commented. Kiera hadn't noticed, but it was true, dark clouds had gathered into shadowy shapes where the water met the sky, so far away it was hard to accept as true when it was so sunny and beautiful now.

Aaron looked genuinely worried. "I'd better go prepare the boat," he told them, and hurried off.

Then it was just Kiera and Evannah, gazing into the distance. Kiera fought the urge to fidget. She had never been nervous around her best friend, but then again, she had never kept a secret this big from her either.

Maybe Evah wouldn't care?

No, Kiera told herself, that was wishful thinking. This was the truth about Evannah's legacy, her entire future. Kiera couldn't meet her eyes. Not today. Maybe not ever.

Until then, Kiera was going to bury all court-related information to the very back of her mind and enjoy the precious time the three of them had together.

It might be the last they ever had.

She tore her thoughts away from that subject and tried to make conversation. "I still can't believe your dad let us do this."

Evannah turned her gaze from the ocean to meet Kiera's green eyes.

"I know, it shocks me too." She was quiet for a few minutes, then added in a lower voice, "I believe he meant it as a test."

"What do you mean?" Kiera asked, startled.

"If we come back, we are worthy. If not..." Her voice trailed off, but the silence spoke for itself.

Against all odds, Lord Cyrus, Evannah and Aaron's father, had approved their solo journey.

The idea had begun at the Blossom Gala, an annual event to honor spring. Kiera, Aaron, and Evannah would all have their eighteenth birthday within the next few months, the age of initiation into the court. And while it should be an honor, it would be the end of their childhood, their freedom, *themselves*.

While it was rare, youths nearing their initiation would occasionally be sent on independent voyages or missions to prove their worth. They'd all felt an itch, a burning desire to get away. So they'd asked for one final adventure: an ocean voyage to explore the unmapped islands far off the coast of Neomerica.

To their astonishment, Lord Cyrus had agreed. A month later, they had set off unaccompanied on a fully stocked boat. They had been at sea for many days, and the islands should be near.

A huge gust of wind blew at the boat, rocking it slightly and causing Kiera's hair to fly wildly around her face. It looked like the storm was headed closer.

"Look!" Evannah said, a bit of excitement leaking into her voice. Kiera followed her pointed finger across the ocean, slightly to the right. There it finally was.

"Land!"

It was just a sliver of land, far away, a tiny silhouette against the now cloudy sky.

"Hmm," Aaron commented, joining them again and following their gaze. "There's something... odd about it, isn't there?"

Kiera tilted her head. The longer she stared at the little island, the more she agreed there was something...off. Maybe it was the way it was shaped, like its edges were flowing into the ocean itself. But it was hard to tell from so far away.

"I guess," she agreed. Just then, another stronger gust of wind shoved the boat, making them rock violently and drift closer in the direction of the island.

"Whoa!" Aaron exclaimed, toppling over. Kiera and Evannah grabbed the railing to keep from falling into the sea, and held tight while the boat rocked for a few more seconds.

"The storm is getting too close," Evannah murmured.

"Yeah," Aaron agreed, "I think we'd better go inside."

They went inside the boat, where through windows they watched the sky get gradually covered with clouds. She fingered the pin on her top nervously. It was the court pin, the symbol of court youth.

Hours passed, and the warmth changed into a cold, and that changed into a freezing cold so sharp that it bit at your face and fingers. The sun began to set and the sky turned dark.

Kiera, Evannah, and Aaron shut all doors and windows in an effort to stay warm. It was by far the coldest night they had had so far on the ship, and it had begun to rain as well. Unable to sleep because of the violent rocking of the boat, they gathered in the sitting room.

Kiera stared out the window, a blanket wrapped around her shoulders. In the distance, a bright, jagged line appeared, blurred among the raindrops, then disappeared just as fast. Lightning.

The waves had begun to pick up as well. The boat was being tossed around now. Waves were crashing onto the deck of the boat, and it was a miracle that the indoor section hadn't been flooded yet. The three friends were quiet throughout this, but when a wave so big it nearly knocked over the boat hit, everyone screamed. Kiera sprang to her feet.

"I think we're going to have to hit the emergency communication button," Aaron told them.

Kiera's voice was steady, but her knuckles were white on the chair arm. "Do it." Hitting the button would let everyone know they couldn't handle themselves out in the world, but right now, staying alive was more important.

Aaron walked to the front of the boat, stumbling with every rock. Kiera sprang to her feet and followed him as he finally reached the control panel and shakily pulled himself onto a chair. He lifted a finger and clicked the big red button.

Nothing happened.

He clicked it again, growing pale.

"Should something... be happening?" Evannah asked.

"It should have started ringing, and opened a communication line to home," Aaron explained agitatedly.

He fumbled with the panel, slick with seawater. The silence after pressing the button once, twice three times, felt like it echoed forever. Then his fist struck the panel with a thud that matched the thunder outside. "Looks like we're going to have to brave this ourselves."

Kiera wasn't easily scared. But here they were, alone, in a dark sea in the middle of an increasingly violent storm, and it was hard not to feel a shiver of fear. She walked back to their spot in the sitting room.

But on her way back, her foot splashed in a puddle. "Wait..." she said, confused. "It's wet," she observed, dipping her finger in it.

Across the room, Evannah's head shot up. "Oh no," she gasped, realization dawning on her.

There was a crack, and water started flooding into the room. The faintly muffled din of the storm grew louder, and the crashing of waves became deafening.

Kiera screamed. "Get to higher ground!"

"What higher ground? We're in a boat!" Evannah yelled back. Water was attacking their legs and swirling around what was previously the pristine floor of their boat. It was up to their ankles and quickly rising.

Aaron cried out as the glass wall protecting the control panel shattered by the pressure of the waves, which knocked him across the room and rushed over him. Kiera struggled to get across the boat to help him, but eventually reached and pulled him up.

There was another loud crack and the sound of shattering glass as the right wall broke and another wave of water flooded in. Now the water had almost reached their knees, and furniture had started floating around alongside pieces of glass. Evannah gripped the sofa desperately to prevent herself from being pulled through the destroyed wall into the ocean.

Outside the boat was tossed from wave to wave, heightening the chaos inside. When the boat was knocked up high by a particularly big wave and fell back down, Kiera was flung into the nearest wall. She slammed into it and collapsed on the ground. Her head was pounding from the impact, and couldn't find the energy to get up against the rushing water on the floor. In a matter of minutes their safe haven had transformed into a nightmare.

"Stay together!" she yelled to Aaron and Evannah, although the sound of crashing waves was so loud that it drowned out all other noise. She could barely hear herself.

A huge wave, the biggest one Kiera had ever seen, lifted up the boat until it was almost vertical. Her stomach lurched as she involuntarily slid across the floor.

Then with a thunderously loud crack, the boat was flipped over and tossed across the waves.

Kiera screamed as the boat fell apart, and she was plunged into the dark ocean.

Chapter 2

Dark water closed over Aaron's head as he was thrown violently into the ocean. The world was pitch-black. He couldn't tell the difference between left and right, up and down. He was stuck in a cold world of darkness. It was so, so cold. He thrashed, unable to breathe.

Kicking his legs, he managed to reach the surface to take a huge gulp of air. Another wave crashed over his head and forced him back under. He was trapped again in the dark space. The shock of hitting the water made his face sting and he flailed to find the surface again. Every time he managed to push himself up, another wave knocked him under, and the current dragged him in different directions.

"Evannah!" he gasped, paddling weakly, trying to stay afloat. "Kiera!"

"Aaron!" came a faint cry from far to the right. Aaron took a deep breath, then started kicking fiercely and propelling himself across the sea.

A sharp piece of debris from the boat struck him in the side, and he cried out in pain. Clutching his side, he pulled the water with his remaining arm in an effort to get to whoever was calling his name. He felt breathless and dizzy, but he kept swimming. It was misty outside, and the fog clouded his vision and made it hard to see.

"Aaron!" he heard again, much closer this time. It was Kiera. She was hanging on to one of the wooden emergency supply crates to stay afloat. Her beautiful braid had unraveled, and her light brown locks were drenched and stuck to her face. Her eyes looked wild and terrified, just like Aaron knew his own eyes looked in that moment, and her face drained of color.

With a last surge of effort, he reached Kiera and grabbed on to the supply crate too. His head spun, and his breaths were coming shallow.

"Where's..." he panted. "Where's Evannah?"

"I don't know." Kiera looked distressed. "I got tossed from the boat. I barely managed to swim up and grab this crate. I don't know where Evannah went! I've been looking for her, and you."

"I'm going to go look," Aaron told her breathlessly. "Stay safe, and hang on."

He paddled out into the darkness again, making sure he remembered where Kiera was floating. "Evannah? EVANNAH! WHERE ARE YOU?" His arms felt like they were going to fall off, but he had to keep going. His sister was somewhere in this vast sea, and he needed to find her.

The mist felt like it was growing thicker, which just increased his panic. With every breath that he inhaled mist, he felt more nauseous.

"Evannah?" He swam in wide circles. The waves were still huge and crashing, causing him to accidentally swallow huge gulps of seawater and get knocked this way and that, but they seemed to be dying down, which was good. Nonetheless, it felt as though he were being smacked every few seconds.

Fighting the pain, he tried again. "EVANNAH?" Working up the courage, he plunged under the water and swam around, occasionally diving deeper. He came up, took a breath of air, then plunged in even deeper, using all his strength to push himself as close as he could to the ocean floor.

His hand brushed against something deeper down underwater, something soft. His heart picked up speed. Kicking harder, he reached out to touch it again. He felt shock and fear strike him when he realized what it was.

Smooth strands of hair.

Evannah! He needed to get his twin to the surface, fast. His fingers closed around Evannah's arm, and he tugged it toward himself. It was heavy and cold. Evannah was completely unconscious.

Or...

No. She was alive, she had to be.

He pulled with all his might, trying to drag her out of the water. Her dead weight was heavy, and Aaron would never have been able to manage it alone, but fear and terror for his sister's life channeled strength into his aching muscles.

Evannah was sinking down even deeper, but Aaron wrapped his arms around her body and kicked as hard as he could to get to the surface. Pain struck his chest. They needed air, or it would be the end of both of them.

With one last furious pull, he hauled Evannah out of the dark depths of the ocean. He carried her like a baby, which was difficult, because they were the same height, and kept her floating on top of the waves, trying frantically to plan his next move.

"Aaron, here!" Kiera's voice rang out. "You're not alone." He turned his head and squinted, the thick mist hindering his vision. She had swum closer to him. One of her hands still gripped the supply crate, and the other held on to a long, broken piece of wood that looked suspiciously like their dining table from the boat.

Aaron closed the last stretch of sea between them, and without saying a word, laid Evannah down on the piece of wood, carefully making sure her long hair didn't catch on the jagged edges. It bobbed gently up and down with the waves, which had grown significantly smaller. He hung on to the piece of wood like Kiera was doing.

Evannah was still and looked peaceful. Her skin was pale, drained of all color, and her lips were almost blue. But she still looked angelic in unconsciousness.

"Evannah," Kiera looked horrified. "Is she... alive?" Aaron picked up Evannah's cold wrist. He nearly fainted in relief when he felt a faint pulse.

"She's alive." He let out a breath he hadn't realized he was holding. "But she drowned, and she's not waking up."

"She probably has water in her lungs," Kiera told him.

"Of course," Aaron had been panicking so much he hadn't thought of it before. "Kiera, hold the plank steady." She obliged, and he climbed onto the slab of wood next to Evannah. He started pressing down hard on Evannah's chest, rhythmically, while the plank wobbled. After about a minute, nothing happened. "Please wake up," he whispered. He pressed again, harder this time. Her body didn't move. "Come *on*, Evah."

Suddenly, Evannah rolled onto her side and began coughing up water.

"Oh!" Kiera gasped in relief. "Thank goodness!"

"It's okay," Aaron soothed his twin. "We're here. You're okay." He clasped her soaked hand.

Evannah opened her mouth to say something but was cut off by another bout of coughing.

"It's okay, take your time," Kiera told her. Evannah took deep breaths, her icy blue eyes staring off into the distance. Aaron coughed. The mist was now so thick he could hardly see in any direction. His head was feeling like it was stuffed with cotton.

In the silence, Kiera exclaimed, "Oh, look, Aaron!"

And then he saw it.

Dark mountain peaks, rising high above his head. Looming larger than life, they looked like magnificent giants watching over him.

"Land!" he breathed.

"It's not too far away," Kiera cried excitedly. "We can swim. Get to safety."

Aaron felt a weak spark of hope. Maybe there was a possibility they could survive this. A possibility they wouldn't end up dying in this dark, foggy ocean.

Next to him, Evannah croaked, "The island."

"She's right," Kiera said. "That's the island we saw before."

Aaron stared longer at the island. He finally realized why it had seemed odd when they were looking at it before.

The entire island was covered in mist.

The white fog was spread out over the isle like a blanket, shrouding it, making it impossible to see anything except shadows of the mountain peaks. The mist flowed into the ocean. There was no telling what was on that island.

"An island of mist," Aaron whispered.

"That's really odd," Kiera remarked. "I've never seen mist like that before, completely covering just the island. It doesn't feel right."

Aaron thought so too. He felt a strange sensation, like a tugging toward the mist-covered isle. "It's still at least a couple hundred yards away."

"It's our only option," Kiera told him. "Evannah needs rest and something to eat. Who knows, maybe there will be people living there."

"Yes," Aaron agreed. "It's weird, I feel like right now—"

"I *need* to be there," Kiera finished. They exchanged a look, full of emotions Aaron couldn't decipher.

There was a groan as Evannah struggled to get up. She finally managed to sit upright on the piece of wood. Aaron tried to reach out to help her, but she swatted his hand away.

"I'm fine," she rasped, then cleared her throat and repeated, "I'm fine."

"We don't have a choice," Aaron muttered hoarsely. He'd lived long enough with Evannah to know better than to baby her. "It's the island or... nothing."

It was only when his legs began to go numb did he realize that they were still treading in the cold water. "I think two of us can float on the wood," he told them. "We can take turns swimming."

"I'll swim first," Kiera volunteered. "You already tired yourself out looking for Evannah." Aaron didn't want to make her swim, but his limbs ached so much he could hardly move. He pulled himself onto the piece of wood and sat beside Evannah.

Kiera began paddling, swimming with wide strokes, one hand holding the piece of wood that Aaron and Evannah were sitting on. Evannah was so weak she could hardly sit up; instead, she rested her head on Aaron's shoulder.

Minutes passed and they hardly seemed to be getting anywhere. The island still loomed in the distance, so close yet so far. The mountain peaks seemed to be taunting them.

"I'll take a turn," Aaron offered, when Kiera paused, gasping to take a breath. He slid into the water, and she smiled gratefully, climbing onto the wood.

As Aaron swam, he realized the gravity of their situation. Their boat had been destroyed in the middle of the ocean, hundreds of miles from the nearest known civilization. Their only hope was an island that had never been explored before, and their only food and supplies were whatever happened to be inside the one emergency crate that Kiera had rescued. Their communication wasn't working, and they had nothing except each other.

Floating in the vast sea, with the dark sky blanketing them, it was hard not to feel hopeless. Especially when they had drifted into the thickest part of the mist, where Aaron couldn't even see his own hands.

The mist almost felt like a barrier, shielding the island, warning them to stay out. But they had to go on. Even though he couldn't depend on his vision, he trusted his instincts and went straight forward, and knew that Kiera and Evannah were with him, from the feel of the wood on his fingers and the sound of their voices.

Then the mist began to clear, and he couldn't believe his eyes.

The light of the moon lit up the mountain peaks still loomed high above them, but now he could see them in detail. The center mountains were jagged and rocky, a beautiful rough purple color. The surrounding mountains were a vibrant, lush green. A majestic waterfall, tiny from this distance, tumbled down from a peak.

And in front of them, but still agonizingly far, the ocean lapped at the sand of the beach, which was backed by an exotic-looking, dense green forest. A *jungle?*

"Oh!" Kiera gasped, overwhelmed by the sight. A place of safety in this sea of danger. Aaron felt himself being drawn to it.

But when he turned back, the mist blocked all view of the outside world. It felt like they had crossed through the barrier, and were now locked inside.

"Almost there," Evannah whispered, when she slid into the water for her turn to swim. The three were exhausted from the swim, bruised and bleeding from the breaking of the boat, and feeling completely in despair. The only spark of hope was the mist-covered slowly growing closer.

And it grew closer indeed, growing bigger and bigger until the sand-covered shores were mere steps away.

And then, after what felt like an eternity, they were able to stand up in the shallow water and limp their way to the shore. Kiera barely remembered to drag along the crate of supplies

They stumbled onto the beach, and collapsed in the golden sand as a single ray of light reached out across the horizon, breaking apart the darkness.

Aaron lay on the ground, cheek pressed to the cold, wet sand. His limbs twitched with leftover tension, breath shaking as it finally came.

They lay there, silent, for a few minutes, but it felt like hours. Finally, Aaron found the tiniest bit of energy to push himself upright. His head spun and he grew dizzy with the motion.

"We made it," he finally said, breaking the silence. "We're here."

As he gazed around the lush, mysterious island, he found the strength inside him to say, "We're going to survive this and return home again."

Chapter 3

T he island was whispering.

Evannah was certain that no one else noticed, or they would have said something. But it was very hard to miss.

Mysterious, quiet words floated through the air. Strange language was entwined into every swish of leaves, and the whispering seemed to carry in the wind.

"Do you hear that?" she asked, after Aaron had talked.

"Hear what?" Kiera asked.

Evannah shook her head. "Never mind." Either she was imagining it, or only she could hear it. This must just be the after-effects of losing consciousness in the ocean.

The whispers seemed to grow louder and louder until they were all whisper-shouting one word in unison, over and over.

Whisperer. Whisperer! WHISPERER!

Evannah's hands flew to cover her ears. Her twin, Aaron, looked at her in concern. "Are you okay?" he asked.

"I'm fine," Evannah reassured him. "I think it's just water in my ears." That seemed to satisfy them, and they stopped looking worried.

"Okay," Aaron said after a minute. "We can't stay here forever. We need to explore a little and find some food and water. Maybe there are people living here, too."

Evannah nodded, and Kiera's eyes shone brightly at the prospect of exploring a new place. She had always loved adventure, Evannah thought fondly, looking at her best friend.

"Oh, the supplies!" Kiera cried. "There might be something useful in there."

"Let's open it," Evannah suggested.

They were all injured in some way, so breaking open the crate took a while. When it was finally open, Kiera dumped out the contents to find a single canteen of water and two sealed plastic boxes of food, that had somehow survived undamaged. There was also a rope and bag, and a small dagger with a holster. At the bottom of the box lay three fresh pairs of clothes and shoes. Thank goodness, because Evannah's dress was completely in tatters. She realized she had lost her court pin in the mess, but couldn't care less at the moment.

They ate and drank their fill. "We need to ration it," Kiera commanded. Evannah looked longingly at the water, but she knew Kiera was right.

They changed into fresh clothes, and Aaron strapped the dagger holster around his waist and slipped the little dagger in. "Look at you," Kiera smirked, slinging the bag with food over her shoulder. "Court boy turned jungle warrior. Try not to stab yourself by accident." Aaron rolled his eyes at her.

Kiera had released her hair and let her locks tumble freely down her shoulders in a wild way. Evannah let her hair fall down too. In their new clothes, light colored shirts and cotton pants, they felt like they were playing explorers. Like it was just a game.

While Kiera and Aaron sat and rested some more, Evannah walked up to the edge of the ocean and dipped her feet in. Now that it was almost dawn, the water seemed to have warmed. The mist still surrounded the island, not allowing them to see past the shoreline.

Would they make it back? They had left with a fully functioning boat, well, somewhat functioning, after Evannah had been through it with, stocked full of supplies and they still hadn't made it. How were they supposed to return now? She supposed they had to think about that plan sometime, but right now, she didn't want to think about home at all.

She turned back to face the island, taking in its foreign beauty. The waterfall immediately caught her eye. It was so majestic. This place seemed so wild and untamed, the complete opposite of the orderly court at home.

From birth, all three had been groomed to inherit that future: silk gowns, jeweled smiles, and a life of rules so rigid it left no room for mistakes. Maybe it was a blessing in disguise they had ended up somewhere so different. Maybe she was trying to convince herself it was because it was partially her fault they had been stranded.

Looking at the falls made her throat ache. The scant contents of the canteen hadn't been enough, and they had to find fresh water soon.

The waterfall, the whispers seemed to murmur.

"Hey," she said, calling the others over. "If there's a waterfall, there has to be a river or at least a pool somewhere."

"Where we can get water!" Kiera brightened. "We can't stay on this beach forever, and it's not like we have a path. So we can just—"

"Walk toward the waterfall!" Evannah finished. They smiled at each other, and it felt like the old days again, when they used to plan all kinds of mischief together.

They agreed to leave after sunrise, and so they sat on the beach, watching the bright sun rise in the sky. The sunrise was a beautiful orange-pink, but something felt off. Why did it feel as though she were being watched?

An hour later, Aaron rose to his feet, gathering their few remaining possessions. "Let's see what this island has in store for us."

They began walking toward the jungle, the sand sticking uncomfortable to Evannah's skin. As they walked, Aaron listed the things they had to do. "First, find water and food. Look for any civilization. If we find food and water, we can work on making a boat or something that will get us back home, or to the nearest inhabited island where we can call for help."

A few more steps, and the jungle surrounded them. They were enveloped by tall trees overflowing with green leaves and vines. Everything was so vibrant, from the dappled sunlight to the growing ferns. Beautiful exotic flowers grew in bright pinks, oranges, whites, and every other color imaginable. Some of them were bigger than they had ever seen, while some were just the size of a finger. The air smelled sweet and earthy and fragrant. It was like nothing they had ever seen before.

"It's beautiful," Evannah breathed. She brushed her fingers across a white flower, and it was paper-thin and soft under her fingers.

"A real jungle," Kiera said. "Like in the storybooks we used to read."

"Oh, I remember those," Aaron added. "I never thought we would actually see one. It's so... intricate. And the weather! It's like the air itself is warm. It's amazing."

Secrets. Power. No one knows what lies here. Evannah hadn't realized that the whispers had gone silent until they started to speak again. Her head darted around, looking for the source of the sound. The otherworldly voice sent chills down her spine.

They are here. They have graced our shores at last. Then the whispering changed into a strange language she couldn't understand.

"Evannah?" her brother's concerned voice jolted her out of the spell. "What's going on?"

She internally weighed the pros and cons to just telling them what was going on. Every part of her wanted to just brush it off and move on. That's how they were taught in the court. Keep pain and problems to yourself, deal with them on your own time, stay disciplined on the outside. Especially for the future High Courtieress. But they weren't in Neomerica anymore.

It took a lot of effort to tell them, "I've been hearing voices. Whispering to me. Do you hear them?"

Kiera and Aaron's eyes grew wide with concern. Aaron was the first to say, "No, Evah. We don't hear anything."

Kiera placed a hand on her shoulder. "Are you feeling okay?"

"I'm fine, it's just..." she trailed off, unable to find the right words for this feeling, which felt like fear and longing and a calling at the same time.

"I think you're still feeling off from the dip in the ocean," Aaron told her. "We're going to find you some food and water, then we'll rest. We'll make it better, okay?" He gently took her hand in his. She nodded.

"Which way?" Kiera asked. "There's not really a path."

"Let's continue in the direction of the waterfall," Aaron decided. "We can go where the ground is the clearest."

They started off walking slightly to the left, on a route that wasn't quite a path, but was free of most foliage. It was dense, and leaves would brush against their skin every few steps, leaving wet dewdrops on their skin.

"What if the plants are poisonous?" Evannah wondered out loud.

Kiera shrugged. "Guess we'll find out."

They had been walking for a short while, but hadn't gotten very far. Evannah could still see a glimpse of the dark gray-blue, mist-covered ocean through the trees.

"Ow!" Kiera yelped suddenly.

"What happened?" Aaron reacted quickly.

"This stupid thorn stabbed me," Kiera hissed angrily, showing them a large, wicked looking-thorn growing from a vine wrapped around a tree.

Evannah felt a sharp, painful prick in her wrist. She looked down to see a huge dark thorn sticking out of her skin. A bead of blood slipped down her stinging arm. "One got me too."

The forest went still.

Then a sinister rustling sound began, slowly. As if something were waking up. "What's that?" Aaron exclaimed, flinching.

Vines studded with hundreds of thorns started curling themselves around the trees, slithering like snakes and creeping over roots and soil until the clearing was completely covered with them.

"They—they're moving!" Evannah cried out.

The vines crept around their feet, causing them to jump back to avoid being stabbed. Even more vines dropped down from the trees to form curtains covered in the sharp thorns, glinting dangerously in the light.

They were surrounded.

Then the deadly point of every thorn slowly turned to face them.

Evannah had just a few seconds to organize her thoughts. Out of the corner of her eye she saw a gap in the thorny vines that they could run through. She met Aaron's eyes and nodded.

For a few moments, everything was deathly quiet. Then Aaron screamed, "Run!" and they exploded into action.

Evannah sprinted as fast as her legs could take her, squeezing through the gap in the vines. Thorns caught in her skin and scratched her, but she kept going. She didn't dare stop, because she could see the dangerous vines moving and chasing after them, slipping over trees and snaking over the ground, their thorns flashing.

She heard thumping footsteps as her friend and brother sprinted for their lives. Evannah wished she could stop for them, but that would slow them all down.

Aaron pulled out his small dagger and started slashing at the vines, cutting right through them. Thorns fell to the ground and vine cuttings lay lifeless. But for every one he took down there were another two rearing up to attack him like a snake about to strike. "Get back!" he yelled.

Evannah kept running. The whispers in her head grew louder and louder until they sounded like screaming. *Use the power*, they said. *Let us come to you.*

A thorn made its way under her foot and pierced her heel through her shoe. Blood dripped on the forest floor as she raced away, in pain.

There was audible pounding in her ears and she ran, and her face began to heat up with fear.

There was a shout as the thorns surrounded Kiera, backing her into a large tree. In one clean move, she snapped off a branch and started hitting them, causing them to recoil. But they were gathering and growing larger in number, and she couldn't keep them all away. Evannah felt sick when she saw the scene and was unable to help.

Aaron was fighting with a fury that Evannah had never seen. He made his tiny dagger seem like five as he pivoted back and forth, slicing at top speed while stopping any vines trying to get to Kiera or Evannah.

In a desperate move, Kiera wrapped her hands around one of the branches of the tree and pulled herself up, trying to climb up it. She managed to reach the branch and scrambled away from the thorns, which were starting to snake up the tree. The branch whirled around in a way that seemed too fast, and Kiera held on for dear life.

She couldn't ignore the whispers any longer. The more they yelled the more that pressure seemed to be building up in her head, until it was throbbing in pain.

STOP FIGHTING.

LET US COME.

Her head was going to burst from the pressure. Dazed and disoriented, she tripped over a root and ended up sprawled on the ground. At a frightening speed, the vines swarmed closer, rearing up like a viper about to strike, nearing its prey, getting closer, closer yet.

LET US COME.

Fine! Evannah thought furiously, pushing herself up. She couldn't block them anymore; she let the whispers flood her mind. The thorny vines were inches away, and she was surrounded on all sides. This was it.

As the whispers in her head multiplied tenfold, singing in strange languages, energy thrummed through her body.

And in the second that the vines were about to strike, the energy exploded in her mind.

It was so intense, she was thrown to the ground again. A blindingly bright light erupted around them and she threw up her hands to shield her eyes. While the light shone, the whispers became yells, and she silently screamed in pain. Her eyes, her ears, her mind, it was all overloaded, she couldn't take it.

She lay there for many long seconds. When the whispers grew silent, she opened her eyes and the light had gone.

The thorny vines lay still and lifeless around them. Cautiously, she reached toward them. "Are they... dead?" She picked one up and it flopped over in her hand, a completely harmless, regular vine.

What had happened? Something had saved them. But the overwhelming energy and power she had sensed... it was unpredictable, dangerous. Maybe it had worked this time, but would the whispers always help rather than harm?

"I...I think so," Aaron responded, from far off. Evannah forced herself to her feet, her head still spinning, and ran over to where Aaron was hobbling. He was cut all over and bleeding, but alive.

She wrapped her twin in a tight hug. "Thank goodness you're okay. Where's Kiera?" They both scanned the forest.

"Up there!" Aaron pointed. They caught a glimpse of light brown hair among the dark green leaves of a tree. Kiera was dangerously high in the branches.

"Oh, be careful, Kiera!" Evannah cried.

Kiera grabbed the trunk and tried to lower herself down. Out of nowhere, one of the branches spun, knocked right into her, and sent her flying off the tree. Aaron and Evannah screamed as she landed with a sickening THUD! She rolled for a few seconds, and landed with a SPLASH, somewhere out of sight.

"KIERA!" they both shouted in unison.

"Hey, look, I found water!" came the yelled reply. They hurried over and found Kiera lying in a small lake. The water was a beautiful crystal clear, and the shores were surrounded by soft grass, smooth rocks, and small pink and yellow wildflowers. Slender purple trees with wispy branches grew around them.

"Are you okay?" Evannah asked, hurrying over to check. Kiera's leg was bent at an awkward angle, and she held it tightly.

"Yeah, I'm fine. My leg hurts, though. Those living snake vine things were CRAZY."

"What even were they, and how were they moving?" Aaron asked.

"Where *are* we? The rules keep changing. So many mysteries," Evannah whispered. She dipped her hand into the pond and let out a sigh of relief as the cool water soothed her scratched-up hand. "How did we not see this before? Was this pond just under our noses the whole time?"

"I have a theory," Kiera said. She paused dramatically, then announced with importance, "This island is *alive*."

There was a moment of silence. "Alive," Aaron remarked skeptically.

"It's true," argued Kiera. "How else would you explain the living vines? And the fact that water appeared just when we needed it? We didn't see it because this pond wasn't here before, I'm sure of it. The island is alive, and it's moving. Maybe it's trying to make sure we survive."

That could explain the whispers I've been hearing.

"I know you feel it," continued Kiera. "That there's something off about this place. Something different. That tree I climbed—it was alive too. You saw the way it moved, and swung me off. No tree does that. How is that explained?"

"Magic?" Evannah suggested, then felt quite silly for saying that.

"Maybe," Kiera went on. "Whatever it is, I *know* it's *something*."

Evannah placed a hand on her shoulder. "Right now, we first need to take care of ourselves. After that, we can find out more about this island."

"Do you think we can drink this?" Aaron asked, tapping the water gently. Small ripples spread across its surface.

"If not, we're going to die of thirst anyway, right?" Kiera remarked. She scooped up water in her cupped hands and poured it into her mouth. "Mmm. Definitely poisoned."

"You need to be more careful, Kiera," Evannah scolded. "We don't know where we are, and *anything* could be dangerous."

You're right about that, a voice murmured next to her ear. She gasped and turned, frantically searching for the source of the voice, before realizing that it was another whisper.

"Evannah, really, what happened? You've been acting odd all day." She snapped out of it and found Aaron staring at her in concern. *Again.*

She scooped up water to drink to avoid answering the question. It was cool and fresh, and eased the aching in her throat.

"Evannah." Her brother was not impressed. "Something happened to you right before the vines died. I saw it. You can tell me."

How can I tell you when even I don't know?

She tried to find the words. "Those voices I was telling you about. I heard them again. They were calling to me, asking me to let them come. I couldn't take it, so I let them. Then there was this flash of light, and the vines were... dead."

She waited for them to brush her off as crazy again. But Kiera just looked stunned. "I believe her," she said. "I think those voices, whatever they were, saved us."

They did save us. They killed the vines. Are the voices I'm hearing good? I hope so.

"You don't think I'm insane?" she asked.

Aaron shook his head. "We were just attacked by living vines. If you're insane, then we all are too."

"Thanks," she said softly. It helped to know that they were there for her.

"Let's rest for a bit," Evannah suggested. "Then we'll figure out what to do."

And far away, someone watching was also figuring out what to do.

Chapter 4

They were playing on the bluffs of West Neomerica, the capital city. A salty wind blew, and they could see the gray-blue waves crash far below the rocky slopes.

"Let's climb down to the shore!" a nine-year-old Kiera suggested eagerly, her eyes sparkling.

"It seems dangerous," Aaron said hesitantly. There was no trail, but there was a narrow, steep path carved into the bluffs. One wrong step and they would go tumbling into the ocean forever.

"But Father isn't here," said Evannah, her hair parted into two little braids. "This might be our only chance!"

Aaron couldn't protest when he was outnumbered, which happened often. "Fine, let's go!"

As they carefully clambered down the side of the sloping cliffs, the castle loomed not too far off in the distance, its tall, gray stone towers watching over them.

They continued scrambling down, shoes skittering and slipping on loose gravel and sand.

Later, they had arrived at the shore, covered in small scrapes from the rocks but feeling like they climbed the highest mountain in the land.

"I told you we'd make it!" Kiera cried happily. It was quite possibly the greatest accomplishment of her short life. She hugged Evannah and high-fived Aaron.

"Okay, you were right." Aaron smiled at her. "Let's play!"

They ran across the sand toward the waves, removing their shoes and rolling up their pants. They happily ran in and began splashing around.

While they played, a dark shadow caught Kiera's eye. A cave! Perhaps nobody had ever seen it, and she'd be the first to discover it.

Then she'd be special and famous, and nobody could yell at her then. All the court members would agree that Kiera's "mischievous tendencies," as they put it, had actually been helpful in the end.

Then maybe she would finally feel like she belonged.

She slipped away to examine it.

The cave was large and dark, a hole carved into the cliff face that yawned its huge black mouth, waiting for prey to step in. Maybe it was a bad idea to go in, but Kiera had never let a dumb thing like logic stop her.

Bubbling with curiosity mixed with a little fear, she headed in, hopping to avoid the puddles that had formed in the wet sand.

Twenty steps in, and she had reached the back of the cave. Though it was dark, the misty sunlight still reached her.

And something on the ground made her do a double take.

There were words written in the sand, as though someone had carved them there with a finger. Kiera kneeled down to read them, whispering out loud softly.

Three born in silk shall flee the storm,

Through wind and waves their fate shall form.

One shall hear the island's breath,

And dance upon the edge of death.

The thorn shall strike, the mist shall rise,

A shadow waits with watching eyes.

But if the wild they dare to claim,

The isle shall whisper their true name.

"Wow," Kiera breathed. Had she stumbled upon a forgotten story? An unfinished poem?

She was momentarily distracted by the loud roar of the ocean. As she turned her head, a mighty wave swept into the cave and washed over the ground. When it receded, the sand was smooth again.

No trace of the words had been left.

She had to tell her friends! "Evannah! Aaron!" she cried, running out of the cave.

The scene that met her was frightening. The twins were together, heads bowed. Their father, Lord Cyrus stood before them, tall and intimidating, his dark hair perfectly combed and his dark blue suit neat. A jeweled brooch with the royal crest was pinned to his collar. It was shining gold, representing his status as High Courtier.

His eyes were sharp as he glared down at his children. "Aaron. Evannah. I expected better from you. Imagine how I must have felt when I arrived early from my journey and found that my two heirs had gone gallivanting by the cliffs."

"Wait!" Kiera yelled, running toward them. "It was my fault, I convinced them."

"Nice try, Miss Carmine," he said. "But my children should have known better. I thought that I taught them better than this."

His eyes bore into their souls. "We are leaving now. You are confined to the castle for the next seven days as punishment. Leave, and you will not like what happens."

They were silent on the climb up. Kiera's only entertainment was watching Lord Cyrus sweat as he desperately tried not to slip.

She had not gotten a chance to share the mysterious words with her friends, but they lingered in the back of her mind, forever imprinted.

Kiera woke up with a start, pushing herself up. The dream, which was more like a memory, was unusually clear in her mind.

They were still in the clearing with the pond. After the vine attack the previous day, they had gone to sleep, exhausted.

Her thoughts flashed back to the dream. Something was poking at her thoughts, something that didn't feel quite right.

It came to her in a flash. The words! She pulled them from the back of her mind.

Three born in silk shall flee the storm,
Through wind and waves their fate shall form.

The words weren't poetry, as she had previously thought.

They were *a prophecy.*

She thought back to that day. She had never gotten to share the mysterious verses with her friends. After they had gotten caught by Lord Cyrus, it hadn't seemed so important to her younger self, and she had eventually forgotten about them.

Until now. The words had come back to her for a reason.

Evannah and Aaron were still sleeping peacefully, so she decided to let them rest for a while longer. They could use it. Getting up, she washed her face and hands in the little pond and drank some more water, wishing for the hundredth time for more food. Going hungry and sleeping in the grass had been uncomfortable, and something she had never experienced before. But they had all been exhausted.

Her leg had thankfully not broken, but still hurt. Sighing, she flopped back onto the grass. If they never made it back, everyone would assume they'd just been lost as sea.

Her thoughts wandered briefly to her parents, Lord and Lady Carmine. She wondered if they were worrying about her. Probably not. In the Neomerican court, families weren't close. Kids were taught by tutors and usually watched by caretakers. Children were more heirs than family members. If she died, would anybody pay much attention? Would there even be a remembrance ceremony for that wayward girl everyone secretly wished to be rid of? She shook off the thought.

She doubted that Lord Cyrus would worry much about Evannah and Aaron. Maybe he would be a little disappointed that they hadn't been worthy, but that would be it. She wondered if Aalliah would have cared about them if she was still alive.

Alive.

Which brought her back to her theory that the island was alive.

It wasn't just that the vines had obviously been living, or that the tree she had been climbing had scooped her up and whirled her around, or that it had tossed her into a water source that definitely had not been there before.

She could *feel* it.

The island felt like one vast creature, watching with a thousand eyes. Some about it vibrated in her bones, like the forest was breathing.

"Island," she whispered, half to herself. "Are you alive?"

Of course, she didn't expect an answer. But when she heard a faint bubbling sound, she turned around to look where it was coming from.

At the rightmost edge of the pond, water was rising to the surface and bubbling out. A tiny spring had appeared, where she was sure nothing but still water had been before. A *response?* she thought, startled.

Had the island heard her, and answered? In a blink of an eye, the spring stopped bubbling. There was no sign that it had ever existed.

But Kiera was sure it had.

While she got up to walk closer, Aaron began to stir. He opened his eyes and pushed himself up, yawning.

He looked around, blinking in confusion. "Oh," he said. "I forgot that we were still here. For a moment when I woke up, it felt like we were still in Neo... still home," he finished abruptly. The word "home" sounded cold and not at all true.

"Is it such a bad thing that we're here?" Kiera said softly, then instantly regretted it. She had the feeling that she had just voiced everyone's inner thoughts that felt shameful to say out loud. Then again, she had never really thought before she spoke.

"Never mind. We should probably look for something to eat," she suggested, before Aaron could respond.

"Yeah. But everything's so different, I don't even know where to start looking. Everything could be edible, or it could be poisonous," Aaron pointed out.

"I can try it," she joked.

"Ha, thanks. We wouldn't want to lose you though," he laughed. Before she could blush, he added quickly, "Evah would be devastated if she woke up and found you poisoned."

"Yup," Kiera agreed. She stole a glance at her best friend. "Do you think she's okay?"

"I don't know," Aaron said, letting a worried edge creep into his voice. "She's never acted like this before. I don't think she would lie to us."

"About the voices?"

"Yes, the 'whispers'. They must be real, at least to her."

Kiera didn't know how to respond to that, so they were quiet for a moment. During that minute, Evannah opened her eyes and sat up, shaking out her long hair. She went to the pond and began splashing her face without saying a word to Kiera or Aaron.

"Good morning to you too," Kiera prompted.

Evannah looked up. "Oh! Good morning." She continued splashing her face. Kiera could tell when Evannah was lost in her thoughts, and today was definitely one of the days. Her friend would probably be trapped in her own mind for the next few hours. Before they left, Kiera had been hoping that this trip brought out signs that the old Evannah was still there. The one who would call out any injustice, even in front of the leaders, the one who would eagerly charge into danger to protect someone else, the one who was so fiery and strong-willed she wouldn't let anybody make her do what she didn't think was right.

It brought her back to the secret she was keeping from Evannah. She had nearly forgotten about it. She shoved that to the back of her mind.

"Now that you're both awake, I have to tell you something," Kiera told Evannah and Aaron. They looked at her, confused. She sat down, took a deep breath, and began to describe her dream.

"Oh! I remember that day," Aaron exclaimed when she set the scene of their rock climbing adventure. "I was so scared, but you talked me into it."

"I can't believe we made it without falling," Evannah commented. "And that Father climbed down himself to get us."

"I was secretly hoping he'd fall on the way back," confessed Aaron. "That would have made things interesting."

"Why are you telling us this?" Evannah asked.

"Well, There was something that I never got a chance to tell you," she said, continuing on.

When she reached the point in the story where she discovered the words, her friends' eyes grew wide.

She spoke the prophecy in a deep, dramatic voice, trying to recreate the feeling she'd had when she'd seen it. As she spoke, she dragged a finger through the mud on the edge of the pond to write the letters out. When it was finished, chills ran up her arm. It looked just like what she had seen that day, brought back after almost ten years.

Aaron and Evannah had twin looks of shock on their faces. They scooted closer and bent over the prophecy to examine it.

"That's... I don't even know what to say," Aaron finally uttered. "I mean... it fits perfectly. 'Through wind and waves? That's obviously the storm. 'The thorn shall strike'? That just happened with the vines."

"And you heard this a *decade* ago?" Evannah asked. When Kiera nodded, she responded, "But that's not possible."

"I know what I saw," Kiera insisted. "I'd just forgotten until now. I didn't think it was important at the time."

"But that means—" Aaron started.

"Our fate was already written," Evannah breathed. She really had a very dramatic demeanor, Kiera thought.

"So what are we supposed to do?" Aaron asked, confused.

"Study the prophecy?" Kiera suggested. "I don't know. It came to me for a reason. We just need to figure out why. Like this, look," she pointed to the words. "A *shadow waits with watching eyes*. Who is that? Oh, *the mist shall rise*. Are we supposed to stop that?"

"Stop mist?"

"Well I don't know, *Aaron*. Do *you* have any other ideas?"

Aaron touched the second to last line. "*But if the wild they dare to claim*. That's basically our only instruction. We have to somehow claim the wild?"

Evannah tilted her head, thinking. "That sounds almost like we're *taking* the wild for our own. Or maybe..." she thought for another second. "Maybe it means we're supposed to *go into* the wild. What if there's something waiting for us there?"

"Someone expecting us," Kiera breathed. "It could be. Maybe we were called here for a reason? Or this was meant to happen. I don't know, I mean, seeing the future? That's impossible, isn't it?"

"Maybe at home," Evannah mused. "Here's something else to think about: who delivered the prophecy? It had to be written by a human, right?"

"Perhaps it was someone who wasn't supposed to reveal themselves to us," Aaron added. "Wait. What if *they're* the person waiting for us here right now? What if they are the shadow who waits with watching eyes?"

"How are we going to find them?" Evannah asked.

"I don't think we can," Kiera said softly. "I think... like when I found the prophecy, the best we can do is trust our instincts, and when the time is right, they'll come to us."

"I don't like this *dance upon the edge of death* part," Aaron interjected. They stared at him for a moment. "What does that even mean?"

"Obviously it means you'll be doing ballet on a cliff," Kiera explained loftily.

"This isn't funny," Aaron rolled his eyes.

"It is if you picture the tutu," Evannah added savagely. It was so surprising that Kiera snorted before bursting out into laughter. Aaron joined in.

"Anyway, I think we should keep moving," Kiera suggested. "Explore, and find out some more. We can leave this afternoon." The others liked that plan, and it was decided that in the afternoon, they would set out to look around the island.

An hour later, Kiera stood up and announced that she was going to go look for food. "I'm coming," Aaron immediately pronounced.

"Me too," Evannah added. Together, the three of them left the little clearing and began walking around in the surrounding forest.

The air smelled fresh and tiny dewdrops had gathered on the vibrant green leaves. Kiera looked around for anything that looked like it could be edible, although she really had no idea what she was doing. Everything she ate back home had already been prepared and cooked. Oh, why hadn't life in Neomerica prepared her for something like this?

"What about these?" Evannah called from further off. Kiera jogged over to see her and Aaron standing by a small tree overflowing with some kind of tropical fruit. She examined the fruit. It was smooth and purple with little blue speckles.

"Looks good to me," Kiera answered.

"Wait," Aaron said. "We don't know if it's poisonous. Let me open it." He used the little dagger to slice the fruit open. On the inside, it was a bright neon blue. "Oh. Definitely poisonous."

"I'm pretty sure it's edible," Kiera argued. For the sake of her empty stomach, it better be edible.

"We should probably be safe. Let's not—" Aaron was cut off when Kiera grabbed a fruit and took a big bite out of it.

"KIERA!" the twins yelled at the same time.

Evannah snatched the remaining fruit from her hand. "Spit that out!" she cried. "It could be poisonous!"

Kiera had already swallowed it. It was juicy and delicious, cool with an exotic taste that reminded her of a plum or a raspberry. "It's okay, it tastes good."

"You can't do that!" Evannah scolded. "Maybe it tastes good now, but it might kill you later."

"You know what will actually kill us later?" Kiera asked, swiping the fruit again and taking another bite. "Starvation."

"I'm serious," Evannah said, looking actually worried now. "It might do some long-term damage."

"Well," Kiera remarked, finishing off the fruit, "while you worry about long-term damage, I'm going to be full and happy." Her friends gave her the death stare while she ignored them and plucked fruits off the tree, stuffing them into the bag that held their remaining food, until it was full.

She took a few more for her hand and continued eating them, finally feeling full. They walked back to the clearing.

After a few minutes of pointed silence, Kiera sighed. "Look, I'm sorry. That was rash, and I shouldn't have done it. Now, do you want one?" She held out a fruit as a peace offering.

"Um..." Aaron was hesitant.

"Come on. I know you're hungry, you can't fool me. Forget about any possible side effects. I'm fine. Now take the fruit."

He took it from her reluctantly and bit in. "This *is* good." Evannah took one too and agreed.

"See? *Thank you Kiera*, you're welcome for feeding us."

"Thank you," Evannah caved in. "But next time, please be more careful. We don't know where we are, or what could hurt us."

Kiera didn't really regret what she had done. She knew the twins needed a push during times like these. But perhaps she had been a little reckless. "Okay. I'll try."

While they ate and drank their fill, the sun grew steadily higher in the sky. "It's afternoon," Kiera remarked, later. "Are we ready to leave?"

"Yes," Evannah responded. The single word was thick with emotion, hope and fear, but most of all, courage.

"Which direction are we going to go?" Aaron wondered.

"I think we should listen to our instincts," Kiera said. "Something called us here, and now we need to figure out what to do for ourselves."

"I have an idea," Aaron added. "Close your eyes, and point to the direction you want to go. We'll see where our instincts lead us."

Kiera shut her eyes, trying to figure out where to point. The safest spots would be the outskirts of the island. But nothing beckoned her like the dense tangles of trees and high mountains in the center of the island. And when was Kiera ever safe, anyway? She swung her hand to point at the heart of the island.

"Open," Aaron commanded. She opened her eyes. All three of them were pointing in the same direction. "I guess that's decided then."

They packed up their things, and holding hands, stepped into the unknown.

In a distant place, high up, surrounding the heart of the island, a figure sat by a small pool of water. Waiting. Watching patiently.

You dealt well with the thorns, my young friends. But will you be any match for what the island and I have in store for you?

The figure watched the blurry shapes of Evannah, Aaron, and Kiera through the water. Curious, they crouched next to the pool when the prophecy was uttered out loud.

Interesting. I have not heard this version of the prophecy.

"A shadow waits with watching eyes."

Well, I guess that's me.

Chapter 5

I t felt like the jungle was eating them alive.

The trees wrapped around them, leaves fanning out in their faces, roots spread out over the ground, tripping them.

Aaron glanced over at the two girls. They were all traveling in silence. When they got a chance back in Neomerica, they would always chat, when a court member wasn't watching, of course. But now everyone was lost in their own thoughts.

Aaron was saddened by how beat up everyone looked after their multiple near-death incidents. Especially his sister. She had scratches and dried blood all down her arms, and a cut under one eye. Her cheeks were flushed red from exhaustion. Kiera still walked with a slight limp from her fall.

Seeing them like this brought back memories from home, of when Kiera or Evannah would accidentally get hurt, and Aaron would be punished alongside them for letting that happen. He felt that he had failed his sister by letting all this happen to her.

It wasn't in his control, though, he reminded himself. This was starting to feel hopeless. The further they walked, the more it became evident that there were no people here. That had been his hope. But he didn't think it was true.

"Do you want a fruit, Evannah?" he asked his twin, offering her one.

"I can feed myself, thanks," she replied curtly. She hated when he tried to take care of her, but he did it anyway.

How long had they been here? Not even two days? It felt a lot longer than that. It was humid, and Aaron's feet were starting to blister.

"What's that over there?" Kiera wondered out loud. She pointed to a gray shape sticking up above the treetops. It was about the width of a tree, and round.

"Probably a rock," Aaron responded glumly.

Kiera sighed. "Wow, what a ray of sunshine you are. What if it's a magical rock? Stop sulking and let's go see!" She tugged his arm forward, and skipped ahead. Evannah quietly followed.

Kiera brushed past a thick spot of foliage, squeezed between two trees, and disappeared from sight. "Whoa!" her voice called. "You have to see this!"

Aaron squeezed between the trees, unsure of what it would be. When he finally saw it, he tilted his head up in amazement.

He had stepped into an enormous clearing, and a massive stone archway stood in front of him, rising above the trees. But the archway was only the entrance. Behind it was a huge structure. Tall, crumbling pillars supported a ruined roof with many layers. Half of it was cracked and large chunks of stone surrounded the ground around it. What was left of the structure was swallowed by moss and wrapped in vines. It looked ancient.

"Wow," Aaron breathed, stunned. "What is this?" The answer came to him in a flash. It was his proof. People lived here, or had, once.

There was a slab of stone on the front of the ruin, almost like a sign. Strange letters were carved into it, in a language they couldn't read.

"Do you... want to take a closer look?" Evannah asked slowly.

"Let's go," Aaron agreed. As they stepped past the archway, the vines began to move, slithering around the stones and curling around the pillars.

"Creepy," Kiera whispered. "Definitely cursed. I want to go in!"

Aaron took cautious steps toward the ruin. It looked older than anything he had ever seen. It beckoned him forward. Slowly, he reached his fingers out and brushed one of the stone walls.

As soon as his finger touched the wall, it was like the ruin sprang to life. The vines began to glow brightly and a strong gust of wind passed through the clearing, roaring loudly.

"Do you feel that?" Evannah whispered. The glowing vines cast an otherworldly radiance on her face.

She didn't have to specify for Aaron to understand what she was saying. The instant the wind had died down, Aaron felt a mysterious presence. It was like the feeling of being watched, except ten times as strong.

Something has awakened.

"Yeah, I feel it."

"The stones!" Kiera gasped, jumping back. Under their feet, a trail of stones had lit up with a blue glow, leading into the ruins.

Above their heads, the strange, foreign language on the sign rearranged into letters they could read.

Temple of Forgotten Fears.

"Should we go in?" Aaron asked. Under normal circumstances, he would never enter a seemingly haunted ancient temple. But it was like the ruin was calling him.

"I think we have to," Kiera replied. They carefully followed the glowing stones between the pillars, where a door might have stood once, and into the temple.

The inside of the temple was just as damaged as the outside. There was no furniture to be seen, and the stone walls and floors were old and cracked. Moss draped over everything. Slits in the stone walls showed places where books might have once rested.

The trail of glowing stones ended in the center of the main room. What was left of the high ceiling arched above them, and unrecognizable, weathered stone statues adorned the walls.

"What now?" Kiera voiced everyone's thoughts as they reached the end of the path. Like it had heard her, the path branched off into three separate trails, leading right, left, and forward. The rightmost path started at Kiera's feet, the leftmost at Evannah's, and the middle path... right under his own feet.

Splitting up in an unfamiliar, dangerous place like this made Aaron want to run away. But they had to stay and follow the path. It was the only thing close to information they had. "Meet right here in ten minutes," he instructed them. "Stay safe." Then they were gone, following their paths out of sight.

Aaron walked along his own trail of glowing stones, through the ruin. It was actually much bigger than he had thought. It must have been beautiful, once.

He walked for a few more steps before his path started to stop. It led him into a separate room, accessible through a doorway on the wall of the main room. The door was long gone, so he stepped through.

Aaron was in a rectangular chamber of stone. Moss swallowed the place just like the rest of the temple. Strange shapes were roughly carved into the wall.

There was a creak behind him. He turned sharply to look. A stone was rolling into place.

"Wait!" he cried, rushing toward it. He was too late. The stone completely covered the doorway, and the space went dark. Aaron was trapped.

"No, no, no," he muttered, trying in vain to push it away. It was no use. He was going to die here like the hapless explorers in stories he had read that fell into a deadly trap.

A rumbling sound began.

"What's that?" he wondered out loud, then began to shout. "HELP! Evannah! Kiera! Anyone!"

"Aaron?" came a faint reply, in Evannah's voice.

"I'm here, I'm stuck, I need help!" he shouted back.

The rumbling grew louder, and he wasn't able to hear the reply.

Then the ground started to shake. "What's going on?" he demanded, although he wasn't sure who he was talking to. The shaking intensified and soon he was struggling to stay upright.

The dark room began to fill with smoke. No, not smoke. It was *mist*. And while the mist moved in, faint whispers began to speak in the background, their words unintelligible. The more mist that filled the space, the louder the whispers grew. It was growing more and more foggy, Aaron couldn't see anything anymore.

Then suddenly, he could see *everything*.

As the mist cleared, Aaron was no longer in the room. There was a *crash* and he was soaked in water up to the neck. The scene before him was familiar, engraved into his memories.

The storm.

The ocean was as dark as the sky, and churned violently, tossing him around. He hung onto the piece of wood keeping him afloat.

Where was he? Had he been sent back in time?

"Kiera! Evannah!" he yelled, trying to be heard over the roaring sea. If this was the past, where were they? This was not what had happened.

"KIERA! EVANNAH!"

"Help, Aaron!" cried a voice, far off. It was Kiera.

"I'm coming, hang on!" Aaron paddled as quickly as he could, fighting the sea again. Where did she go?

"Kiera, where are you?"

There was only silence in response. Aaron looked around desperately.

"Kiera? Kiera! Where did you go? Talk to me!" Only the waves responded.

He continued screaming for his sister and friend, but neither answered. If this was the storm, this was the point he had found Kiera and set out to find Evannah.

He dived under the waves a few times, reaching around. Nobody was there. He was alone.

Lightning flashed in the distance and illuminated an object floating nearby. He swam toward it, and picked it up.

It was a shoe, a white one. He recognized it immediately. It was Evannah's shoe. Next to it floated a tiny metallic object. Her court pin. "No, Evannah, where are you?" he yelled to the wind.

A few yards away, another gleam of light on a court pin. It was Kiera's this time. Her shoes floated next to the pin, but she was nowhere in sight.

"Please, where are you?" he called desperately. "Please be alive. I'm coming."

He was slammed into the water by a wave, and surfaced, gasping for air and still searching hopelessly when an odd shape caught his eye. He swam over, and the shock brought tears to his eyes.

The body of Kiera lay in front of him, floating on the sea. Her skin was tinged with gray and was cold to the touch. "Kiera, no. Wake up!" he cried. She was not breathing, and had no pulse. He knew immediately that she was dead. Tears began to drip down his cheeks.

Another body floated nearby, and he knew instinctively that it would be Evannah. One look confirmed his prediction. Her corpse was lying on its side, looking eerily similar to when she had drowned, but much paler and colder. Death had sucked all the color from her.

"Evannah, please, you can't be dead." He shook her. She was not breathing and had no pulse either. "Get up!"

His friend and sister were dead. And he had let them die.

His arms were burning from the effort to keep himself afloat. He couldn't take it anymore. The ocean was dragging him down.

The weight of the guilt, shame, and pain pulled him under. Why did he deserve to live when he couldn't protect those he loved the most?

You couldn't protect your own sister. Useless. Weak. The thoughts echoed around his head as if they had actually been spoken.

He was drowning and couldn't do anything about it. He closed his eyes and succumbed to the pain.

Then from a far corner in his mind, an echo of a memory. Kiera's voice, during this same storm. *You're not alone.* And something clicked. *You don't have to do this alone.*

With renewed strength, he pulled himself back up. Kicking hard, his head burst through to the air above. Cracks began to form in the sky, and the whole scene began to look distorted.

He didn't have to be strong. He didn't have to protect anyone.

He just needed to *forgive himself.*

With that resolution, the world around him began to shatter into pieces. Shards of sky fell into the ocean, which was getting sucked into the ground. In a matter of moments, he was standing back in the stone room, completely dry. The boulder covering the door slid open.

Evannah watched in horror as a large stone rolled to cover her door. She was stuck.

"HELP! Evannah! Kiera! Anyone!" She could recognize Aaron's faraway voice. Oh no, what danger had he gotten into?

"Aaron?" she yelled back. As she yelled, a rumbling noise began. She heard his voice again, but couldn't tell what he was saying. "I can't hear you!"

As the rumbling grew louder, the room began to shake. Mist filled the area, growing thicker and thicker.

When it cleared, she was in a room she recognized. The Neomerican throne room, with its arching ceiling, formal silver chairs, and walls patterned with gold filigree.

How did I get here?

Her friends were nowhere to be seen. Realizing that she was now sitting, she tried to stand up, but something blocked her.

Looking down, Evannah found out that she was sitting on one of the many large, throne-like chairs in the room. Chains wrapped around the chair and her body, strapping her in place. She strained, trying to free herself, but had no success.

"Hey, let me out!" she shouted, although she couldn't see anyone around. "Why am I here?" It was definitely not possible that she had been sent back to Neomerica in the span of a couple seconds.

The grand doors at the opposite end of the room opened, and Evannah fell silent. A regal procession of leaders and court members entered, taking their seats. All eyes were on Evannah as she struggled to get free, chains rattling.

The last person who entered made Evannah's breath catch in her chest. It was her father, Lord Cyrus. As he drew closer, she realized that he looked different. Older. His dark hair was streaked with gray and his stare looked even colder. He took a seat closest to Evannah.

"Father," she tried. "Help me. Get me out of here." Her pleas were only met with silence.

"Father, please. What's going on?"

Lord Cyrus held up a hand, motioning for her to stay silent. The chains, as well as fear, made her skin feel scratched and raw. What was happening?

One of the court advisors stood up and turned to address the rest of the court. "The Whisperer has fulfilled her role," he announced.

Who do they think I am? The Whisperer? I don't even know what that is!

I have been hearing those voices though...

"Wait," she cried. "I don't know what you're talking about; that's not me."

Evannah was met with hard glares. She had talked in court without permission. *I think being chained to a chair is permission enough!* Her arms hurt in the places where the cold metal dug into.

The advisor continued. "The Island's power is ours."

Evannah froze. *What?* What did this have to do with the island?

She twisted desperately, trying to escape the uncomfortable chains. On her right side stood a tall, elaborate mirror. She turned to meet the eyes of her reflection and realized that the girl in the mirror looked significantly different.

In her reflection, she looked a few years older, taller, with longer hair that fell past her waist. She looked a lot thinner, too, like she had been starving. With a desperate look, chained to the chair, she looked completely hollow.

Controlled.

But what stood out most were her eyes, which were not the blue she remembered. The eyes in the reflection were pale and glowed with a misty silver light. She looked inhuman.

Her father stepped forward and met her gaze. "You belong to the court," he told her. "Your gift saved us. Your freedom is the price."

My freedom?

Evannah's fingers began to tingle. She looked down to see them radiating the same glow as her eyes. *I could break out.*

But wait. This was her home. Her court. Her father. She had finally done something right, she had helped them, even if she didn't know or remember what she had done.

Every instinct from her childhood screamed at her to stay, to be obedient, to listen. *Am I worth saving?*

Then the whispers began, once more. But this time they weren't speaking to her. They were commanding her.

Wake up! Fight! Open your eyes!

And Evannah made a decision. *I am not going to accept being used any longer. It's time to fight for myself.*

With that resolve, her entire body began to glow brightly. She held up her hands, and the chains melted away.

The people of the court began screaming as she stood up, free at last. Lord Cyrus shook his head, looking disappointed. But she couldn't care less.

She raised her glowing arms, and the brightness intensified. She closed her eyes as the world grew blurry. When she opened them again she was standing in the room.

"Hey, let me out!" Kiera kicked the rock that was covering the entrance. *Ow, that hurt.* "Dumb rock! Aaron, Evannah, are you there?"

A deep rumbling started to shake the room. *Earthquake?* The ground shifted.

The chamber started to fill with mist, until she couldn't see.

When the mist receded, she was not in the room anymore. The wind whipped against her face. She looked down, and screamed.

Kiera was on a ledge sticking out from a cliff. It was so narrow that her toes hung over it.

And below the ledge awaited at least a five hundred foot drop.

Panicked, she pressed her back and arms against the smooth rock of the cliff face, trying not to feel like she was about to fall to her death at any moment. Her heart thumped painfully. The ledge felt awfully fragile.

Mist sprayed, and she turned to see an enormous, spectacular waterfall dropping over the cliff, rushing into the river underneath. The ledge extended behind the waterfall, into a cave. A *safe spot.*

She tried to edge toward it, scooting sideways. Her heart was pounding from the dizzying height. She was grappling for a handhold on the rock when she brushed skin.

It was Aaron, next to her. Evannah was on her other side. They both looked awful, with scratched up faces and arms, torn up clothes, and starved eyes.

"Aaron," she cried. "How did we get here?"

Aaron turned to her slowly, to reveal dried blood on one cheek. His eyes were dark with hatred, an expression she had never seen on him. It was terrifying. "Aaron," she said again. "*What happened?*"

"Are you kidding?" he snapped. "You don't remember what happened?"

"What happened," Evannah interjected angrily, "was that you had one of your brilliant ideas and decided to lead us out here. Now we're all going to die!" She pressed closer to the face of the cliff.

"You wouldn't take no for an answer," Aaron added. His voice raised to a shout to be heard above the roaring waterfall, "You never did!"

"Wait," Kiera said. "I don't even know what I did!"

"That's the problem," Evannah retorted with a cruel edge to her voice. "You never think. You just act. And you drag us down with you!"

What is going on?

"Were we not just in the ancient temple?" Kiera asked.

"The ancient temple? That was ages ago," Aaron replied. "So much has happened since then. Too much. What happened to you? You weren't the smartest in the first place, but this is a bit much."

Kiera flinched, stung. She knew immediately that this was not the real Aaron. He would *never* say something like that.

She took a deep breath, trying to sort out her thoughts. The treetops were hundreds of feet below her. Moving meant certain death. The ledge was barely big enough for the three of them.

She had just been in the temple. She had somehow been transported here. Now she just had to figure out what to do.

"Remind me," she said to Evannah. "What did I say when I brought us here?"

Evannah glared at her. "You said that there was something here that would save us. Something in that cave." She gestured to the cave behind the waterfall. "I don't know why we ever believed you. All you've ever done is lead us into danger!"

Kiera fell silent. She had been hurt before, but nothing hurt as much as these cruel words from her two best friends.

"Let's try going to the cave then," she said finally, trying to edge to that side.

Aaron stopped her. "No. We're done listening to you Kiera. Look where we ended up!"

Evannah chimed in again. "Look what you've done."

"Come on," she told them. "It's our one chance for survival!" They reluctantly started scooting toward the cave. If it weren't for the thin strip of rock under their feet, it would have almost looked like they were flying.

Evannah let out a cry that echoed around them. One of her feet slipped and she slid off the ledge.

"Evannah!" Aaron screamed.

Evannah's hands were clinging desperately onto the rock. "Help!" she cried, her legs flailing in the air, panicked. Her fingers were starting to slide off the ledge. She screamed louder.

"Evannah, hold on!" Kiera cried. Carefully, she bent down and grabbed one of her friend's hands. Aaron grabbed the other. They started hauling Evannah up.

A cracking noise made the rock beneath Kiera shake. Part of the ledge was breaking off! "Get to the cave!" Aaron yelled.

"We can't leave Evannah," Kiera shouted back. Evannah was almost there, just a strong pull away.

The ledge broke into pieces, and Aaron went tumbling off. Without his weight helping, Evannah fell back down, her hand slipping out of Kiera's.

"No!" Kiera shouted.

The twins screamed as they fell down, down, down. Hundreds of feet. They grew into tiny specks, far, far away.

They landed in the river with an inaudible splash. Kiera waited, clinging to the tiny bit of ledge left, watching to see if they would surface.

They never did.

No. They couldn't be dead, after all they had been through. What had even happened? Was this real?

All you've ever done is lead us into danger. Evannah's harsh words were trapped in her mind.

One last chance to get to the cave. Holding her breath, trying not to shake, she tried to make her way over.

It looked like she wouldn't make it, but finally, she stepped inside, safe at last. *Unlike Aaron and Evannah.*

But there was nothing inside. *How?*

Evannah had told her that Kiera herself had said there was something inside, something that could save them. She had been wrong.

She had failed her friends. She brought them into danger, acting before thinking, even if she didn't remember it.

She dropped to her knees in the empty cave. What was she going to do now? Die here alone?

Words caught her eye on the ground. It was the words from the prophecy she had discovered.

I found the prophecy. It came to me.

Kiera stood up, clenching her fists. *I found the words. I'm not a mistake.*

She had saved her friends by finding them water. Her courage and determination outshadowed her recklessness.

I led us this far.

With that resolve, the cave lit up. She turned quickly to see that a beautiful diamond had appeared, floating in the middle of the cave, gleaming with light.

I was right. There was something here!

She lunged toward the diamond, her fingers wrapping around the shimmering object. The minute she made contact with it, the air twisted.

The world whirled around in a dizzying blur of motion, and soon she was standing back in the room of the temple. The stone rolled away, letting her go free.

Chapter 6

Evannah bolted from the room. Images from whatever illusion she had been in still flashed in her mind. Had Aaron and Kiera been through the same ordeal?

"Kiera? Aaron? Are you there?"

Aaron jogged out of his own room, his face lighting up with relief when he saw his sister. "Evannah, you're safe!"

Kiera walked in their direction, meeting them in the main part of the temple. Her face looked paler than usual, and sweaty. Her eyes were wide. She almost never looked this scared. "Thank goodness you're here," she declared. "The weirdest thing happened."

"You were somehow transported back in time?" Aaron guessed.

"Almost!" Kiera replied, looking surprised. "I was suddenly on a cliff. With both of you. Then..." her voice trailed off.

"Me too," Evannah added quietly. "I was somewhere completely different. What happened?" The whispers still chattered in the back of her mind.

Congratulations. A deep, rich voice echoed loudly around them, seeming to come from everywhere at once. The whispers fell silent.

Aaron shrieked and grabbed Evannah's arm. Kiera snickered at him. "Who was that?" he called.

You have survived the Temple of Forgotten Fears.

"Who are you?" Evannah asked.

I am the spirit of the temple. I have stayed dormant for many years, watching, waiting for someone to step inside me.

"You show people their greatest fears?" Kiera said. "That's horrible."

I show people their deepest fears that they themselves don't know about. A long while ago, people would journey to find me, to prove that they were worthy and conquer their terrors.

You can only truly have courage if you once had fear.

I exist to help individuals overcome the burdens of their mind, to guide them toward the light that exists inside of them.

"I see," said Evannah. "That was like a test. An illusion. None of it was real."

You are correct.

Kiera was steaming mad. "Okay, Mr. Temple. For putting us through all that, how about you answer some of *my* questions."

I will gladly provide you with the knowledge that I am able to.

"Good. Starting with: where on Earth are we?"

You are currently located on the Isle of Whispers.

"The Isle of Whispers," Evannah murmured. It fit so well. Yet so much was still a mystery.

The Island has not had human visitors in a long while.

"Yay for us," Kiera retorted. She was still angry. "Now: what's happening? Is this real? Is this magic? Is this place alive?"

I cannot disclose all secrets of the Isle. What I can tell you is that powerful forces work here. It is not so much magic. More like nature that has reached its full potential. The power of the wild.

And yes, it is common knowledge here that the Isle of Whispers is alive. That is all I can tell you now.

"I knew it," Kiera crowed. "It *is* alive!"

Evannah was more stuck on the *powerful forces.* What were they, and what did that mean? *Nature that has reached its full potential. The power of the wild?*

As a reward for being mentally strong enough to complete my challenge, I will provide some guidance.

A glowing ball of light the size of Evannah's fist descended from the roof above them, shining so brilliantly she almost couldn't look at it.

Touch the light.

"This seems suspicious," Aaron muttered.

The light seemed to draw Evannah closer. "I'll try." Hesitantly, she reached her hand out, slowly moving it toward the ball of light.

Her fingers brushed the light. It was pleasantly warm, but not burning hot, and smooth and solid under her touch. The contact filled her with warmth.

All at once, the whispers were back, but she could understand them. All of them. The ones that had been speaking in a strange language melted into a language that she could understand.

"What happened?" she asked the temple. She didn't know where to look, so she just looked at the cracked roof.

You have been bestowed with the power to comprehend the language of the Island. It will prove useful on your journey.

"It's safe," she told Aaron and Kiera. They reached out and touched the ball of light too.

"Hey, that feels good!" Kiera remarked, examining her hand. The ball of light disappeared. "How do we know if it worked?"

It worked. You now instinctively know the language of the Isle.

"Thank you?" said Aaron. "Um. Can I call you Mr. Temple?"

Please don't. The Temple of Forgotten Fears will suffice.

"That's a bit of a mouthful," Kiera retorted. "Mr. Temple it is!"

The structure shook with what Evannah assumed was a temple's equivalent of a sigh. **Kings and queens used to voyage to me once. Very well, call me what you wish.**

One more thing. I can sense that you are completely, hopelessly, lost.

"It doesn't take a genius to figure that out," Kiera whispered dramatically.

You are both mentally and physically lost. I will start you on your journey. Get to a high place, and find the Flowering Tree. It will rise high above the other trees, and bloom with beautiful blossoms of each color. You will know it when you see it.

Find the Flowering Tree, and start traveling toward it. The rest is up to you.

"Thank you," Aaron told the temple earnestly. "Anything else?"

A perilous path unfolds in front of you. Have courage. Farewell.

The voice quieted, and Evannah could sense that the presence they had felt earlier had disappeared. The spirit was dormant again.

They stood in stunned silence for a second. "Well," remarked Aaron. "At least we know where to go now."

They walked out of the temple together. Kiera sighed. "I'm kind of going to miss Mr. Temple! He was mean at first but at least he helped us."

"As far as we know," said Evannah. "We have no idea what's waiting for us at this Flowering Tree."

"We need to find a high space first," added Aaron. "So we can find this tree."

Kiera's eyes lit up in excitement. "Yes! Let's—"

"You're not climbing, Kiera," Aaron told her. "Remember last time?"

She pouted. "Hey! Not my fault. The tree flung me off!"

"The tree," Aaron remarked, raising one eyebrow.

"Yes," Kiera said confidently. "The tree flung me off because the island is alive. How about this: we all climb, and whoever spots the tree first wins!"

"Great idea," Aaron said, voice dripping with mock praise. "Now we can all break our necks together!"

"Well, I'm not hearing any better ideas from you. So let's climb!"

Kiera led them a little further through the woods, to a patch of trees that were covered in branches and handholds, great for climbing. "Perfect! Let's climb."

"Um," Evannah interjected, her cheeks turning red. "I can't climb trees."

Kiera elbowed her. "Sure you can! We did it all the time together as kids!"

"That was so long ago!" Evannah protested.

"It's just like this," Kiera instructed, scrambling up a tree with a thick trunk. "Find branches. Pull yourself up. That's it!"

"Okay, I'll try," Evannah said hesitantly. She stepped onto a branch. The forest was so dense that with every step she took, a leaf or branch whacked her, leaving scratches across her face.

She wrapped her hand around a higher branch and stepped onto a nook between the branch and trunk. Slowly but surely, she was working her way up.

After a few minutes, she looked at the ground, and was shocked to see it so far away. She never really had a fear of heights, but to be stuck on a tree so high off the ground was terrifying.

She gulped, and continued working her way up. One more minute, two, then the bright explosion of treetop leaves came into sight.

She had made it! Perching on a high branch, she could survey a good part of the island in front of her. It was beautiful, with lush green forests spanning miles. In between, there were some odd spots of white trees she couldn't explain.

Evannah swiveled her head, trying to look for the tree. There! Rising high above the treetops, a huge, majestic tree overflowed with flowers of every color imaginable. It was the most colorful thing she had ever seen. "I found it!" she called.

Kiera's laugh rang out. Aaron and Kiera were already sitting on top of trees of their own. "Sorry, Evah. We already found it five minutes ago. Nice job though!"

Evannah sighed. She really was a slow climber. At least the view was pretty. The whispers seemed to be laughing at her. It was even more intense, now that she could understand all of them. It was still hard to comprehend, though.

She began the climb back down, feeling a tiny bit more confident now that she knew the tree. At least every step she took down brought her a little further from death. Evannah was never happier than the moment she touched the ground again. She almost wanted to kiss it in relief.

"I guess we need to go that way now," Aaron said, pointing toward where they had seen the Flowering Tree, even closer to the heart of the island. They began walking in that direction. Kiera linked her arm through Evannah's, and began skipping excitedly. Evannah wondered if she ever ran out of energy.

An hour later, they were only a little bit closer. Aaron and Kiera were up ahead, involved in a heated debate about something pointless, when the voices that Evannah had buried in the back of her mind came back again.

The Whisperer has faced her fears.

She can understand all of us now.

Hello, Whisperer.

She looks just like...

Hush, not now.

I guess I'm the Whisperer, Evannah thought. She didn't know what that meant, other than she could hear the voices, and it made her nervous. *I guess I have to deal with the whispers eventually.* "Hello," she whispered under her breath so Aaron and Evannah wouldn't hear.

No need to speak out loud, we can hear your mind, an otherworldly voice directed.

Okay, Evannah thought. *What do you want?*

A ghostly laugh rang out. *No, the question is, what do you want? Whisperer, would you like to learn more about your abilities?*

Evannah's breath caught in her throat. The power of the whispers felt dangerous, even too much for her. But a part of her did want to know more. Perhaps learning about them could help her control whatever "abilities" she had. "Yes," Evannah replied quietly, forgetting that she could use her mind. She definitely wanted to know more about these strange voices.

Close your eyes, they commanded.

Evannah closed her eyes, and crashed into a tree a few seconds later. "Ow!"

Aaron and Kiera turned around in concern. "Are you okay?" Aaron asked, helping her to her feet.

"Yes," Evannah coughed, completely embarrassed. "Just, um, didn't see that tree." That was technically the truth. They continued walking.

The whispers laughed. *Perhaps we should keep our eyes open instead.*

Yeah, perhaps, Evannah thought in annoyance.

Reach out with your mind, Whisperer. Do you feel our presence?

No.

Concentrate. Try again. Reach out and feel us, the voices instructed.

Evannah didn't know what "reaching out with her mind" would feel like so she just scanned her surroundings, trying to sense something, anything.

She didn't feel anything, then, there! The slightest hint of a feeling that reminded her of when the temple had awoken. The watched feeling. She prodded the feeling, until sensations she couldn't explain began pouring in.

She could somehow sense the presence of a being, or multiple nearby.

I feel you!

Good job, Whisperer. Now feel our energy.

Now that Evannah had sensed the whispers once, it was easy to find them again. She concentrated on them with her mind and felt a well of what felt like energy.

I found it, she told them.

Good. Now pull some of that energy toward your hand.

That instruction confused Evannah. She found the energy again, but had no idea how to "pull" it. She settled for imagining she was grabbing it with her mind and dragging it toward her hand. She felt something happening but didn't know what it was.

Her right hand began to tingle fiercely.

Now what? she asked.

Let the energy rise to the surface, and release it. You will see what happens.

Evannah relaxed her hand and tried to release the energy. Her hand lit up with a brilliant glow, like a miniature sun.

She gasped, and hid her hand behind her back so Aaron and Kiera didn't see. She sneaked another peek at her hand, which was still radiating light.

What was that? she thought at the whispers.

Congratulations, Whisperer. You have begun to tap into your power.

Ah, the beginning of the end, a voice murmured cryptically.

I see that she is not like that, a whisper argued. *She's not like the other one.*

How do I make it stop? Evannah wondered, trying to puzzle out the individual voices.

Douse it with your mind. It takes significantly more energy to create the light than to destroy it.

They were right, Evannah found. It took little effort to dismiss the light, and her hand went back to normal.

What else? Evannah asked, excited now.

That is all for now. You may keep practicing. We are always here, Whisperer. Then the voices faded to the back of her mind again.

Evannah stared at her hand. The whispers were helping her. What was she capable of doing?

Then the whispers suddenly grew silent. She was jolted from her thoughts back to the present. Her surroundings looked completely different.

"Whoa," Kiera whispered. She and Aaron had stopped. "What happened here?"

Evannah looked around. In contrast to the beautiful, colorful jungle, this stretch of forest was sparse and colorless.

The few flowers that remained were brown and wilted. The stark trees were bare, their trunks bleached white. The shrubs were gone, leaving the ground bare, covered in a white-gray dirt. It looked like an entire part of the forest had died.

"Did it die?" Aaron voiced her thoughts, touching a tree trunk. It looked rough and dry.

"Like all the life's been sucked out," Evannah murmured. The whispers were completely silent here. That was both a relief and completely terrifying at the same time.

"Let's cut through as fast as possible," Kiera proposed. Evannah nodded, and they started moving faster. This place was making them all uncomfortable.

"Look," Aaron pointed out. "It's spreading."

He was right, at the very edge of the bare stretch, the white was slowly creeping into the dense jungle, draining its color.

"Slowly," added Kiera. "But yeah. That's really weird." She touched a withering flower and shuddered. "I think it's dying."

"Let's go," said Aaron, leading them past the withered path as quickly as possible. Evannah could see the lush jungle on the other side. This must have been one of the odd white spots she had seen from the top of the tree. If so, how many more of these were there?

Evannah was sure this was not a normal occurrence.. The whispers had fallen silent, the destruction was spreading, and life had been taken from the jungle.

Something unnatural was happening, and she would find out what it was.

Chapter 7

Kiera stepped out of the dead patch of forest, relieved. She couldn't shake off the hollow feeling she had gotten inside when she had touched that wilted flower. The only way she could describe it was feeling drained. It was odd. She tried to brush it off and forget about it.

"I think we're halfway there!" Aaron announced. Kiera sighed. It had been at least two hours of walking, and they were only halfway? Not to mention that it was getting really hot and sticky. She almost missed the cool ocean winds in Neomerica.

Kiera put her hand in her pocket, fingering the small object in there. Her court pin, which had somehow survived the storm and the journey. She couldn't decide whether to keep it or throw it deep into the jungle. Maybe keep it, for now.

The pin made her think of Lord Cyrus's conversation that she'd overheard. She had to tell Evannah eventually. Every second she kept the secret only made it feel worse.

"Come on Kiera," Aaron beckoned, and she jogged ahead to join him. Speaking of secrets, Aaron was definitely hiding something. Kiera had known him for a long time, long enough to know he was terrible at keeping secrets.

Every so often in a conversation, he'd glance away like he remembered something and look around really awkwardly. It was suspicious, but Kiera would get to the bottom of that later. Whatever it was, it couldn't be too important, or Aaron would have already shared it.

Deciding to tease him a bit, Kiera skipped ahead and elbowed him in the side. "Aaron," she whisper-yelled in his ear. "I know you're hiding something..."

It had the intended reaction. Aaron stiffened. "What? I'm not hiding anything."

"Come on," Kiera rolled her eyes. "I've known you literally my whole life! You're keeping a secret. Want to tell me?"

Aaron looked away. "It's nothing." Evannah had turned large, watchful eyes on their conversation.

"Fine," Kiera muttered. "But you have to tell me eventually."

"I will," Aaron agreed, which was basically a confession. He wrapped his fingers around her hand. "I promise."

"Hey," Evannah pointed at something in the distance. "Over there."

Kiera dropped Aaron's hand, staring in that direction. There were some trees, and flowers, and look, more trees! "What?" she asked.

Evannah's voice dropped to a whisper. "Right there, between those huge trees."

"Oh, I see it!" Aaron exclaimed quietly. "What *is* that?"

Kiera finally noticed it too. Between two trees stood a dark, shadowy figure.

It was vaguely humanoid in shape, but definitely bigger, and a wispy midnight black, almost translucent. Besides its silhouette, Kiera couldn't see any other features. It looked like a living shadow.

"Creepy shadow guy," she shuddered. "Let's move."

"Great, it's coming toward us!" Aaron whisper-shouted.

"Go, go, go," Kiera commanded. "Let's get out of here." They began stealthily bolting away from the shadow, as it approached them, moving slowly and dramatically.

Its pace increased the closer it got to them, not so much walking, but gliding over the ground.

"Shoot, it's here," Aaron cursed. The shadow was too close for comfort.

"Hide!" Evannah cried, pressing herself to the opposite side of a tree.

Aaron dropped to the ground and took cover behind a large patch of ferns. Kiera pondered over whether she could climb a tree fast enough, but eventually ducked behind a large, sturdy tree next to Evannah's. She held her breath, chills creeping up her arm despite the heat. Beside her, Evannah shivered.

The shadow glided into the patch of trees, its presence commanding. Kiera held still, stiller than she had in her life, willing the shadow not to come any closer.

The shadow moved in a slow, wide circle. It was on the opposite side of Kiera's tree. She could have reached out and touched it.

Please don't look around any more, she silently begged. *There's nobody here.* She squeezed her eyes shut. If the shadow moved *one more foot* in her direction it would all be over. Her breaths came quickly.

The shadow moved back into the center of the patch of trees, standing still now. Kiera wondered whether they could make a run for it.

"*Don't think I can't see you,*" a voice rang out, echoing around the forest. It had come from the shadow, who, as far as Kiera could tell, didn't have a mouth or ears or anything.

"*It will be much easier if you don't hide from me.*" The voice was dark, and menacing.

Kiera's breath caught in her chest. *Breathe, breathe!* she reminded herself. Never had she been in such real danger before.

"*Do you know who I am, young adventurers?*" Gulping, Kiera closed her eyes. When she opened them, she was staring into an emotionless, shadowy face. "*Nice to finally meet you.*"

Kiera screamed, a scream laced with fear and horror, as she bolted from the dark figure. Aaron and Evannah were hot on her trail, following behind as they raced to put distance between themselves and the shadow.

"*I have been watching you,*" the shadow called, easily keeping up with them. It looked like it was putting in no effort at all to move that fast.

That's ominous, Kiera thought.

She kept running, crashing through the forest as Aaron screamed, "Leave us alone!" *Really scary, Aaron. I'm terrified.*

"*No need to run,*" the figure glided smoothly behind them. "*I simply want to introduce myself.*" Kiera ran until she thought she was going to collapse. She risked taking a moment to look behind her.

The shadow had vanished.

"Evannah! Aaron!" she panted. "It's gone!" She doubled over, hands on her knees, and took gasping breaths.

They had emerged into a spot covered in huge, thick trees that stretched up to the sky. The ground was mostly clear here, with a few large ferns spotting the place.

"Let's... hide," Evannah suggested breathlessly, gasping. "Just in case."

"Here!" Aaron called. He pointed to a small ditch in the ground next to a fern. They ran to slide into the ditch, and Aaron pulled the giant leaves of the green fern over their heads.

There they sat, squished into one another, not daring to move. It was silent, except for the noise of their own pounding heartbeats.

Kiera pulled her head down to her knees, staring at the soil. Dirt and dew dusted them as they huddled together, waiting out whatever monster was hunting them.

Minutes that may have been years passed. After a while, Kiera whispered, quiet as the wings of a butterfly. "I'm going out to check."

They nodded. "Be careful," Aaron told her. Stealthily, Kiera crawled out of the ditch, getting to her feet and raising her head.

The shadow creature stood watching her, staring directly into her soul.

Kiera screamed. "It's here!" Evannah and Aaron scrambled out of the ditch, trying to flee.

"*There is nowhere to run,*" the shadow's voice resounded. It was a whisper and a yell at the same time. "*I am everywhere.*" Kiera started to run, when the shadow disappeared and reappeared directly in front of her. She scrambled to change directions.

The shadow caught up to her in no time. With nowhere to run, Kiera impulsively picked up a stick she spotted lying on the ground and bashed the shadow over the head with it.

Surprisingly, the stick hit something solid, and didn't pass straight through the shadow like Kiera was expecting. The figure clutched its head and stumbled back.

Recovering quickly, the shadow vanished and appeared in front of Aaron and Evannah. Curling its fingers into long, deadly claws, it swiped at them. Aaron jumped in front of Evannah, and got the worst of it. Blood dripped from long gashes up his arm and neck. Holding his arm, he collapsed while Evannah screamed and dropped down to check if he was okay.

Still clutching the stick, Kiera twisted it so that the pointy side faced the shadow, shot toward it, and stabbed in through the back.

Bent over, the shadow removed the stick protruding from its stomach, and it dissolved into dust in the shadow's hands. It didn't look hurt in any way. It gazed into the distance intently for a moment, as if looking or listening for something.

"*Fine,*" the shadow murmured angrily. "*You don't want to talk now? Then I will be back. Next time your circumstances will not be as favorable.*" It glided away before disappearing altogether.

Kiera stood still for a few moments, her breath coming in short gasps. "What just happened?"

"You saved us!" Evannah rushed toward Kiera with bright eyes, wrapping her in a big hug. *I'm not so sure I did, Kiera* thought. *The shadow wasn't hurt. Something else clearly made it leave.* Had it just been trying to scare them? Or spy on them? In any case, she wasn't going to scare her friends any further.

"You were amazing, Kiera!" Aaron congratulated her, still lying on the ground. "But I think that shadow just threatened us."

"Wait," Evannah paused. "A *shadow waits with watching eyes!*"

"Oh!" Realization dawned on Kiera. "I didn't think it would be that literal. An *actual* shadow? What happened to metaphors?"

"And why was it stalking us?" Aaron wondered. "We'd better keep our guards up now." He groaned, twisting onto his side. His shirt was stained with blood, a lot more of it than Kiera had first realized.

"Are you fine, Aaron?" She rushed over to check on him.

"I'm great," he responded sarcastically, trying to get up, clutching his neck in pain. "I'll live, I think."

"We can't keep going, can we?" Evannah asked. "Not with Aaron in this condition."

"I think we should try to keep moving, reach the Flowering Tree," Kiera answered hesitantly. "It's our one lead. Maybe we'll learn something to protect ourselves from Shadow Guy. But *only* if Aaron is fine." She paused. "Maybe we should rest for today, and leave tomorrow."

"No!" Aaron interjected. "I don't want our journey to be compromised because of me. We don't know what's at the Flowering Tree; we might need to get there today."

"Fine," said Evannah. "Let's take care of those wounds first."

Evannah poured water over his injuries while Aaron winced in pain. He was losing a lot of blood, quickly, and was starting to look pale. Kiera found some moss, which would have to do for bandages for now, and wrapped it around Aaron's arm and neck.

He pushed himself to his feet. "Let's leave now. I don't want to keep us behind."

This time, they were all on the alert, talking minimally and instead keeping watch for threats, specifically shadowy dark threats. Aaron's arm was around Evannah's neck as she supported him through the long walk. He was looking more pale and sweaty with each step.

"Almost there," Evannah commented, after a prolonged journey. They were now able to see branches laden with flowers towering above the treetops.

Luckily, they hadn't seen the shadow figure since their encounter. But Kiera had been jumpy around her own shadow all day because of that.

"Finally!" Aaron cheered, then stumbled awkwardly. "We've been walking for *so long*." He was really not looking good.

Kiera agreed. She couldn't believe that it was only that morning that she had remembered the prophecy.

A minute later, they emerged into a large clearing, clear of most plants and shrubs except one glorious tree in the center.

The Flowering Tree towered above them, its trunk unbelievably broad and its long, ancient roots stretching around the clearing. It towered high above them, majestic branches draped with flowers.

And the flowers, they were unlike anything Kiera had seen, in all shapes, sizes, and colors. She saw blues, reds, oranges, whites, pinks, yellows, and more, including colors she couldn't begin to name. "Wow," she breathed. It was nearly sunset, and the rays of golden-orange light made the tree look even prettier.

"It's beautiful!" Evannah added, her eyes wide. They all gazed up at the tree.

"Now what?" Aaron voiced the question that they had all been thinking.

"Let's go see," suggested Kiera. They moved closer to the tree and began to examine it. Aaron and Evannah walked in a large circle around it while Kiera lay her palm on the trunk.

The second her hand touched the tree, energy coursed through her. She could feel life and vitality blooming inside her, and felt instantly connected to the tree in front of her.

She jerked her hand back and the feeling faded.

"Guys!" she called. "Something happened when I touched it. You should try it too."

Evannah and Aaron both touched the tree. Aaron looked puzzled. "Nothing happened."

"Nothing for me either," Evannah said. "What happened to you?"

"I felt...something," Kiera tried to explain. "It was like I could sense the tree somehow."

"Hmm," Evannah nodded, looking thoughtful. Aaron tilted his head.

"Maybe you're meant to touch it then," Aaron proposed. "Try it again." His breaths were coming shallower now.

Kiera closed her eyes, laying her hand on the tree again. The feeling came back even stronger, and she tried to make sense of it. It was like the tree was a living creature and she was communicating with it.

What are you trying to tell me, Flowering Tree? she wondered.

"Aaron!" Evannah cried, jerking Kiera from her thoughts. She whirled around to see that Aaron had collapsed to the ground, his arms splayed and his eyes closed, unconscious. Blood still dripped down his neck.

"No!" Kiera cried. She started to run toward him. Aaron couldn't die, he *couldn't*.

The branches of the Flowering Tree moved, stretching toward her, as if they were calling her forward. Like a sign. She hesitated, looking toward Aaron.

"Go see!" Evannah shouted desperately, tears streaming down her face. She seemed to read Kiera's mind.

While Evannah tended to Aaron, Kiera rushed back to the tree, willing it to tell her something.

She touched it again, thoughts of Aaron taking over. And as soon as she closed her eyes, an image flashed into her mind.

She could see it as clearly as if she had eyes open. The image was of a flower, small and blue, with distinctly diamond shaped petals that formed a small bowl.

Like the tree had told her, she immediately knew she *needed* it. And she could find it on the Flowering Tree.

Kiera had never climbed a tree this big, but she was up to the challenge. Not to mention that this was an emergency. She grabbed a thick limb and started to climb.

Within moments, it was clear that she could not climb this tree. The next branch was many feet above her head. She groaned in frustration.

"Come on!" she shouted. "Work with me here, tree!" The branch under her feet started moving, and Kiera nearly fell off.

She dropped down to lay on her stomach and hugged the branch, hanging on for dear life as it twisted around. This was just like what had happened in the fight against the vines, when the tree took on a life of its own.

In a terrifying ride, it whipped her around, turning and twisting as it stretched downward, slowly bending back, almost like... A catapult?

That registered just a moment too late, as the branch snapped forward, sending Kiera flying through the air. She screamed, flailing in midair for something to grab onto. Her fingers closed around another branch above her head.

She dangled from it, hanging on, her legs suspended. Great. She was stuck.

Evannah, who had seen what happened, left Aaron and rushed toward her. "Hang on, Kiera! I'm coming!"

Kiera had two options. Option one: hang there like a clumsy squirrel and hope that Evannah could save her. Option two: try to save herself and hope that she wouldn't die in the process.

She sincerely doubted that Evannah, who had just learned how to climb trees today, would be able to reach her. So it was up to her.

Kiera swung back and forth, trying to work up enough momentum to flip onto the tree. It would be an acrobatic feat like she had never pulled off, but it was worth a try.

A few swings later, she pumped her legs and attempted an awkward backflip. Her head collided with the branch and she nearly fell, but her arms grasped the branch at the last moment. She was saved! She was on top of the branch! But, ow, her head *really* hurt.

I'm alive! Time to find that flower.

Closing her eyes, she pictured the blue flower with the diamond shaped petals. A short search revealed a small cluster of them growing on a branch *just* out of her reach, to the right.

"Please, tree," she begged the plant. "Can't you bring those a *little* closer? I know you can move."

The branch was still for a minute. Then the branch with the flowers began to move, drawing closer until Kiera could reach out and pluck one, which she did.

That actually worked! Kiera was one hundred percent sure it wouldn't have. "Thanks, tree!" She patted its trunk.

While the branch she was standing on gently lowered her to the ground, she examined the flower. Its blue petals faded to white around the edges, and its center was as deep and shimmery as a sapphire. Its bowl-shaped insides were coated in a thick layer of dusty pollen.

Safely on the ground, she touched the tree again. "Now what?"

A picture entered her mind, of pouring the pollen over wounds. *This could save Aaron!*

After seeing that Kiera was safe, Evannah had gone back to Aaron. Now, Kiera charged over to her, yelling, "Evannah, move!"

A confused Evannah sprang out of the way, revealing an unconscious, bloody Aaron. Without hesitating, she poured the pollen over Aaron's wounds.

"What is that?" Evannah asked, while Kiera worked.

"The tree showed me this flower," Kiera explained. "I think it could heal Aaron." It was a true testament of their friendship that Evannah didn't ask about the tree "showing" it to her.

Kiera continued dusting the pollen over him. *Come on Aaron, wake up. Come back to me.*

She didn't check his heartbeat, too scared of what she might find. Red soaked his shirt and dripped down his arm.

She leaned over his closed eyes, willing them to open. *Please, please.*

Then they opened.

Kiera and Evannah watched, stunned, as his wounds closed up and skin grew over them. His brown eyes, layered with a golden shimmer, opened. Color returned to Aaron's cheeks, and he looked as healthy as before. He sat up, examining his arm. Only a scar remained.

"Aaron!" Evannah and Kiera wrapped him in a bear hug, throwing him back to the ground.

"Whoa, let a guy breathe!" Aaron looked around. "How long was I out?"

"Three years," Kiera told him solemnly.

"WHAT?"

Evannah rolled her eyes. "It's been five minutes! Quit the drama, Aaron."

After Aaron checked for any traces of his wounds and found none, they decided to use the leftover pollen in the flower to dust their own wounds, the various small cuts and scrapes they had picked up, and Kiera's remainder of a hurt leg. She hadn't even realized that the pain had persisted until it went away.

They all looked and felt healthier than they had for a while. Kiera explained what had happened with the tree, omitting the part with the disastrous acrobatics, which Evannah filled in.

"Wow," Aaron uttered. "Thank you for saving me, Kiera. *Again.* I hate being indebted to you!" She shoved him.

"It sounds like the tree spoke to you," Evannah mused. "Interesting."

"Yeah, it was like it communicated straight into my mind," Kiera explained.

"Hmm," Aaron tilted his head. "Well, the tree also saved my life."

"How do you thank a tree?" Kiera wondered. "Water it? Give it a big hug?"

Aaron laughed. "I'm just glad we can move on from this. We found the tree. Where to now?"

"Look, Kiera," Evannah told her. "The tree looks like it's calling you."

The Flowering Tree was stretching colorful branches in her direction, as if it was beckoning her. Kiera walked up to it. Slowly, a curled branch reached out. Kiera reached her hand out to it. It uncurled, dropping something in her hand.

It was a small seed. As Kiera's fingers brushed the branch, she heard a message. *Plant it later, protector of the wild. We are happy to help in return when you must help us soon.*

Confused, Kiera dropped the seed into her pocket.

"What is it?" Aaron asked.

"A seed," Kiera replied, wondering what it grew. She turned it over in her pocket. It was small, white, and smooth. She would need to find somewhere to plant it later. "And it called me *protector of the wild*."

"Hmm," Aaron commented, impressed. "I don't know what that means, but it sounds very dramatic."

"Guys," Evannah began, cautiously.

"Apparently I have to plant this somewhere," Kiera displayed the seed.

"GUYS!" They turned to look at Evannah. "I think we're under attack."

Chapter 8

It had been merely moments since Aaron had come back from the brink of death, and they were already facing another crisis. Or, was this even a crisis?

"What now?" he complained.

"Look," Evannah pointed. He looked. It was... some small animals. A group of three long, little mammals with pointy faces and little whiskers.

Kiera laughed. "An attack? You got me, Evannah."

"I'm not joking," Evannah looked serious. "I think they're dangerous. Something tells me."

Kiera and Aaron exchanged a look. Was Evannah all right? Evannah pressed her hands to her ears and squeezed her eyes shut like there were loud noises in her head.

"Come on, Evannah," Kiera went a little closer to the animals. "They're cute! They look like the weasels back home, except black."

Aaron did have to admit that they were a little cute. Definitely not dangerous. Definitely not an attack. One of them blinked its small brown eyes at him innocently.

"See, look!" Kiera called as she approached them. "Aww, they're not dangerous at all! They're adora—"

Mid-sentence, the weasel-like creatures' eyes turned red and they opened their mouths to bare long, shining fangs. As they hissed, long claws extended from their small paws.

Kiera stumbled away. "Aah! The weasels are evil! Never mind, you were right!"

Their red eyes flashed dangerously as they advanced on Kiera, Aaron, and Evannah, tongues licking their sharp teeth.

Kiera and Evannah began to back away. *Wait a minute. Why are we running from these little guys?* Aaron thought indignantly.

He unsheathed his dagger. "This time we won't run! We hold our ground and fight!" He stepped closer to the weasels, aiming his dagger threateningly toward them.

Then, *hundreds* of the demented creatures emerged, slinking out of the shadows, crawling down trees, burrowing out of the dirt. Soon, the clearing was filled with black fur and gleaming eyes.

And they were the targets.

Aaron backed away from them again. "Never mind. We run, we *definitely* run!"

As they attempted to flee, the weasels rushed toward them with frightening speed, while even more emerged out of nowhere.

Every direction they turned, another creature was ready to come at them. They moved in groups, their tiny bodies made large by the sheer amount of animals in the clearing. There were now so many, Aaron thought, that it would take a miracle for them to escape. Several swarmed up his body, and he shook them off, yelling. Their claws and teeth left tiny marks in his skin. For every weasel he threw off of himself, another replaced it.

Finally removing all the weasels, he bolted in the only free direction, toward the Flowering Tree. The weasels pursued him, slinking in their direction. The pitter-patter of hundreds of little claws made him shudder.

Evannah, Kiera, and himself backed toward the Flowering Tree. They were now surrounded by weasels on all sides.

The creatures slowly slinked toward them. It seemed like they had evil smiles on their faces. The ground was completely covered in rippling black bodies that churned like waves. Black, furry waves coming to sweep them away.

"Stop!" Evannah cried. She held up a hand, which lit up with a bright glow. The weasels skittered away for a moment. *What is happening?*

Aaron pressed himself closer to the tree but there was nowhere else to go. There were weasels in *every direction.* They advanced closer.

"Aaron!" Kiera cried. "If we die, I want you to know—" She was interrupted by a weasel, who looked like the leader of the pack, jumping onto her foot. She yelled, trying to shake it off, and it was followed by several more. Soon Kiera was covered in the little creatures and was pulled down to the ground.

"Kiera!" Aaron hurtled to help her, grabbing weasels and throwing them into the pack. He gasped as a burning pain ran up his arm instantly, where the shadow had scratched him. The sudden shock sent him thudding to the ground.

Now the weasels were coming for him and Evannah, raking at them with sharp claws. He was covered, he was suffocating.

"STOP!" A new voice roared. It was deep, rumbling, and fearsome. The loud voice rang out around the clearing, making the weasels stop in their tracks.

"STOP THIS MADNESS! Back to the shade where you belong!" A gigantic dark creature, the biggest he had ever seen, crashed into the clearing, easily swiping aside the smaller animals with its broad paws.

"*What* is *that*?" Kiera screamed, her eyes huge. "And is it trying to kill us as well?"

The enormous animal bared its fearsome teeth at the weasels, knocking them aside and chasing them. They fled, terrified.

The weasels that covered Kiera, Evannah, and Aaron dropped and ran in the other direction.

When the clearing was finally free of the black weasels, the creature prowled the edges of the clearing, snarling. After it was sure no weasels were left, it advanced toward them.

"Run!" Aaron cried. He scrambled up, clutching his arm, and they began to bolt away. There was no way they could take on this mighty, fearsome creature.

"Wait," the creature rumbled. "I'm not here to hurt you."

"We thought the same about the weasels!" Kiera yelled. "Then they became demented."

"Don't converse with the monster, Kiera!" Evannah scolded quietly.

The creature let out a shaking growl that he realized was a laugh. "Shadestalkers are not usually a threat, but—" it glanced around. "We can't talk here; it's unsafe."

Aaron took a moment to examine the size of the animal. It was immense, as big as a Neomerican horse, but with thick muscles.

Then it stepped out of the shadows, and into the light, and Aaron gasped.

It was a black panther, the biggest one he had ever seen. Its gigantic head could have devoured him in one bite. Its black pelt was studded with tiny dots of light, like stars in a dark sky. It was actually beautiful.

"Who are you?" Aaron wondered. If it wanted to hurt them, they would be dead by now. And it had saved them. Maybe it really did want to help them.

The creature bowed its mighty head. "I am called Night Star," he growled in a voice that Aaron realized was male. "I am here to help. There is much that I need to tell you."

"I think it's safe," Aaron told the others, approaching Night Star. He stopped right in front of the panther's face. He looked down at Aaron.

"He is right," the panther agreed. "I am going to check that it is safe to proceed. I will return momentarily. I have somewhere I must take you." With that, he gracefully bounded into the forest.

"Do we trust him?" Kiera still looked suspicious.

"I think so," said Evannah. "He hasn't done anything yet. And I bet he can hear this whole conversation."

"Correct!" Night Star called from far off, unseen. "But I will pretend I cannot."

"Evannah," something nagged at Aaron. "How did you know that the weasels were dangerous?"

Evannah was quiet for a moment. Then she finally replied. "The voices that have been speaking to me... they told me."

"And what was with that glow?" Kiera asked. "Do you have magic powers now?"

Aaron had almost forgotten about that, but the confusion now rushed in tenfold. What was going on with Evannah?

Evannah bowed her head. "The voices told me how to do that." She held out her hand, which began to shed light again. Then she closed it into a fist and the light cut off. "I don't know what it means. And I can't do anything else."

Aaron could sense that she was a bit scared, even though it didn't show on her face. It was the twin connection. "We'll figure this out, Evah," he reassured her. "We have help now."

As if on cue, Night Star reappeared, the dots of light in his pelt twinkling. The sun was setting now, and the sky was tinged purple. It had begun to grow darker.

"Come with me," the creature called. "We must go now, quickly."

The three exchanged a look. Though it was unspoken, they all trusted Night Star and were willing to go with him.

"Climb onto my back," Night Star instructed as they walked over.

Of course Kiera was the first one. The panther lay down so they could easily climb on. "Wow," Kiera beamed. "We're riding a cat!"

"Panther," Night Star growled.

Hesitantly, Aaron swung his leg over Night Star's back. He was big enough to easily seat all three of them. His fur was surprisingly soft, and the dots of light didn't feel hot, like Aaron was expecting. They were pleasantly warm. Evannah joined them too.

Night Star stood up, and Aaron gripped the cat for dear life. He was in front, so he wrapped his arms around Night Star's neck. "Hang on!" Night Star instructed.

Then he leaped forward. They didn't touch the ground, like Aaron was expecting. They leaped straight *into the sky*.

The panther wasn't quite flying, it was more like he was bounding through the sky. Like the air was firm under his big paws. Each leap took them higher and higher up, into the twilight sky.

"We're flying!" Aaron cheered, and Kiera whooped. Even Evannah joined in to the cheering, joy displayed in her bright eyes.

Soon they were bounding above the treetops, the entire island spread out underneath them. The sunset painted the land in beautiful hues. Aaron felt comfortable on Night Star's back, not at all scared of falling off. He could see the silvery ocean from up here, but anything past that was cloaked with mist.

"Where are we going?" he asked Night Star.

The cat replied in his gruff voice, "We're going to Fenlithra, one of the forest villages."

Fenlithra. "People live here?" Aaron asked, curious.

"There are multiple civilizations here," Night Star responded. "Each is different. Perhaps one day you will see them all. But for right now, Fenlithra is the safest."

"Safest?" Aaron asked. "Is there danger here?" He remembered the dead, withered patch of forest.

"More than you can imagine," the great cat growled. "You have arrived in a time of chaos and instability. It will only be safe to say more in Fenlithra. I am sure we are being watched here."

Aaron cast a glance around the sky. There were no living creatures in sight that he could see, except maybe a few birds in the distance.

As time passed, the sky grew darker, and stars began to appear. The night sky perfectly matched Night Star's pelt, and Aaron guessed that they now appeared almost camouflaged against the sky.

"Isn't this crazy?" Kiera whispered. Her cheeks and nose were pink from the wind. It wasn't a cold night, but it was windy when soaring through the sky. Her hands were wrapped around Aaron's waist, keeping herself steady. "We're actually flying."

"This is amazing," Aaron responded. "What are those?"

In the distance, he could see flashes of multicolored light. As they drew closer, he could tell that they were enormous birds, with feathers that softly glowed in vibrant colors, and changed every few seconds. "They're beautiful."

Night Star plummeted into a steep dive that made Aaron squeeze his neck so tight that he was sure he had strangled the cat. Everyone screamed.

"What happened?" Aaron yelled.

"Lightning birds," Night Star snarled. "Usually peaceful, not a threat, but... they could be to us, today. We'll have to stop for the night; I know a spot nearby." He continued to bound downwards, heading toward the ground.

"Something's controlling them, right?" Evannah asked. "The vines, the weasels, these birds. Something's wrong." Night Star nodded but didn't say anything more.

Soon, they had reached the ground. The forest was dark, which made the various swishing and rustling noises, as well as the birdcalls, frightening.

They slid off his back, and followed Night Star as he padded along. "Stay quiet," he warned. After a few moments, he murmured, "We are here."

They had reached a small, grassy hill surrounded by tropical trees. A large, gaping hole was carved into the little hill, which turned out to be hollow.

"My old den," Night Star announced. "I stayed here a few times, back when the first leaves fell. It should be comfortable enough for you. I will stand guard outside, and we will leave again in the morning. Goodnight." He nudged them inside, then retreated outside to stand guard.

Aaron looked around the cave. It was actually quite large and spacious, blanketed with soft grass with smooth rocks lining the edges. It was dark, but moonlight streamed through the entrance.

"Evannah, can you do your magic hand thing?" Kiera requested. Sometimes it seemed like nothing fazed her. Evannah sighed but lit up her hand, casting light around the cave. Kiera used the light to distribute fruits and water canteens.

They lay down, spaced out, on the grass. It was soft and fairly comfortable, but thinking about the dangers waiting for them made the ground turn rock-hard under Aaron's head.

"What do you think?" Evannah's voice whispered through the darkness.

"About?" Aaron asked, lying on his back.

"This place. This whole situation. Everything."

He hesitated. "I don't know. The Isle of Whispers. We've never heard about it." He paused. "Maybe... maybe there's a reason that nobody's explored these islands before. It's dangerous here. Different. But we were called here for a reason. We ended up here for a reason."

He reached out to grab Evannah's hand to give her a reassuring squeeze. It reminded him of when they would sneak into each other's rooms in the castle to talk at night. "We'll be okay," Aaron told her. "I'll make sure of it."

And with that, he fell asleep.

Sunlight streamed into the cave as Aaron stretched awake. He had been in a deep sleep the entire night, exhausted.

"Finally up!" Kiera commented. "Sleepyhead."

Evannah offered him a fruit. "Breakfast?"

"For breakfast we have fruit, with a side of fruit. Also, if you want to get fancy, we have fruit juice," Kiera joked. "When you mix the fruit with water."

Aaron accepted one. "That fruit juice sounds delicious but I'll have to pass." The fruits had tasted good, but he was getting really sick of eating them.

"Ah, you're awake," Night Star poked his head into his old den. "It is time to leave."

After packing their things, they climbed onto his back, and he bounded up into the sky again.

Soaring through the sky was very different in the daytime. The land under him was a deep green spotted with white, and mountains rose in the distance. He could see a river winding through the trees.

"We're meeting people from the island!" Kiera exclaimed excitedly. "Are you ready?"

"I'm a bit nervous," Aaron admitted. "I don't know what to expect. I mean, what will they think of us?"

"We must be so odd to them," Evannah commented. "But it will be interesting. I think I'm ready to meet them."

"They have been waiting a long time to meet you," Night Star rumbled.

"What does that mean?" Aaron asked curiously.

"You will see. Fenlithra awaits!" The panther loped through the sky. "We are nearly there!"

Night Star dipped over a cluster of tall trees, and started descending toward a thin river. "Prepare yourself." He gracefully touched down on the ground and ran to a stop. "Let me scout ahead."

He walked ahead, sniffing the air for threats. The three waited nervously behind him.

"I think we've faced all possible threats," Kiera said playfully. "The vines, the weasels, the shadow guy..."

"There is always more danger," said Night Star solemnly. That quieted them. They walked along the little river for a few moments. It bubbled over rocks, clear and inviting, but the mud caked on Aaron's shoes.

Night Star motioned ahead with his head. "You have arrived at Fenlithra."

Aaron stepped forward, unsure as to what to expect. A row of primitive little shacks? A shockingly advanced civilization? A group of outcast explorers? His imagination got the best of him for a moment.

He looked up, and gasped.

Dozens of tree houses, large and small, all expertly crafted and placed, sat in trees, which were connected by long walkways and bridges. Ladders and steps were connected to the trees, turning the treetops into a complex but perfect home. Some trees hosted multiple houses, at different levels.

Down at ground level, people dressed in natural, earthen tones tended to plants and splashed in the river. Clusters of large ferns sprang up near the base of trees, and stepping stones formed different paths. Brightly colored birds perched on trees and people's shoulders. It was a wondrous place. His eyes darted around, trying to take it all in.

A woman with long brown hair, wearing green robes embroidered with silver stepped forward. "Welcome to Fenlithra!" She shook Aaron's hand, then Kiera and Evannah's. "It is incredible to meet you at last." She seemed to be in her late-twenties, and wore a headpiece that looked like twisting silver vines studded with small jewels.

"At last?" Aaron asked.

"My name is Jannary Everdawn, I am the leader of Fenlithra, the forest village. Come, we have a lot to talk about," Jannary beckoned for them to follow her. "What are your names?"

"I'm Aaron, and this is Evannah, and Kiera," Aaron replied.

"Kiera can introduce herself," Kiera retorted.

Jannary laughed. "I can tell we're going to have trouble with this one." She turned to the panther standing behind them. "We are in your debt, Night Star. I can take it from here."

"Very well," Night Star rumbled. "I will meet up with you momentarily." He padded away.

They walked on one of the stepping stone paths while Jannary narrated with a practiced voice. "Fenlithra is one of the two main forest villages on the Isle. We are also known as 'Village of the Treetops' because we have made our home high above the ground. Many people live here, and have various professions such as taking care of the plants, maintaining the treehouses, and defending our home."

A different woman rushed up to them, much younger than Jannary. She seemed to be not much older than Aaron, and her long hair was in a braid. Curiosity glimmered in her fierce light brown eyes. "Is it true? Have they really arrived?"

"Patience, Khalisse," Jannary laughed. "This is Aaron, Evannah, and Kiera. For you three, this is Khalisse, Head of the Warriors."

"Nice to meet you," Aaron shook her hand.

Many people had started to gather around them, murmuring in hushed tones and pointing. He heard multiple cries of "They're here!" Shocked and curious faces stared their way.

"What's going on?" Kiera asked.

"You'll have to pardon my peoples' enthusiasm," Jannary explained. "We have been waiting for you for over a hundred years."

Chapter 9

People crowded around Evannah. "I must ask you to move away for now," the leader, Jannary, commanded. "Our guests need space, but you will meet them later."

One of the people pointed excitedly at Evannah. "Whisperer!" they exclaimed. "It's a real Whisperer again!"

The rest of them clamored to get closer. "Whisperer? I don't believe it!"

"What are they talking about, Evah?" Aaron questioned.

Evannah only backed away amidst the calls of, "Whisperer! Whisperer! She's come to save us from the Watcher!"

"Enough!" Jannary's stern voice rang out. "Leave them alone." Her command was enough to make the people back away. "Get back to your work." They did, but kept shooting glances in Evannah's direction and muttering with interest.

"Your presence has caused some excitement," Jannary explained.

"What's this about a hundred years?" Kiera questioned. "We haven't even been alive that long!"

Jannary nodded. "Khalisse, meet me in the Great Tree," she addressed her friend. The warrior ran off. "Your existence has been written in the fates. That is how we knew you were coming, and how we know what else shall be."

Written in the fates? I didn't think we were that important.

"Wait," Kiera said. "Will someone please explain what is going on?"

"It will all be explained at the Great Tree," replied Jannary calmly. "Come along." She guided them further along the path, until they reached a remarkably large tree, with roots hanging off its branches and descending to the ground. It reminded Evannah of drops of rain falling from the sky. Perched in the tree was a grand, multi-story treehouse with spiraling steps, rope walkways connecting to other trees, and raised towers.

"This is the Great Tree," Jannary told them. "This is where the Everdawn, or the leader, lives, among the other important people in the village. This is my home." She gracefully climbed up a series of steps attached to the tree.

Evannah began climbing. It was a lot harder than Jannary made it look. They got to their feet on a platform overlooking the village. "Let's go inside," encouraged Jannary. She led them through an archway to a surprisingly spacious room made of wood.

The room had multiple seats around a wooden table. Roots from the tree climbed up the walls, making the room feel like part of nature.

"Cool room," Aaron muttered.

Jannary smiled. "Everything in this village is connected to the natural world." She retrieved three cups made from leaves from shelves carved into the back of the tree and placed them on the table. "Please, have a seat. Water?"

Evannah sat down. She had only been here for a minute, and it already felt a lot more welcoming than the court room in Neomerica. She drank the water gratefully.

A curtain of hanging moss that served as a door parted as Khalisse stormed in. She was now dressed in golden armor, which set off her bronze skin, and also took a seat. She tilted her head at them. "Hmm. Are you really as amazing as they say you are?" she asked skeptically.

"Be kind," Jannary scolded. "Ah, here is the last member of our party." Night Star had leaped onto the platform, and curled into the far corner of the room, his massive body taking up most of the space.

"So we meet again," he greeted them.

"We must talk," Jannary said. "Let me start with this: what questions do you have?"

Aaron raised his head. "Why is everyone treating us like we're famous?" Evannah had been wondering the same thing.

Jannary nodded. "Good question. That is one that involves a long story." She stood up and began to walk around the room.

"A century ago, the Fate-readers from every village came together, as they usually do when they read something important in the stars. They had all gleaned the same prophecy." She stared directly at them. "And that prophecy was about you."

"Us?" Evannah felt her arms tingle.

"Yes. The prophecy told us tales of three young strangers, from a faraway land, arriving on our shores in a time of great peril.

Each with a special connection to the Isle, and each with special abilities." They were silent for a moment.

"I'm sure you've seen this for yourself, but... a dark power has gotten hold of the Island. He's been corrupting it, controlling it, stripping it of its power."

Her voice lowered to a whisper. "He can see us and hear us almost anywhere now. It is only really safe to talk within the protections of Fenlithra."

"The Watcher," Khalisse said darkly, and Evannah shivered a little. "The Isle of Whispers was beautiful before he came along."

"It's still beautiful," Evannah murmured.

"Yes," said Night Star. "To outsiders, yes. But much of the island's beauty has been stripped away. The forest is dying." Evannah remembered the dead patch of forest spreading.

"Many creatures have turned dark." *The weasels.* "The mist that once shielded our coasts from the world is growing thicker and thicker, until it will suffocate our shores and strangle our island *forever*." Evannah flinched at his harsh words and tone. Even Jannary looked a little alarmed.

"Let me put it this way," Khalisse interjected fiercely. "The Island is *dying*. And we can't do anything about it."

"Why not?" asked Kiera. "You can always do something! Fight back! Save your home!"

Khalisse smiled. "I like her spirit!"

"We cannot do anything," Jannary explained, head ducked. "Years ago, when the Watcher first came to power, Fenlithra did not support him. As a result, he used his powers to separate every

Island village, and confine the citizens of Fenlithra to their home. We have not left Fenlithra in years, because we are not able to."

She patted Night Star's large head. "Night Star is our connection to the world, but he can only do so much."

"So this Watcher *trapped* you here?" Aaron exclaimed. "That's terrible." He clutched at his arm again, and Evannah could tell that it was still hurting him.

"*And* separated the Island villages," Khalisse hissed. "We used to meet and trade, and work together. But we haven't seen another soul for years."

"Clever strategy," Night Star rumbled. "The citizens can't fight if they can't communicate."

"How is he so powerful?" Evannah asked.

Jannary met her gaze with brown eyes that glimmered with gold. They looked so familiar. "The Watcher is a Whisperer. Until you arrived, he was the last one left on the Island."

Evannah recoiled. Did she have something in common with this villain from the stories? "What... what exactly is a Whisperer?"

"We are called the Isle of Whispers for a reason," Khalisse explained. "One thing sets us apart from every other island in the world. The Whispers."

She leaned forward dramatically. "Powerful spirits of nature, eternal, ethereal beings that are intertwined into the fabric of the Isle. They flourish with the Island and draw their power from the natural world. While the Island lives and breathes, they roam and change. Most people cannot see them." It sounded as though she were quoting a well-known story.

"Like ghosts?" Kiera breathed.

"No." Jannary took over. "Ghosts, if they were real, were once alive. Whispers never had a life. They were born from the power of the Island, and live here forever. I'm sure you have noticed that the Isle of Whispers is unlike any place you've ever seen. The life of the Island and the power of the Whispers combine to form a unique paradise."

Khalisse leaned back and broke the spell. Jannary continued. "Whisperers can harness their power. We will explain more during training, Evannah."

Training? Evannah didn't know how to feel about that. Did she really want to use this power that she had not asked for, that she knew so little about?

"Remind me your names," Khalisse requested. "Full names."

"Kiera," she introduced herself.

"Full name?" Khalisse raised an eyebrow.

Kiera groaned, pausing for a minute. "Kieralyndria Carmine! It's Kieralyndria. Are you happy now?" she shouted. "But don't you dare call me Kieralyndria! It's just Kiera." Evannah snickered. Kiera had hated her full name so much that she had had it officially changed to Kiera three years ago. So technically it was just Kiera now, but nobody had forgotten her original name. When she was eight, she had stood up on the dinner table and shouted to the entire court that if anyone called her Kieralyndria, she would punch their face in.

"I was just asking your last name." Khalisse looked a little traumatized.

"Oh," Kiera blushed. "Um, Kiera Carmine."

"Aaron and Evannah Farrah," Aaron gestured to himself and Evannah amidst the awkwardness. "We're twins."

"Farrah?" Khalisse asked curiously. She looked at Jannary, who shook her head.

"What?" Evannah asked.

"It's nothing, It can't be." Jannary replied curtly, ending that conversation. She paced elegantly around the room before adding, "The prophecy has foretold that you will save us all."

That simple sentence hit them hard. Aaron stood up, Evannah gasped, and Kiera exclaimed, "What? You must be joking!"

"I'm afraid not," Jannary looked down at them with sorrowful eyes. She was young, but at that moment she looked much older, like her responsibility had aged her. She adjusted her headpiece. "I know you didn't ask for this, but destiny has written it for you. What may be shall be. You'll just have to see how fate plays it out for you."

Evannah took a deep breath. They had washed up on a mysterious island, had no idea what was going on, and now they had to save everyone?

"I don't think you have the right people," she started cautiously.

"It couldn't be clearer," Night Star argued in his deep voice.

"Right," Jannary agreed. "You are obviously a Whisperer; any experienced Island citizen can tell. I'm guessing you," she pointed to Kiera, "have some sort of connection to the Island's wildlife. As for you," she looked at Aaron, "I have a hint of an idea, but I'd rather you discover it on your own."

Aaron looked annoyed. "You aren't able to tell me?"

"No, I could," Jannary said pleasantly. "But things only really have meaning if you discover them yourself. Do not worry, I am sure you will learn soon." Aaron sighed.

"Can we hear the prophecy?" Evannah asked.

"Maybe later," Jannary replied curtly, and sat down again. "I know you must be wanting to get back to your home. Do you?"

It was quiet for a few seconds. "Yes," Evannah replied hesitantly, breaking the silence.

"I will not hold you here," Jannary continued. "You are free to go, if that is what you desire. But the Island is in a lot of trouble, and like it or not, you are involved. We would love it if you could stay here and help, however you can. But I don't want to force you. So I am asking you, as an Islander and Emberdawn of Fenlithra, are you willing to fight?"

The air felt thick with tension. It was true, they were confused and conflicted, but they had been called here for a reason. They had felt a call. And now they were needed.

They exchanged a glance, unspoken words traded, before Aaron spoke for them. One word, but it held all the words they weren't willing to say. "Yes."

"Excellent!" Jannary clapped and stood up. "A few of our people have prepared a guest house for you. There will be a feast tonight to introduce you to the rest of the village. Khalisse or I would be more than happy to give you a tour."

"I can take them," Khalisse offered.

"Thank you, Khalisse." Jannary said graciously.

Night Star stalked out of the room. "I will see you again," he promised them.

"Thank you, Night Star," Kiera laid a hand on his side. The cat nodded, a rare glimpse of kindness flashing in his normally gruff eyes, and bounded away.

"Come on," Khalisse began climbing down the Great tree, her long braid swinging. "Let's go see your new, temporary, home!"

"Do we get a treehouse?" Kiera's eyes sparkled.

"Yes! You'll see!" Khalisse seemed equally excited to show them around. "We've prepared a great guest house."

"Better than sleeping on grass," Aaron joked.

"How long have you been here?" Khalisse questioned, skipping forward.

"Two days," Evannah responded.

"Wow. It's actually a miracle you survived that long." Khalisse said frankly. Kiera shot Evannah an indignant look. "Are you starving?"

"We ate this blue fruit thing," Evannah explained. "For every meal. *Every meal.*"

"Ouch," Khalisse laughed. While they walked, she pointed out various parts of the village, like the healer's treehouses, the food gardens, and watch platforms, mounted on the very tops of the trees, to see into the rest of the forest. "How is the rest of the Island?" she asked them longingly.

"You've never seen it?" Evannah asked, shocked. "Your own home?"

"The Watcher separated the villages ten years ago," Khalisse explained. "I explored this area before that, but I was too young to go very far. I've never even seen the other villages!"

"We haven't either," Aaron reassured her. "The rest of the island is beautiful. We arrived on a beach, and we've been in the forest ever since."

"How does the ocean look?" Khalisse asked. "I've only been there twice, both before I was ten. You can't even see the ocean from the watch platforms anymore; the mist covers everything. I just want to see outside this place. Anyway, here we are!" She pointed to a tree.

Steps led up to a beautiful multi-level house, with little flowers growing in the windowsills. Fenced platforms overlooked the forest floor, and swings and hammocks hung down from the house.

"It's so pretty!" Evannah breathed. She couldn't believe they were going to stay here.

Khalisse gave a small smile of pride. "Our houses *are* very unique. It should be fully stocked, but you can find me if you need anything. See you later!" She ran off, effortlessly taking long strides.

The treehouse was like a home straight out of a fairy tale, wrapped in vines, with a living room, dining room, and bedrooms for all of them.

"Almost makes you forget the last two days, huh?" Kiera said. "The mud, the heat... the scratches, the blisters..."

"It's a lot," Evannah agreed. "I don't know what to think. Especially with all this Whisperer stuff."

Aaron patted her shoulder. "You have to let me know if it's ever too much for you. If you can't handle it... we can leave. I don't know where we'd go, but we can leave."

Evannah flinched. "Don't baby me! I can take care of myself." She softened at Aaron's hurt look. "Sorry. I'm fine, and I will be. Don't worry."

"Look, lunch!" Kiera broke the tension, gesturing to a basket on the table. It was stuffed with bread, nuts, and unrecognizable, colorful vegetables.

They sat around the wooden dining table and began to eat. Kiera created a sandwich from the bread and vegetables, and the others followed.

With no warning, a feathered creature flew through the open doorway and crash-landed on the floor.

Everyone screamed, and Evannah jumped back, alarmed. "What. Is. That?" The creature was relatively small, chubby, and covered in yellow, brown, and white feathers.

"I told you to close the door, Aaron!" Kiera scolded.

"You never said that!" Aaron defended himself. "It almost looks like the marmots from the Neomerican mountains. But with wings. And feathers."

The chubby creature scurried toward them happily.

"What if it tries to kill us?" Kiera cried. "I don't even know what's cute and what's deadly anymore!"

"You're the one who's supposed to be connected to wildlife, or something like that," Aaron retorted. "Do something!"

Deciding that neither of them were going to do anything, Evannah stepped toward it. "Shoo!" She tried to scare it off. Luckily, the creature hopped outside, and Evannah closed the door. "How hard was that?"

"Our savior, Evannah!" Kiera cheered. "My lunch awaits." She picked it up, and bit into it.

She was mid-bite when the creature flew in again, through the window that they had forgotten to close, swooped past the table, and grabbed Kiera's sandwich right out of her hands. "HEY!" Kiera yelled. "Catch it, it's evil!"

Kiera jumped up and began to chase the creature around the room with fierce determination. Aaron tried to jump in and help but got smacked by a wing and fell onto the couch.

Evannah got up to help but lost sight of Kiera as she ran after the creature up the stairs. There was a CRASH and moments later, she came barreling down and nearly ran into Evannah.

"Let it go, it's just a sandwich!" Aaron shouted.

"IT'S MY SANDWICH!" Kiera yelled back furiously, still chasing the creature with outstretched arms. There was another BANG and a CRASH as she careened into the table and ended up sprawled on the floor.

"Help me corner this thing, Evannah!" Kiera called. Evannah sprang into action, leaping up on one side of the kitchen while Kiera regained her footing and blocked the other.

The creature, caught in the middle, looked from Evannah to Kiera, dropped the sandwich, and cocked its head innocently. It seemed to be smiling with its chubby cheeks.

"Thanks," Kiera swiped the sandwich, which was now a soggy mess, and promptly dropped it in the trash.

"You didn't even want it?" Evannah asked indignantly.

"Of course not! It's all gross now. It's the thought that matters anyway," Kiera explained as though she knew everything.

"I couldn't let that little guy get away with stealing from *me*." Evannah sighed, shooing the creature out of the open window and making sure *all* entrances were closed this time.

They finished up lunch, laughing about the whole sandwich-stealing incident. Evannah told everyone that she was going to take a much needed nap, and retreated to her bedroom.

She shut the door and flopped onto her bed, limbs outstretched. Then she closed her eyes, and let the whispers come to her.

Hello, Whisperer. I see you know what we are, now.

Yes. I wanted to know, what does it mean to be a Whisperer? Evannah asked. A hint of pain lingered in her temples, threatening to turn into a headache. The onslaught of voices was still too much.

Ah, the mind wonders. It means you can hear and understand us, like nobody else can. Once you get experienced, you can even see us.

What do you look like?

You will find out, once the time comes. The most important power of a Whisperer is the ability to harness our energy and use it to manipulate and change the world around you. You can use our power as your own.

I don't want to hurt anyone, Evannah thought.

You don't have to. In fact, just the opposite. Your powers can be used to create and protect. You are not evil. Each individual has choices to make.

Am I the only one? Evannah asked.

The one they call 'The Watcher' is the only other Whisperer currently in existence.

What happened to the others? Evannah wasn't sure she wanted to know the answer.

The Watcher killed them.

Chapter 10

Kiera stared at the mirror. Jannary had had clothes delivered earlier that day for the feast they would be going to in minutes. She had been given dark green robes shot through with gold and a simple gold headpiece.

She looked like a real Island citizen now.

"Are you ready?" Aaron called from the main room.

"Coming!" she responded, hurrying out. Aaron and Evannah were dressed in matching robes and headpieces, but Aaron's was mahogany and gold and Evannah's was dark blue and gold.

"Hey, who made us match?" Aaron complained. "Evannah and I matching was bad enough." Evannah elbowed him. "I'm just kidding," he laughed. "You look really pretty, Kiera."

"Thanks," she responded. "Are we leaving now?"

"Yup!" Aaron replied. "The only direction the person who dropped off our clothes gave me was to *follow the crowd.*"

She glanced out the window. Sure enough, every person in the village seemed to be heading in the same direction. "Thankfully it's on ground level. You can get lost in those treehouses."

"It's a maze," Evannah agreed, glancing upwards at the intricate levels of treehouses. "I don't know how anyone finds their way around."

"I hope the food is good!" Kiera remarked cheerfully, as she ran down the steps. Sunset had painted the sky with beautiful smears of light pink and dusky purple.

They began walking in the same direction as everyone. Was the *entire village* attending the feast?

A couple with two young children approached them. "Welcome, we're so glad that you're here!"

Aaron grinned in response. "We're happy to be here!"

"I hope the village is treating you all right," an elderly woman said, beaming at them. "Are you enjoying your stay?"

"Yes, it's a very pretty place," Kiera replied. Something was off. Their bright eyes, their too-wide smiles. *This is wrong.*

The people moved away, and Kiera shifted closer to her friends. "Doesn't this seem weird?"

"What about it?" Aaron asked, puzzled.

"They're *too* friendly. Like they know something that we don't."

Aaron brushed it away. "I'm sure they're just trying to be kind."

But Kiera couldn't help but notice that the villagers who were not talking directly to her were muttering in groups, casting them wary looks.

"Hello!" Khalisse, dressed in gold, jumped off a treehouse platform and landed directly in front of them.

"Aah!" Evannah jumped back. She laughed when she realized who it was. "You scared me!"

"You should have seen the look on your faces," Khalisse grinned. "How was lunch, was the house okay?"

"Great," Kiera responded. "Except a feathered *monster* broke in and stole my sandwich!"

"Oh, a quangle!" Khalisse snickered. "They love to steal food. If you leave a door or window open you'll have an invasion in no time. But they're kind of cute, some people have them as pets." Kiera shook her head in disapproval.

"So where is the feast at?" Aaron asked.

"It's held at the Gathering Place," Khalisse explained. "Community gatherings, meetings, and large get-togethers are usually held there."

"That's a creative name," Kiera commented, rolling her eyes.

"That's what I've been saying!" Khalisse agreed in surprise.

"You're young to be Head of Warriors," Aaron noted. "You don't look much older than me."

"Yes," Khalisse said, fingering the edges of her braid. "Jannary was made Everdawn, which is what we call our leader, really young. We were always close, so she picked me as the new Head of Warriors when the time came. She thinks youths have the best ideas." She winked. "And I was the best warrior in my batch."

"Is that it?" Kiera pointed.

"Yup! This is the Gathering Place."

The Gathering Place was a large clearing, apparently large enough to fit the entire village. Rows of wooden tables and woven mats had been set up around the space, and dozens of tiny wildflowers grew all around. The place had been made beautiful by softly glowing flowering trees, and little balls of light hovering above to illuminate the area.

Loud chatter filled the place as Khalisse showed Kiera, Evannah, and Aaron to their special seating area near Jannary and herself. More people continued to stream in and fill up the space. Kiera felt awkwardly on display in the front of the crowd, as all the Fenlithra citizens talked and pointed at her.

When everyone had arrived and had taken their seats, Jannary stood up and hushed the crowd. There were hundreds and hundreds of people there.

"Welcome, everyone!" Jannary announced with widespread arms. "Tonight, we celebrate the arrival of Evannah, Aaron, and Kiera, from the faraway land of—" She looked toward them.

"Neomerica," Kiera filled in.

"Neomerica!" Jannary continued. "As you know, we have been waiting for these three for a long time. I have hope that the end of the Watcher's horrible reign is on the horizon." Kiera winced, feeling the pressure of the hopeful stares.

"Please be kind to our distinguished guests and treat them with the respect they deserve. We will now feast!" She clapped, and the citizens began standing up to get food.

"Front of the line for you three," Night Star, who had melted out of the shadows, nudged them. "You are the guests of honor."

"Nice," Kiera remarked, walking with her friends to the food tables.

The food was laid out like a buffet on tables set up in the corner, and shielded under a covering woven of leaves and mounted on poles.

There were dozens and dozens of giant pots and plates filled with cooked vegetables, breads, fruits, and many types of unique dishes that Kiera had never seen before. It all looked amazing. She inhaled the delicious scents, and grabbed a wooden plate, ready to dig in.

Then, the ground began to shake under her feet.

She stumbled back and forth as it rocked. The dishes clattered and several plates fell off the table. The world was moving, it was shaking.

"GET DOWN!" Night Star sprang to his paws and yelled. "Earthquake!"

People started screaming, pulling their children close and ducking for cover under tables. Kiera tripped, trying not to lose her balance.

Evannah grabbed her hand. "Come here!" She pulled Kiera and Aaron over to a table to try to take cover.

"You three, here!" Night Star called. They tried to run over to him, holding on to each other. Finally, they made it. Night Star pushed them, Jannary, and Khalisse together, and curled his great body around them to protect them.

The clanking and crashing sounds continued, but Kiera couldn't see anything past Night Star's fur. He shielded them loyally.

After a minute, the shaking finally stopped. Night Star cautiously uncurled himself. People slowly crawled out from their hiding spaces and uncovered their heads.

The damage had been minimal. A few dishes had fallen and a small tree had collapsed. Already, people worked on carrying it away. Thankfully, there were no injuries.

The citizens began murmuring in concern. Everyone was shocked by what had happened. Night Star shot a significant look at Jannary, and Kiera caught it. What was that?

"Are earthquakes common here?" she asked.

"They happen," responded Night Star simply. "This one, though... it was unnatural."

"Oh—you mean," Kiera began.

"It was most likely caused by the Watcher."

"He can summon earthquakes?" Evannah's knuckles gripped her empty plate so hard they turned white. "The Whispers were screaming in pain."

"He's never done it before," Night Star explained gruffly. "I don't think he meant to do it."

"Then why—"

Jannary lowered her voice, touching her headpiece nervously. "We feared this was coming. The Watcher has pulled so much power from the Island that it is becoming unstable."

"So this may happen again?" Kiera questioned.

"We predict it will happen more and more frequently, until the Island finally collapses," Night Star let a little emotion leak into his gruff voice.

"But—" Khalisse interjected. "This is *way* earlier than we predicted."

"Yes," Jannary looked grave. She turned to the three friends. "When the Watcher first started taking power from the Isle, we knew that it would cause the Island to become unstable. But we thought we had at least a year or two from now to deal with the problem."

"How long until the Island collapses?" Kiera asked.

"It could be anywhere from a few days to a few months," Jannary sighed. "Unfortunately, we have no research on this topic. For good reason!"

People were starting to look anxious, turning to Jannary for solace.

"For now," Jannary ordered. "Put on a smile and enjoy this feast. My people need reassurance, and you need a celebration, and a break. Enjoy tonight. We will deal with this tomorrow."

She turned gracefully back to her citizens. "We apologize for that disruption. I hope we won't let it ruin our night that we worked so hard to prepare for! You may continue to feast!"

People began lining up for food again. Kiera heaped her plate high, and Aaron and Evannah followed, selecting whatever looked good to them.

They took their food back to the table and began eating with everyone else. If Jannary had been trying to lift her village's spirits, it had worked. Happy chatter and conversations filled the air. It was dark now, and little glowing fireflies flew around.

Curious people approached Kiera, Evannah, and Aaron to ask them questions, such as: "What was your home like?" "What parts of the Island have you seen?" "Are you really from the prophecy?" They tried to answer the questions as best as they could. Aaron especially seemed to enjoy talking to everyone, and it felt like he was already forming a bond with the Fenlithrians. But it did feel odd that the villagers were already so kind to them. Shouldn't they have been at least a little suspicious of the strangers?

An elderly woman with a silver bun came up to Evannah. "You're so pale, haven't you been getting any sun?"

"Um," Evannah looked confused. Kiera giggled.

The woman patted her on the cheek. "And skinny. You need to eat more!"

"Thanks? Wait, no, I mean..." Evannah fumbled for the right words. The woman walked away and Kiera and Aaron burst out into laughter.

"Yeah, eat more," Kiera teased, patting Evannah on the cheek like the woman had done. Even Night Star let out a snort that sounded suspiciously like a laugh.

"It's time for tonight's tale," Jannary announced to everyone.

"Tale?" Kiera asked.

"At big gatherings like this, it's tradition to tell a story," Khalisse explained. Everyone started pulling their mats into a big circle. Kiera found a mat and did the same, until everyone had formed a giant ring.

Sitting on the ground with everyone in a circle, sharing food and laughing, Kiera felt a sense of community that she had almost never felt before.

A big bearded man wearing a golden medallion stepped into the center of the circle. "My name is Aremor Talesharer," he introduced himself. "And for our new guests, I am one of Fenlithra's storytellers. We are tasked with passing down history and tales from our people over time. I have a story for you today."

Kiera clapped with the crowd, looking forward to the tale.

Aremor gestured passionately as he announced, "Today's tale will be one of sorrow and loneliness, of a broken heart and a thirst for power." He had an expressive voice that immediately drew Kiera in and got her interested.

"Once, there lived a young boy named Naharan," Aremor began.

Jannary stood up. "I hardly think this tale is appropriate for the occasion!" she exclaimed in concern.

"The children need to know," Aremor argued. "Stories cannot be withheld from anyone. They must be shared."

"Fine," Jannary conceded. "Have caution while sharing this tale."

What could be so bad about a story that even Jannary didn't want them to share?

"As I was saying," Aremor continued. "There once lived a young boy named Naharan. Long ago, but not as long as you may expect, Naharan lived on this Isle with his parents and sister. They lived peacefully and happily, sharing with the earth and learning and teaching one another.

"One day, there was a storm on the Isle. A fierce storm, and the rivers and lakes began to flood. The rain pelted down so hard they could be shards of glass. And while getting their children to safety, Naharan's parents drowned and departed from this life.

"Naharan and his twin sister, both young at the time, were raised by their entire village, even their entire Island, for the Isle cares for everyone. As they grew older, it became clear that they were both Whisperers, an ability that even their parents had not possessed."

Aremor paused for dramatic effect. "As you know, even back then, Whisperers were rare and special, each one unique in the gifts that they brought to the Isle and to their people." Many stares went to Evannah, and she shifted awkwardly.

"Naharan and his sister continued to grow, from young children to young adults, and their powers developed over time. They grew into fine Whisperers, knowledgeable and confident in their abilities.

"They used their powers to expand villages, heal wounds, and create wonderful things. They left their home and began to travel around the Isle of Whispers, exploring and creating, helping and trading. They became well-known across the Isle, and had earned quite a reputation.

"Naharan started to get more and more interested in what his abilities could do, realizing that as a Whisperer, he could do things that mere men had only dreamed of. While he was like fire, fiercely passionate, his sister was like water, steady and gentle, with much determination and strength. It was no surprise that they began to get into arguments about how to best use their power.

"However, both his sister and he had a fascination with life beyond the island. They began to explore the ocean further and further away from the Isle. They announced, one day, that the two of them would be taking their boat and sailing far across the sea, to lands that nobody had seen before."

Kiera leaned forward, entranced. The story had captured her attention, and everyone else's. The entire clearing was silent, except for the passionate voice of Aremor.

"They had not announced a date for their journey, but rather were waiting for the right opportunity. But before they had a chance to depart, something new had come to the shores of the Isle.

"A group of people, who looked and acted like nobody they had ever seen before. Who arrived in a big boat, eager to explore and learn all about this new, different place. But little did they know how different it would be. The things that set the Isle of Whispers apart from every other place in the world.

"Naharan and his sister, who were regarded as something close to leaders now, welcomed the strangers, excited to learn about the lands beyond their island. They began to show them around, to trade with them and let them live as citizens do for many days. They even shared some of the Island's secrets, like the presence of the Whispers.

"But now that the strangers had seen this land, they wanted it for themselves. They wanted the resource-rich mountains, the lush rainforest, and the beautiful sea. They had gotten greedy.

"Naharan and his sister were shocked at their change of behavior. After all, they had only treated the guests with kindness. Negotiations opened, and the fiery Naharan swore to come out victorious at all costs.

"Fights broke out. Small fights, nothing like the battles that could have happened. All Naharan wanted to do was scare these strangers away, and for them to spread tales to stay away from his island.

"But the conflict had unintended consequences. The intruders took Naharan's sister by force and attempted to leave the island. Despite Naharan's best efforts, they had a huge head start and escaped the island with his sister, killing her in the process.

"Heartbroken and alone, Naharan swore that the Isle would stay hidden from the rest of the world for all of eternity, and sought to make good on that promise.

"He began to experiment with his powers, doing something that no Whisperer had even done before. He attempted to draw his power *directly from the life of the Island.*

"It took an enormous effort, and a big toll on the Isle, but he eventually succeeded. He had gained access to abilities that no Whisperer had ever gotten before. He was more powerful than ever. But the Isle was beginning to become unstable."

A knowing murmur went around the crowd, and Kiera began to suspect that she knew who this story was about.

"He continued to gain in power, while the Island continued to slowly wither. The life in the rainforest started fading while the ocean coves and lagoons suffered.

"Eventually, Naharan created a home for himself in the tallest mountain on the Isle of Whispers: Watcher Peak. He adopted its name for himself, and was known since then as the Watcher, claiming that like the mountain, he watched over the safety of the Island. But taking the life of the Island had taken its toll. He was too far gone, barely human anymore.

"The other Whisperers protested about how he was hurting the Island, tried to rally the people and stop him. But they were no match for him. He killed them all.

"With nobody to stop him, the Watcher separated the villages so that they couldn't fight back again. He believed that the Island would only be safe while he was the leader.

"And still today, the Watcher rules with an iron fist, crushing anyone and anything who dares get in his way."

Kiera stood in the clearing, waiting for someone to show up.

She could still feel chills from the story the previous night. After the tale, they had started playing music and celebrated into the night. They had gone to sleep late, and awoken to instructions the next morning.

A note had been slid under their doorway with separate directions for each of them. Kiera had followed the directions to an empty clearing on the outskirts of the village, and was told that someone would meet her there. She wasn't sure who, and when they were coming.

"Hello," an older man walked into the clearing. Spectacles framed his kind brown eyes and his neat black hair was streaked with gray. "It is a pleasure to meet you at last."

He held out his hand to shake, and Kiera took it. "My name is Tovan Smallsprout."

"Kiera Carmine," she introduced herself. "What are we doing here?"

Tovan laughed gently. "They didn't tell you?"

"No. I was just given a note with instructions."

"Oh," he replied. "We're training, of course."

"Training?" Kiera asked, surprised. She knew Evannah, the supposed Whisperer, needed training, but she hadn't expected to need it.

"Yes," he answered. "Both your friends are in training right now, with different mentors. I was selected because of our similarity in abilities."

"Abilities?" What abilities did this man have? What abilities did she even have?

"In the prophecy, you supposedly have a special connection with the Island. Night Star has told me that you have started to connect with these abilities to save your friends."

"I'm not magical," Kiera told him. She knew it wasn't like that.

"Not magic," Tovan agreed. "More like a bond with the Island. You ask, and it listens. A friendship. An understanding. Even for Island citizens, that's very special."

"Oh." Kiera had never been special like that in her life. It was a lot to wrap her head around. "Wait, you said you have abilities? What kind?"

"You have to know," Tovan explained, "that many children or relatives of Whisperers have small abilities. Sometimes unrelated individuals that the Island has chosen have them too. Nothing as large as the power of Whisperers, much more limited and focused."

"Can you show me?" Kiera asked eagerly.

"Of course." Tovan removed a handful of something from the pocket of his simple, earth-colored attire. Seeds. He dug a small hole, poured the seeds in, and covered them with dirt.

He closed his eyes and waved his hand over the hole. After several moments of concentrating, a small green sprout shot up and unfurled tiny leaves. Tovan opened his eyes, exhausted and panting. "Wow. I've never grown a plant that fast before, but I wanted to show you. It usually takes several hours."

"That's so cool," Kiera exclaimed. "You can grow plants?"

"I can help them grow," Tovan corrected, "just a little bit faster and healthier. Nothing too intense."

"So you had Whisperer parents?" Kiera asked. She hesitated. "Were they—"

"Killed by the Watcher?" Tovan's face darkened. "Yes. I was part of the force to stop him, back when I was a warrior. They died in front of my eyes."

Kiera reached out and patted his arm. "I'm sorry."

"Don't be," Tovan assured her. "We're going to take him down. All of us, together. The prophecy will guide us."

"What is this prophecy?" Kiera asked. "I keep hearing *about* it but I've never heard it."

"Perhaps another time." Tovan placed another seed in the dirt and covered it up. "For now, let's start off simple, and see if you can grow this seed."

"Um," Kiera said. "How do I do that?"

"Ask the Island," Tovan instructed. "Channel its force through the seed and let it grow."

"Okay..."

Feeling quite silly, she crouched down by the seed. "Um, Island?" she whispered. "Can you make this seed grow?"

Of course, nothing happened. She looked questioningly at Tovan. "Try to connect with the soul of the Island," he suggested.

Kiera didn't have the faintest idea how to do that. She closed her eyes and placed her palm on the ground like she had done to the Flowering Tree.

A presence. She couldn't describe it, but she could feel a presence, enormous and ancient, always present, watching and breathing and listening with a thousand eyes and ears. "I think I feel the Island," she breathed.

"You're on the right track," Tovan reassured her. "Any Islander can feel the presence of the Island, so this is a good first step. Now you need to ask it a favor. Remember, you have a bond. It will likely listen, if you ask with enough conviction."

Feeling the presence with her mind, she asked again, quietly murmuring, "Can you make this seed grow?"

So slowly she thought she imagined it, a tiny green bud shot up. She jumped back, surprised.

Tovan applauded. "Good job! We're on step one of beating the Watcher."

Chapter 11

Where was everyone? Aaron whirled around. He had followed his instructions to a clearing that looked like it was used for training. Weapons were mounted on racks and various obstacles lined the area.

A sword was tossed to his feet. *What?* He looked around for anyone who could have tossed it. There was nobody. Aaron carefully picked the sword up. His arm was feeling much better after a few days, and he was now able to use it properly.

"THINK FAST!" Khalisse jumped from the nearest tree holding a sword of her own.

"Yaaah!" Aaron screamed. When he recovered from his near heart attack, he found Khalisse charging toward him, ferociously waving her sword. He started to run away.

"Don't run, you idiot! Fight back!" Khalisse yelled at him.

Reluctantly, he stopped, and turned to face the fierce warrior. He brandished his sword awkwardly.

She moved to strike him, and he blocked it. She tried that a few more times in various positions, and he blocked all of them, quickly moving around.

Aaron tried thrusting the sword and striking her, but she avoided it with lightning-fast reflexes. After a few minutes of back and forth, Khalisse took a swipe at him with so much force that his sword clattered to the ground.

Khalisse held the blade inches from his neck. "I win!" She picked up his sword and handed it back. "Good fight, but get a grip on that handle or you'll lose your head. Have you had any training before?"

"A little bit," Aaron replied. "Barely any."

"Well, you held the sword very comfortably," Khalisse said.

"Really?" Aaron laughed. "I thought that was terrible."

"It was really good for a beginner," Khalisse remarked. "Have you ever *really* fought someone before?"

Aaron thought about that for a minute. "Well, there were those enchanted vines. I cut up a few but I don't know if that counts as fighting. There was also this shadow guy. He mainly chased us, but Kiera stabbed him."

"You fought a Shadow?" Khalisse looked incredulous.

"We mostly ran," Aaron admitted. "Do you know... what it was?"

Khalisse looked solemn. "Shadows are agents of the Watcher. They used to be Whispers, but were changed when the Watcher pulled out the life of the Island. They killed Jannary's aunt, the previous Everdawn."

"It spoke to us," Aaron told her.

Her eyes grew wide. "Shadows can't speak by themselves. That must have been the Watcher, speaking directly to you."

Chills ran up Aaron's arm. He didn't know what to say, except, "Oh."

"And if you survived, it's because the Watcher wanted that. A Shadow could have easily killed you. Anyway, let's try a few different weapons." Khalisse moved on quickly, rapidly changing subjects in her usual manner.

She pulled a few more from the rack and tossed them into a pile at his feet.

Aaron tried daggers and spears, bows and arrows, and more swords, while Khalisse watched and gave advice.

Finally, exhausted, he reracked them all.

"You're an intuitive fighter," Khalisse commented. "I suspected as much."

"So... what?" Aaron asked. "Does that have something to do with the powers that I'm supposed to have?"

"I would think so," said Khalisse cryptically. "Honestly, I don't know all too much about the prophecy. That's left to Jannary and our Fate-reader, Nyevia. You'll probably meet her eventually."

Aaron's mind ran, trying to collect his thoughts. "I can't be some fighting prodigy. I don't even like to fight!"

Khalisse plopped down on a nearby rock and folded her legs in. "I'll tell you a secret. I didn't want to fight either."

"Really?" Aaron couldn't believe that.

"Really. When I was little, *really* little, I wanted to be a gardener," Khalisse laughed. "I can't imagine that now. But when I got a bit older, around eight, my parents would take me to watch their training. They were warriors, really good ones. They talked all about how important it was to defend the village and protect our people, and I got interested. Then being a warrior became my new life goal."

"Hmm," Aaron nodded. It was hard to picture Khalisse wanting to be anything except a warrior. "I guess I would if I had to... if I could save someone."

"That's the spirit! Come on, pick up the sword," Khalisse encouraged. "We'll train until lunch."

So they continued for a few more hours. Khalisse showed Aaron how to wield each weapon, and the tricks of fighting a live, moving opponent. She was right; Aaron was a natural. He picked up the precise techniques as quickly as she could teach them. And although he didn't want to fight, he had to admit that it was a useful skill.

"Okay," Khalisse looked at the sun. "It's about noon, so we'll gather for lunch." She led him away from the training clearing.

They walked through the village, finally reaching an area close to the center of the village. Tables were laid out and canopies provided shade. It was the perfect, picturesque picnic spot.

"Hey Aaron!" Kiera waved. She was already sitting at one of the tables. "How was training?"

"Good, I think," Aaron replied. He didn't really know what to make of the session. Evannah approached and sat down next to them. "How was yours, Evannah?"

"Interesting," Evannah said. "They don't have another Whisperer to teach me so I'm just learning from books."

"Ouch," Kiera winced. "That just sounds painful."

"It's not too bad," Evannah shrugged. She'd always liked reading. "What are you learning, Aaron?"

"Fighting," Aaron responded unenthusiastically. "With weapons and stuff."

"Ooh." Kiera's eyes lit up. "That sounds so fun!"

"You can switch with me," Aaron tried immediately.

"Why do you want to switch?" Kiera asked. "All I'm doing right now is growing plants!" An older man standing a few feet away gave her a look out of the side of his eye. "Um, I mean, it's a very useful and important job."

A few villagers sat down on the tables around them, and someone started passing around plates of food. A villager with a long reddish-brown ponytail served them some kind of red drink, which Aaron became immediately obsessed with.

"The food here is so good!" Kiera exclaimed. "I don't think I'm ever leaving." Quangles, the chubby little sandwich stealing creatures, had begun to bounce innocently around the edge of the picnic spot, and she gave them a suspicious look.

Aaron laughed in response but it brought a question to his mind that he hadn't thought about in a while. How and when were they going to get home? They had to go back eventually, didn't they? There was no telling when this whole crisis with the Watcher would end. Honestly, it was hard to think of it as his crisis, even though he was connected to it. The Watcher seemed like a faceless being he had never met.

Was Lord Cyrus missing them? Probably not. As High Courtier, he was in charge of the court, and had devoted his life to that. Maybe Aalliah, the mother he never knew, would have. She had been High Courtieress when alive, and the court had decreed that someone from the next generation of children would be the next High Courtieress. Everyone knew it was going to be Evannah.

"Did you hear that Aaron?" Khalisse asked.

"Huh?" Aaron had been lost in his thoughts.

Khalisse rolled her eyes. "I said, you and Evannah will be training together this afternoon. It might be helpful!"

"Oh," Aaron replied. "Yay? I think?" Evannah just sighed.

"Can I join?" Kiera asked immediately. "I don't want them having too much fun without me!"

The older man shook his head. "We have a lot to work on." Kiera groaned, but they were both smiling. He introduced himself as Tovan, Kiera's mentor. Aaron could see that Kiera genuinely liked him.

Khalisse left, and they started chatting about their sessions. Aaron recounted the fact he had learned, that the Shadow had been a fallen Whisper and that it had been the Watcher talking to them.

Soon, some curious villagers scooted closer to join the conversation.

"Hi, what's your name?" Aaron asked a kid, probably around ten years old. His face lit up at having been acknowledged.

"I'm Kairen," he responded happily.

"Aaron," he introduced himself in return. "Do you want to sit with us?"

"Yes!" Kairen's eyes brightened.

A teen with a mischievous smile and gold streaks in her black hair came over. "Kai, don't bother the guests. I'm sorry about my brother."

"Don't be," Aaron reassured her. "He's very sweet. You're welcome to sit with us as well."

"Oh! Thanks," she looked surprised. "I'm Auri. You must be Aaron."

"That's me," he admitted jokingly.

Three other villagers joined and introduced themselves: Thalen, a bearded village guard; Liora, who was another storyteller; and Barbenne, the chef who had served the red drinks.

"Tell us," Thalen asked. "Where did you come from, and what is it like there?"

Aaron looked to Kiera, who had made it clear that she spoke for the group. "All you," she said, busy guzzling her drink.

So Aaron launched into a description of Neomerica, from the court to the gray ocean, from the castle where they lived according to their traditions.

"Wow," commented Liora. "That sounds so... rigid."

"Yeah," Barbenne agreed. "Here, we do what we do, whenever we want. The Everdawn guides us, but doesn't control us."

"Our real leader is the Island," Tovan chimed in with a poetic voice.

"But I'd love to see Neomerica!" Liora said dreamily. "Or any place, other than this village."

"Staying in the same place for ten years gets really tiring," Auri explained.

"I've *never* seen anywhere else!" Kairen complained. "How am I supposed to train as a warrior or brave explorer if there's nowhere to go?"

"Aaron!" Khalisse's voice called from faraway. "Evannah! Training time!"

"I guess we'd better go too," Tovan told Kiera. She grabbed one more cup of the red drink for the road and followed him.

"Come on," Evannah tugged Aaron forward. "It might be fun?" Even she sounded unsure. They caught up to Khalisse and walked to a spot near the river.

Liora, the storyteller, had brought Evannah a stack of books and ancient looking scrolls. She struggled to carry them all. "Here's everything I have on Whisperers! Ancient tales, biographies, and even some books that were meant to teach other Whisperers."

"Thanks," Evannah took an armful of books and Khalisse stacked the rest of them on a rock.

"Get reading," Khalisse suggested.

Liora explained that she had been helping Evannah learn through the books. "I think we left off here," she held up a book-marked page. "The chapter about light."

"We finished that one," Evannah held up her hand and created floating balls of light that flew around the clearing before winking out. Aaron watched, amazed. Evannah seemed much more in her element here.

"Okay, moving on," Liora flipped the page. "To... levitation!" She continued to read, and Evannah moved closer to listen.

"While they're doing that," Khalisse jabbed Aaron's leg with the hilt of a sword.

"Ow!"

"Stay vigilant at all times!" she barked, jabbing him again, before handing it to him. "Move your feet!"

Aaron groaned, before obliging.

While they sparred, Evannah and Liora were working on making things fly. She started with one book, and soon multiple were soaring around the area.

Khalisse had just shoved him into the river for the third time, and he was hauling himself out, dripping wet, when the books started to attack him.

"Ack!" he shielded himself from the books flying at his face.

"Oh, sorry Aaron!" Evannah didn't sound sorry at all. "It's hard to control so many!"

He tried to run to get away from them, but so many books were flying around the area that many kept crashing into him.

He held up his hands to block his face, and his head pounded.

Then, every book suddenly fell to the ground.

"Oh no!" Liora ran to pick them up, stroking their spines lovingly. "Are you okay?"

"What happened?" Evannah's head tilted in confusion. "I can't hear the Whispers anymore." She put a hand to her ear.

Liora and Khalisse exchanged a joyful look. "This is better than we hoped for!" Khalisse exclaimed. "Our plan was to advance Evannah's skills enough that she could break the curse and get us out of here. But Aaron—you have the ability to bind powers. You can temporarily take them away."

"Aaron—you're our key out of here."

Aaron stood up and quietly walked to the door. It was the middle of the night, the only noises were the tweeting of birds and the rustling of leaves. Shadows cloaked the world.

He couldn't sleep, so he got dressed and went to stand on the platform outside their treehouse. It was a beautiful, clear night. The moon illuminated bright stars and he could faintly see swirls of purple galaxies.

After their discovery that afternoon, that Aaron could somehow bind magic, Jannary and Night Star had immediately started to make plans. They were to embark on a journey the next morning, of which he knew no details. There had also been a second earthquake that evening, which just made everyone more anxious.

Right now, he just needed a moment to himself.

A shadow caught his eye. In the distance, on a small hill dotted with glowing flowers, a figure sat, head tilted back, staring at the sky.

Curious, Aaron silently descended from the treehouse and walked over to look.

The figure was a young woman with long, streaming black hair. A glowing flower was tucked behind her ear. As he got closer, he realized that unlike the rest of the village, her eyes were blue. A cobalt blue that reflected the stars.

"The stars tell me what I need to know," she murmured in a melodious voice, not bothering to turn her head to see him. "But they do not need to tell me that sometimes, someone needs a minute away from reality. Come, sit with me, and we'll escape into the sky together."

Aaron climbed the small hill and sat down on the soft grass next to her. "Are you..." he hesitated, "Nyevia?" He recalled Khalisse mentioning the name.

"Yes," she replied. "The Fate-reader. I'm very sorry we haven't met before. I prefer to be outside at night."

They were quiet for a minute. "How old are you?" Aaron asked. She looked young, but seemed much older than that.

"My soul, as the soul of every Fate-reader, is as ancient as the planets."

"Were you one of the original Fate-readers who heard the prophecy? About us?" Aaron wondered.

"I was not around a hundred years ago," Nyevia told him. "That Fate-reader has moved on from this life. But I've been educated in that prophecy, and am very familiar with it."

"I've never heard it," Aaron admitted. "Nobody is telling us, and... it feels like they're keeping it from us on purpose. I don't know."

"Would you like to hear it?" Nyevia offered gently.

Aaron shifted a little on the grass. "Yes."

Nyevia took a deep breath, and launched into the prophecy. She almost sang it, with a melodic, mysterious voice that seemed to echo through the night sky. Her eyes looked like they faintly glowed.

From distant shores three strangers come,
Young hearts drawn where old songs hum.

By root and flame and whispering stone,
They walk a path not walked alone.

The Whisperer shall wake the past,
The Wanderer tread truths once masked,
The Warrior rise where others fell—
And break the Watcher's binding spell.

Not born beneath our sky or sea,
Yet called by fate, by land, by plea.
One shall fall, one shall fade,
One shall see the darkness slayed.

Aaron sat straight up. "So that was why nobody wanted to tell us. One of us is going to die! And the other will fade, whatever that means."

"Warrior," Nyevia addressed him using the title from the prophecy, "If something is fated, it will happen. But we can control *how* it happens."

"I... I don't know anymore," Aaron confessed. "I don't know how much longer I can put on a brave face, when I know that I've dragged my sister and my... my friend into danger. And if one of them were to die? I don't think I would survive that." He wrapped his hands around his knees. "I'm no Warrior."

The Fate-reader turned to him, compassion in her striking eyes. "A great warrior is not born, but made. I see the fire within you. The passion that drives you forward. That is all you need."

Aaron brushed the grass with his fingertips, feeling vulnerable at having spilled his feelings to a stranger. "Sometimes it feels like the world is against us."

"It may feel like that now," Nyevia reassured him. "But even on the darkest nights, you can see the stars. It may be midnight, but it will be dawn soon. The sun will rise and brighten the world once more."

She turned to Aaron, and the starlight illuminated her youthful features. "I know that you did not ask for your destiny. No one does, but the heavens weave them anyway. I believe in fate, but I also believe in choice. Freedom and destiny go hand in hand."

Aaron tilted his head. "I'm not sure if I understand."

"What I'm saying," Nyevia expressed, "is that you can never truly change who you are. So live the life you were meant to live, and live it to the fullest. The stars do not bind you—they remind you. Fate is not a chain, but a lantern, and it is yours to carry."

Aaron pondered that. It was a lot to think about, but he thought he understood, deep down. "Thank you," he whispered. "I need to ask you one more thing. Many years ago, when we were in Neomerica, we found a version of the prophecy."

He recounted the prophecy to her, and she looked thoughtful. "I was wondering, who sent that prophecy?"

Nyevia stroked one of the glowing petals of the flowers growing on the hillside. "I believe you know the answer to that question."

It seemed clear all of a sudden. "The *Island* sent it to us, didn't it?"

"Yes. A preparation for the years to come ahead. A warning."

"We were nine," Aaron remarked. "Only Kiera saw it, and she didn't understand it. Why would it send it to us then?"

"The Island works in mysterious ways," Nyevia gave him a faint smile. "It was just a clue. The smallest hint about who you were meant to be."

They were quiet for many minutes, watching the twinkling stars amidst the dark skies.

Finally, Aaron got up. "Thank you for talking to me, but I should probably get some sleep before the journey tomorrow."

"Good bye," Nyevia said melodiously. "And remember—the stars do not tell you the path to walk—they only show you that you are not walking it alone."

Chapter 12

"We leave in five minutes," Night Star growled, padding around the Great Tree. They were by the trunk of the enormous plant, getting ready for a mission that they had no idea about.

"Can you tell us where we're going now?" Evannah asked. "And why couldn't we know?"

Night Star glanced around and sighed. "I guess it's late enough now. Fine, we're going to find a secret path called the Trail of Truth. Legend states that you can find an answer to any question there. We couldn't tell you earlier, because we're afraid the Watcher might try to attack you, and we didn't want to give him any time to think or prepare. We know he can see us. The borders of Fenlithra are usually protected against his magical sight, but after all the earthquakes, we no longer know."

There had been a third earthquake, very early in the morning. Evannah, along with the village, had woken to the rattling of her bed and the shaking of the ground. Nobody wanted to say it, but everyone knew what it meant. The quakes were getting more and more frequent. The Island was destabilizing.

"We've prepared a team," Night Star continued. "Only the best, of course. Myself. Khalisse. We also have two warriors, Orin and Marra." He introduced the two new faces.

Khalisse climbed down from the Great Tree's houses. "Are we ready?"

"They need weapons," Night Star responded.

"Right!" Khalisse dashed off, presumably to find some.

"Listen," Night Star sat back on his haunches. "The Trail of Truth hasn't been found for over a century. This could be a fool's quest. But we're going to try. According to the myths, a person with a great need and great desire will find the path."

"So this trail might not even exist?" Kiera asked.

"Maybe," Night Star rumbled. "But again—we'll try. We're bringing a small party, and walking instead of flying, so as to not attract too much attention. But if the Watcher finds out, it could be dangerous. It could come to a fight."

Evannah glanced at Kiera and Aaron, and knew that, like her, they were thinking about the prophecy. Aaron had told them about his midnight meeting with the Fate-reader. He had recounted everything from the words of the prophecy to the fact that the Isle had delivered their original prophecy.

"That's why everyone was acting too nice to us," Kiera had exclaimed. "They know we're going to die!" Now, the words lingered in the back of their minds. *One shall fall, one shall fade. One shall see the darkness slayed.*

"But don't worry," Night Star finished. "We should be well prepared. That reminds me. Was there anyone else that you wanted for our group? Someone else that you trust that you've met, perhaps?"

"Barbenne," Kiera said immediately, very solemnly.

Night Star sighed. "Barbenne is a chef. What is she going to do?"

"Make us food of course! We need her."

"I am sorry for asking," Night Star groaned.

Khalisse reappeared, cradling the weapons like they were beloved stuffed animals. "I've got swords, spears, bows and arrows, all the good stuff." She handed Kiera and Aaron medium-sized swords. "Do you think you can handle a bow?" She handed one to Evannah. "You look like an archer to me."

Evannah had shot a bow a few times back home. The court members had thought that the next High Courtieress, female leader of the court, should have those skills, but it had been a while. She accepted it hesitantly. "I guess we'll see."

"Let's leave," commanded Night Star. "The sooner the better."

They walked until the border of Fenlithra. The little river burbled, inviting them to follow it. Evannah, Aaron, Kiera, and Night Star stepped forward easily, but Khalisse, Orin, and Marra were unable to move further, like an invisible barrier was trapping them.

"This is your turn, Aaron," Khalisse prompted.

"Okay," Aaron sounded a little unsure. "Um, just a warning, I haven't practiced much."

"You can do it. Come on," Khalisse encouraged him.

"YEAH AARON!" A high pitched squeal rang out. Kairen, the little boy, had been following Aaron around the previous day. Evannah and Kiera burst out into laughter.

"Someone has a fan," Evannah commented jokingly. Auri appeared, chasing her brother, and eventually caught him and dragged him away.

"Hurry up and do the thing," Kiera told Aaron impatiently.

"I'm getting there!" He held up his hands. After discovering that Aaron could temporarily stop magic, he and Evannah had practiced for hours on end. She had continued learning from the books, and the Whispers, and he would try to pause her powers for as long as possible. They had no idea if he would be able to do the same to the Watcher's curse, but he had to try.

He closed his eyes and took a deep breath. Moments passed. Then there was a slight flicker in the air.

Khalisse stepped forward, followed by Orin and Marra.

Aaron looked shocked. "I did it!"

Wonder spread across the Fenlithrians' faces. Marra gave Orin a hopeful glance. "We're out!" Khalisse exclaimed. "I can't believe it. It's been so long!" She looked at Aaron. "Is the barrier down for good?"

"I don't think so," Aaron admitted. "It seemed too powerful. I could only stop it temporarily to let you out."

"It's a start," Khalisse reassured him. "We haven't stepped foot out of the village for ten years. This is huge!"

"I never thought I'd leave again," Marra said. It was the first time Evannah had heard her speak. "It feels like a miracle."

"We could unite the villages again!" Khalisse's eyes were shining. "This changes everything."

Interesting. The brother of the Whisperer is the only one who holds the power to stop her.

Aaron wouldn't do that! Evannah mentally scolded the Whispers.

"Hush," Night Star warned. "We can't speak too loudly of that now."

"Right," Khalisse remembered. "I guess it's time to go, then." A group of villagers had gathered and were watching the party leave the village with shocked, excited murmurs.

They followed the river until the village was out of sight. Then it was only them, and the jungle breathing and singing around them.

"Night Star, what did you mean when you said the Trail hadn't been found in over a century?" Evannah sidled up to the great cat and asked.

"The Trail only appears for a person with a great need. Someone who is searching for a vital truth. It is nearly impossible to find, and could be anywhere on the Isle."

"Then where are we going?" Aaron asked.

"We're going to the Pool of Glass," Night Star responded. "That is where the most witnesses have spotted the trail appear. It's not too far from here; about an hour's walk."

Orin and Marra flanked them, holding long spears, while Khalisse led the patrol with a sword strapped to her hip.

After a few minutes of silence, Kiera finally asked, "What would you ever do if we got back to Neomerica?" It seemed like the question had been weighing on her for quite some time.

"Enjoy the peace and quiet," Evannah quipped. It was odd, though. It had only been a few days and already she couldn't remember a time when the Whispers had not constantly been talking in the back of her mind.

"Hmm," Aaron wondered. "Tell my dad, ha, we survived, against all odds." Evannah allowed herself a small laugh.

"I'd wait a few more days before confirming *that*," Night Star grumbled. Kiera elbowed him in the side. Well, his side was really shoulder-level for Kiera.

"What *are* you, Night Star?" Evannah asked. "You don't seem like a regular panther."

"Quite right," Night Star rumbled. He seemed pleased with the question. "I'm a Guardian, one of the sacred protectors of the Island. We're not quite animals, more so ancient beings of great power."

"There are more of you?" Kiera questioned.

"There are more Guardians, yes. Each one is different, with unique abilities and forms. We used to meet frequently to share tales and happenings across the Island. But I haven't seen most of them in over a decade. Most have been in hiding during the Watcher's reign, but I chose to stay with the villages. I have a long history with them."

"How old *are* you?" Aaron asked. "Sorry—I hope that's not rude."

Night Star let out a gruff laugh. "I'm older than you could possibly comprehend. I've seen it all, so I can tell you; nothing like this has happened to the Isle before."

"Yes," Marra chimed in. "It's been many years since I've been outside the village, but I still remember it. It's so different now. The forest used to be full of life, but I don't see a single animal now. I can clearly see that the Isle is—well, it's dying." She patted a tree and Evannah could see streaks of gray-white climbing its sickly trunk.

"The rumor is that the jungles around the shores are still beautiful," Khalisse added. "They haven't been completely damaged yet. Those areas were probably what you saw when you arrived."

"Yeah," Kiera admitted. "It does look a lot worse here." She was right. The branches of the sparse trees bent in a crooked way. It wasn't completely dead, like the stretch of forest they had seen, but it was getting there.

"Hang on," Aaron said. "We passed through this place two days ago on the way to the village, and it looked perfectly fine."

"That's right," Evannah recalled.

Khalisse blanched. "That means the Watcher's moving faster than we thought."

"Nearly twenty years," Night Star murmured. "And the Island's been slowly losing its life. It seems that it's reaching the end now." He bowed his head solemnly. "As a Guardian, I would give up my life to save my home."

It was quiet for a bit. They walked through the rainforest for minutes, until Night Star broke the silence. "While we travel, would you like to hear a story from the Isle?"

"Yes!" Kiera responded eagerly, and Evannah and Aaron followed.

"It has to do with the Trail of Truth," Night Star started. "You should probably get some background about it."

"It starts with a young man, long, long ago, not too long after the Island was created.

"The people who lived here didn't live in large villages like they do now. They were few in number and lived in small groups, spread out across the Isle."

"This young man lived with his family, along with a few others. They led a simple life, living off the land.

"The man was around eighteen when he started hearing voices. They were soft at first, but always there, whispering in his mind. Everyone he talked to said he was crazy, but he knew that he wasn't."

This story was starting to sound a little familiar, Evannah thought.

Night Star continued, "The man took to wandering outside his home, eager to have some time to himself. He felt like nobody understood him, like he didn't quite fit in with the world. After exploring for many days, he found a pool of water, not too far from his home. The Pool of Glass.

"It was a beautiful, peaceful place that would soon become the young man's second home. Every day for one hundred days, he visited the Pool of Glass, and asked why he was hearing voices.

And everyday, when he didn't get an answer, he would swim in the pool.

"Rumor says that he carved a mark for each of those hundred days into a rock. I have seen it myself.

"Close to day ninety, his family, and everyone he lived with, fell sick. They were horribly ill, and it seemed sure that they would never recover. The young man was devastated, but he continued his pilgrimage to the pool every day.

"It was no surprise that he caught the sickness too. He weakened considerably within days.

"But on day one hundred, he dragged his sickly body to the Pool of Glass. Weak, feverish, and close to death, he threw himself in it one last time, begging for answers.

"And that day, the Island responded. As he swam in the pool, a path opened up next to him where one had not been before. He found enough strength inside him to walk the path, not knowing where it may lead.

"Nobody really knows what exactly he found at the end of that path. What we do know is that he found what he was looking for: answers. He had become the Island's first Whisperer.

"When he came home to his family, strong and healthy, they thought it was a miracle. He was able to heal them, and explain what he had discovered. From that day, he was not shunned, but rather became the most respected and beloved man in the land. His name would go down in history.

"As for the Trail, it has only been discovered and documented seven times since then, many millennia ago. Four times around the Pool, and the other three times, a mile or less from the pool.

And that is where we are headed today." He ended the story with a bow of his head. They applauded.

"Almost there," Khalisse remarked.

"That went fast," Evannah commented. It didn't feel like they had been walking for almost an hour.

"Stories do that," said Marra.

"Ah, here we are," Khalisse announced. "The Pool of Glass." Eager to catch a glimpse of the legendary pool from the story, Evannah walked quickly ahead.

The ground sloped sharply down, many feet below, to a large pond. It was clear and glassy, with hints of dark blue that shimmered from the depths below. A waterfall, about ten feet tall, crashed into it from above.

A small, smooth area of soil and grass stretched out by the far edge of the pool, the only way to access it that wasn't on a steep slope. But there seemed to be no way to get to that area, at least not without taking a long detour around the forest.

"It's beautiful," Kiera said. "But how are we going to get down there?"

"We jump!" Khalisse exclaimed. "Obviously."

Evannah looked down apprehensively. It was not a deadly drop, only ten to fifteen feet, but still high enough to look terrifying.

"Not it!" Kiera and Aaron called in unison.

"You cowards." Khalisse shook her head in disappointment. "Real warriors would be fighting over the honor!"

"We're not warriors!" Kiera and Aaron spoke again in perfect unison, then burst out laughing.

"Fine," Khalisse sighed. "Then *I'll* choose."

Evannah had only registered these words when hands shoved her roughly in the back, forcing her body over the small cliff.

She dropped through the air, her screams rivaling the thunderous waterfall. Her stomach pounded with a frightening free-falling sensation, before she was plunged into the water.

The cold of the water shocked her, and she sank down deep below the surface, to the sapphire-blue depths, while bubbles from her crash billowed around her.

Regaining her wits, Evannah swam to the surface and stuck her head out of the pond, treading to stay upright while water streamed down her features and her hair stuck to her face.

Up above, the others were laughing. She scowled. "Who did that?"

"Sorry," Khalisse called from the top of the slope. "Somebody had to go first." She shrugged unapologetically.

"It's not funny, Aaron!" she scolded her brother, who was doubled over with laughter. "Push him in, Kiera!"

"Wait, wait, wait!" Aaron dodged Kiera's outstretched arms and evil look. "I'll jump myself. See?" He walked to the edge, sizing up the jump.

He prepared himself, getting in position for the jump.

"Hurry up!" Kiera yelled impatiently.

"I'm getting ready!" Aaron argued. From far down below, Evannah could see him get into a beautiful diving position.

He even did a little twirl before getting into the neatest position, about to execute the most perfect dive in history, when

Kiera shoved him off the edge. He fell several feet, screaming and flailing, before eventually flopping with a splash into the water.

Kiera and Evannah cheered loudly. Aaron surfaced. "Hey, I wasn't ready!" he muttered angrily.

"You snooze, you lose!" Kiera taunted. She jumped and tucked her legs into a cannonball, sending a mighty wave of water across Aaron and Evannah's heads when she landed. Aaron tackled her and forced her head underwater.

Leaving them to their antics, Evannah paddled gently around. It was so peaceful that she could almost pretend it was just a beautiful day at a swimming hole. This would have been an idyllic place to swim, if they weren't under the current circumstances.

"Incoming!" Khalisse was followed by the two warriors as they jumped neatly into the pond and began to swim elegantly toward the narrow strip of shore. Night Star descended after them, leaping through the air and landing on the shore gently, without ever getting wet.

"What if we can't find a way back up?" Evannah floated to the small shore.

Khalisse shrugged. "No big deal. Night Star will just fly us up."

"Hey, couldn't he have just flown us down here in the first place?"

"That spoils the fun!" Khalisse explained mischievously, reaching the shallows and walking out. Evannah followed.

"So," she wrung out her long, wet hair. "Now what?"

"We search," Night Star growled. "For the path. For any clues. Spread out and start."

They split up and began to search the place. Some searched in the water, while others fanned out in the forest.

Evannah found herself drawn to the smooth boulders around the shore, curious to find the one from the story.

She trailed her fingers over their surface, trying to find the marks. She checked every possible rock, but found nothing.

Undeterred, she checked again. She found something promising on a large gray rock right next to the pond.

It looked like the rock had been lightly scratched. The marks were so faint, she almost thought she was imagining it. But then again, they had survived for hundreds or even thousands of years.

"Hey, Night Star," Evannah called the cat, who was leaping through the air above the waterfall. He bounded over at the sound of his name. "Is this the rock from the story?"

"Yes," Night Star answered. "I believe so, at least."

Evannah counted the marks. "Exactly one hundred."

Night Star put his paw on the rock. His huge paw covered half of the large boulder. "It's always incredible to see how history has been preserved this way."

"It's not perfect marks," Evannah observed. "They're all over the place. Some are sideways, some diagonal, some are curved."

"Mmm hmm," Night Star agreed. "There are some theories that it's a secret message."

"Really?" Evannah was intrigued. She traced them with her fingers. *A secret message. Could it be possible that it wasn't discovered for all these years?* "Has anything here been enchanted by Whisperers?"

"No," Night Star shook his head. "They considered it sacred, especially the rock, because of its ties to the first Whisperer."

Secret message. Never been touched by Whisperers. The pieces were coming together in Evannah's head.

She closed her eyes. "Well, first Whisperer, I'm sorry about this." Taking energy from the Whispers, she pushed it into the rock. Her hand tingled, and the rock lit up.

Night Star jumped back. "What are you doing?"

Evannah didn't answer, but watched as the lines rearranged themselves into letters. She read the message out loud. "*Below still glass the keeper calls from siltbound dark in the pond's far deep seek downward only the secret waits in sleep.*"

"It was true," Night Star murmured.

"Come here!" Evannah called the others. "I found something!" They raced over. She read the message again.

"I can't believe a clue has been here all this time," Marra remarked in surprise.

"It doesn't even make sense," Aaron groaned. "I thought we were done with cryptic messages."

"Come on Aaron, I thought you were smarter than that." Evannah whacked him on the arm. "This one's so clear. 'Below still glass?' 'In the pond's far deep?' 'Seek downward?' There's *obviously* something at the bottom of the pool."

"Would it be that obvious?" Kiera wondered. "Maybe it's a trick."

"I don't believe so," Night Star said. "I think the hard part was figuring out the message. After doing that, you get the reward."

"I can look," Evannah offered, stepping into the shallows of the pond.

"Don't worry, we can do it," Khalisse gestured to herself and the two warriors.

Night Star interrupted, "Evannah should go. She found the message. She may notice things that we won't."

"Of course," Khalisse responded. "Can you swim?"

"I can swim," Evannah answered, deciding to leave out the part where she had drowned before reaching the Island.

"Good luck!" Kiera said. "Don't drown!" Aaron rolled his eyes. "Too soon?"

Taking a deep breath, Evannah plunged into the water, pushing herself down. Sounds grew muffled and the light changed to a dark blue.

It was much deeper and more vast than she had expected. She kicked upward as hard as she could, but still missed the bottom of the pond by several feet. She quickly swam back up to take a huge, gasping breath.

Before her friends could express concern, she dived down again, pulling in with her hands and drifting downwards.

The surface was high above her now, dangerously high. The pressure squeezed at her ears as the water became colder. She was getting deeper and deeper. She *needed* to get out now.

But over there! Something glinted on the floor of the pool. She kicked furiously, trying to close the distance between her outstretched arm and the bottom.

She was running out of air. Her lungs began to ache. *Just a little closer.*

She scrabbled at the rocks, her fingers finally closing around the glinting object.

Growing faint, she kicked with all her might, propelling herself to the surface.

Her hand shot out of the water triumphantly, throwing droplets everywhere as she clutched the glimmering key.

Chapter 13

I t was a key.

Kiera stared in wonder as Evannah swam back to shore with the key clutched in her hand, gasping for breath. Everyone cheered, and Kiera helped her to shore.

"A key!" Aaron exclaimed. "What does it unlock?"

Evannah, who was bent over and trying to catch her breath, managed a weak, "Don't know."

"I might have the answer to this one," Night Star interjected. "I spotted an odd hole near the far end of the pool while I was flying near it. Let me take a look. Does one of you want to come?"

"Evah's in no shape to go," Kiera said. "I'll come."

Evannah handed her the key, still gasping, "Thanks."

Kiera turned it over in her hand. She knew it was ancient, but the heavy golden key was still in fairly good shape. It had probably been preserved, somehow.

"Ready?" Night Star lay down.

"Let's go!" Kiera pulled herself onto his back and wrapped her arms around his large neck. Night Star pushed off and leaped through the air, reaching the far end of the pool within seconds.

"See it?" Night Star asked.

Kiera scanned the area. "I think so. Can you get closer?"

He obliged, swooping closer. The hole was carved into the stone on the edge of the pond. She pulled out the key, but knew even before sticking it in that it wouldn't fit. "Just a weird shaped hole."

"Let's look around a little longer, then." Night Star dived further down, gliding along above the ground.

Kiera wondered briefly if her supposed powers could help her, then decided to just do it herself. She hadn't had much training, after all. At her last training session, they had planted the seed the Flowering Tree had given her, and she was still waiting to see what grew from it.

After finding two more holes that turned out to just be holes, Kiera decided to be smarter about this. She pulled out the key and examined it.

It looked like a regular key, maybe a bit oddly shaped, with a looped top, long handle, and an extending tip. Kiera flipped it over, trying to look at it from different angles.

She turned it upside down so the loop was facing down and the tip facing up. Wait, something looked familiar.

That was it! The key was a map! The loop was the pool, the handle was the waterfall, and the tip was the ledge on the top of the waterfall that extended into the forest.

Which means there must be clues on it. It was a little weathered, but she brought it closer to her face. At the top of the handle, there was a tiny engraving of a keyhole. *Found you.* "Night Star, can we go closer to the waterfall?"

"Of course." Night Star flew to the waterfall within seconds. Down below, the rest of the group was resting and watching them intently.

"A little closer to the top," Kiera shouted over the roar of the waterfall. Mist sprayed her face, and she wiped her eyes furiously. If the waterfall was the handle, the keyhole should be *right there* above it. "Found it!"

"Yes!" yelled Night Star triumphantly.

Kiera pushed the key into the hole. Perfect fit. She turned the key, and there was a *click*. The key was sucked into the hole and disappeared from sight.

Then the waterfall parted.

There were gasps of awe as Night Star swooped back to rejoin the group. "The waterfall!" Aaron cried. "It's open!"

"Wow," Evannah stared in shock. "Amazing job, Kiera."

Behind where the waterfall used to be gaped a large, dark tunnel entrance. The falls streamed to either side of it.

"What are we waiting for?" Khalisse said impatiently. "Let's go!" They began walking into the pond again.

Something furry brushed Kiera's foot, and she screamed.

Everyone immediately jumped and turned, weapons out, ready to fight. "Kiera, what?" Night Star started, then broke off as he saw what it was. "Oh."

A little creature was snuffling at her foot. It looked exactly like a puppy, except bright blue, with small golden antlers like a deer.

"A puppy!" Kiera cried. She bent down to let it sniff her hand. It licked her hand with a little pink tongue. "Aww, it's adorable!"

"Careful," Aaron warned. "You don't know what that thing is."

"Come on, Aaron," Kiera rolled her eyes. "It's a puppy. A baby!"

"It's no baby," Night Star said ominously. "Boundingwolves can be very dangerous."

Kiera scooped up the animal. It wriggled happily, little antlers poking her gently, and licked her chin. "Let's keep him!"

Aaron sighed. "We're on a mission, not a vacation! You can't keep it! You heard Night Star; it's dangerous."

"I know this is important," she snapped. "Fine. Good bye, little guy." She set it down on the shore, and began wading in like the others.

When she made the mistake of looking back, her heart clenched at the sight of the puppy sitting and staring with the saddest expression she had ever seen.

Feeling guilty, she turned back and continued swimming to the waterfall. There was a splash beside her. The puppy had swum to her!

"He's following us!" Kiera cried. "Come on, guys. Look at his face."

Khalisse relented. "Fine, keep it. But we have to keep moving. If it slows us down, we're leaving it."

"Of course," Kiera promised, scooping up the puppy again. The water was getting deeper and colder closer to the waterfall.

Night Star, who had flown and was waiting for them by the entrance to the tunnel, frowned. "Be careful. Boundingwolves are extremely unpredictable." He narrowed his eyes. "What's more, it's a *dog*," he spat out the word with disgust.

"Cats and dogs can't get along, I know," teased Kiera. "I'll keep him, and you won't have to see him again." She followed Khalisse's lead, pulling herself up to the entrance of the tunnel. She was considerably shorter than the others, so she struggled a bit, eventually rolling awkwardly across the floor of the tunnel before springing to her feet.

The dark tunnel stretched and twisted before them, its stone walls slick with water and moss.

"It is a bit cute," Evannah stroked the puppy's head, climbing up beside Kiera and jerking her from her thoughts. "What are you going to call it?"

"Hmm," Kiera pondered. "Something island related, probably. Ocean? No. Tree? Definitely not."

"Sky?" Evannah suggested. "Because of the blue fur?"

"That's cute," said Kiera. She looked around the tunnel. "How about Moss?"

"Oh, I like that!" Evannah replied.

"Moss it is, then," Kiera bent down to stroke her new pet's ears. "Hi, Moss. Sit. Good boy!" Moss shook out his wet fur.

Aaron was the last to climb onto the tunnel entrance. "Whoa. Is this the Trail of Truth?"

"Possibly," Khalisse answered. "Or it might lead to the Trail. Ready?" She checked the two other warriors, and put her hand on the hilt of her sword. "Evannah, some light would be nice."

Evannah lit up the tunnel with her enchanted light, illuminating the dark passageway.

"Much better. Night Star, watch the rear," Khalisse commanded, starting forward. The cat padded behind them, eyeing the puppy with disdain.

"Come on Moss, heel," Kiera tried.

"Great time to train your new dog," Aaron commented teasingly. "In a dark tunnel on a mission vital to the life of the Island."

"He's a good boy!" Kiera argued. "Look, he knows sit already. Sit!" Moss gave her a blank look. "Come on, you're making me look bad!" He nudged her leg with his wet nose.

"Keep up!" Khalisse called bossily from far ahead. They scrambled to catch up.

The tunnel went on for many, many feet, so many that Kiera couldn't see any sign of light other than Evannah's. The only other life was the moss growing on the walls. The stone floor was slippery, and she had to slow down so she didn't fall.

After many minutes of walking, the tunnel began to slope up. "We're getting somewhere," Khalisse commented.

"Finally," replied Kiera. "Moss needs the sun." The puppy jumped in agreement.

"It's only been five minutes and she's already obsessed," Aaron stage-whispered to Evannah. Kiera kicked his foot lightly.

Up ahead, the walls and ground under them changed from a dark gray stone to bright white, a material that looked like quartz.

"Whoa," Kiera whispered. The tunnel was now reflecting light in a rainbow of colors. It was dizzying.

"I think this is the start," Khalisse explained, "of the Trail of Truth. Congratulations, we are the first group to walk it in over a century."

Kiera cheered. "We make it look so easy, sometimes."

"No wonder nobody had found it," Aaron joked. "They just needed us!"

Night Star gave a gruff laugh.

"As exciting as this is," Khalisse continued, "we have to be careful. Nobody really knows what happens on the Trail, but we know that it can be confusing. Dangerous, sometimes. Disorienting. So keep your eyes open, and stay focused. Don't forget why we're here."

As if on cue, the ground gave a small shake under them, and everyone fell silent. "And whatever happens, we stick together."

The ground sloped upward, sharply this time, and they emerged from the tunnel.

The path was the same glimmering white stone, and sprawling boulders of the same reflective white lined the trail, making it almost impossible to see past the path. They could only see the sky, and the very tops of the trees.

Moss looked around and whimpered, pressing closer to Kiera's foot. She ran her fingers through his fur, whispering, "It's okay, it's okay."

"This is weird," Aaron looked around. The rainbow refractions were even brighter in the sunlight. It should have been beautiful, but it just seemed strange.

"Yeah," Kiera agreed. Her hand found Aaron's, and she clasped it for comfort. Aaron wrapped his other hand around Evannah's, and they walked together.

Step by step, they would make it through this, together.

Something flickered in a stone to their right, and Evannah pulled her hand from Aaron's. "Did you see that?" she asked.

"It was just the light, Evah," Aaron tried to coax her back, but she was already kneeling by the stone.

Evannah stared, transfixed, at one of the boulders, her eyes wide and shocked.

Night Star stopped. "Is she okay?"

"I don't know," Kiera knelt down by Evannah, trying to see what she was looking at. All she could see was small flickers in the stone. She shook Evannah. "Evah? Hello?" Reflected in Evannah's eyes were unfamiliar colors and shapes that were not part of their surroundings.

She waved to get the attention of their leader. "Khalisse! Something happened to Evannah!"

Khalisse whirled around. "Oh no. Evannah!"

Evannah's shoulders began to shake, then her whole body trembled. She turned back to look at them, and her eyes overflowed with tears.

"I'm sorry," she sobbed.

"What is it?" Aaron asked in horror. He put his hands on her shoulders. "What happened?"

"I should have told you earlier," Evannah ducked her head in shame.

"What is it?" Kiera instantly felt cold.

"It's my fault we crashed," Evannah confessed, tears streaming from her eyes. "My fault that we got stranded here."

"What are you talking about?" Aaron looked confused.

"Back home, before we left... I disabled the tracking feature on the boat and broke the communication button," Evannah trembled. "That's why we couldn't call for help, and why we can't be rescued now. I think I damaged the boat somehow too, while doing that, and that's why it broke so easily during the storm."

Kiera reeled, shocked. That had been an unexpected confession. She pulled Evannah into a hug. "It's okay," she soothed. "We don't blame you for anything."

Evannah sniffed. "I didn't want any contact with anyone back home. No dad constantly giving us orders; no court member tracking our journey and reporting about it."

Aaron hugged Evannah too. "Don't worry. Remember the prophecy? We were destined to come here. It was going to happen anyway."

"Yeah," Evannah murmured. "But it doesn't change the fact that it was my fault." Moss curled up at Evannah's feet, laying his head on his paws.

Khalisse chimed in with a surprising amount of compassion. "It was a *good* thing you landed here. Otherwise, the Island would have been destroyed in a matter of days, and we'd have been unable to leave our village for the rest of our lives."

"Thanks," Evannah wiped her tears with the back of her hand. "Let's keep going; I don't want to slow us down."

They began walking again. Kiera moved to her side. "What did you see?" she asked Evannah softly.

"I saw images in the stone," Evannah explained. "Scenes of when I damaged the boat. I remembered it all over again, and I felt so guilty. I had to tell you now, or it would be my burden forever."

"The Trail of Truth," Kiera said. "It must have encouraged you to tell the truth, somehow."

"That makes sense," Evannah replied. "I think we should avoid looking at the rocks, just in case. Keep focused ahead."

Kiera relayed this message to the group, and everyone faced ahead while walking. It was still hard to avoid looking at the glimmering rocks.

Orin, the warrior, stopped to face the stones. He didn't kneel like Evannah had, just stared at them in a stunned way.

"Oh, no," Khalisse groaned. "Orin, not you too."

He didn't tremble or begin to cry like Evannah had. Instead, he just gazed openmouthed at the stone, at whatever scene he was watching, looking shocked.

He turned back to the group and swallowed, looking at his feet. He cleared his throat several times, and Kiera realized she had never heard him speak.

Quietly, he whispered, "I love you, Marra."

Marra's jaw dropped, and she opened her mouth and closed it many times, not knowing what to say. Her cheeks flushed red. "I...," she trailed off.

"You don't have to say anything," Orin said immediately. "I just wanted you to know."

"Oh," Marra still looked stunned.

Khalisse looked between the two warriors, unsure what to do. "Um, okay. How about... how about we keep moving?"

"Yes," Orin bowed his head solemnly and resumed his position flanking Kiera, Aaron, and Evannah.

After that, Kiera became even more focused on trying to avoid looking at the stones. She couldn't spill her deepest secret, not here, not now.

The stones glinted, beckoning her to gaze into their depths, to lose herself in them. No! She squeezed her eyes shut. It was a trick. Eyes ahead.

Only one foot after another, one foot after another, one step, another step, keep going.

Then their path was abruptly blocked. A wall halted them, made of the same white material, but so thin that it was translucent. They could see the path continue on the other side.

"Come on!" Kiera complained. "All that and they're not even letting us pass?"

Khalisse knocked the wall. "There must be some way through. We made it this far, after all."

"Some kind of password?" Aaron suggested. "A special code?"

"Or a secret," Evannah spoke up. "This is the Trail of Truth, after all."

It was now so clear. "Small wall, small secret, I'm guessing," Khalisse remarked. "Who wants to take this one?"

Nobody moved. The warriors stood stoically, pretending they hadn't heard. Aaron sighed. "I'll take this one. At least it's small."

He stepped up to the wall, and placed his hand on it.

"Do you see anything?" Kiera asked.

"No," Aaron replied. "I guess that means I get to choose the secret." He sighed, then thought for a moment. "When I was ten, I stole Kiera's cupcake at dinner."

"That was you?" Kiera cried, outraged. "I beat up poor Hadrian Crestwell over that."

"Well he stole my cupcake," Aaron explained. "Then I stole yours. So it was all fair."

"I don't think I can ever forgive you," Kiera sniffed teasingly.

The wall had begun to break under his hand, cracks shooting through the material. "Oh, I guess that wasn't enough," Aaron sounded disappointed. "I thought that was a great secret."

"I can finish it off," Khalisse offered. She tilted her head, pondering. "Until I was twelve, I was scared of the water."

"You live on an island!" Aaron remarked, startled.

"Well, I got over it long ago," Khalisse told him. "But before that, I *hated* the water. I would sweat every time I had to swim. Nobody knew except Jannary."

Kiera was actually surprised by this; Khalisse seemed like the type of person who wasn't scared of anything.

"That did it!" Khalisse exclaimed. The wall had cracked apart and dissipated in a cloud of glimmering dust. "We're back on track."

They continued walking, avoiding the stones. Kiera tried to distract herself by counting her steps and making sure Moss was following them. One foot after another, just one more step.

The second wall shouldn't have surprised them, but it still did.

This one was much bigger than the first, and so solid that it felt like nothing could break it.

This would need a *huge* secret.

"Anybody have a secret that big?" Khalisse asked. "That was my only one."

Aaron and Evannah shook their heads. Orin and Marra did too.

"Kiera?" Khalisse asked.

Her heart began to pound. No, no, no. She couldn't say hers now. Not here. Not in front of everyone. Not without an explanation.

"You do have one," Khalisse accused, responding to her silence.

"I... yes," Kiera admitted, realizing she couldn't get out of this. "Give me a minute."

She stared at Evannah's face, knowing that after she shared the secret, she wouldn't be able to look her in the eye.

Kiera turned to the wall, and pressed her hand against it. Images began to flash in the stone, and she couldn't tear her gaze away.

Evannah and Kiera growing up, attending lessons together, Evannah ushered away by her father to take part in special lessons befitting for her future status.

Lord Cyrus sharing tales of his late wife, the High Courtieress Aalliah, while Evannah watched with wide eyes.

Evannah staring down her father with steel in her eyes as he scolded her, screaming that she was a disgrace and failure.

Kiera crouched behind a door, ear pressed to the wall as she listened to a conversation between Lord Cyrus and her dad, Lord Carmine, a conversation she shouldn't have heard.

She was vaguely aware of the others speaking to her, asking her if she was all right, shaking her, but she only snapped back to earth when the images stopped.

"Kiera, you need to tell us," Evannah placed a hand on her arm. "I know how it feels."

The overwhelming guilt bubbled inside her, and she yanked herself away from Evannah, turning the other way.

She began in a whisper, "A month before we left for our journey, I heard a conversation between your dad and mine. He said," she swallowed, forcing the words out. "Your dad said that the time had come to choose the next High Courtieress."

Evannah became silent and still.

"He told my dad that it would be me." She had to say the rest of it. "He said that he didn't want to reward his failure of a daughter, give her a position she was unfit for." Now the words were out, and there was no going back. "It's not true, Evannah. Please believe me."

Slowly, she turned her gaze to Evannah. She was pale, eyes wide and filled with tears. She turned back, she didn't want to see that, she *couldn't* bear to see that.

"I'm sorry," Kiera choked out.

It wasn't so much that Evannah hadn't been given the position, it was that Lord Cyrus had picked Kiera, the troublemaker of the court, over his own daughter. He had picked Evannah's best friend, just to spite her. He wanted to tear Kiera and Evannah apart, watch his daughter live her life in competition with Kiera, just as part of one of his twisted punishments.

It wasn't fair that Kiera had come in the middle of it, or that she had to carry the burden of the conversation and be the one to tell Evannah, but someone had to do it.

The life Evannah had been working toward for her entire childhood, the legacy she had been promised, would never be hers.

And it was Kiera's fault.

Evannah took a shaky step back. "So all this time... you knew what I was meant to be."

"No," Kiera's voice was hard. "I knew what they *wanted* you to be, but I also know that that's not you. It was never you, Evah, and that's a good thing."

Evannah looked away, blinking furiously. "You should have told me."

The silence felt deafening as Kiera stared at the ground, tears pricking her own eyes, too full of heavy guilt to look up. She didn't even notice as the giant wall cracked into dust, the barrier breaking, letting them through at last.

But she did notice the Shadows descending from the sky.

Chapter 14

They had stepped into a circular chamber, with no ceiling, and short walls, so short that they could see outside at last. The end of the Trail.

In the middle, on a gleaming white pedestal, rested an ancient-looking brown journal.

But it was obscured by the swooping Shadows, the agents of the Watcher who had found them at last, and were here to finish them. The sight of them made Aaron's stomach twist, remembering his last, nearly fatal encounter with the dark creatures.

"We're under attack!" Khalisse cried. "Weapons out!"

Aaron yanked out his own sword and brandished it, stepping in front of Kiera and Evannah. They were standing apart, the reveal of Kiera's secret having torn a hole between them.

Aaron didn't know if that hole could recover, but right now, they needed to fight. Their lives were on the line.

Evannah blinked away her tears and got out her bow and arrow. Kiera got her sword ready and stepped up beside Aaron.

"The journal!" Aaron cried, pointing to the notebook on the pedestal. "Do we need that?"

"Get it if you can," Khalisse instructed. "It's important; it's what we walked the Trail for. But your lives are more important."

Aaron started toward the journal, when no less than six Shadows landed in front of them.

"Hello *again*," they all spoke at once with a chilling voice. Remembering that it was the Watcher speaking through them, Aaron backed away.

"*Thank you for leading me to the Trail of Truth. That helped me very much.*"

"Step back!" Khalisse barked, brandishing her sword, which was long and narrowed to a deadly point. The warriors stepped forward with their spears. "Leave us or we'll have no choice but to kill you."

"*Funny,*" the shadowy figures, dark silhouettes with no discernable features, gathered together. "*I was about to say the same to you.*"

Khalisse leapt forward, sword in hand, and chopped the head off the nearest Shadow. "Run!" she shouted.

The head dissolved into darkness, and simply reformed on the Shadow's shoulders. "*Now you're just making me mad.*"

Then the world trembled as the Shadows grew, lengthening in height until they towered over the group, at least seven feet tall each.

"He's taking power from the Island," Aaron realized.

Kiera's eyes grew wide, and Evannah pressed her fingers to her temples, hearing noises that none of them could hear.

The ground began to shake harder. It was by far the biggest earthquake they had experienced so far. Cracks shot through the walls and stones of the path, with pieces splintering and littering the ground.

"*I just need one thing,*" the Shadows spoke again. "*If you three would accompany me back to Watcher Peak to talk, I will spare your companions.*"

Aaron doubted he just wanted to "talk." Night Star sprang into the sky, landing in front of the group and baring his teeth. He growled menacingly.

"You have to get past me first!" He lunged at the tallest Shadow, bringing it to the ground and ripping at it with his sharp fangs.

"Get them!" the Watcher commanded through the Shadows. At once, the Shadows were on them, pursuing the group with dark, outstretched arms.

A Shadow lunged at Aaron, towering above him, as the world continued to shake. He struggled to regain his footing, stumbling as he swiped at the figure with his sword, avoiding its deadly-sharp fingers. He had been there once already, after all.

There was a shattering noise, and the walls of the path fell apart completely, the glimmering shards falling to the ground as the forest scenery around them was revealed. The pedestal with the journal still stayed standing.

"Run!" Khalisse tried to warn them again, engaged in a fierce battle with two Shadows, a sword in each hand. "You're more important! We'll handle this!"

Aaron didn't have to check with his friend and sister to reply, "Never! We fight together!"

Aaron and the Shadow engaged in a sort of dance, with the Shadow viciously swiping at him, and him blocking it with his sword. When he tried to slice the Shadow, it easily avoided the blow.

He could see Evannah and Kiera fighting. Kiera wasn't very adept with a sword, but she fought with a kind of chaotic fury that just confused the Shadows, sending them scrambling for a new plan.

A Shadow was slowly approaching Evannah, and she fumbled with her bow and arrow. She tried to nock an arrow, but it failed. The second time she succeeded in nocking it, but when she released it, it flew into the sky, many feet away from the nearest Shadow, and landed in the dirt beside Aaron. Evannah gave up, grabbed a handful of arrows, and started stabbing the Shadow with it.

All this time, Moss was running around people's feet and barking madly in confusion. A Shadow came closer to him, and in an instant, he had grown into the biggest blue wolf Aaron had ever seen, with enormous fangs and long, golden antlers. He snarled and pounced on the Shadow, easily ripping it apart.

Kiera screamed, shocked. "Um, good dog? I think?" The wolf was monstrous, nearly as tall as her. She stared in fear at the gleaming fangs.

The earthquake stopped, and Aaron thought it was finished. But seconds later, it started again, this time ten times more intense. He fell to the ground, scrambled back up, and fell again, all while fighting off the Shadow pursuing him.

A thunderous CRASH echoed across the forest as a mighty tree smashed to the ground, displaced by the strong shakes. Its branches stretched out, trapping Night Star in place.

"Night Star!" Aaron cried. "I'm coming!" Amidst the confusion, he crawled over the cat, and tried in vain to pry the thick branch off his paws.

"No, child, save yourself!" Night Star growled.

"Someone help!" Aaron called out, ignoring the cat's words.

Evannah appeared out of nowhere at his side, yanking at the tree with all her might. "Come on Aaron, one, two, *three!*"

They gave a final burst of effort, and the branch moved just enough for Night Star to pry himself free, racing off to tackle more Shadows with a gruff, "Thank you."

The world was moving so much now that it was blurry. A second tree fell, and it would have fallen on top of Aaron if Night Star hadn't doubled back and pushed him out of the way, sending him flying.

"DUCK FOR COVER!" The cat roared. Trees fell left and right as Aaron, who was sprawled on the ground, curled into a small position with his hands covering his head.

"Aaron, can you block them for a minute?" Khalisse cried.

"Oh, I'll try!" Aaron called back. He hadn't used his binding powers against actual Whispers or Shadows, but it was worth a shot.

Flicking the ability on was like someone had tied a knot in his stomach: strange, but not unpleasant. He gave a cry as he targeted the Shadows, holding their magic in place.

They froze, growing less solid, and more translucent, not moving at all.

"Brilliant!" Khalisse responded. "How long can you hold it?"

"Not long!" Aaron yelled. Already his head was starting to pound, and he was breathing hard. "Get the journal!"

Kiera sprinted for it, leaving behind the now frozen Shadow she had been grappling with. Her fingers closed around the ancient-looking notebook just as Aaron couldn't hold it any longer, and the Shadows sprang back to life.

The Shadows fumbled for a minute, confused by what had happened. By the time they had regained their bearings, the entire group was armed and ready to take them on.

"*Nice trick,*" the Shadows hissed. "*But no match for real power, I'm afraid.*"

And with that, the earthquakes were back, but now, massive cracks started appearing in the ground.

The crack slithered through the forest like a snake, opening deep chasms that would surely kill someone if they fell inside.

One of the cracks was following him, traveling after his footsteps, waiting for him to slow down so he would fall in and be lost forever. It was so deep he couldn't see the bottom.

A crack raced under Kiera's feet, throwing her off balance. As the crack widened, she hung on to the edge of what was now a cliff, desperately.

"Kiera!" Aaron raced to help her, grabbing her hand and pulling her out of the chasm.

Her face was flushed with fear. "The journal is gone!" Indeed, Aaron could see it hurtling into the chasm, lost forever.

Then it reversed course, and flew back into Kiera's grasp. Aaron looked up to see Evannah, her hand outstretched. "Thanks, Evah!"

"Kill some Shadows for me in return!" Evannah responded slyly.

A Shadow had snuck up behind them, and Aaron twirled his sword, then whacked it in the face. It fell over, seemingly unconscious. He stabbed it with the sword just in case, but it didn't seem to leave any mark.

Another deep chasm ran through the forest, separating Evannah and Marra from the rest of the group. The Shadows abandoned Aaron, Kiera, Orin, Khalisse, and Night Star, and began to swarm toward them, gliding over the abyss easily.

They moved toward Evannah with outstretched hands, long claws curling. "Evannah!" Kiera yelled.

Marra was fighting as hard as three people, shielding Evannah, fighting both with her swords and with her fists. But there were just too many Shadows. They crowded around her, and one produced a long sword made of darkness, and stabbed Marra through the chest.

"No!" Orin cried, going pale.

The Shadows now surrounded Evannah, grabbing her arms as she tried in vain to escape. Their numbers easily overpowered her, even as she tried to fight back.

Night Star, the only one of them who could cross the chasm, flew over it to attack the Shadows. Every Shadow stretched their hand out at the same time, and dozens of streaks of darkness appeared, hitting Night Star in the side and blasting him back to the other side.

He lay on his side and groaned. Khalisse hurtled to him, checking if he was okay.

The Shadows had restrained Evannah's movements, two holding her arms behind her back while one covered her mouth so she couldn't scream.

Another Shadow brought out a strange looking object, a circle of glass outlined with gold. It held it up to the sun, and as light passed through the glass, it created a portal in front of them.

Aaron raced toward them, but he couldn't do anything more than stand at the edge of the chasm, shouting, "Leave her alone!"

Then the Shadows had dragged Evannah through the portal and they were all gone, the portal closing behind them.

Aaron stood in shock. Evannah was gone. Taken.

Feeling cold all over, he walked back to Kiera. He had failed as a brother, and now his twin would pay the price. She might die.

"She's gone," he whispered hoarsely, sinking to his knees.

Kiera grabbed his hand and pulled him back up. "We'll get her back!" Next to them, Moss the wolf approached, as tall as his shoulder, shrunk back into a puppy, and began licking his leg.

It was as though all his limbs had gone numb. "It was my fault."

Pain blossomed in his cheek as Kiera slapped him across the face. "Stop that! If we have any chance of getting her back, you need to stop blaming yourself and move on!"

They were interrupted by a cry of despair that rang out loudly. Aaron raced over to see that Night Star had gotten up and flown Marra back to their side of the chasm. "Is she...," he asked softly.

"Barely," Night Star rumbled. "I don't think she can hang on for much longer."

Orrin had sunk to her side, and was sobbing, tears running down his face onto Marra's body.

Khalisse was crouched over her, trying to heal her with the medicines she had been carrying, but it was clear that it was too late. The shadowy sword still protruded from her chest, and blood pooled on the ground. Eventually, Khalisse gave up and backed away.

Marra took a shallow breath, the effort rattling her chest. "Kill... him," she breathed, and Aaron realized she was talking to him about the Watcher.

"We will," he promised.

She reached a pale, shaking hand up to Orin. "Orin," she croaked.

"Shh, I'm here," Orin hushed. "It's okay."

"I... I love you too." With those last words, Marra's chest fell still and her eyes gazed off into the distance, staring at nothing.

"No," Orin sobbed. "No, please." It was heartbreaking. Aaron had barely known Marra, but tears still sprang to his eyes.

Fury blazed in Khalisse's sharp eyes. "Marra was a brave warrior, and she died a warrior's death. I will not allow the Watcher to kill any more of my people."

"You need to go, *now*," Night Star growled. "Before they can come back."

"But, Evannah!" Aaron protested.

"I'll stay," Night Star told them, lying down next to Marra's body. "I'll search the area. But it's not safe for you. I'll be back in a day if I can't find her, and I'll bring Marra's body."

"We can't leave you here alone!" Kiera cried.

"I'll be fine," Night Star rumbled. "I live alone; I'm used to this. I can handle the Shadows. What's most important is that you head back."

"He's right," Khalisse gave in. "Come on, let's go quickly. Night Star, come back soon."

"Bring her back, *please*," Aaron added, ice still trickling down his spine.

"I'll do my best," Night Star promised. "Go, now."

Moss leapt at Kiera's leg, eager to be picked up again. "I don't know," Kiera muttered. "You didn't tell me you were a huge wolf." The puppy gave her an innocent look. "Fine," she picked him up and he gave a happy bark.

The journey back to Fenlithra was a lot shorter than it had been getting to the Pool of Glass. They ran for five minutes at a time before slowing back down to walk again, not wanting to get ambushed by the Shadows again.

They reached Fenlithra just as noon passed, and Aaron couldn't believe that it had only been a few hours.

Jannary had brought them back to the Great Tree and sat them down in the visiting room that they had been in before. Plates of lunch were laid out before them, untouched.

"I'm sorry to hear about Evannah," Jannary said, sitting next to Khalisse. "But I have no doubt we'll get her back. She's a survivor."

"That girl is stronger than you think," Khalisse agreed.

"In the meantime," Jannary continued. "I hate to ask this of you."

"What is it?" Aaron asked. Did he even want to know?

"Our researchers estimate, based on the increase of earthquakes and Island instability that the Island," Jannary's face turned grave, "has less than a week."

"What?" Aaron stood up. "So soon? That can't be possible!"

"What'll happen if the Island falls?" Kiera asked quietly, which was out of character for her.

"We will all die," said Khalisse solemnly. "The entire Island will collapse. The mountains will come crashing down, the forest will wither, and the mist will suffocate every creature who remains. Whatever is left of the Island will be sucked into the sea, never to be seen again."

There was a stunned silence for a moment. "What can we do?" Aaron asked.

"That is what I needed from you," Jannary explained. "You see, it is time to unite the villages once more."

Unite the villages.

"It has to be you two," Khalisse told them. "You are symbols of hope to the people of the Island. They may not trust us, especially since we haven't met in a decade."

"Will they listen?" Aaron wondered. "Even if they do, is it enough?"

"We need to hope," said Khalisse. She rested her hands on the table. "We never thought we'd be counting down the days that the Isle has left to live. We need to act, now or never."

"We're in," said Aaron, and he knew Kiera felt the same way.

"Excellent!" Jannary exclaimed. "Again, I am so sorry to be rushing you into this so quickly. But it needs to be done."

She got up, walked to the corner of the room, and pulled down a rolled up map that Aaron hadn't noticed hanging on a wall. She unfurled it, revealing that it was a large map of the Island.

"Island geography lesson." Jannary tapped a spot at the top of the map. "This is Watcher Peak, and the surrounding, tallest mountains are called 'The Eyes of the Island.' The rest of the mountain range is smaller, and called the Mistveil Mountains."

She tapped a spot lower down, in the green colors of the forest. "Here we are, Fenlithra. There are four main villages on the Island. Fenlithra, Vahari, Cressiara, and Silverspire."

Aaron gazed at the map. It was beautiful, painted with light, detailed strokes, with each location labeled underneath it in a swirly script.

"Fenlithra and Vahari are the two forest villages," Jannary continued. "Cressiara is the ocean village. They live near the shores, and are the biggest village, because the ocean provides for all. Silverspire is in the mountains, and they usually prefer to keep to themselves. As such, we don't know too much about them, except that they own the biggest library on the Island."

"Only four villages?" Kiera asked. "It's a big Island."

"Four *main* villages," Jannary corrected. "The Island has many, much smaller villages, but the Watcher has swayed many of them onto his side. They are his only human army, his supporters."

"Who would support him?" Kiera looked disgusted.

"Many of them didn't have a choice," Khalisse explained. "Because of their small size, they couldn't fight back. The Watcher was strategic. He separated them like he did to us, then recruited them one by one. Not all of them joined him, but many did."

"Where are we going first?" Aaron studied the four main villages.

"Vahari." An odd expression flashed in Jannary's eyes. "They are the closest to Fenlithra, and have a powerful army. But...," she trailed off.

"What?" Kiera demanded.

"That is the village that the Watcher was born into," Jannary traced the map with a finger, not meeting their gaze. "Many people still feel the slightest bit of loyalty to him, and they fought with him for a time. But it's been many years of confinement, so they may have changed their mind. But we can't be too sure."

"They might all be Watcher sympathizers?" Kiera exclaimed. "Then why are we bothering?"

"Like I said, their army is powerful." Jannary drummed on the table in an unusually nervous way. "They had a good leader, the last I heard. One who was firmly on our side. But I'm not sure what's happened since then."

"Your job," Khalisse told them, "is to get them *all* on our side. Show up and give a nice speech, act all powerful. Any questions?"

Aaron and Kiera exchanged a look. "When do we leave?"

"Here it is," Khalisse announced. "Vahari." After an hour-long journey by foot, they had arrived at the second forest village.

To avoid getting caught or captured, they had snuck around the back of the village, and climbed a tree. No guards had stopped them. Defense was lacking, probably because of the fact that there were no other villagers that were able to attack.

Not wanting to put any others in danger, the group consisted of only Khalisse, Kiera, and Aaron, who were currently crouched in the leafy branches, spying on the village.

"It's beautiful," sighed Kiera. She caught Khalisse's look and quickly added, "But not as beautiful as Fenlithra, of course."

She was right; while Fenlithra was of the treetops, Vahari was of the earth. Every building looked like it had grown rather than been built, with twisting structures covered in vines, to smooth, natural shapes and spirals. Complex arrangements of flowers and plants covered the ground, framed the houses, and contributed to a truly unique look.

"That's right," Khalisse winked. "Okay, this is the plan. We're going to climb up even further so they can't reach us, then you're going to talk to them."

"Okay," said Aaron hesitantly. Sounded like a totally foolproof plan, he thought sarcastically. They scaled the rest of the tree and perched in the highest branches.

"All right, your turn," Khalisse shoved Aaron forward.

"Why me?" he protested.

Khalisse ignored him. "Go get them!"

Aaron nervously walked forward on a thick branch, gripping a smaller branch for support. He emerged from the leaves into sight of the village.

"Citizens of Vahari," he tried slowly. Nobody looked. He cleared his throat. "Citizens of Vahari!"

People passing by underneath, in the village looked up. There were several screams when they discovered a strange person standing in a tree.

Kiera gave him an encouraging nod, and he continued. "My name is Aaron. I come from lands far away with my friends, Evannah and Kiera. You may have heard of us; we are the three from the prophecy."

An arrow bounced off a branch near his ear and fell back to the ground. It was followed by three more. Aaron ducked, gripping the branch for dear life. "They're shooting at me!" he yelled.

"Deal with it," Khalisse told him. "The amount of times I've been shot at, you wouldn't believe." Kiera snickered.

"Kill me and you'll be stuck with the Watcher forever!" Aaron shouted. He rolled to the side as several more arrows were launched at his head. "I got my allies in Fenlithra out of their village. Wouldn't you like to escape too?"

Murmurs and gasps echoed from the people. The crowd had grown, and the arrows stopped as they stared up at Aaron. It seemed like the whole village was gathering.

He stood back up, satisfied. "That's what I thought. Please, just listen for a moment." They grew quieter. It seemed like the promise of freedom had caught their interest.

"I only arrived here a few days ago. But already, I feel like a citizen of the Island. And I know it is in danger. I'm sure you've all felt the earthquakes." There were mutters of agreement.

"The Island is reaching the end of its life. The Watcher is taking so much power from it, that it is at the brink of collapse. And we can't just sit here and watch it happen!" Wide, shocked gazes looked up at him.

"I know I'm not from here, but I wouldn't sit back and watch my home die! I wouldn't support someone who is killing us all!" His voice increased into a yell. "We have only one chance to stop this! And it takes all of us!"

He pumped his fist into the air. "We rise together, or not at all!" With that, the village erupted into loud cheers.

"Nice job," Khalisse said, over the noise of the excited chatter of the crowd. "I think it worked!"

A young man in gold and green robes and a headpiece that resembled Jannary's had emerged into the front of the crowd. Feeling like it was safe now, Aaron climbed down the tree to meet him. "Aaron?" he asked. "Nice to finally meet you. I'm Neyric, the Everdawn." They shook hands, and Neyric gave him a good-natured smile.

"I have to admit, Aaron, my people were torn. We've had a lot of internal conflicts, being the village that the Watcher was born in. But between the earthquakes and your arrival, I think we're starting to come together again."

"That's great," Aaron responded. "We need to come together in times like these."

"We would be glad to support you," Neyric said solemnly. "Is it true you can get us out of the village?"

"Yes," Aaron answered. "I can show you now."

"One more thing," Neyric looked hesitant. "Is Jannary still Everdawn of Fenlithra?"

"She is," Aaron said. "She spoke highly of you."

Neyric turned red. "I'm glad to hear." Aaron had to stifle a laugh. It was obvious what was going on here. The leader had a crush!

"Let's go to the border," Neyric suggested. "I will bring my best warriors, and myself." He turned to a woman behind him. "Aelra, you're in charge while I'm gone. Wait here," he told Aaron.

Kiera slapped him on the back. "Wow, surprisingly good speech Aaron. You owe me, Khalisse."

Khalisse sighed. "Fine, fine."

"Wait." Aaron said, offended. "You bet against me?"

Khalisse shrugged. "Someone had to."

Just then, Neyric appeared again, followed by a mighty army of hundreds strong. "I've brought a majority of my warriors. The rest will stay here and guard the village. This is no time for holding back."

"Wow," Aaron was shocked by this. "Thank you."

"Thank me when you get us out of here," Neyric said.

As they led the warriors out of the village, for the first time in many days, Aaron felt like they might have a chance.

Chapter 15

"Let go of me!" Evannah screamed, kicking and thrashing as the Shadows gripped her. Nobody could hear her because of the dark hands covering her mouth. "I'll kill you!" she threatened, although she had no idea how she was going to do that.

They forced her through the portal they had created with their device as her friends watched, helpless, from the other side. Aaron screamed, but there was nothing anyone could do.

Then she was falling through the portal, still flailing as the Shadows shoved her through. Everything felt warm for a second, then she crashed through the other side.

She had merely a moment to take in her surroundings before the Shadows were on top of her again. They were by a small lake, at the foot of a tall, rocky purple-gray mountain that loomed overhead, casting its shadow across the forest. She had no doubt it was Watcher Peak. The air was cooler and damp here.

A Shadow slammed her head against the ground. "Ow!" she cried. Tears of pain and anger sprang to her eyes.

She rallied her strength and gave the Shadow a vicious kick. It stumbled back momentarily, but was back again in no time.

"Wait!" she yelled. "I'll come with you, I promise. Just please get off me!" The Shadows looked at each other like they were communicating, then slowly backed away, forming a circle around her.

Evannah had been planning to run, but now she could see that there was no possible way to escape. There was a Shadow waiting in every direction to intercept her, and they were *so tall* now. She wiped blood from the side of her face.

A Shadow pointed forward, and the circle started moving toward the mountain, shoving her forward against her will. "I'm coming!" she shouted as they forced her ahead.

Her mind started spinning out possible ways to escape. She needed to stay calm and collected. Make them think she was harmless. Then use her powers to break her out and run.

"Are we going to the Watcher?" she asked. There was no response; the Shadows just continued walking.

Kiera and Aaron must be worried sick. She hoped that Kiera was keeping Aaron from spiraling into hysterics. He could be so dramatic, sometimes.

Kiera. The thought stabbed her heart. The reveal of her secret was still fresh, and sent shocks of pain down Evannah. She was angry, but not just at Kiera, at her father. She couldn't believe it. How could he have done such a thing?

She let the tears come now, streaming down her cheeks while she sniffled quietly. Choosing Kiera over his own daughter, after she had spent her entire life training to be High Courtieress. It was more than mean, it was cruel. She didn't know what to say to Kiera, if she ever saw her again.

But it was only Evannah now. Evannah, and the Shadows, and the pain that would live in her forever. The pain of betrayal.

She couldn't count on her friends to rescue her now, not when they didn't even know where she was. It was up to her. She wiped her tears and lifted her head defiantly.

After a few minutes of walking next to the lake, they stopped at the very base of the mountain. The Shadows pointed at the ground, prompting her to sit, probably rest before the rest of the walk.

She plopped to the ground, wrapping her hands around her knees and looking innocent. She closed her eyes and rested her head on her knees.

The Shadows stared down at her with their featureless dark faces, daring her to try to run. She sat still.

All the Shadows suddenly turned their heads toward the mountain, no doubt hearing a command from their master, the Watcher.

Evannah waited for a moment. Then, seeing an opportunity, she quickly sprang to her feet and took off.

Not daring to breathe, she darted over the soil by the lake, as fast as she could possibly go.

There was a crash as the Shadows realized and were on her path, gliding over the ground with an otherworldly speed, gaining on her.

She kicked the speed up a notch, racing away. She was nearly past the lake. She needed to escape into the forest, hide, then figure out how to get back to Fenlithra. *Run, Whisperer!* The Whispers urged her on.

Her breath was failing. She needed to stop. *Take our energy,* they suggested. She located the Whispers and borrowed their energy. Rejuvenated, she kept running.

But the Shadows were getting closer and closer. She could feel them drawing nearer, easily catching up.

She tried to put on one final burst of speed, but a streaking force of fury knocked her to the ground.

The Shadows had caught up. "Get away from me!" Evannah threatened, scrambling to regain her footing. She wasn't backing down without a fight.

She swung a punch at the first Shadow that had knocked her over, and kicked the next one that tried to grab her. A third approached, but she elbowed it in the stomach, and it crumpled.

They recovered as quickly as she could take them down, easily standing up straight again as though nothing had happened. More kept approaching and appearing, until she was surrounded by a crowd of Shadows so thick it looked like night.

Okay, Whispers, she thought. *This is where you come in.* She used her power to light up her hand, and turned the brightness up so high that she had to close her eyes. Several of the Shadows flinched, and backed away as the bright rays hit them.

It wasn't enough, though. More Shadows kept appearing, and moving toward her. With a burst of energy, a fiery ball of light shot from her hand and hit the nearest Shadow in the stomach. She looked at it triumphantly. "Ha!" Her powers just kept surprising her.

Shooting off another round of streaks of light, she managed to take down the first row of Shadows. She whipped around, shooting them in every direction. The Shadows were stumbling back, tripping over themselves, and falling to the ground.

Then she spotted the transporting device in the hand of the original Shadow that had kidnapped her. *That's my way out of here!*

Evannah fought her way in that direction, finally reaching the Shadow, who she finished off with an intense burst of light. It fell to the ground, and she picked up the transporting device.

It was a circle of glass rimmed with gold, and Evannah tried to remember how they had used it. She held it up to the sun, and a ray passed through it, tearing a circular hole in space.

Take me back! She thought furiously. The remaining Shadows were approaching, getting closer and closer. They descended on her right as she escaped through the portal, free at last.

The last thing she saw was a cloaked figure standing high above, on a mountain ledge, watching her.

Evannah fell through and landed on grass, breathing hard. She lay there for a minute, in shock. Then she got up and rubbed her arms. It was colder here. Was she back in Fenlithra?

She looked around, taking in the crashing waves of the ocean, the rocky bluffs, and the castle in the distance. A cool, salty wind blew at her face. The voices in her mind were silent.

Oh no.

Evannah was back in Neomerica.

Her thoughts of Kiera, and her father's betrayal must have led to a portal being created back to her home.

She held the circle of glass up to the sun again, but then thought better of it.

While she was here, she had some things to take care of...

Evannah marched across the grassy slopes to the gray castle, a sight she had been familiar with her entire life, kicking up pebbles and dirt. The dark blue Fenlithrian robes she had been wearing blew out behind her.

Within moments she had reached the grand doors to the castle. Two armed guards waited by the door to protect it. "Name?" one of them asked, bored, not bothering to look up.

"Evannah Farrah."

They finally lifted their heads, startled looks on their faces. "Miss Farrah? But—"

"Aren't you—"

"How?"

"I'm back," Evannah said irritably. "For a little bit. Are you going to let me through?"

They parted and allowed her to step through, still confused. As she walked through the doors, she heard one of them whisper. "But I don't see a boat!"

She gave a satisfied smile. Let them wonder. Let them gossip. It didn't matter to her anymore.

She stormed through the long gray stone entrance hall adorned with gold filigree patterns and gorgeous paintings. She had stopped noticing the attractiveness of the castle a long time ago. This formal style couldn't compare to the wild beauty of the Island.

Luckily, there was nobody there who noticed and stopped her. She made her way to the twisting staircase, and began climbing up the second tower.

Fury encouraged her forward, driving her every step, filling her with energy when she should have been exhausted.

Nothing was going to stop Evannah.

She had the path memorized, climb the staircases up the second tower, take a turn on the right corridor, then walk down the hall to the third room.

Lord Cyrus's study.

He was often there, at his mahogany desk, working on something, or meeting someone, or writing away on a paper that Evannah was sure was not as important as he believed it was. She hoped it was where she could find him today.

She poked her head through the open doorway and sure enough, that's where he was. He was dressed in perfectly pressed navy finery, his usual color, with his gold High Courtier brooch shining. Lord Cyrus's sharp ice blue eyes were focused on a paper on his desk.

Evannah had never liked how she resembled Lord Cyrus, with her blue eyes, dark hair, and pale skin. She envied Aaron, forever linked by looks to the mother they had never known.

She stormed through the doorway. "Hello, father."

Evannah relished the look of shock on her father's face, how he knocked over all his papers and fell backward in his chair.

"Evannah!" he cried. "What are you doing here? You're supposed to be—"

"Out at sea, I know," Evannah said vaguely. "Clearly I'm not."

Lord Cyrus looked Evannah up and down, from her blue Island-style robes, to her disheveled hair and wild eyes, to the blood crusted on the side of her face. She must have looked completely deranged.

"There were no reports of any boats arriving." Lord Cyrus gave her a searching look. "I must be dreaming," he said finally.

"Believe that if you want," Evannah responded coolly. "How could you, father?"

"Whatever are you talking about?" Lord Cyrus fumbled to pick up his papers before dropping them again.

"You chose Kiera as High Courtieress," Evannah shouted. "It was supposed to be me!"

"I was under the impression you never wanted it," her father responded coldly. "I was doing you a favor."

"Don't try that," Evannah growled. "Yes, I never wanted it, but I spent my whole life training for that moment. It was what I was meant to be. And you took that away."

Her father was speechless for a moment.

She continued. "And the title doesn't even matter to me. What does matter is that you chose Kiera over your own daughter. Why?"

Lord Cyrus narrowed his eyes. "You must know that you were never fit for the job. Spouting your opinions off everywhere, never listening to anybody." He met her gaze for a moment then broke it, gazing passively at the old books and maps tucked into shelves on the wall of his study.

"And Kiera didn't?" Evannah cried. "It was never about her being better than me. It was about you. Always another test, another punishment. It was only Kiera because she was my best friend. You wanted me to live my life watching her in my position. Why?"

Lord Cyrus stared at her with blazing eyes, standing up from his chair to face her. "I—"

"No, this is about you," Evannah shouted again. "You just couldn't *bear* to see me live my life happily. I was never good enough for you. I don't know what happened to you to make you like this, but I will *not* have you taking it out on me!" She slammed her hand down on the wooden desk.

Lord Cyrus swelled. "How *dare* you speak like that to me? I've done nothing but prepare you, and train you, and take care of you for your entire life. It wasn't my fault I was given a worthless child, but I tried. I did everything I could, but it seems that it wasn't enough. Nothing can fix you."

"Don't start," Evannah warned, rage making her face heat up. "You can't talk back to dreams. And I did everything I could, too! I tried to fit in your mold. I changed. I gave up everything. I gave up my real self. And it wasn't enough. It was never enough."

She stepped closer to Lord Cyrus, giving him a dangerous look. "I know now that it was never going to be me, at least not for a long time. You're so stuck in your ways. You would *die* if you knew what was out there in the world, beyond your neat little room in your perfect castle. Things you can't control. Things you couldn't even *comprehend*." Her voice rose to a shout. "WELL, I'M DONE! I'm done with you, and done with Neomerica!"

Her father looked around hurriedly. "Lower your voice! What if there are—"

"Court members around?" Evannah sneered. "I DON'T CARE!"

Lord Cyrus took a stunned step back. Evannah took a breath. "You know what?" she said softly. "I forgive you, father. It wasn't all your fault. You can't control where you live or how you were brought up. And I suppose I love you on some level; you're my father. But just *think* about what you are doing. It's possible to change."

Evannah edged toward Lord Cyrus's window at the back of his room as he stared, speechless. In one swift move, she opened the window, pulled out the circle of glass, and held it up to the sun, picturing the Island.

Lord Cyrus gaped. "What? Now I *know* this is a dream." He blinked several times as a portal opened up in the sky, a swirling image of dense forests and towering mountains.

"Goodbye," Evannah said firmly, with a finality as she vaulted over the window and leaped through the portal.

She landed on her shoulder, and rolled to avoid hurting herself as she jumped to her feet. The change in her senses hit her immediately. The temperature was now warm and humid, the scents strong and fragrant, the colors many shades brighter, and the noises wild and loud.

In her hands, the teleporting device crumbled into dust, the glitter covering the ground. She supposed that it had had a limited amount of leaps through space.

She had landed in a patch of flowers, crushing several as she regained her footing. The ocean crashed in the distance, which meant... *oh no.*

This was definitely not Fenlithra.

She walked toward the noise and emerged onto a small beach, thick with mist. The silvery ocean lapped at her feet. Khalisse was right; the damage didn't seem to have reached the coast quite yet.

But this wasn't the beach they had landed on when they reached the Island. So where was she? She didn't even have the teleportation device to get her back anymore.

She had hardly noticed the murmurs of language in the back of her mind, sounding like they were talking far away. "Whispers?" she asked out loud. "Can you help me find Fenlithra? Where on the Island am I?"

The Island surrounds you... they hummed. *The Island is all. We are all part of the Island...*

Okay, so they weren't going to be any help at all. What did that leave her with?

Evannah squinted at the mountains. There was Watcher Peak, tall and menacing, and its surrounding jagged mountains. The other mountains were smaller and green, but were they more to the right than they had been when she arrived?

Hmm... Watcher Peak did look more at a right angle, and so did the waterfall. But she really had no idea. She picked a path that looked correct, crossed her fingers, and began stumbling through the undergrowth.

Evannah was lost and alone, and nobody would be able to help her.

Chapter 16

"Faster, faster... brilliant!" Tovan applauded Kiera as the vine she was encouraging wrapped itself around the tree at the quickest pace she had managed yet. "Let's take a break."

They went to sit at a nearby rock. "What's wrong?" he asked. "I know that something's the matter."

Kiera sighed. "Evannah," was all she had to say. She felt so guilty, first about the secret, then about having lost her best friend to the Shadows.

Tovan put a hand on her shoulder. "Don't panic. She will come back, I'm sure of it."

"I hope so," Kiera responded glumly. "But—the prophecy! It says one of us will fall." Her voice cracked and she cleared her throat. "What if it's too late for Evannah?" Or... what if the reveal of her secret would be the last time they met? What if their friendship was never mended? She wished Moss was here to make her feel better, but he was being fed and taken care of by some villagers while she trained.

"You can't think like that!" Tovan scolded gently. "You *must* hope for the best. Anyway, you can't be upset when you're doing so great." Kiera did enjoy the sessions with him. Already he felt like a good friend, or almost a father figure. And she liked connecting to the Island. She didn't care about not having any "powers" when she did have such a special bond with the Island itself. She was able to ask, and it gave her something in return.

Although, she had felt its presence weakening slowly these past few hours in a way that scared her. The damage seemed to be increasing at an increasing rate, and it hurt that she couldn't stop it.

"I guess so," she replied finally.

"I think I know something that will cheer you up," Tovan told her, standing up. "Your seed is just about ready to be harvested."

"The one from the Flowering Tree?" Kiera stood up so fast she nearly fell over. "What did it grow?"

Tovan gave her a mysterious smile. "See for yourself. I had some hunches. Come on." He beckoned her forward, and together they walked to the little patch where they had planted the seed that the Flowering Tree had gifted her.

Kiera stopped. "Whoa, what *is* that?" From the seed had grown a green cocoon made of large leaves, as tall as her waist. It swayed gently in the wind.

"Want to pick it?" Tovan suggested.

Kiera hesitated. "I don't want to break it. Maybe you should do it?"

"Don't be silly," he said. "We'll do it together." They both bent down to the base and tried to lift the large cocoon. It was quite heavy. They eventually plucked it out of the soil, and Kiera hefted it into her arms.

"It's big," she grunted. In her arms it reached taller than her head. "But I still don't know what it is."

"Open it," Tovan told her.

She laid it down on the ground and began peeling the long leaves of the cocoon off while it became skinnier and skinnier. Finally, she stripped the cocoon of its last layer, to reveal a shining object.

"Wow," Kiera gasped. The cocoon had been wrapping a long sword, as tall as her waist. The beautiful sword was a burnished gold, and the handle and blade were wrapped in dark green vines, which twisted slowly. Flowers blossomed along those vines, making the sword seem like a living entity or a plant. "A sword? I was not expecting that."

"Not just any," explained Tovan with wide eyes, "The Blade of the Wild. One of the ancient swords, specifically linked to the wildlife of the Island. The Island has given you a gift, a fighting chance."

Kiera turned it over in her hands. "It's amazing." She gave it a small twirl, and flowers shot up around her feet. "Whoa! How do I use it?"

"I'm afraid you'll have to figure that out," Tovan winked. "Nobody has seen the sword in a long, long time."

Kiera experimented, slashing the sword in different ways. Sometimes the plant life around her changed, sometimes it didn't. It was hard to figure out what to do.

There was a rustle as Thalen, the big village guard with the impressive beard brushed past the new flowers to meet them.

"Aaron is bringing in the last Vahari warriors, we thought you should be there."

"Oh!" Kiera exclaimed. "Coming!" Sword in hand, she energetically followed the big warrior through the village until they reached the border, where she could see glints of armor in the distance.

"Exciting!" Tovan remarked. "We haven't met the Vahari Everdawn in many years."

Indeed, a small crowd had gathered, both on the ground and in the treetops to watch them arrive. Aaron had been in Vahari all day, binding the Watcher's curse temporarily to allow the troops to leave while also practicing his abilities. Kiera had wanted to help, but in the end, it was more useful to spend the time training. This was the last batch of the best warriors, led by Neyric Everdawn himself.

"I see them!" a villager shouted excitedly. Jannary herself had emerged to see, leaning over a treehouse railing which she was gripping hard. Her long hair swept over her shoulders and barely hid her face, which was flushed with anxiety.

The previous groups of Vahari warriors had consisted of dozens, but this group contained *hundreds*. Their armor was bronze, in contrast to the Fenlithra gold, and a little thicker and blockier, which made sense, seeing as they didn't have to climb trees to get around.

Aaron led the group, his eyes tired from the many journeys, but his walk strong and confident. "Aaron!" Kiera called, waving madly. His face lit up and he waved back.

It turned out the curse only applied to leaving villages, so Aaron didn't need to use his power to get them in. There were hopeful murmurs as the mighty horde marched in, led by a young man in gold and green robes. He adjusted his headpiece, looking boldly at the village.

Neyric's eyes darted around the village, looking for something. He finally met Jannary's eyes, and it was like someone had given him the sun as a present. His face brightened as he looked on in shock and happiness. "Jannary!"

The same expression was written all over Jannary's face, making her look years younger, a girl in love instead of an anxious leader in peril. "Neyric?"

She quickly climbed down from the treehouse and ran to the other leader, throwing her arms around his neck. "I thought I'd never see you again!" she murmured in his ear. Kiera could only hear because she was so close.

"I won't leave this time," Neyric promised, hugging her back. "We'll stay together. Always." They broke apart. There were some startled glances, but not too many. Kiera thought that many villagers had suspected the leaders' relationship.

"Your warriors can mingle with my citizens," Jannary said. "I expect they'll be wanting to meet after so long. As for you, we have much to discuss. Come to the Great Tree." She pointed at Aaron and Kiera. "You too."

Aaron came up to Kiera's side as they began walking. "What's with the sword?"

"Surprise! It was in the seed the Flowering Tree gave me. Apparently it's an ancient sword called 'The Blade of the Wild,'" Kiera grinned.

"Wow!" Aaron exclaimed. "Want to let me borrow it? I *am* the Warrior, after all."

"Find your own weapon!" Kiera scolded. "This one's mine."

"Fine, fine," Aaron scowled.

A loud THUD frightened them, making them jump back as a dark shape dropped from the sky. Night Star landed in front of the Great Tree.

"Night Star!" Kiera exclaimed. "You're back!"

"What happened?" Jannary asked, as dread spread across her face.

Night Star bowed his head. "I've just dropped Marra's body off at the burial grounds, and I come with news. Evannah has been found."

Kiera shrieked and grabbed Aaron's arm with joy, as he went limp with relief. "Where?" he demanded.

"I haven't seen her, but I've heard reports from the birds," Night Star explained. "She was seen wandering around the southeast beaches."

"Thank goodness," Jannary sighed. "How did she get so far?"

"We don' t know. I was just on my way to get her," the cat said. "But Fenlithra was on the way and I thought you'd want to know."

"Yes," Kiera breathed. Evannah had survived. "Thanks."

"One more thing," he added. "Chasms like the ones that opened up in the battle against the Shadows have been appearing all across the Island."

"Another symptom," Neyric murmured. "Another sign of the end."

"So many animal casualties," Night Star remarked solemnly. "So much life lost, fallen down the abysses."

A cold dread seized at Kiera. "What can we do?"

"What we're doing," Neyric assured. "Connecting the villages. We're going to make a stand, and soon. We don't have much time."

"Less than a week," Jannary agreed.

"For now, I will retrieve Evannah, and see you soon," Night Star took off into the sky without another word. They watched him grow smaller and smaller, until he was finally swallowed by the clouds.

"What do we do?" Kiera complained. She knew the answer before Jannary said it. "Back to training, I guess."

They spent the afternoon training halfheartedly while really waiting for Evannah to get back. Every time Kiera heard a noise, she tilted her head to the sky to look for Night Star.

The eighth time she did so, a couple of hours later, after lunch, she nearly fainted in relief when she saw the great cat soar through the air and land a little ways away.

Kiera abandoned her training and ran through the village, just in time to see a disheveled and exhausted looking Evannah slide off Night Star's back.

She sprinted to her side and tackled in a hug, nearly toppling them both over. Aaron wasn't far behind. "Evannah!" he cried, hugging her so hard she had to pry him off.

"Whoa, I need to breathe," she laughed.

"I can't believe you're back!" Kiera exclaimed, scanning her friend for injuries.

"Neither can I," said Evannah. Then she looked at Kiera differently, as though remembering something again.

"I'm so sorry Evannah," Kiera said softly. "But remember: we can't change what others do, only how we react to it." The line was a little too poetic for her, but she still loved it. It had been Evannah who had told her that, long ago, after reading it in a story.

Evannah sighed, immediately recognizing her own words. "I'm sorry too. I overreacted, and... I realized it doesn't even matter. When the entire Island is going to be brought down, what difference does a little title thousands of miles away make?" She wrapped Kiera in a hug.

"What happened?" asked Kiera, and so Evannah told them the whole story as villagers brought her fresh clothes and food. It was a detailed and interesting story, from escaping the Shadows to storming the castle of Neomerica.

Aaron actually choked on his sandwich when she said that. "*What?*" he exclaimed. "I can't believe you actually did that."

"You better believe it," Evannah grinned slyly. "I think I gave father dearest the fright of his life." They all began laughing, and Kiera felt the tension she had held onto for so long finally fade away.

They told Evannah the many things that had happened in the hours she had been gone, from recruiting the Vaharians to finding her sword, which Evannah was very impressed by.

"Oh," Evannah remembered. "What was in the journal? The one we walked the Trail to find?"

Aaron and Kiera exchanged a look. Kiera pulled out the journal, which she had been carrying around with her. It looked old, with a brown cover and weathered edges. "Here's the thing. We don't know."

"You haven't opened it?" said Evannah, startled.

"We can't," Kiera admitted. She handed the book to Evannah. "Check it out."

Evannah tried to open the pages, but just like when Kiera and Aaron had tried it, it was stuck, like every page had been glued together. "You're right. Seriously? All that for nothing?"

"I guess so," Kiera muttered. "Maybe we'll need it later?"

"There you are!" Jannary's voice called. She was accompanied by Neyric, Khalisse, and Night Star. "Come, we need to talk." She led them to the nearest treehouse, a guest house where Neyric had been staying, which was as lavish as theirs, and high up in the treetops.

Kiera looked down at the long fall to the ground as Neyric spoke. "We need to discuss next steps."

Night Star was draped across a branch in a neighboring tree, his long tail swishing. "I believe we need to recruit the other villages as fast as we can, before the Watcher stops us."

"Tomorrow we strike back," Jannary agreed.

"Tomorrow?" Kiera gasped. "Already? But—we aren't prepared at all!"

"We have no choice," Night Star growled. "We'll send a small group, attempt an assasination. It needs to be done quickly. We fight or we die."

"I'll make the announcement to the Fenlithrians and Vaharians," Jannary said gravely.

Just then, there was a soft whooshing that made them all turn their heads. It grew louder and louder, until a shape was barreling through the trees, coming straight at them.

They screamed, trying to jump back, but there was nowhere to go. The shape stopped, floating in the air, right in front of Night Star.

It was a cloud of white smoke, forming the rough shape of a towering bird's head, as though someone had carelessly sculpted it.

"What is it?" Kiera asked.

The bird shape opened its beak and began to speak. The voice seemed like it wasn't working, it started very soft, and cut off in some places. "All Guardians... captured... Tharros Peak. Not much time." Then the smoke bird fell apart, rapidly dissipating.

Night Star jumped to his paws, nearly falling off the tree.

"What happened?" Kiera demanded.

There was a look of panic in the cat's eyes that she hadn't seen before, as he dug his claws deep into the bark. "The other Guardians—they've all been captured. That was a message from Streakwing, a sky Guardian."

"Oh no," Jannary murmured. "That's horrible. I think we need to focus on taking out the Watcher first, though."

"You don't understand," Night Star explained agitatedly. "If the Watcher converts the Guardians to shadow, or kills them before we reach him, it's over. There's no hope for the Island anymore."

"We must get them back," Khalisse announced with determination. "Did it say Tharros Peak?"

"I'm afraid so," Night Star responded. Then everyone looked at Aaron, Kiera, and Evannah.

"What?" Aaron asked.

Khalisse sighed. "The Eyes of the Island, the tallest range, is protected by a powerful blood curse. Anyone with pure Island blood cannot enter, or they die."

"It's how the Watcher protects his home," Night Star said darkly. "It's protected against Guardians as well. Unless he captures them, of course."

"We have to do this," Kiera realized. "We're the only ones who can get past the blood curse."

"Hang on, can't I undo it?" Aaron asked. "At least temporarily, and let you through?"

Jannary shook her head. "A blood curse is too powerful. You can't undo it, or stop it at all. The curse has been created by the blood of his victims."

"It's too dangerous," Neyric argued. "We can't lose them."

"What choice do we have?" Khalisse responded desperately.

"I don't know," Jannary murmured. "I couldn't send them into danger like that, without any support. Not only is our cause lost without them, but I wouldn't be able to live with myself if these youths got killed because of our decision."

"Wait," Kiera interjected. "Do we have a say in this? Because I want to go."

"You can't!" Jannary cried.

"But it sounds like if we don't rescue the Guardians, our cause is hopeless anyway, right, Night Star?" Kiera argued. The cat nodded gravely. "So we have to go."

"I'm afraid they're right," Night Star said sadly. "I'm not saying this out of concern for my fellow Guardians, but we can't win without them. And especially if they get converted to shadow..." he trailed off. "I shudder to think."

"So we'll go," Evannah declared firmly, with Aaron and Kiera nodding along.

"She does have one of the ancient swords," Neyric mused. "That itself proves she's worthy."

January sighed. "I guess there's no choice. We'll prepare you the best we can."

"They need an All-Key," Night Star said anxiously.

"An All-Key?" Evannah asked.

"A key that can open any lock," Night Star explained. "The only way that the Watcher could neutralize the Guardians' abilities would be by keeping them in a powerfully enchanted cage."

"Is there any spell that can open it?" Evannah asked.

"We don't know," Jannary admitted. "And we don't have the time to search for one. I don't know where we can quickly find an All-Key, though."

"I have an idea," Neyric offered. "The Serpent of Song lives somewhat near our territory, and he collects special, magical objects. It's rumored he has an All-Key."

"Brilliant!" Jannary took Neyric's hand. "You three and Night Star can go meet him immediately, while we prepare the warriors here."

"All right," remarked Aaron. "Who is this Serpent of Song?"

Night Star grumbled. "Technically, he is a Guardian too, but he gave up on protecting the Island a long time ago to 'devote his life to music.' Now he lives a futile and purposeless life alone."

"Sounds like you're best buddies," Kiera teased. The cat groaned.

"Good luck!" Khalisse called as they started to leave, Kiera and Aaron both armed (Evannah had given up on her bow), and Night Star by their side.

"So," Kiera asked, walking through the forest. Many of the remaining trees and plants looked withered and infected, another sign that they needed to move quickly. "What should we expect? A fight to the death?"

"I wouldn't expect a fight from the Serpent," Night Star remarked. "More along the lines of a bargain, maybe a test. We need that key at all costs. Oh, and you'll have to go by yourself. He's not interested in meeting other Guardians, and we don't love him either."

"Great," Kiera grumbled.

Along the journey, they were able to see the many chasms that Night Star had told them about, that had spread across the Island, deep scars in the Earth that would remain forever. Earthquakes, chasms... what was next?

They walked a while longer, until they reached a place that looked better than the rest of the forest. The trees were a bit healthier, and a few clumps of flowers covered the ground. "This is where I leave you," Night Star said. "Keep going, and you'll find the Serpent's home. May luck stay with you."

They kept walking. "I'm a bit nervous," Evannah commented. "A test scares me more than a fight, honestly."

"I think this is it," said Kiera. They had walked into a clearing, where a small river cut through, and a large cave was on the other side. The Serpent's den, likely. It was like a place of paradise in the middle of a crumbling island: warm, damp air and flowers, a crystalline stream, and flourishing trees.

"Do you hear that?" Aaron asked.

Kiera tilted her head, before she noticed it. Everything in this clearing sounded musical, from the melodious birdsong, to the bubbling brook, to the wind echoing off the stone cave. "It's like one giant song."

"I like it," Evannah began to hum softly. "What was that?" She turned her head abruptly.

A flicker of movement in the trees. A loud rustle. A flash of white.

Kiera twisted around as the same sounds rang out from the other side of the clearing. She subconsciously backed away, until she hit something and screamed.

It was only Evannah. She and Aaron had already backed into the clearing, standing still in fear. "Is it the Serpent?" she whispered.

Whatever was moving around had to be *huge*.

"Look!" Aaron pointed frantically. Enormous coils of white were wrapped around the nearest tree, unbelievably big.

Then a colossal snake head pulled out of the trees and turned to face them, rising high above their heads. Kiera let out an involuntary shriek.

The rest of its body slithered out, and began to circle Evannah, Kiera, and Aaron, coming closer and closer.

"Who do we have here?" the great serpent asked, flaring its hood. Kiera was surprised to hear that it had a sophisticated, rich male voice with an elegant accent. He was quite beautiful, actually, with milky white scales that shone in different colors, and golden eyes. His scales were patterned with music notes that changed every few seconds.

Evannah and Aaron turned to face her. Wow, some friends she had. "Hello, dear Serpent of Song," Kiera began smoothly. "We came to meet you."

"Hmm," the Serpent towered above them, his head as big as one of their bodies. He could probably swallow them in a single gulp. "And what do you want?" His body was curling around them, squeezing tightly and holding them in place. Kiera let out a choked grunt as she was squashed into Evannah and Aaron.

"We need your help," she gasped. "We need an All-Key."

The Serpent released his hold on them slightly, allowing them to breathe, while still trapping them. "Interesting. What for?"

Aaron decided to chime in. "The Watcher is destroying the Island, and we don't have much time. The Guardians have been captured, and we need the All-Key to release them so we can fight against the Watcher and win."

The snake looked thoughtful. "Well... I certainly don't like the Watcher, he's ruining the music of the Island. But I don't care much about the Guardian's whereabouts. Those bunch of ruffians only care about fighting. They don't appreciate the arts like I do," he sniffed.

"Please," Kiera begged. "We need them to win."

"Who *are* you?" the Serpent's eyes flashed dangerously. "You're not from the Island."

"I'm Evannah, she's Kiera, and my brother is Aaron," said Evannah. "But you may know us as the Whisperer, the Wanderer, and the Warrior."

The snake's huge tongue flicked out, and he arched his head down to study them. He brought his face near them, his golden slitted eyes as large as their faces. "From the prophecy! One of my favorite works, I have to admit. What are you willing to give for the key?"

"What do you want?" Kiera asked boldly.

"I have only one request, and I will not settle for anything else," the Serpent's mouth curled into what looked somewhat like a smile. "It's been *soooo* long since I've heard a human sing." He dropped his hold on them, and slithered in front of them, allowing them to walk around once more. "Take it or leave it. But I hope you'll take it! I have no use for the All-Key; I don't have fingers to work it with. But I would love a good song again." His scales' music note patterns flashed in excitement.

They were quiet for a second. "I can't sing," Kiera said hurriedly.

"Well, we can't either," whispered Aaron to Kiera. Evannah nodded rapidly. "We have to try."

"Ready?" the Serpent asked.

"Wait," Kiera hesitated. "I'd like to preface this. I'm not very good..."

"Go on, try," the snake insisted.

"Um," she glanced around. "I don't know any songs..."

"You must know something," the Serpent commented in annoyance. "*Think.*"

Kiera wracked her brain, but in the end, the only thing she could think of was a creepy lullaby that court parents would sing to their children. Well, at least she'd give it a try. Blushing bright red, she opened her mouth and began to sing in an off-key voice.

"*Twinkle, twinkle, court pin, how good have you children been?*

"*Act proper, put on a show, or in the dungeon you will go.*

"*Twinkle, twinkle, court pin, how good have you children been?*"

She finished the horrible sounding song in her screechy tone. The Serpent was staring open-mouthed at her, his music note patterns flashing red and breaking. Aaron let out several coughs that sounded suspiciously like laughs.

"Suns and stars," the Serpent muttered, horrorstruck. "You poor child."

"Do we get the key?" Kiera asked eagerly. That embarrassment had hopefully been worth it, at least.

"In no world did that count as singing," the Serpent hissed. "Oh, my poor ears..."

"It wasn't *that* bad," Kiera protested weakly.

"Anyone else?" the Serpent of Song asked.

"Aaron plays the violin," Kiera offered with an evil laugh.

"Shut up," Aaron grumbled. When he was ten, he had taken up the violin for a few months. It had been so ear-splittingly awful that Lord Cyrus had forbidden either of his twins from touching another string instrument as long as they lived. "I guess I can try to sing, though. For the *good of the Island*." He cleared his throat. "*Twinkle, twinkle*," he began in a voice nearly as awful as Kiera's.

The Serpent's music notes turned red again. "No, no! Not this song again. Your turn's done," he told a very relieved Aaron. "Last try," he said to Evannah. "I'll even make it a little easier for you: I'll give you the words this time." He flicked the end of his tail and a thin paper came flying from inside his cave, straight to Evannah's hands.

"I really don't know if I," she began.

"Hush, and sing," the Serpent of Song demanded.

"*Ode to the Serpent of Song*," Evannah started, reading off the paper. "*The greatest creature in the world...*"

Wow. Evannah could *sing*.

Not just sing, she was amazing at it. Her voice was bright and clear, resonating loudly and powerfully, but still gently and melodiously on the soft parts. She had one of the most beautiful voices Kiera had ever heard, even more silky and rich than the professional musicians in Neomerica.

She finished at last, faint traces of her vibrato still ringing in the air.

There was a moment of silence.

"Wow," said a shocked Aaron. "Evah, I didn't know you could sing!" Evannah ducked, hiding her blushing face.

"Wow," the Serpent echoed. "That one makes up for the horrible singing from you two. The key is yours!" He flicked his tail again, and something came flying from the cave, landing in

Kiera's hands. It was a finger-length golden rod that was oddly soft. She could bend it if she applied enough force.

"This is the All-Key?" she checked.

"Yes," the Serpent answered. "Put it in any lock, and it will take that shape."

"Thank you!" Aaron said politely.

The Serpent of Song flared his hood with satisfaction. "Please come back any time you like!" He bumped Evannah with his tail. "When you're done saving the world, you would be the perfect voice for one of my pieces."

"Noted," remarked Evannah, a little embarrassed. "That sounds like an... interesting opportunity."

They said goodbye to the snake, who slithered back into his cave, humming the ode to himself that Evannah had sung.

"Night Star!" Kiera called the cat over, waving the little object. "We got the key!"

"Congratulations," Night Star said. "We must go quickly. I fear Fenlithra is in danger."

Chapter 17

"What happened?" Aaron asked anxiously.

"I believe they are under attack," Night Star growled. "Or will be soon. Look at the birds; they are all fleeing from that direction. I was flying around a bit while you were gone, and I noticed the route between Watcher Peak and Fenlithra was darker than usual, and withered. Shadows have passed through."

"Could you be wrong?" Kiera asked.

"Perhaps," Night Star responded. "But I don't think so. I have very strong instincts, and this feels wrong."

"Let's go," Evannah suggested.

"We'll fly back," said Night Star. "Forget about stealth, we need to be there as fast as we can." They climbed onto his back, and he took off.

Seeing the damage from above made Aaron's breath catch in his throat. They had flown mere days earlier, and the Island had been lush and beautiful. Now, the white patches of death and decay had spread to cover the Isle, and the stretches of green forest were small dots on the map. "It got so bad so quickly," Aaron whispered.

"Yeah," Evannah responded. "We have to fix this."

"I'll have you back in a few minutes," Night Star called over his shoulder. "We'll see what this is about."

"I think I see what this is about," Aaron replied, horrorstruck, as he pointed to some motion below. Night Star swooped a little further down to see.

A massive gathering of Shadows, towering bigger than Aaron had ever seen. They marched slowly in the direction of Fenlithra.

"There must be hundreds of Shadows," Kiera gasped. They stared at what were small black dots from here, but were soon to be a village-ending threat.

"Why are they moving so slowly?" Aaron questioned. "Couldn't they just teleport?"

"I took their teleporting device," Evannah reminded him.

"With so many Shadows, it takes a lot of power to control them," Night Star explained. "He's moving them slowly to save energy."

"For the attack," Aaron finished for him. The poor, innocent Fenlithrians and Vaharians. He had grown close to them over the past couple of days, the danger bringing them together.

"At this rate, we'll reach much before them," Night Star assured them. "Then we can decide what to do."

They flew for a few more minutes, before Night Star announced, "Fenlithra ahead!" They swooped down, landed, jumped off Night Star's back and went running into the village.

Night Star leaped up in the air. "ATTENTION, EVERYONE! SHADOWS ARE MOVING THIS WAY!"

People began to scream and run around. Jannary emerged from the Great Tree with Neyric and Khalisse. "What's going on?"

Aaron rushed to explain. "An army of Shadows is coming toward here, the biggest gathering I've ever seen."

"Revenge for uniting the villages," Night Star growled.

"Can we fight?" Khalisse's hand went immediately to her weapon.

"No chance," Night Star told her.

"There's too many of them," Kiera jumped in.

"Then we must evacuate." Jannary's dark eyes gazed around at her panicking citizens. "I hoped it wouldn't come to this. Will you make the announcement, Night Star?"

"Of course," the cat rumbled. He leapt up again, standing in the air above their heads, and called out in a booming voice. "WE ARE EVACUATING! THE SHADOWS WILL REACH IN ONE HOUR, OR LESS! GATHER YOUR FAMILIES AND YOUR MOST PRIZED POSSESSIONS! THIS IS AN EMERGENCY!"

Children began to cry, and their parents scooped them up, carrying them away in a hurry.

"Where will we go?" Evannah asked with a distant look. "In only one hour?"

"We have to go before it gets dark," Jannary said. "And there's only one place where the Shadows can't follow us."

"The ocean," Neyric and Khalisse said solemnly at the same time.

"Shadows can't leave the Island," explained Khalisse. "They'll die."

Jannary began to pace. "We'll need to swim around the perimeter of the Island and look for somewhere safe. An outer island, perhaps. But some Fenlithrians can't swim! The elderly and the young. Many kids have never even *seen* the ocean before."

"We'll build rafts," Aaron suggested. "We'll get *everyone* to safety."

"This is my fault," said Neyric. "I brought my warriors here. He was watching."

"It had to be done!" Night Star snarled. "We're striking back for the first time in years, and he couldn't handle that. Now are you going to give up now, or are we going to get through this?"

"We'll get through," Jannary declared.

"What about the Guardians?" Kiera asked. "We still need to go for them."

"This is more important," Neyric said firmly. "We'll rescue them as soon as we can."

"Gather your things," Jannary commanded. "I'll need some help organizing the people—we don't have much time." She wrung her hands as she walked off, starting to group families together to get a headcount of everyone.

The next half-hour passed in a blur. The threat of Shadows had brought everyone, Fenlithrian and Vaharian, together in a way that they had never been united before.

Aaron joined a group of woodworkers who were binding logs at a frantic pace, trying to make rafts for the very young and old. He chopped wood and vines and tied them together at top speed, working until his arms felt like they couldn't move anymore, like they were going to fall off, but he kept working.

Evannah was working with Jannary, counting everyone, dividing them into groups, and assigning those who needed it to rafts.

Kiera helped Fenlithrians pack up a few possessions each and leave their homes, maybe for good.

Throughout it all, Night Star bounded around the village, helping get the warriors armed and ready, while shouting out the time they had left. "FORTY-FIVE MINUTES! HALF AN HOUR!"

Five minutes passed. Then ten. And before Aaron knew it, their hour was up.

"Everyone to the border!" Night Star called. "Aaron will let you out!"

Aaron helped drag one of the rafts to the border of the village. It all depended on him now. "Is everyone ready?" he yelled.

Loud screams of terror resounded, and Aaron followed many people's gazes. Hovering in the air several yards away, clumped together to form a dark haze was a great mass of Shadows.

"Go, now!" Khalisse shouted. But before Aaron could do any-thing, all the Shadows reached up toward the sky.

Lightning plunged down from the clouds toward the earth at a frightening speed, lighting up the sky in a dazzling flash. Blinded, Aaron closed his eyes.

When he opened them, the air smelled like smoke. "Fire!" several people shouted. Tongues of flame licked at several buildings.

"Get us out!" Jannary shouted. "Quickly!"

Aaron closed his eyes, and halted the Watcher's spell. "Run!" he yelled back. "It's open!"

While there was a thunderous stampede to exit the village, the Shadows continued to summon lighting. Fires erupted where the lighting struck, reducing treehouses to charred piles of ash.

Tears ran down the Fenlithrian's faces at the sight of their home being destroyed.

"There's still people in there!" Neyric screamed.

Without another word, Aaron ran back into the burning village, dodging smoldering branches and flying sparks. Small groups of people ran toward the border, coughing from the smoke.

"Everybody run!" he commanded in a hoarse voice. "The exit's that way!"

A group of young children was huddled on the ground, casting frightened looks around at the blazing village, which was now lit up with an orange glow. Aaron pulled them to their feet. "Go to the border and leave! Find your parents!"

It was so hot he thought he would melt. The smoke was in his eyes and his throat, and he coughed roughly.

"Get out, Aaron!" Kiera screamed from a distance. He pulled his shirt up to cover his mouth and nose, and ran toward her voice, swiping at his watering eyes.

The flames made the air waver and the heat seared his skin. He couldn't see anything. He kept following the faint voices calling him, barely audible over the crackling and sizzling.

He stumbled. He was on the ground now, crawling to the border, the village collapsing behind him. It was all feeding the hungry flames. He would become the fire's next meal.

Then Kiera and Evannah were both there, grabbing his arm and hauling him to his feet. "Keep going," Evannah murmured. "Only a few more people need to leave." Kiera pressed her hand to the ground and began to murmur a plea to the Island, and the banks of the stream flooded, putting out many of the flames.

So he mustered his strength to break the barrier again, and the remaining people bolted out, burnt and terrified. "That's everyone!" Night Star called from above. "Let's go!"

As they shot into the slowly darkening forest, Aaron dropped his hands and took a deep breath. The smell of smoke was stuck in his nose, and his clothes were covered in ash.

"The Shadows are on us!" Jannary cried. "Move faster!"

Then they were running, Night Star at the back, encouraging them forward. The Shadows hovered overhead, moving behind them, sending strikes of lightning that set fire to trees and plants. Occasionally it struck a person and they collapsed, unconscious, but there was nothing that they could do now.

Aaron grabbed one of the rafts again, and with aching arms, pulled it forward. It was growing close to night, and the Shadows blended into the dark sky.

Evannah was sending streaks of light at the Shadows, causing them to flinch and back away, buying more time for the members of the two villages to run.

"Go, go, go!" Night Star urged. Families carried their small children, hushing them, and Kiera and Evannah helped the elderly forward. The massive group of evacuees ran from their crumbling home, the only place they had known for a decade, toward the ocean, their only hope. Moss whimpered as he bumped against Aaron's leg. He had forgotten that the puppy was there.

Then there was a roaring in Aaron's ears. Against all odds, pursued by vengeful Shadows, they had reached the ocean.

"The ocean!" Khalisse called. "Everyone in, as fast as you can!" There was a huge stampede to reach the shallows.

The Shadows raced to stop them, but Evannah and Night Star held them off, fighting with all their might as the villagers stumbled into the water. Aaron dragged the rafts into the ocean as the salty water crashed at his ankles.

"Almost there, come on!" he shouted at the terrified horde. Then everyone was in the water and Evannah and Night Star were sprinting in, and they were finally safe, standing in the cool ebb and flow of the water.

The Shadows reached out with their spidery fingers, fighting to get into the ocean, but an invisible barrier had blocked them. They couldn't pass. Frustrated, they threw lightning strikes into the water, but they were weaker now, unable to hurt them.

"Get away from the coast!" Night Star commanded. "We're going to swim away from the Island. If you can't swim, get to your assigned raft!"

Aaron began running out, the water causing him to move in slow motion, then started swimming when his feet wouldn't touch the ground anymore, fighting against the waves to get as far as possible. The cold water soaked his clothes and left him shivering. At least it got rid of the smell of smoke and the ash.

"Stay together!" Khalisse yelled. The mist was thick out here, and it was growing impossible to see everyone.

Aaron and a few warriors helped villagers onto the rafts, and tied the vines to themselves so they could pull them. He couldn't see Kiera or Evannah anywhere, so he had to hope they were nearby.

"Pull!" encouraged a warrior beside him. He strained to keep swimming and towing the raft ahead, but the weight was so great it was a struggle to just keep his head above the water.

He turned around, and one look at the terrified civilian's faces was all the motivation he needed. Aaron swam as hard as he could. The gigantic group of thousands swam together, a surging, churning mass of faces and hands, clothes and kicking feet.

"We're far enough out!" Night Star called from somewhere ahead in the mist. "We're going to go around the coast. Follow me!"

From the shore, the Shadows stood, watching them. As they paddled around the coast of the Island, the Shadows walked, following them, just waiting for them to step foot on land again.

Around twenty minutes later, Kiera's voice rang out, and Aaron realized she was riding Night Star. "Stop at that islet!" There was a small landmass ahead, too small to support the thousands of villagers currently swimming beside them, but perhaps enough for a short break.

The villagers stumbled eagerly toward it, able to stand in the shallows. The tiny islet was only big enough to fit less than a hundred people, so those who couldn't fit collapsed in the sandy shallows.

Aaron sank to his knees on the islet, panting in exhaustion. "Aaron!" a voice called, and Kiera rushed to his side. "Are you okay?" she asked.

"Yeah," he gasped. "Just tired. Everything hurts." The sand made everything feel scratched and raw.

"We'll be there soon," Kiera said sympathetically. "Hang on a bit longer."

"Where's Evannah?" Aaron looked around frantically, but Evannah appeared next to him just then. "Thank goodness you all made it."

"Look at them," Evannah commented in disgust. Aaron first thought she was talking about the villagers, but realized she was looking at the Shadows clustered on the shore. "It's like they're hunting."

They were interrupted by screams in the distance. There was a large splash, and the people that had been floating in the outermost shallows came frantically running to the islet. "What's that?" Kiera asked, squinting.

A massive head surfaced, eyes gleaming, before submerging again. Aaron had never seen a shark before, but he guessed the Island versions were at least double the size. It was colored like molten silver, with a metallic sheen, and the moonlight reflected off its many rows of teeth.

Evannah paled. "It's so big. Why is every creature so big here?"

"Silversharks are usually harmless to humans," Night Star scowled. "There have been people swimming in this sea for centuries. No surprise why they're deciding to attack them now." *The Watcher.*

"Can we lure it away, somehow?" Aaron asked. "We can't go any further with it guarding our escape like that, but we can't stay here either. Nobody can fit, and we'll starve."

"I'll try," Night Star offered before raising his voice. "Everyone get ready to swim! Get to your rafts if you need them. I will distract the silvershark while you go. Aaron, Kiera, and Evannah will lead the group in my absence."

It was a big responsibility, but they had to do it. After a few minutes in which the Islanders dragged their exhausted bodies back to the rafts and prepared to continue the journey, Aaron called, "Ready?" There was a weak murmur of agreement. "Come on!" he yelled. "The Shadows may have forced you out of your home, but they can't break your spirit! We're together, and we're strong!" Cheers resounded. Aaron liked leading the Islanders—it gave him a purpose to be actually doing something meaningful.

"I'm going now!" Night Star growled. The shark was showing its teeth and splashing around the outskirts of the islet. He leaped into the air and swooped over its head. "Come get me, you great beast!"

"In the water!" Aaron yelled. There was a dash to start swimming and get as far as possible from the shark as they could. Aaron grabbed the raft's vines again, this time leading the party, and dragged it over the sand into the dark ocean.

The shark snapped at Night Star's ankles, but mostly ignored him, swimming with interest toward the large group that had taken to the water. "No!" Night Star cried. He lunged at the shark's head, smacking it hard with one large paw and knocking it backward. The shark recovered and jumped at him, mouth open.

"Faster!" Evannah commanded. Night Star was doing his best to hold back the shark, but it kept moving forward. "We need to go, quick!"

"It's not working!" Night Star called. "It's not interested in me!"

"Quick, Evannah," Aaron asked. She had always been the one who had loved books the most, the smart one. "What attracts sharks?"

Evannah met his gaze before solemnly admitting, "Blood."

Aaron had one moment to think about his plan, before extracting a dagger from his holster. It was the small dagger that he had started this journey with, and would perhaps end it now.

"No!" Kiera cried, knowing what he was about to do.

"Aaron, don't," Evannah begged.

"Just get them to safety," Aaron told her. He used the dagger to draw a mark from his wrist to his elbow, shallow enough so that it wouldn't be fatal, it would just bleed a good amount.

Kiera took over his spot pulling the raft while he swam in the other direction. Between the night and the mist, he could hardly see a thing, save for moonlight gleaming on a silver body.

"Hey! Over here!" He waved his blood-soaked arm.

"Aaron, you fool!" Night Star called, still grappling with the shark. "What are you doing?"

"Grab me when I tell you to!" he responded.

He paddled closer to the shark, and it turned, attentiveness in its deep-set eyes. It dove under the water and swam expertly toward him.

With all the swimming for his life Aaron had done the past few days, he was getting pretty good at it. The shark was big and heavy; it wouldn't be able to maneuver as well as him.

Then it reached him, its snapping jaws merely inches away from Aaron.

It was like someone else had taken over his body. In that instant, Aaron knew just what to do. He dove down below the shark, and twisted to escape the many teeth. Annoyed, the shark came for him again.

Aaron curled up into a ball. Confused, the shark prodded him with its nose. Aaron quickly uncurled and started swimming away, using its confusion as a distraction.

Now the shark was enraged. It widened its jaws menacingly as it swam toward him, flicking its tail from side to side. Aaron plunged to his right, twisted to avoid being bitten, and emerged behind the shark.

He strained to catch a glimpse of the fleeing villagers, and let out a sigh of relief when he saw that they were a good distance away. *At least this wasn't for nothing.*

Aaron had always wondered what kind of person he'd turn out to when it came time to step up, to defend, to survive. He knew now.

He continued dodging the shark's teeth, using his speed and reflexes to avoid the shark's large, brute strength.

"Ready, Aaron?" Night Star called, hovering overhead. "They're far enough! Hang on a little longer!"

"Ready!" Aaron confirmed.

"Hold out your arm!" Night Star commanded. "I'll come get you!"

Aaron lifted his arm out of the water, watching the shark swim closer, his heart pounding. *Come on, Night Star.* The beast was getting closer, closer, closer...

Night Star's jaws closed around Aaron's hand and pulled him from the water with a mighty splash like a geyser of water, droplets flying everywhere. The shark leaped, trying to grab onto his leg, but Aaron kicked at its face, and knocked it backwards into the water.

Aaron whooped as they flew into the sky, watching the shark gnash its teeth. He rose upward like a creature that had burst from the depths of the sea. The shark grew tinier and tinier until eventually Aaron couldn't see it.

Aaron used his other arm to pull himself onto Night Star's back, and they soared toward the group of rafts and swimmers.

Kiera and Evannah cheered as they rejoined the group. "You're alive!" Evannah congratulated him.

"While you were off battling the shark, we found a possible place to stay," Kiera said, straining to pull her raft. "Looks like there's a bigger islet ahead."

Night Star gazed into the distance. "Ah, Bluedawn Bay. Calm waters dotted with many little islets. We'll need to stop here, out of necessity," he gestured to the exhausted, panting mass with one paw. "I don't think anybody can swim further."

"Almost there, everyone!" Aaron yelled. "Let's stop at that islet!"

The last few minutes of the journey took forever. Every moment it seemed like the islet was so close, but not coming any closer.

Finally, they reached the sandy shores of the islet, and dragged the rafts to shore. This one was big enough to accommodate them, although it would be crowded; it was small enough to see straight across to the ocean on the other side. It was covered in grass and dotted with tropical trees, with a few rocky hills.

All around, people murmured in concern, exploring their temporary little home, while hugging their children and unloading their few possessions. Warriors began to try to craft weak shelters. The little Kairen came up and gave Aaron a hug while Auri watched silently, saying nothing but feeling everything.

"We need to take a count," Night Star told Khalisse.

"On it," Khalisse started to organize the groups they had counted before, getting a quick census. After a few minutes, she came back, wearing a grim look.

"What happened?" Aaron asked.

"Twelve lost. A small amount, given what we've been through. Casualties, I'd have to guess. And…"

"What?" Kiera demanded.

"Both Jannary and Neyric didn't make it."

Chapter 18

"We're surrounded," Khalisse said simply. They were enjoying a breakfast of unevenly cooked fish while sitting on the beach. "They're waiting for us."

The Shadows had gathered on the coast of the Island, across the bay, their numbers larger than ever. "No way to escape," Evannah murmured. She prodded the cold fish.

It had been a rough night. Most of the Island citizens had lost everything they had, and had been too tired to do anything except cry themselves sick and sleep in the grass and sand, under the shoddy palm leaf covers the warriors had built. Many of them, including Evannah, had woken up early with the sun, and decided to fish to try to get them some food. At least they had found a tiny pool of water at the center of the islet for a water source.

Not to mention that Jannary and Neyric were nowhere to be found. No one had any idea if they were alive, and where they'd been lost. The last Evannah remembered seeing them was when fleeing the village. The responsibility of leader had fallen to young Khalisse's shoulders.

"But we can't stay here forever," Kiera tightened her grip on her new sword. Moss was splashing around in the small waves.

By some miracle, the villagers that had been taking care of him had made sure he survived the journey. Evannah wasn't sure why Kiera was still so attached when Moss had shown his true colors as a huge, deadly wolf, but maybe she just needed a companion.

"And we need to rescue the Guardians," Aaron added. The pressure just kept building up, adding more and more weight on their shoulders.

While lying awake last night, Evannah had thought for a long time. Why were they risking their everything for an Island they had only been on for five days? Then she realized something. They were connected to the Island in ways they could barely understand. This was what they were meant to do, something bigger than themselves. More than that, this was the only place that had ever really accepted them for who they were. They had a responsibility to fix this.

"We have to get you out of here," Khalisse decided. "Maybe we can distract the Shadows for long enough."

"We couldn't put you in more danger," Evannah traced patterns in the sand with her finger. "Everyone has been through enough already."

"We'll all die soon anyway," Khalisse responded darkly, looking away. "We need to do something." When Evannah had been awake last night, she had heard Khalisse crying quietly, the only time that Evannah had seen her fierce warrior facade crack.

"I still have the All-Key," Kiera reminded them, tossing and catching it.

"And the journal," Aaron added. He handed it to Evannah. "I know it's important, somehow."

Evannah tried again to open it, knowing she couldn't. *What was inside those bound pages?*

They were interrupted by Night Star leaping to join them, and laying down on the sand. "The other Guardians are weakening. I can feel it."

"Night Star," Evannah hesitated to ask. "Why weren't you captured?"

"I've been with the villagers since the separation," Night Star explained. "It made it harder to find me, and I suppose it wasn't worth it." He stared across Bluedawn Bay. "But I should've been taken with the others."

Nobody knew what to say to that. Finally, Aaron broke the silence. "It sounds like freeing the Guardians is our next step then."

"We'll make a distraction," Night Star promised. "And I'm sure the villagers will want to help too." He glanced at the ramshackle shelters. "They've been calling this islet 'Desperation.'"

"Accurate," Khalisse muttered, curling her fingers into a tight fist.

"How will we get all the way to the mountains without being attacked by Shadows?" Evannah asked. "They're not close by."

Night Star and Khalisse shared a look. "Crystal River."

"We swim," Aaron confirmed. "But how is that going to protect us?"

"Crystal River flows from Heart Falls," Khalisse explained. "The main waterfall, in the heart of the Island. I'm sure you've seen it. But Heart Falls flows from the first water source on the Island,

and so it's sacred. Because the Crystal River carries that sacred water, it's impossible for dark creatures to attack you while in it."

"Oh," Evannah understood. "The river is our protection."

"Where is Heart Falls?" Kiera asked.

"Watcher Peak," Night Star grumbled. "I'm sure the Watcher has tried to corrupt it, but he hasn't reached that level of power quite yet."

"Anyway, Tharros Peak, where the Guardians are being held, is directly next to Watcher Peak," Khalisse added. "Remember the blood curse?"

"Hard to forget," Aaron said sarcastically.

"I can't come with you," Night Star looked at his paws, starry pelt blinking. "If I get captured, or leave the Fenlithrians and Vaharians alone, there's nothing to protect them. But I'll get you past the Shadows. Unfortunately, we can't fly over them. If we took a hit in midair, it would be fatal."

"I guess we have to leave now," Evannah ignored the twisting feeling in her chest she got when looking at the Shadows lying in wait across Bluedawn Bay.

"That's right," Night Star rumbled. "The sooner the better. Are you well-rested and fed?"

Evannah forced herself to swallow a few bites of fish and nodded. It was slimy and tasteless, but it would keep her alive. How quickly her life had changed.

"I'll gather the able-bodied people," Khalisse offered, pushing herself to her feet and heading toward the cluster of shelters. "We'll create a distraction to end all distractions."

True to her word, within twenty minutes, Khalisse had gathered a group of at least a hundred warriors and villagers wanting to help. They gathered on the shore with their weapons, talking excitedly.

The only good thing, Evannah thought, that had come out of this disaster, was the unity it had brought. Fenlithrians and Vaharians alike were standing together and conversing as friends. You could hardly tell who was from which village anymore. Everyone was eager to be finally doing something helpful, to have some hope at last.

"We're ready," Khalisse announced later. "Here's the plan. The group is going to head close to the land and taunt the Shadows, engaging them in a fight. We'll conceal you in the center of the group, then Night Star will lead you to Crystal River. From there, follow the river, and you'll reach Watcher Peak. The mountain to the left of it is Tharros Peak. Can you remember that?"

"Yes," Kiera confirmed.

"And this is most important," Khalisse said solemnly. "Do not. Leave. The river. *Ever.* The second you step out of it, the Shadows can get you. You lose all protection, then it's all over."

"Where will we know where the Guardians are?" Kiera asked. "It's a big mountain."

"You are the Wanderer," Khalisse told her. "Protector of the wild. It is likely they will reach out to you and call for help. You may be able to sense their presence."

"That's a lot riding on *may*," Kiera commented.

Khalisse sighed. "I'm afraid it's the best we can do." She handed them each a small bag. "Here, we've packed up whatever we can find. Food, supplies if you need to set up camp for a night, all waterproof. You shouldn't have to rock climb, just find a trail up the mountain to follow." She looked at Evannah. "If you need help, ask the Whispers to send a message to Night Star. He can't come to Tharros Peak, but if something happens and you need to turn back before that, come back. Your survival is the most important."

"Thanks, Khalisse," said Evannah quietly. "I hope we see you again."

"I hope so too," Khalisse murmured. "One more thing: keep an eye out for Jannary and Neyric, will you? Just in case..." *Just in case they're alive.*

"Of course," Aaron promised.

"It's time," Night Star boomed. They met the warriors at the shore, and began to swim toward the mainland, across Bluedawn Bay. The mist was still thick during the day, as Desperation grew smaller behind them.

Finally, they reached the Shadows, standing as unnaturally still as statues, waiting to strike.

"Hey Shadows!" Khalisse taunted. She unsheathed her sword with a metallic sliding noise. "Want a piece of this?" She lunged out of the water and stabbed the nearest Shadow.

The Shadows exploded out of their stillness and everything descended into chaos. Streaks of shadowy substances flew around, while warriors dodged them and fought.

"Come on!" Night Star yelled over the din. "Let's go quickly!"

They ran around the fighting mass of warriors, villagers, and Shadows. Every sound Evannah heard behind her made her flinch, and she didn't breathe until the Shadows were out of sight, and they reached the riverbank.

"Listen to me," Night Star growled quietly. "Don't leave the river. Don't engage with Shadows. If you can't free the Guardians, come right back."

Kiera hugged the cat's neck. "Bye, Night Star."

"Luck be with you, Whisperer, Wanderer, and Warrior," Night Star wished, before disappearing back into the fight.

The screams and shouts of pain made Evannah want to turn back around and fight, but she couldn't look back, they had to keep going. Aaron stiffened beside her, obviously having the same train of thought. "We need to go," she urged softly.

They stepped into the river, letting the cool water wash over their legs. It was only knee-high at this spot. The name Crystal River was accurate, it was a beautiful clear color and reflected the light like a diamond. It looked so pure compared to the rest of the Island tainted with darkness.

"Follow the river," Aaron murmured Night Star's instructions as they splashed onwards, against the current. Evannah's wounds felt much better, and she wondered if these sacred waters had healing powers as well. In this water, the Whispers seemed to be at peace.

"I think we can reach the mountain by the end of the day," Aaron said. "If we swim all day."

"Hopefully," Kiera responded. "I keep thinking about those poor people we left behind."

"They'll be all right," Aaron assured her, but he ripped at some riverbank ferns in anxiety.

Kiera gasped. "Shadow!" A dark figure was standing by the riverbank, reaching forward desperately, but unable to touch the water.

"Many Shadows," Evannah corrected. The whole horde of Shadows had gathered on the riverbanks, watching them, trying to get to them. Shadowy streaks, fire, and crackling bolts of electricity were all launched their way, but they disappeared before reaching the area where the river was as though an invisible barrier had stopped them. "Ignore them; don't let them see us scared."

The Shadows followed them for the next hour, walking alongside them, as the river grew deeper and wading grew to swimming. It was quite eerie having them so close, but knowing they were safe. Wherever they stepped, the bright ferns and flowers extending into the river withered and died, crumbling to black dust. Eventually, the horde grew smaller and smaller, until they couldn't see any more Shadows.

"Do you think they've gone?" Aaron asked hopefully.

Evannah shook her head. "I'm sure they're still watching."

They stopped for lunch on a cluster of rocks, trying to eat among the sprays of water drenching them. Then it was back into the water, which now reached their chins. It was quite peaceful without the Shadows, drifting through the clear river in the rainforest with the cool water kissing their skin, and little glimmering fish darting around their toes.

An hour after lunch, Kiera commented. "This would almost feel like a vacation if it wasn't for the evil creatures chasing us."

"And the entire Island depending on us," Evannah added.

"Why us?" Aaron blurted. "Why do you think we were chosen for the prophecy?"

They thought for a moment. "I don't know," Evannah responded after a minute, dragging her fingers through the smooth surface of the water. "I guess... fate picks what it wants."

"And you're okay with that?" Aaron asked.

"What can we do?" Evannah argued. "We have to help the Island. We can't leave these people and creatures by themselves." And there was more, she didn't want to say. This was a place where she could be herself, think and say what she wanted to. Her self-identity had been completely destroyed in Neomerica. Although she wasn't really sure who she was on the Island either. Truth was, her powers still scared her, and she didn't know if she was the right person to have them.

She knew she could do so much more with her powers, if she didn't hold back as much.

"Yeah," Kiera was uncharacteristically quiet. She turned over and floated on her back, staring at the sky.

"I guess...," Aaron murmured. "This whole 'fate' thing is bothering me. Of course I want to save the Island, but is the only reason that I was destined to do it? I don't know." They went quiet for a while after that, listening to the soothing sounds of the river, swimming along.

"Come on," Kiera said eventually. "We can't keep brooding like this. We need to face the evil creatures with high spirits!" As she was the smallest of them, the water reached her chin and her loose curls floated around her.

"Yeah? How are we going to do that?" Evannah flicked a dripping lock of hair from her face.

"We'll play a game!" Kiera exclaimed.

"I don't think this is the time for games," Evannah sighed in exasperation.

"No, it's the perfect time!" Kiera argued. "We're going to be swimming for the next few hours anyway. We need to distract ourselves."

"She's actually right," Aaron admitted. "I could use a distraction."

"Oh, all right!" Evannah gave in. "Make it quick."

"Hmm," Kiera gave a little spin in the water. "All right—if you could get one wish, what would it be?"

For my powers to go away. The thought jumped into Evannah's head, surprising herself. Yes, they were a big responsibility, but didn't they help sometimes? She didn't know anymore. *To say whatever I want to say and be my own person?* She couldn't admit that out loud. "Um... to travel more," she finally said lamely.

"Come on, Evah, you're not even trying!" Kiera scolded.

"I don't know!" Evannah sighed.

"For the Island to save itself, so we didn't have to," Aaron joked.

"Good one!" Kiera commented. "Okay, that died pretty fast. Let's do... who's most likely to!"

"How about who's most likely to climb a waterfall?" Aaron remarked.

Evannah looked in front of her and groaned. A slope of rocks and crashing water was ahead of them. Since they were traveling upstream, it was splashing toward them. They would have to figure out how to overcome it. Luckily, it wasn't steep.

"We can't leave the river," Kiera reminded them.

"We're got to climb," Evannah concluded. The water was now up until their knees and they tromped toward the falls.

"Hang on to the rocks under the water," Aaron suggested. "We should be able to climb those. Don't get swept away."

"Helpful," Kiera remarked, trying to pull herself onto the first rock, while sputtering through a mouthful of water. "I have a different game!" she yelled over the roar. "It's called, who's going to die first?"

"Kiera, don't say things like that, remember the prophecy?" Aaron cried, slipping down several feet before he got a grip on a branch extending over the falls. His feet continued to slide out under him as he hung on for dear life.

"Don't let the prophecy get in your head!" Evannah said with a quiet resolution, struggling to find her footing. The heavy spray drenched her from head to toe. "It can only harm you if you let it."

"I think I'm going to be the first to go!" Kiera yelled from several feet above. She had found a way up on a series of rocks that jutted out like steps. "Take care of Moss for me!"

"Well, if I die first, say something heroic about me!" Aaron called. He lost his grip on the branch and slid down the waterfall before landing hard on a rock. "Ow!" Evannah and Kiera laughed at him.

"Give me a nice remembrance ceremony if I die first," Evannah stopped for a moment to rest her exhausted arms. She was *soaked*. Water streamed into her eyes, and she could hardly see anymore.

"Made it!" Kiera called triumphantly. She stood on a ledge on the top of the falls, waving in victory. "See you later, losers!" She sat down in the spray and watched Evannah and Aaron struggle.

After many tiring minutes, Evannah reached the ledge, followed closely by Aaron. "Finally," she grumbled.

"We're getting closer," Aaron remarked. Watcher Peak looked much bigger now, looming high above their heads, Heart Falls sparkling like a jewel in the sunlight.

Hours passed, and the sky began to darken ever so slightly. Evannah thought she had known exhaustion before, but it was nothing compared to spending an entire day swimming against the current. The knowledge that the Island and the Guardians were suffering was the only thing that kept her arms and legs moving.

"Watcher Peak," Aaron announced finally. "Here we are." The river had opened into the lake that the Shadows had brought Evannah too. Heart Falls crashed overhead, contrasting with the dark purple Watcher Peak.

"That should be Tharros Peak, then," Evannah pointed at the gray-purple, rocky summit to the left of Watcher Peak.

"Not too far a walk," Kiera commented. "If we don't get attacked by Shadows."

"Let's make a run for it," Aaron suggested. "One, two, three... go!" They splashed out of the water, dripping wet and ran toward Tharros Peak. It was further than it looked; it took them almost ten minutes. Upon reaching the base of the mountain, a strange shock wave passed over them. "Whoa! What was that?" Kiera asked, shuddering.

"I'm betting that's the blood curse," Evannah murmured. "At least we survived." They began to search for the easiest way up.

"There's a sort of trail here!" Aaron called from further away. They caught up to him to see a winding, rocky path, steep and overgrown. It was not a man-made trail, but had perhaps been carved out over time from journeys up the mountain.

"Good. Let's go?" asked Kiera. "The Guardians are waiting for us."

The beginning of the hike started out easy, but quickly became more draining. The path sloped upwards and grew narrower as the trail went on, until they were all panting with exhaustion. "At least no Shadows!" Aaron pointed out. The forested surroundings slowly changed to open stretches of rock, as the temperatures grew cooler.

"Maybe we should find a place to stay the night before night falls," Evannah suggested. "I don't think we'll be reaching the mountaintop today. Or maybe even tomorrow." They were already fairly high up, but the peak didn't look much closer.

So they climbed for another half hour, until the sky became streaked with orange and pink, until they found a suitable shelter.

It was a small cave carved into the face of the mountain, just enough for them to fit in. A small ledge protruded out of it, overlooking the tall cliffs and providing a clear view of the hundreds of feet below them. "Wow," Kiera said. "If we roll in our sleep, we'll fall to our deaths. Aaron gets the edge!" she declared immediately.

"What?" Aaron looked offended.

They unrolled the thin mats that had been packed in the bags Khalisse gave them, and rolled them out, trying in vain to move a few rocks in front of the cave entrance so there wouldn't be any deaths that night. They pulled out a few waterlogged pieces of food for their dinner. Kiera experimented with flicking her sword different ways until a curtain of vines grew in front of the entrance.

When sunset was at its peak, Kiera slid out of the cave and sat on the ledge outside, arms hugging her knees, watching the vivid, fiery sky with a vague expression. The Island extended for miles underneath them, all red and orange and pink in the waning light. Aaron and Evannah joined her. "What is it?" Evannah asked.

Kiera gazed into the distance. "Don't you feel like we've just been thrust from one destiny into another?"

"I was thinking the same thing," Aaron let his legs hang over the edge, staring at the tiny trees and rivers below. "From the role we were supposed to have in court to this mysterious Island prophecy. It's the same, in essence. Our lives are laid out for us."

"I don't want to believe the prophecy is real," Evannah admitted, rubbing her chilled arms. "Not if one of us is going to die."

"I don't see how it couldn't be real," Aaron tilted his head back to look at the orange clouds. "So much of it has come true already. I just don't like it. What kind of power can take away the most basic human right, choice?"

"We can't go against the prophecy," Kiera said. "Not when there's so much at stake. So what can we do?"

"I don't know," Aaron admitted.

They stayed out there until night fell and the stars began to shine in the sky, thinking about destiny, and fate, what it all really meant. Evannah rested her head on Aaron's shoulder as he let out a troubled breath. What did destiny really mean? Was it a path laid out for you to walk, or was it a map of events that would happen no matter what? Was Evannah wrong for believing in the prophecy because she wanted a purpose?

Multicolored, glowing shapes started to dot the sky. "Lightning birds," Evannah remembered. "Let's go inside."

As they lay shivering on their thin mats in the dark, on the mystical mountain out of stories, Evannah closed her eyes and listened to the wind.

Nothing was certain, in this world of prophecy and power, but Evannah knew that she would be doing whatever she could to save the Island she had called home for the last few days. She closed her eyes and drifted off into an uneasy sleep.

Not too far away, the Watcher sat on his self-erected throne, surveying his kingdom with a satisfied expression.

It is nearly done. Soon, the Island will be safe and protected forever.

He gazed down at his pool of water. As he grew stronger, the clarity of the shapes within increased. He watched the three youths' chests rise and fall with sleeping breaths. Soon he would be strong enough to harness the power of the first source of water on the Island, and wouldn't have to bother with this little pond.

After all my work, I won't let three children stop me.

Especially not these children, he thought with disgust.

They think their mission is a secret.

They shouldn't have been foolish enough to think they could keep a secret from me.

Chapter 19

A rustle of wings, a flash of fur. *Tharros Peak.* The blinding darkness. *Not much further.* The oppressive cages. *Follow the path, you'll know you're there when you overlook the valley.*

A scream, a roar. *Be careful, don't—*

Kiera woke up with a start. Seeing the startlingly long drop next to her, she almost shrieked, but stopped when she realized where she was, her heart pounding.

Evannah and Aaron were just waking up, and she shoved Aaron in the shoulder just because she felt like it. "What?" Aaron mumbled sleepily.

"Khalisse was right. The Guardians did reach out to me."

Evannah sat up immediately, all traces of sleepiness gone. "And?"

"Apparently we're on the right track. We'll find them when we 'overlook the valley.'"

"Good," Aaron commented. "Finally Kiera was useful." He rubbed the shoulder she had smacked with a grouchy expression.

"Like *you've* done anything useful this entire time," Kiera retorted.

"Come on," Evannah encouraged. "Let's leave." After they had all woken up a little more, they packed their things and left the little cave behind. Kiera was not going to miss it.

The hike going forwards was definitely more treacherous. The trail was narrow and was growing narrower still, as the sloping sides of the mountain became steeper and steeper. A cool breeze whipped at their faces and Kiera was sure she wasn't imagining tiny tremors under her feet.

"Do you feel that?" she asked after the fourth time.

"Yeah," Aaron replied. "I think it's just the wind."

So they continued on, as the hike became more of a climb. The path was so steep in places that they had to pull themselves up with their hands and feet. In one spot, it was so narrow that they had to edge sideways, in fear of falling right off the cliff and plunging until their deaths. It reminded Kiera unpleasantly of the illusion in the Temple of Forgotten Fears.

For one terrifying moment, her foot slipped over the edge, but Evannah and Aaron reacted so quickly in grabbing her arms and pulling her up that she was slammed into the wall of rock behind her. They stood there in shock for a moment, with Kiera thanking the world for the miracle that she was still alive.

Evannah looked up at the summit of the mountain and groaned. "We're not getting any further."

"We'll get there," Aaron assured. "One step at a time." One step at a time became their new motto. One step at a time, one step at a time. They murmured it as they climbed on, trying to ignore the long drops and steep trails, the jagged rocks and sheer cliffs.

"Where is this valley?" Aaron voiced the question that was in everyone's minds.

"I think we'll know it when we see it," said Kiera wisely. "I hope."

The hours went on and the sun climbed higher in the sky. It was about noon when they had crossed to the other side of the mountain, the side not facing the forests, and spotted the valley at last.

They had walked onto a viewpoint overlooking the spectacular valley. It dipped down below, between the two mountains, a long expanse of vibrant green grass. They could faintly see the other side of the ocean, the north coast.

"There's the valley," Evannah pointed out, wind blowing her long hair out in front of her face. "Now, where are these Guardians?"

"Um, I think I found it." Kiera slowly turned to face the other way.

Tall, jagged rocks behind them partially obscured a view of a set of stone doors, much further up the mountain, tiny-looking from here.

Evannah squinted. "Are those Shadows?" Sure enough, there were two little dashes of black next to the doors.

"Guards," Aaron remarked. "Now we have to get past *them*, too."

Now that the destination was in sight, the climb didn't seem so long anymore. In fact, it seemed too short, and as the doors grew larger and larger, the trio became more nervous.

"Do you have the All-Key, Kiera?" Aaron checked for what felt like the hundredth time.

"Yes I have it!" Kiera fumed. "Ask me one more time and I'm hurling it off the cliff!"

"Sorry," Aaron muttered.

"What's our plan?" Evannah asked. "Distraction, or go straight to fighting?"

"Let's skip straight to the fighting," Kiera decided. "The Shadows know us, they're not going to be fooled. Maybe if we surprise them we'll have an advantage."

"Good plan," Evannah answered. She looked ahead. "There it is."

Built straight into the side of the mountain, the doors to one of the Watcher's domains were massive. Made of heavy-looking stone, they were at least four times the height of Kiera and incredibly wide. Two Shadows guarded the doors, along with two humans, clad in silver armor with an insignia of an eye centered on a mountain silhouette etched on their chests.

Now in sight of the doors, they crouched down behind a boulder. "There's people!" Kiera whispered.

"That must be the Watcher's recruits from the smaller villages," Evannah remembered. "Jannary told us about them."

"Right," Kiera realized. "Well, now that I'm looking at it, it seems impossible to break it."

"We have the key," Aaron reminded them. "If we can get the guards away from the door, we can sneak in."

"I have an idea," said Kiera with a smirk. "Change of plans..."

Kiera threw a bundle of sticks onto the pile. "That should be good!" she announced happily. They were on the plateau that was the beginning of the slope into the valley, but still close to the doors to the Guardians' prison, just out of sight of the Shadows.

"Are you sure you can start the fire without any materials?" Evannah tilted her head.

"Tovan taught me a trick or two about Island survival while you were out gallivanting in Neomerica," Kiera grinned. "Here's where they come in handy."

She searched for a few minutes before finding a pair of what Tovan had called striking rocks, the types of rocks that could be used to start a fire. These ones were gray and nondescript, with a white shimmer.

"Come on," she pleaded, striking the rocks together with as much force as she could muster. Nothing happened. A few more strikes, and a tiny flicker of golden-orange appeared between the rocks, accompanied by the faint smell of smoke. "Did you see that?" she asked. "Oh no, it disappeared."

"Do it again," Aaron urged. "Come on." She struck it again, and the spark appeared again. This time, she quickly held it to the pile of twigs and leaves they had gathered, and the edge of a leaf began to smoke and char.

"That's it!" she cried, holding the burning leaf to the other branches in the pyre. The fire was transferred, and the pile began to blaze with tiny flames.

"I got the leaves!" Evannah cried, holding an armful of large, flat green leaves. Just enough to produce smoke, but not set the whole area on fire.

"Perfect, put them on," Kiera told her. "Then we hide." The plan was stealth. With the guards distracted with the fire, they would use the All-Key to sneak in.

Evannah dumped the leaves on, and a thick column of gray smoke rose into the air. "Hide!" Aaron urged, and they ran to their previous hiding spot behind the large boulder, the doors in sight once more.

The sight of the entrance to the Watcher's lair was intimidating, a massive access in the middle of the rocky mountains, the rest of the Island far below. It was a few minutes before they heard any commotion from the entryway.

"I'll be lookout," Kiera suggested in a whisper. "Here they come."

The Shadows were creeping down to the plateau to investigate the mysterious pillar of smoke that had appeared, along with one of the human guards. "Shoot, they left one behind!" Aaron whispered frantically.

"It doesn't matter, we have to go now!" Evannah commanded. "Quick, before they come back!"

They creeped toward the entryway, as quietly as they could, while Kiera kept watch.

The Shadows moved toward their pyre, as Evannah and Aaron made their way toward the door. With one last glance at the Shadows, Kiera followed.

Sure enough, the last human guard was still waiting there, the insignia that Kiera assumed was the Watcher's symbol prominent on his armor. His eyes widened. "What are you—"

He hadn't even finished his sentence when Aaron, Evannah, and Kiera were on him. Aaron brought him to the ground while Evannah shot blasts of light at him, which seemed to daze him. "We can't kill him!" Aaron said at once.

"Let's knock him out," Kiera pulled out her sword and whacked the guard's head with it. His eyes snapped shut and his head flopped to the side. The sight of him lying there made her feel very guilty, but this was something they had to do. At least they had left him alive.

Evannah let out a breath. "Thanks."

"Wow," Aaron looked impressed. Kiera immediately brought out the All-Key and inserted the soft golden rod into the keyhole on the enormous door. It slowly melted into the shape of a key, and Kiera turned it with a click.

There was a rustle in the background. "I'll go check," she said. "Open the door." She quickly jogged to a view of the pyre, and the view that met her made her stomach sink.

The Shadows were gliding back toward the door. The twigs and leaves were scattered, and the grass withered under their feet. "They're coming!" Kiera called quietly. "Open the door quickly!"

She turned back to see Aaron and Evannah straining to pull open the large doors. "They're too heavy!" Evannah was tugging so hard that her knuckles had turned white.

"Pull harder!" Aaron tried, and Kiera joined them. Every moment the Shadows were getting closer and closer, coming to discover them...

"They're going to find us!" Kiera said anxiously. "We have to do something."

"It's opening!" Evannah cried. They had pried open the doors so that a little slit was visible between them. "Keep pulling."

The Shadows heads were becoming visible over the rocks. They were going to be discovered any minute. Kiera didn't have any time to think before she bolted. "Open it while I distract them!"

"Kiera, wait—" Aaron tried, but it was too late. Kiera was dashing toward the Shadows, sword in hand.

She picked up a rock, and flung it at them. It slammed into the nearest Shadow's head, and it turned. "Hey!" she called.

The Shadows and human guard immediately turned, getting into an attacking position.

She lunged toward them with her sword, and roots exploded out of the ground, knocking one Shadow across the plateau, hitting the other in the face, and causing the human to go unconscious. "Yeah, Blade of the Wild!" she cheered to her sword.

But the Shadows got back up easily, starting the chase once again. Now the smell of smoke from the pyre lingered in Kiera's nose, and she realized she had only one option. She picked up a still-flaming stick, and hurled it at a Shadow. It missed, and the grass caught fire instead. "No!" she muttered.

Kiera plunged the sword into the grass almost instinctively, using its power to guide the flaming plants toward the Shadows.

Although it didn't seem to harm them, they paused for a second to destroy the pyre more thoroughly.

"Come on!" Evannah called, and Kiera began sprinting. She *just* needed to get to those doors...

Closer, closer.

The Shadows were getting closer.

The distance was closing.

The Shadows were gaining on her, their spidery fingers reaching out.

She burst through the doors just as the Shadows caught up, and they wrenched the doors shut, which was luckily much easier than opening them, right as the Shadows pounced and the plateau went up in flames.

Evannah bolted the door as there was a frantic thumping and scratching from the outside, breathing hard. "That was close," she shuddered. "I thought the plan was to be stealthy!"

"Well, plans have to be changed. At least we're in!" Kiera exclaimed. "But the fire..." the guilt caught up with her, "it'll hurt the Island."

"You did what you had to," Aaron reassured, but Kiera shuddered, remembering the burning stretch of mountains. It wouldn't have bothered her normally, but she had felt the life of the Isle these past few days, and now knew that this would bring harm, on some level, to the Isle of Whispers. *Please forgive me.*

Everything was dark; she could hardly see a few feet in front of her. "No guards?"

"I guess they assumed nobody would make it past the blood curse," Aaron remarked. "So they relaxed security."

Evannah created an orb of light that illuminated a long expanse of dark hallway. The faint light looked eerie bouncing off the stone walls. "Let's rescue these Guardians," she said determinedly.

Every step down the dim hallway was a step closer to saving the Island. Their only hope lay in front of them, trapped in cages, waiting to be rescued.

At the end of the long hallway was another set of doors. Kiera used the All-Key, and it opened with a click. "Weapons out," she suggested. It was funny how comfortable the sword felt in her hand now, when it had felt so foreign just days earlier.

They pulled the doors open, and the silence shattered with a loud roar. The walls vibrated from the sheer volume, shaking loose billowing clouds of dust. They screamed as the ground trembled under their feet again. "I know I'm not imagining that!" Kiera cried.

"It's the Guardians," Evannah breathed. "They know we're here."

"I really hope they're on our side," Aaron added nervously.

The room they were in was the biggest Kiera had ever seen, a stone chamber so large that she couldn't see the far walls. The ceiling curved overhead, fragile, twisted stalactites extending from it.

But even before she saw the cages, she felt it. The unnatural silence, the stench of blood and metal.

The feeling of being watched.

"Wanderer!" a low voice resonated from further away, mournful and desperate. "Please, unlock the cages. We don't have much time."

Kiera raced toward the voice. "We're coming!" A row of huge stone cages with thick bars filled the cave, the faint glow betraying the fact they were enchanted. She caught her first glimpse of the Guardians: pelts cloaked with shadows, eyes bleak, lying still in the cold air.

Inside the first cage, an enormous female tiger the size of Night Star gazed at her with blazing eyes full of a painfully strong hope. She was a burnished orange-gold with flames dancing down her back and tail, and breathed raggedly. "How could they do this to you?" Kiera murmured angrily.

She jammed the All-Key into the keyhole, and waited until it took form, praying that it would work. She pulled at the door of the cage, and her stomach clenched as it merely rattled. No. She waited a few more seconds, taking uneven breaths, then tried again. The door swung open. *Thank goodness.*

The tiger stepped out, head high, and took a long breath. "Freedom. At last. Thank you." The flames on her pelt grew taller. "We need to hurry." The ground trembled again.

"What's happening?" Aaron called anxiously, waiting by the second cage. "Another earthquake?"

The tiger shook her head. "The Island is starting to collapse. The mountain will fall."

"No, not already?" Evannah asked.

"The Guardians have failed," the tiger admitted. "All we can do now is flee this mountain and rescue the villagers. Perhaps we can make it out before we are all buried."

There was a much stronger tremor in the ground, and a sudden crack as a hanging spear of a stalactite dislodged itself from the ceiling and crashed to the ground next to Kiera. She shrieked. "Shoot! Let's move quickly."

She moved onto the next cage, unlocking it to release the next Guardian. The shaking grew stronger, and she coughed on the dust billowing from the stone walls in thick clouds.

The next cage's occupant was a giant white bird with a long, elegant beak and cloudy wingtips. It was Streakwing, the bird who had contacted them. He scrambled up, shaking dust off his wings. "You got my message!" he exclaimed, eyes alight.

"Yes, thank you," Kiera told him. "We have to get out, quick."

"I got it, Kiera!" Aaron held up his hand, shouting over the din of the rumbling mountain. "Toss me the key and look for a way out!" She threw the key to him and he caught it, beginning to move toward the fourth cage.

"There's an exit on the other side," Streakwing told her. "Let's lead the others to it." They ran as stalactites plummeted from the roof, shattering around their feet. Chunks of the ceiling began to fall, exposing tiny holes to the sky. "There!" He gestured with a wing.

So close to freedom, so close to an escape. "Guardians, this way!" she shouted. The liberated creatures prowled toward her.

Then— "Get down!" cried Streakwing. The mountain gave a mighty shudder as large boulders crashed down the mountainside.

Avalanche. Cave-in. Kiera had only ever heard of these.

Streakwing flung a large wing over Kiera as she fell to the ground, hands wrapped over her head, pelted by small pebbles and choking on dust. Her throat itched, then closed off completely, leaving her clutching her neck and gasping.

The dust cleared, leaving them with the horrifying truth. The exit was blocked, boulders piled up in the entryway. Kiera took one shuddering breath before the realization dawned on her. They were trapped.

"Kiera!" Evannah screamed from far off. "There's another way."

She pulled herself up on trembling feet, running toward the voice. A stalactite grazed her arm on its way to the ground, tearing open her skin in a white-hot line of pain. The world began to waver in front of her eyes as it bloomed crimson and the blood trickled down her forearm. She refused to look at the wound, gritted her teeth against the pain. She couldn't collapse, not here, not now.

Aaron appeared, atop the last Guardian's back, a large gold and silvery wolf, as it bounded toward them. He tossed her back the All-Key, and she caught it. "Here!" Evannah called, motioning to a large chunk of cave that had fallen off the mountain, leaving a gaping hole in the wall. They could see straight out to the Island below.

But it was a sheer drop, a fall to their deaths. "Can you carry us?" Kiera called to Streakwing in a hoarse voice.

"Not so fast!"

There was a moment of silence. Then a cloaked figure, accompanied by an army of floating Shadows, soared through the opening. "It's the Watcher!" Aaron screamed. Even the Guardians paused, flinching back as though they'd been struck, a startling movement from creatures so big.

From the other side of the room, a small army of human warriors marched in, spears raised. They were trapped.

"On my own mountain?" The Watcher asked, a cruel edge to his voice. His dark cloak rippled, hanging around him like a cloud of smoke. "Did you really think I didn't know what you were up to?" Kiera's nails dug into her palm as she clenched her fists.

He had been waiting for them.

Then his army swarmed in.

The only sound that Kiera could hear was a ringing in her ears; the Shadows became streaks of black and the Guardians rampaging streaks of color. Evannah and Aaron were quickly lost in the mess. *Think!* She urged her disoriented and heavy head to function. If they couldn't get out now, not only would it be the end of them, it would be the end of the Guardians, the villagers they needed to save, and the entirety of the Island.

A Shadow rushed toward her with frightening speed. Her arm burned as she held up her sword, slashing the air to try to drive the dark humanoid figure away. She squinted through the cloudy air as she skittered through the battle, attempting in vain to find a way out. Every way she turned there was a Shadow or a weapon pointing her way, a blast of fire from the tiger Guardian or a falling rock.

"GO!" yelled Aaron, atop the wolf Guardian's back. The immense creature snarled and whacked away soldiers with its boulder-sized paws, trying to clear a path. Kiera met Aaron's eyes, and gave him a quick nod of thanks. He nodded in response, eyes soft.

The mountain is falling.

The escape was right there, just a few steps toward it, just a few more.

The wolf Guardian Aaron was riding swerved to the side to avoid a dropping stalactite, and Aaron was thrown from his back. His hand went to his sword and he started to fight, the spirit of the Warrior evident.

The exit was so close. She needed to get to it, find a way, then come back for Aaron.

Yes! Now she was out in the open. The sunlight hit her face, promising, but still weak. But now she had the sheer drop underneath her... how was she going to get out?

"Going somewhere?" The sinister voice of the Watcher cut through the air like a knife and made her turn rapidly. A mass of Shadows accompanied him, and they were converging on her.

A scream. Aaron's voice. A group of Shadows were binding him in a shadowy substance as he struggled to get out.

Evannah was running toward the escape too, unaware what was happening to Aaron. The Shadows shot a blast of darkness at Aaron, and he went unconscious, limbs going limp. They dropped him at the Watcher's feet, and he smiled. "Ah, thank you, my friends."

Evannah stopped dead in her tracks, her breathing growing uneven as she took in Aaron's unconscious body. "No!"

"Your turn," the Watcher told her. "Now, you can come quietly, or I'll have to do the same thing to you."

In front of her, the legendary Watcher himself, surrounded by a powerful army.

Behind her, a shockingly long fall to the earth, the promise of an instant death. A sheer cliff, falling rocks.

It's all falling. Cracks were appearing in the mountain, it was going to come down.

In front, the Watcher. Behind her, death.

Kiera made her decision. "You'll have to get me first!" Then she turned, took three sprinting strides, and hurled herself off the cliff.

Then she couldn't hear anything except the wind in her ears, and the plummeting sensation as she fell through the sky. Her mind raced too fast, filling with terrifying images of the ground below to process any last thoughts.

She couldn't hear the shocked gasps of the warriors, the outraged yell of the Watcher, and the cries of Evannah. Her stomach dropped and her eyes began to water.

Then a white blur swooped elegantly under her, catching Kiera and interrupting her fall. It spread its great wings and shot upward into the sky.

"Yes!" Kiera screamed. Her crazy plan had actually paid off! She wrapped her arms around Streakwing's neck as he twisted and flew vertically upward. "Thanks, Streakwing!"

"You really do have a death wish! It was lucky I saw you. Hang on!" Streakwing warned. He soared toward the shaking mountain. Kiera whooped as they shot through the sky.

"Evannah!" Kiera called. Evannah had broken through the barricade of Shadows and was trying to get to Aaron. "You have to jump!"

Evannah cast one last hesitant look at Aaron, then hurled herself off the cliff. Streakwing swooped to catch her in his beak, then deposited her on another flying Guardian, one who looked similar to a dragon with beautiful jewel-bright scales. The other Guardians were hot on their tail, the ones who didn't have wings bounding through the sky as Night Star often did.

"The mountain!" Evannah yelled to Kiera over the wind. Streakwing banked and turned to get a view of Tharros Peak. The mountain was horribly disfigured; the peak had fallen, it was shot through with cracks, and it was still shaking. In front of their eyes, the mountain began to collapse, crumbing to the ground until it was just a gigantic pile of rocks. The surrounding mountains were affected too, cracking and crumbling, but Tharros Peak took the worst of the damage.

The fire was nowhere to be seen; all the falling stones must have put it out. Now Kiera's worries about that seemed so small compared to the destruction of these vital pieces of the Island.

The Watcher had created a shining bridge to Watcher Peak, and Kiera and Evannah watched him recede with his army back to his domain. The small shape of a still unconscious Aaron floated through the air in front of him. "We have to get him!" Evannah cried.

"No," Streakwing commanded. "It's too dangerous. We can come back, but we can't go now."

"But, Aaron—" Kiera protested.

"It's too late," Streakwing said firmly. "I'm sorry. But we have to save who we can. We need to get you two to safety." With that, they turned around and began flying away from the mountain. The feeling was exhilarating; soaring through the air on a giant bird, the wind rushing past her face, the sky surrounding her.

A multitude of glowing dots were becoming visible further off in the sky. "No, not now," Streakwing muttered.

"Lightning birds," explained the wolf Guardian. "They're coming for us."

Chapter 20

Pain. His head ached, and everything felt heavy.

Aaron forced his eyes open, still feeling dizzy and dazed. What had happened? Right, the Guardian rescue. The mountain had started to collapse and the Watcher... oh no.

He struggled to get up, then realized he wasn't even on the ground. His arms and legs were tightly bound by some kind of dark substance, and he was currently floating in the air. "Help!" he screamed, with this realization.

Craning his neck, he could see that he was floating over some kind of bridge, connected to Watcher Peak.

The Watcher's voice rang out. "There's nobody around, no point screaming."

"Where are Evannah and Kiera?" Aaron demanded.

"That's not important," the Watcher murmured. "Do you know where we're going?"

"Watcher Peak," Aaron spat. He tried again in vain to squirm free.

"I don't want to hurt you, Aaron," the Watcher said from behind. "If you stay still, this will be a lot easier for you."

"Yeah right," Aaron muttered. He could've bound the Watcher's powers, but he was too weak right now.

"I am serious," the Watcher warned. "I know you better than you think."

Defeated, Aaron let his head flop over. It hurt so badly, it was like his whole body had been smacked around by a giant. The world became blurry as he lost focus and drifted into an in-between state, somewhere in the middle of consciousness and unconsciousness. At some point, he thought he heard the Watcher murmur, "*One is enough.*"

Then the light grew dim and changed to darkness, and he mustered the strength to lift his head again. *We must be inside Watcher Peak.*

They walked for a while longer, and Aaron tried to create a map in his head for a future escape, but it was no use. There were so many winding tunnels, and it was too dark to see anything properly.

After a few minutes, Aaron was unceremoniously dumped to the ground. "Hey!" he complained. The bindings around his body loosened, then disappeared, and he stretched out. He immediately jumped to his feet and tried to run, which was more of a wobble at this time, but was stopped by a slamming door. He was imprisoned.

The cage was remarkably like the one the Guardians had been in, stone, but with bars, so he was able to see outside, except much smaller. Human sized.

"Get comfortable," the Watcher suggested from off to the side. He swept into view of the cage and lowered his hood. "I'll be back to chat, eventually."

Aaron gasped.

His own face stared back at him from under the Watcher's hood.

Aaron lay on the ground. It hadn't been very long since the Watcher had trapped him here. Was that even the Watcher?

The image of Aaron's face under the Watcher's hood had been haunting Aaron for every waking minute. Was it some kind of trick?

Am I the Watcher?

No, that was ridiculous. Aaron shook his head. It was a mind game, it had to be. The Watcher was a powerful magical being, he was just trying to throw Aaron off. That had to be it. Yes, that was it.

Unless...

No. He shut down the looping thoughts in his mind. The Watcher had deliberately removed his hood, he wanted Aaron to see his face. And that had to mean he was tricking Aaron. "That's it," he told himself out loud.

He turned his attention to his surroundings. His cage was in a cave, with one whole side open, his front facing side, which was how Aaron could see that the cave was at the very peak of the mountain, the very top of the summit.

In fact, Heart Falls flowed from this very cave, and the cave was directly on top of it. A river rushed through the cave, and Aaron could see it drop over the cliff on the open side, plummeting as Heart Falls down to the Island, and hear it roar.

The river must start at some water source behind his cage, but he couldn't see. He remembered Khalisse and Night Star mentioning it was the first water source on the Island, so it was sacred. *Ha,* he thought. *All this power and the Watcher can't touch it.*

The only other things the mountaintop cave contained were a golden, large, and elaborately carved chair, and a small pool of water next to it.

I have to escape. He had to get back to Evannah and Kiera. Or were they being held somewhere in here, too? "I'm going to escape," he murmured to himself, just to make it real.

A small rustle interrupted his thoughts. Aaron sprang up, trying to find the source of the sound. Peering through the bars, he could see another cage on the other side of the cave. Two people were huddled inside. But who were they? "Hello?" he called, cautiously.

Two pairs of eyes widened at the sound of his voice. "Aaron?" a familiar voice called back.

"Jannary?" Aaron exclaimed. "You're alive!"

"I can't believe you're here, Aaron," a second voice chimed. Neyric.

"Me neither," Aaron cried. Squinting, he could see bindings wrapped around their arms and legs. "Are you tied up?"

"Yes," Jannary answered. "The Shadows caught us during the evacuation, and nobody noticed through all the chaos. We've been here since."

"I'm so sorry," Aaron said. Khalisse would be overjoyed. "The Fenlithrians and Vaharians made it to safety. Minimal casualties."

Jannary let out a breath. "Thank goodness. And the Guardians?"

"We freed them," Aaron explained. "But the mountains fell."

"We felt that," Neyric interjected.

There was a patter of footsteps as a guard emerged, going to Jannary and Neyric's cage. "That's the end of meal time for you two." She entered the cage quickly, gagged them, and walked over to Aaron's cage. She had the Watcher's logo on her chest, an eye on a silhouette of a mountain. Aaron sat upright and tried to look undaunted and courageous. "Hello."

The guard held a plate and a glass of water. "I have food and water for you," she said gruffly.

"Thank you," Aaron said politely. He needed the guards to start liking him, eventually trusting him. The guard thrust the glass and plate through the gaps in the bars, and Aaron took it, careful not to spill anything. He took a sip. The water tasted fine, and the plate held bread and some unfamiliar sliced vegetables.

"What's your name?" he asked the guard.

"Ihiria," the guard told him, looking a little awkward.

Aaron lowered his voice. "Is the Watcher forcing you to work for him? I know he threatened the smaller villages."

"I don't—" Ihiria stammered, looking away.

"It's okay," Aaron smiled. "We're..." This was a risky gamble. "We're going to take him down, all the villages, together. We're going to free the Island once more."

Ihiria froze. "You shouldn't say that around here," she said in a furious whisper. "You don't know who to trust."

"I can trust you," Aaron told her offhandedly. "Don't you want to fight for what's right?" There was a beat of silence. "Could you just tell me one thing? Are my sister and Kiera all right?"

Ihiria glanced around before answering. "They escaped. I must go now." She dashed off.

Thank goodness. At least Evannah and Kiera were all right. Maybe they could continue the fight without him.

Because of their gags, Jannary and Neyric couldn't talk to him, but their presence comforted him. As the time continued to pass, Aaron slowly ate the meal. Maybe he should have been afraid of being poisoned, but he had a feeling that the Watcher could have killed him a lot sooner, if he wanted Aaron dead. No, he wanted Aaron alive.

He searched every square inch of the cage, trying to find some way to escape, trying to make a plan. The cage was solid, and the gaps in the bars so small that there was no way he could squeeze through.

"Don't bother," a familiar voice resonated. The Watcher flicked his hand, and the door of the cage swung open. Aaron was finally able to get a good look at the Watcher. He wore a dark purple cloak decorated with golden patterns that looked like ancient runes. Gleaming, thorny vines twisted around his robes and body, constantly in motion.

Aaron hovered in the doorway, wondering if it was a trick.

"Come out," the Watcher coaxed. "Nothing will happen." His hood was still on; Aaron couldn't see his face.

Feeling a little bolder, Aaron stepped out of the cage. "What do you want?" he demanded. "Kill me now, if that's what you're after."

The Watcher chuckled, a low, sinister sound. "Oh, dear Aaron, that will come much later, if you do not behave. For now, you are my guest."

He led Aaron out to where the waterfall tumbled over the edge of the cave cliff and watched it fondly. "Isn't it beautiful? You can see the whole Island from here."

Aaron stared out at the withered forests, the fallen mountains, the mist covered sky. "It was beautiful once, but you've ruined it," he snapped. If he were to push the Watcher over the edge, would it kill him? Or would he fly back up and kill Aaron instead? He was too powerful, Aaron decided. It wasn't worth it.

"No," the Watcher hissed. "I've saved it. You see that mist?" he pointed at the horizon. "It grows thicker by the day. Shielding our borders, protecting us."

"Killing us, you mean," Aaron growled.

The Watcher sighed. "I knew I'd have trouble with you. The rest of the Island... they just don't understand. They could never comprehend it. They're not bold enough, not willing to take the necessary steps, not ready enough to do what has to be done. They're stuck in the past, all of them. Whereas I... I have figured out how to use my power in a new, greater way. I've done things that have never been done before. I am the one leading us to a better future."

"You're lying," Aaron spat.

"I'm not killing the Isle, Aaron. I'm saving it in the only way anyone could—by becoming strong enough that nothing will ever threaten it again. I'd just like somebody to know that." The Watcher turned away from the view to face him instead, and asked, after a second. "What is your last name?"

"Farrah," Aaron told him hesitantly.

"Aha," the Watcher sounded satisfied. "You see..." He removed his hood in one swift motion. "My real name is Naharan Farrah."

Aaron stepped back, reeling. Upon closer inspection, the Watcher didn't have Aaron's face, but his features were so similar that had they been closer in age, they might have been identical. The only difference were his startlingly green eyes, the same vibrant green as the forests of the Island.

The Watcher shared a last name with him? They looked so similar too... the only explanation was... surely not...

"Yes," the Watcher smiled, and Aaron shuddered to see a face so closely resembling his light up. He was much older than Aaron, but still looked young and fairly handsome. "I am your uncle, Aaron."

The world shattered around Aaron and spun at the same time. His fingers and face went numb with shock, and he struggled to form words. "What? What are you talking about? I'm not—"

"My nephew?" The Watcher tilted his head. "I know, we can't pick our families, but I *am* hoping to get to know you."

"You're lying," Aaron said again, at a loss for anything better to say. He clutched his spinning head.

The Watcher conjured a smaller, carved wooden chair next to the throne-like chair. "You should probably have a seat for this." Aaron sunk into the chair, his legs wobbling.

"How?" he whispered, barely audible over the crashing of the waterfall.

"Your mother, Aalliah, was my sister," the Watcher elegantly placed himself on the throne next to Aaron and surveyed him with intrigued eyes. "My twin. I'm sure you've heard the story by now. Two Whisperers, the most powerful on the Isle, destined to rule. Then they took her." His eyes flashed dangerously, and the thorned vines curling around his body shifted. Aaron suddenly recognized them as the thorns that had attacked them their first day on the Island.

"Who?" Aaron asked, although he was sure he already knew. He just needed to hear it.

"The intruders. Outsiders. Strangers. Whatever you wish to call them, they sailed our shores. Shocked, the bunch of them, that they had discovered such a place, ever so *delighted* with every unique part of the Isle we showed them, every secret." The Watcher looked away, a distant look in his eyes. "And there were so many secrets to show. Come on, Aaron, you grew up in Neomerica. You've seen it for yourself. You must agree that we have to stay protected against them."

"This isn't happening," Aaron murmured to himself. Yes, Neomerica might have metaphorically suffocated him, but the life of the Isle was no price to pay for that protection.

"We were young. We were naive," the Watcher continued. "We told them too much. They wanted it. Conflicts ensued. I wanted to scare them off, but if that didn't work, I was willing to do whatever it took, even if I had to end them all. The Isle comes first. They would have ruined us, killed us, destroyed the Island. I saved us, but…"

"You lost your sister," Aaron prompted. Even though he was in a state of shock, he wanted to hear the entire story.

"They took Aalliah," the Watcher clenched his fists. "They took her, and they killed her. Or so I thought."

"She lived," Aaron said softly.

"I've known of the prophecy for a long time," the Watcher dug his fingers into his throne. "I didn't know quite who it was about, but then you showed up on my shores. And I knew *exactly* who you were." He reached out to tilt Aaron's chin toward himself, and Aaron tensed. "The resemblance is striking."

Aaron pulled back, as the Watcher went on. "No one except my blood relative could look like that. And the other two… yes, I recognized their look immediately. So similar to the intruders." His face contorted into a scowl. "How *dare* they mix their filthy foreign blood with the pure blood of a Whisperer, and more than that, hurt my beloved sister? They kidnapped her, controlled her, I *know* it. And they forced her to have you two."

"She died," Aaron murmured slowly.

"I know," the Watcher smiled sadly. "Otherwise she would have come back with you. But I had already believed her dead, and mourned her. It didn't make a difference to me."

"This can't be true," Aaron protested. "If I *am* your nephew, then why could I enter the Eyes of the Island? Isn't there a blood curse on it so anyone with Island blood will die?"

"*Pure* Island blood," the Watcher corrected. "A technicality I had not foreseen when I spilled the blood to set this curse."

"I don't... I can't..." Aaron stammered.

"So now you understand," the Watcher said curtly. "And we can finish this together."

"Finish what?"

"The process," the Watcher gestured grandly. "When I have taken the remaining power from the Island, the plan will be complete. Nobody will ever harm us again."

"You really can't see?" Aaron burst out, standing up. "How do you not see that you're killing the Island? And everyone and everything on it?"

The Watcher just calmly gazed at him. "You see this?" he asked, pointing to the small pool of water by the throne.

"Yes," Aaron answered warily.

"This is how I am able to watch over the Island," he explained. "Look." He waved a hand over the clear pool, and an image shimmered into view, appearing in its depths.

It was Night Star and Khalisse, standing on the sandy shores of Desperation. "*The Guardians are free,*" Night Star growled. "*I felt it when the mountain fell.*"

Khalisse looked relieved. "*Thank goodness. Are the three with them?*"

Night Star hung his head. "*I couldn't tell. I can only hope they survived that.*"

Khalisse gazed at the mountains. "*The Eyes of the Island are almost gone. Watcher Peak is all that remains.*"

"*We must hope for the return of the three,*" Night Star rumbled. "*Without them, all hope is lost.*"

Khalisse sighed. "*Even if they don't come back, we must strike soon. We stand much less of a chance, but...*" her voice trailed off. "*Oh, they have to be all right.*" Then they faded from the pool. Aaron watched in horror. The Watcher truly could see anywhere.

"That scene was from a little while ago," the Watcher explained. "I thought you'd want to see it."

Aaron's head turned toward Jannary and Neyric, whose eyes were wide, still unable to talk. "Ignore our other guests," the Watcher commanded sharply. "I had them silenced especially for you, so as to not manipulate you."

"What are you talking about?" Aaron shouted. "I will *never* join you."

"I thought you'd say that," the Watcher remarked. "I have one last thing to show you. You may call me Naharan, by the way. I assume you're not ready for 'Uncle,'" he finished with a smirk.

"You're right about that," Aaron snapped.

"Come on," the Watcher beckoned. He led Aaron out of the cave, and they walked along the river flowing through the mountain. "You know what will happen to you if you run."

They walked next to the crashing river for the next few minutes, before emerging out of the series of tunnels and caves, into open air.

Surrounded by stone and mountain on all sides, the lake stood alone. It was the same diamond-clear as Crystal River, with a faint flow, surrounded by flowers and thriving wildlife.

"The first water source on the Isle," the Watcher explained. "And the most sacred place here."

"Wow," Aaron breathed. The air was crisp here, and he couldn't explain it, but he truly *felt* the presence of the Island at that moment. "Why are you showing me this?"

"I wanted you to see," the Watcher said calmly. "What we are trying to accomplish. I have been here many times. *This* is what we are trying to protect. The power of the Isle."

The power. Of course. For one startling moment there, Aaron thought the Watcher had been trying to protect the purity of the Isle, the life. No, this had just cemented Aaron's stance against the Watcher. But did he have a choice?

"We can't touch it," the Watcher continued. "It's just too much. I haven't managed to control it yet, but soon. Perhaps even in a day or two, at this rate." He pulled up the sleeve of his robes to reveal a marred patch of skin, blackened and scarred. "This is what happened the one and only time I made contact with the lake."

Aaron was silent. "We shall go back," announced the Watcher, and they walked back to the cave.

"I will leave you here," the Watcher told him. "The door to the tunnels will be shut, but you don't have to be in your cage. That was simply to hold you temporarily. You are free now. I mustn't imprison family."

A lot of good that did him, Aaron thought glumly. He couldn't escape; the one exit was over the cliff.

As the vines on the Watcher's robes twisted, Aaron finally understood. The vines, the green eyes the same color as the Isle's forests... taking power from the Isle had affected him. He was lost, hardly human anymore. He had taken from the Isle, and the wild had claimed him in return.

"Now, after all my explanation, I have one last thing to ask," said the Watcher, turning his back on Aaron to face the sprawling Isle. "Will you join me?"

Chapter 21

"They're coming!" Streakwing shouted. "Brace yourselves!"

Evannah tightened her grip on her Guardian's neck, leaning forward as they hurtled through the sky at top speed. Between the scales, the reptilian body, and the wings, it almost seemed like the creature was a dragon.

Part of her heart had been left behind with Aaron, and she ached to know if he was okay. She was sure he was still alive, she could feel it as a twin. But what was the Watcher doing to him?

"Can we fight them?" Kiera yelled from the side, pointing at the glowing dots approaching them.

The tiger Guardian shook her head. "It's too dangerous while we're carrying you. We'll try to avoid them."

Evannah's eyes watered from the sheer speeds they were traveling at, and her hair streamed out behind her. The lightning birds, glowing dots in the distance grew bigger and bigger until she could see them perfectly.

They were huge birds with long, pointed heads and streaming tail feathers. They glowed softly in a multitude of hues, changing colors every few seconds, and their wingtips crackled with electricity. The bird in the lead opened its beak and let out a fearsome screech.

"Hang on tight!" Streakwing command. "This may get risky!"

Evannah hardly had any time to prepare before her Guardian rapidly twisted to the side, avoiding an incoming bird. Kiera cheered as Streakwing folded his wings into a dive under another lightning bird.

Evannah screamed as her Guardian followed, plummeting into a drop that made her stomach twist and her heart nearly leave her body. There were flashes of light as the ever-growing swarm of birds flew after them.

"Don't let go!" her Guardian advised, executing a series of twists and turns that turned the world into a blur as Evannah gritted her teeth and tried her best not to throw up.

The air was thick with lightning birds and buzzing electricity, as they focused their laser-sharp eyes on the Guardians, and dove claws-first toward their bodies, screeching madly.

"FASTER!" Streakwing yelled over the rushing wind and bird cries.

There was a distant cry of "Yeah!" from Kiera. *Faster is good,* Evannah tried to convince herself. *Faster means a better chance of survival.* But it was hard to believe herself when her Guardian pulled into a loop-de-loop that flipped her world upside down, arms and legs clenched desperately around the great creature. The ground was so far away. They were only surrounded by a vast blue sky.

The dragon Guardian tore two lightning birds out of the sky with one talon and tossed another aside with her mouth.

They were beginning to converge on Evannah and Kiera, and the Guardians shot up into the sky in an effort to throw them off.

"It's too dangerous!" Streakwing called. "Jewelclaws, I'll need to take them down to the Isle while we continue the fight! We can hold them off!"

"What?" Evannah cried, confused.

"Evannah!" Streakwing addressed her. "Jump off Jewelclaws and I'll catch you!"

"Are you joking?" she called, but the words were lost in the cacophony.

Okay. I can do this. Slow... She carefully edged off the dragon's back, safely...

The dragon reached up with one large claw, grabbed Evannah, and chucked her into the air.

Evannah screamed as she free-fell for the second time that day, lightning birds turning into a glowing blur, until Streakwing snapped her up in his beak, and soared down toward the Isle.

She lay between the mandibles of his beak as the fighting Guardians grew further and further away. Finally, Streakwings touched down smoothly, depositing the disheveled, crumpled heap that was Evannah onto the ground.

Kiera slid smoothly off Streakwing's back. "That was amazing!" she cried. Evannah groaned weakly.

"Listen," Streakwing said. "Don't go far. We'll come back to get you as soon as the coast is clear." He turned his head, and plucked a feather off his wing, handing it to them. "I can keep track of you with this. Send a message immediately if something happens."

He took off into the battle with a concerned but determined backward glance.

Then it was just Evannah and Kiera. Evannah stood up and brushed several dead leaves off her body and out of her hair. Then she saw the fallen Tharros Peak and it was all she needed to break down again.

"Aaron," she cried, leaning against the nearest trunk for support.

"I know," Kiera said softly. "But we can't do anything right now except hope for the best. You were captured too, and you escaped."

"I didn't really get captured!" Evannah argued. "I got away before it was too late. The Watcher himself got Aaron. There's no escaping from that."

Kiera huffed. "I had to put up with this when you were taken too. Just think about this: what better way to get Aaron back than to take down the man who took him?"

"Yeah," Evannah admitted quietly, wiping her wet face.

"And for that, we need to stay alive," Kiera said forcefully. "I want Aaron back as much as you, but we can't go storming into danger like I know you were planning on doing."

"That's funny coming from you," Evannah muttered.

"Exactly. If even I'm saying that, you know it's right," Kiera smiled.

"Okay," Evannah admitted. She looked around for a minute. "Does this place look familiar to you?"

"I don't know," Kiera scanned their surroundings as well. "Maybe?"

A patch of withered trees and grass, a massive chasm open in the ground in the distance... every place on the Isle could have looked like this. But it was *just so familiar.*

"Oh!" Evannah finally realized. "I think we're near the Trail of Truth." The place where she had been taken.

Kiera reached into the bag that she still had with her and pulled out the old-looking journal. "I still have this from the Trail." It had been wrapped in leaves to protect it, but now the leaves had fallen off and the book was damp.

The feather in Evannah's hand began to glow and vibrate slightly, distracting them. "*Lightning birds are attempting to get to you. We are holding them off. Find cover, but don't go too far.*"

She glanced around the sparse, dead trees. At the moment, she would like nothing better than to get captured again and reunited with Aaron. She had escaped once, maybe she could do it again. No. She shook off the thought. The Watcher was more powerful than ever and she had to protect herself so she could fight back. "Come on," she beckoned Kiera.

Together, they ran further into the woods, shrieks and roars still echoing from high in the clouds. There were occasional flashes of color, but it seemed like the Guardians were successfully holding off the birds.

"What's that?" Kiera asked, stopping in her tracks.

"What?" Evannah asked back.

"That," Kiera pointed to a tiny clearing. In the center of the clearing stood a large boulder, as tall as themselves. Carved into the rock were three handprints, filled with a blue glassy stone and patterned with swirls.

"I don't know," Evannah responded. "Let's go."

"Let me see, one second," Kiera went over to the rock and placed her hand on the handprint. Nothing happened.

"Kiera," Evannah rocked on her feet anxiously. The flashes of lightning bird colors were getting closer and closer. "Come on!"

"Okay, okay." Kiera came back to join her, and they continued forward through the woods.

"Whoa," Evannah stopped this time a few minutes later. "Look."

They had reached the same clearing again, with the hand-printed rock. "That's not possible," Kiera exclaimed. "We just walked away from that!"

A talon became visible in the sky, and disappeared quickly in a blaze of fire. "Doesn't matter, let's go," Evannah argued.

So they traveled further, looking for some kind of shelter that would hide them from the Watcher's birds. "Oh no," Kiera groaned a little while later.

"Did we reach the same rock again?" Evannah knew it before looking up.

"Yup. Looks like the Island really wants us to see it."

Evannah sighed. "Okay, let's go see." She walked up to the rock. Besides the handprints, it looked completely normal. She placed her hand on the smooth, swirl-patterned handprint. Nothing.

"Three handprints," Kiera pondered. "Three of us?"

"Only two now," Evannah gazed at the fallen mountain.

"Try it at the same time," Kiera suggested. She placed her hand on the handprint the same time Evannah did, and the rock began to vibrate slightly. "Something's happening!"

"I think we need Aaron," Evannah said sadly.

"Why don't you try it?" Kiera asked. "I'm sure your hand is a similar size. And you're twins, maybe it'll count."

"Okay," Evannah agreed hesitantly. And she put her hand on the third handprint.

Almost instantly, many things happened at the same time. The wind picked up, and a transparent, golden dome formed over the little clearing. Evannah jerked back her hand as an electric current began to run over it.

The rock split in two, and a familiar-looking pedestal rose from the depths of the earth. "It's the pedestal from the Trail of Truth," breathed Kiera.

"Wait." A thought struck Evannah. "Do you have the journal?"

"Here," Kiera handed it to Evannah. She stepped forward, and placed the journal onto the pedestal.

The book flipped open, and its pages began to rustle, flipping at top speed until they became a blur. "It opened!" Kiera cheered, as Evannah watched the book intently.

As the pages flipped faster, a shape started to rise from the journal, growing bigger and forming into the figure of a person.

Kiera and Evannah stumbled back. "What is *that*?"

The figure became even more defined, forming eyes and a face and long hair. Then it stopped, and Evannah tried to puzzle out what she was looking at.

It was a woman, floating above the book as though she was really in front of them, but semi-transparent, so that Evannah could see the forest through her body. She had long, wavy black hair, golden-brown eyes, and a kind smile. Evannah recognized her immediately from portraits. Aalliah.

"Is that?..." Kiera whispered hesitantly.

"Yes," Evannah nodded. It was possible that she had never been more confused. Why was a magical image of her mother floating in front of her, on an Island so far away from home?

"What?" Kiera voiced her thoughts.

Aalliah's image gazed down on them. "Hello," she began to speak.

"The book is talking!" Kiera clutched Evannah's arm tightly.

Evannah shushed her. "Listen!"

"I know you may have questions," Aalliah continued. "First, I'd like you to know that I'm not really here. This is a message I left in my journal for you, my children. I assume you're here too, Kiera." Kiera looked startled at being named.

As Aalliah looked at them, Evannah could see a clear resemblance. She looked exactly like Aaron. But there were traces of her in Evannah too, from the shape of her eyes to subtle similarities in their faces.

"Let me start at the beginning," Aalliah said. "You must be on the Isle, and I don't know how much you've found out. You have to know about the Watcher, perhaps you've heard his story already. How he nearly went to war with the intruders, and how his sister was captured and killed. Well, I was the sister. His twin."

"What?" Evannah and Kiera exclaimed at the same time.

"We imagined ourselves as leaders of the Isle," Aalliah told them with a distant look. "Naharan once did great things with his power. But even before the foreigners came, he started to get greedy. But I was always there to curb him, keep him in check."

Aalliah disappeared, and a scene appeared before them. A ship sailing to the shores of the Isle, the shores that the trio had landed upon. A group of men and women climbed out of the ship, staring at the Isle with undisguised wonder mixed with a kind of hunger.

Two men were featured prominently, heading the group, and they were immediately recognizable. The first man was Lord Cyrus, his slick black hair without any traces of gray. The next was Lord Carmine, holding hands with a woman with the same light brown locks as Kiera.

"Our dads?" Kiera asked.

"I think so," Evannah murmured, in shock. Her mind had connected the dots already but not quite accepted it.

"They were kind at first," Aalliah's voice narrated. The semi-transparent scene showed two Islanders coming out of the rainforest to greet the newcomers. They were both young and good-looking, wearing dark blue robes. "We showed them around. We became friends. Almost... more than friends.

"Cyrus began to fall in love with me, but I never returned his affections. I wasn't interested in a partner. We continued to show them the Isle as they settled in and explored. But we were young, and we didn't have caution. We showed them too much. They wanted it. This I'm sure you've heard. Let me tell you the part you haven't."

Evannah stared into Aalliah's eyes, willing her to acknowledge Evannah, longing for the mother she had never known to speak again in her melodious voice.

"There were fights, conflicts. It was clear this was going to escalate into a full-scale war. There was only one way to prevent this without bloodshed, to save my beloved Isle, my home."

The scene showed Aalliah running through the forest, covered in a cloak, under the guise of night. "Very early that morning I went to the Neomericans' camp for the last time. Cyrus had been asking me to come back with him to Neomerica for many days, and finally, I agreed. I agreed on the one condition that they had to leave immediately.

"His companions were not satisfied, but Cyrus argued that they would come back with reinforcements and a better army. Now that they had me there was nothing to worry about.

"I couldn't tell my brother what I was doing of course. He could never lose me. He wouldn't have allowed me. But this was the only peaceful plan. That night I had said goodbye to him for the last time."

The image showed the ship sailing away from the Isle, Aalliah staring longingly back at the mountains. "As we sailed away, I cast a memory spell on the entire crew, making them believe they had just visited a small, uninhabited and unimportant island. This was my plan. I knew I had to stay with them to make sure it worked and make sure that they never returned.

"We reached Neomerica, and were married." A white-dressed Aalliah, glassy-eyed under her veil, with sadness, not happiness like one would expect on a wedding day. "I was given an important court position so Cyrus could show off his exotic new wife. He even took my last name, Farrah, just to prove that point. But I played my role.

"All this time, the effort of keeping the memory spell on the explorers was weakening me. The further from the Isle, the harder it is for a Whisperer to use their power."

The image blurred into a picture of three babies lying in elaborate cradles in one room. "Then you were born, and my life changed. When I had twins, and Kiera's birthday was so close to yours... I knew. We all knew the prophecy. I knew that you three had to be the trio that it talked about. I could recognize the signs of a young Whisperer from birth. I knew you'd be like Naharan and I, Evannah. I needed to keep you away from the Isle as long as I lived, for your own safety.

"I also knew that, as the prophecy said, you were to face a dark power and try to save the Isle. I didn't know at the time that the dark power was my own brother. The Whispers brought me messages occasionally, telling me how Naharan wasn't doing well without me, how he was losing himself more and more. But when I got the message about his declaration as the Watcher, it was too late for me. I was too weak to go back, and I couldn't leave you."

Aalliah herself appeared once more. "You don't understand how sorry I am that this has to happen to you. My own family, fighting itself... when the Whispers brought me that last message, I was torn. I did everything I could to buy myself more time, but it wasn't enough.

"As I got weaker, I knew what I had to do. It was what I had been afraid of doing, but it was time. I used my remaining strength to make the memory spell permanent. It was the biggest memory spell that had ever been cast, and the effort killed me.

As I lay on my deathbed, I sent this message to the Isle with my last bit of power, for you. So you could understand, someday."

The picture showed Aalliah lying on a bed, weakened, but still beautiful. A crowd of Neomericans surrounded her with bowed heads, Lord Cyrus dressed in black heading them. In his hands, young Evannah reached her hands toward her mother. With great effort, Aalliah tried to reach back, but within seconds, her hand dropped to her side and her chest fell still.

Tears dripped down both the real Evannah's and the memory of young Evannah's cheeks, who didn't understand, but obviously sensed the mood of the room. A young memory Aaron cried quietly, while a little Kiera with short light brown curls twisted frantically in Lady Carmine's arms.

Then it turned back to Aalliah again. "I don't know where I'll go in a few moments, but I will always be watching over you. Kiera—you are so young, but you already brighten the room. May your spirit stay strong forever, and your light guide others forward. Aaron—you are braver than you know. Never doubt yourself. Use your thoughtfulness to keep the others on the right track. Evannah—I wish I could be there to watch you grow up and come into your own as a Whisperer. You will face challenges, but remember this: your power is what you make it. You have the chance to use your ability only for good, and I know you will. Stay strong, my child. Good luck, and good bye. I love you so much."

Then she disappeared, leaving behind deafening silence and an empty feeling inside Evannah. After several moments, Kiera reached out for the journal and pulled it off the pedestal, rifling through the pages. "It's open now." She handed it to Evannah.

"Looks like her diary," Evannah murmured, tracing her mom's neat handwriting with her eyes. The pedestal slowly receded back into the earth, the rock sealed itself up, the wind died dome, and the golden dome shimmered into nothingness.

The forest was surprisingly quiet. The feather glowed in her hand, sending them a message. "*We fought them off. Coming back now.*"

Evannah sat down on the soft forest floor, still staring at the diary, feeling disbelief. She didn't want to believe this, but at the same time, it made so much sense. Everything was explained. "I get it now," she said quietly. "Why we were chosen."

Kiera sat down next to her. "Why?"

"It's our responsibility. Our families tore the Isle apart. Both sides of my family did this. It's not *our* fault, really, but we inherited the burden. And now we're the only ones who can fix it." And, oh, this shouldn't have been important, but no wonder the villager's eyes had looked so familiar. They were Aaron's eyes, her mother's eyes. They were really from the Isle.

"You're right," Kiera murmured. "I guess that's the reason we stayed to help. Deep inside, we knew we had to."

There was a loud whoosh as Streakwing landed next to them, stirring the dead leaves into a little tornado. "We got rid of them," he grinned. "We Guardians haven't fought anyone in a while, but it all came back pretty quickly. Ready to go?"

"Yup." Evannah mounted his back. They took off into the sky, the other Guardians floating along. They skimmed the treetops, flying directly above them so they weren't seen by the Watcher.

"*Attention.*"

Evannah screamed and nearly fell off Streakwing's back as a booming voice echoed throughout the Isle, so loud that she could feel the vibrations through the Guardian's feathers.

Streakwing paused in midair, twisting anxiously. "What is *that?*"

A giant square had become visible in the sky, floating directly above Watcher Peak, like a moving portrait, or a window into a different scene. It showed the Watcher standing at the edge of a ledge, overlooking Heart Falls. Every detail was magnified hundreds of times, so that the huge scene was clearly visible anywhere on the Island.

"*I am giving you one last chance,*" the Watcher thundered. "*All I have tried to do is protect your Isle. Lay down your arms, find your family, and face the end with dignity. Know that your sacrifice is to protect generations of Island people and magic. You have the chance to be part of a noble cause, and yet you resist.*

"*You think your precious Warrior, Wanderer, and Whisperer will save you. Your Guardians are weak. Your people are scattered.*"

And across the Isle, humans and creatures alike stopped in their tracks and turned their heads toward the floating scene. Animals stopped dead in the middle of their chases, while the residents of Desperation froze. The Isle held its breath.

"*Your Warrior has picked the right side.*"

Out of the dark cave behind the ledge stepped out a smaller cloaked figure. But Evannah knew, even before the hood slipped to reveal golden-brown eyes.

It was Aaron.

Chapter 22

It couldn't be real. Kiera rubbed her eyes, but the more she stared the more she knew. Even with the cloak, she could recognize Aaron anywhere.

She gripped Streakwing's feathers so hard her knuckles turned white. "Why?" she whispered with a dry mouth.

Evannah shook her head. "Aaron? No. It can't be!" Then after several seconds she added. "Oh. The prophecy, remember? *One shall fall, one shall fade.* He's faded into the shadows. The darkness."

"We need to get back as soon as possible," Streakwing commanded the other Guardians. As they flew away, Kiera saw the floating square disappear out of the corner of her eye.

"Bluedawn Bay," Kiera said numbly. "That's where the Fenlithrians and Vaharians are taking refuge."

Streakwing turned to the Guardians "Bluedawn Bay, as fast as possible."

Under any other circumstances, Kiera would have enjoyed the flight. But instead of the lush and beautiful island they had seen just a few days prior, the place was dead and desolate. It was almost too late. The image of Aaron in that hood, standing next to the Watcher as friends, as *equals* haunted her.

The silver-gray ocean came into view, and Streakwing skimmed its surface as they glided toward Desperation, feeling the salty spray.

Cheers resounded as Streakwing landed on the beach of the islet. Kiera and Evannah slipped off his back and went running over the sand.

"Kiera? Evannah?" Khalisse cried, and ran toward them. "We thought you were dead!" She hugged them, then stepped back a little awkwardly.

"We brought friends," Kiera gestured to the group of mighty Guardians who had touched down on the sand.

Night Star came bounding out of the crowd toward the Guardians, who touched noses with him excitedly.

Evannah took a breath. "Did you know?" she asked Khalisse.

"Know...what?" Khalisse tilted her head.

"Aaron and I are the Watcher's niece and nephew," Evannah told her. "My dad, and Kiera's, were part of the group of 'strangers' from the story."

Khalisse stepped back. "*What?*"

A memory resurfaced. "When you heard the last name Farrah," Kiera pointed out, "you recognized it."

"I knew Farrah is an Island surname," Khalisse explained. "And I suspected you and Aaron might be related to someone from here. He looked so similar to us. But I didn't know... so your mom was Aalliah Farrah?"

Evannah nodded.

"Wow," Khalisse blinked. "That's... unexpected. Is that why Aaron...," she trailed off, not wanting to say it. Everyone had seen the Watcher's announcement.

"We don't know," Kiera broke away from her gaze. "He got captured, and we were going to go back for him, but we didn't know that he would...*betray* us."

Night Star padded back to rejoin them as the Guardians began to greet a crowd of villagers. "I couldn't believe my eyes," he growled. "I can't believe he would *dare*... something has to be wrong."

Kiera blinked back tears and swallowed hard. "The Watcher could be enchanting him, right? Mind control, or something?"

"It's possible," Khalisse ventured. "But Aaron can protect himself against that, remember? It's likely that... that he decided that it would be better to join the winning side."

"He wouldn't!" Evannah cried.

"We must prepare," Night Star warned solemnly. "You might find yourself facing your own brother in battle."

That was too much for Evannah, who stood shocked for a moment, then went running off toward an abandoned patch of rocks in the shallows.

"Let's leave her for a while," Khalisse suggested. "She's been hit the hardest, although I *never* thought Aaron could do this. How could he?" Anger radiated from her dark eyes.

Kiera shook her head, speechless. This was Aaron. *Her* Aaron, the one she'd known for years and years, the one she'd grown up with. She wouldn't accept it; something had to be wrong.

The day rushed past and simultaneously seemed to take its own time. Kiera helped Khalisse and Night Star organize the warriors for battle, while Evannah quietly assisted in fishing. She kept her mother's journal in her hand just as Kiera kept her sword, more for support than anything else. It became clear that even the supply of food in the ocean was depleting and couldn't feed such a large party for so long.

Moss bounced around her feet. He had been following Kiera around during that day, happy to see her again, comforting her. While Kiera was gathering wood from the few trees on the islet, Moss gave a short yap and ran off. "Moss?" Kiera called. "Where are you going?"

Moss turned his head to look back at her, then continued running. Kiera began chasing after him. "Come back, you silly pup!" she shouted at him while he led her on a chase across the beach.

He finally came to a stop next to Evannah, who was standing in the shallows of the ocean, the water lapping her feet. The pink sunset contrasted with the dark Isle and the jagged shapes of fallen mountains.

Evannah reached out to pet the puppy, who was jumping by her feet. "Hi Moss," she remarked. She turned around. "Kiera! There you are. I need to talk to you."

"What for?" Kiera asked.

Evannah took a deep breath. "It's Aaron. I figured out how to communicate with him."

"What?" Kiera splashed into the water beside her. "How?"

"The Whispers," Evannah explained. "Aaron knows I can hear them, so he asked them to send a message. They brought it to me."

"What does it say?" Kiera said, starting to get excited.

"I'll see if I can somehow play it out loud," Evannah closed her eyes for a second. "I think I got it." She waved her hand and there was a little flash of light.

A voice as soft as a gentle breeze was able to be heard. It was Aaron, whispering, "If there are any Whispers around, please take this message to Evannah. Tell her I'm sorry, I'm not actually on the Watcher's side. It was the only way to find out his plans. He's still not telling me much. But I'm going to find a way out soon. If you can, get to Crystal River tomorrow. If there are no Whispers around, I must look really odd right now." The voice faded away.

"See?" Evannah looked delighted.

Kiera hesitated. "I don't know. This could be the Watcher. I *really* want it to be Aaron, but at the same time... I don't know."

"We need to go to Crystal River tomorrow," Evannah said in determination.

"Evah, wait," Kiera stopped her. "We don't know about this. Let's check with Khalisse first." What she really wanted was to jump right into the action, but the part of her newly shaped by the Island's dangers held her back.

Moss tracked down Khalisse, and Evannah played the message. Khalisse tilted her head thoughtfully. "It does sound like him. Then again, the Watcher is one of the most powerful Whisperers who ever lived. And he does control the whole Island right now. Let's be safe."

Evannah was quiet for a few moments. "Fine," she finally huffed, and had no more to say.

As they lay in their makeshift beds that night, a plan formed in Kiera's mind. If there was even the *smallest* possibility that it was really Aaron who sent the message, she needed to check. It would be just her, the only member of the trio who had no family connection to the Watcher. If it was just her, who would even notice? Yes, she would go herself to Crystal River. If anything, Moss would protect her.

The first rays of early morning hit Kiera's face, and she woke easily, remembering her plan. Just a quick swim to the Isle and back, and nobody would notice. She rolled over to double check if Evannah was still asleep.

The bed was empty.

She knew, immediately. Evannah must have had the same plan, and beaten her to it.

Kiera scrambled up, waking up Moss who gave her a confused, ruffled look. "Come on," she whispered to him. "We're going to swim." She picked up her sword.

Sure enough, there was the tiny figure of Evannah swimming in the distance. Kiera waded in, getting soaked, and paddled desperately to try to make up the distance. Moss floated beside her, shaking drops of water of his little golden antlers happily.

"Evannah," she said, in a whisper-yell once they were close enough. No response. "Evannah!" she tried, a little louder.

Evannah turned around. "Kiera? What are you doing here?"

"I'm rescuing Aaron," she said.

"I was doing that too!" Evannah muttered. "I thought you said it was too dangerous!"

"Yeah, too dangerous for you," Kiera argued. "Not for me."

"That's just unfair," Evannah sniffed. "I can take care of myself very well."

"Fine, let's both rescue him," Kiera remarked firmly. "I'm still ninety percent sure this is a trap. You can fight Shadows, right?"

"Yes, but not the Watcher."

"Ok," Kiera still felt uncertain, but they had to do this. "Let's make this quick. And try not to get attacked." Moss licked her in response.

They reached the Isle, and no Shadows emerged to attack them. That was a start. They walked toward Crystal River, the same way they had just two days prior. Still nothing. "This is too easy," Kiera commented.

"Don't jinx it," Evannah warned. They stepped into the river, and Evannah suddenly gasped. "He sent another message." She waved her hand, and Aaron's voice rang out.

"If you're there, Evannah, I made it out. I'm coming. I'll be at the point in the river where there are three giant rocks near the riverbend."

"I remember that place," Kiera said. "It's further along." They waded the familiar route, through the river, until they reached the rocks.

There they waited, for many minutes, until an hour had passed. Then another hour. But Evannah refused to leave, and Kiera didn't want to abandon Aaron anyway. Plus, Moss had settled down for a nap and was not going anywhere.

Finally, after two hours, there was a commotion, and a hooded figure came around the riverbend. "Watcher!" Kiera cried.

The figure took off his hood. "Calm down, it's just me."

"Aaron!" Evannah ran to hug him, and so did Kiera. She didn't even notice the people that he had brought with him.

"Jannary? Neyric? You're alive?" Kiera exclaimed happily. "This is amazing!"

A few more people followed, wearing armor with the sign of the Watcher on their chests. There were six of them in total. "Who are they?" Kiera questioned. "What happened? Wait—are you really Aaron?"

"Of course!" Aaron responded.

"Tell me something only you would know."

"Your real name is Kieralyndria," he admitted solemnly, and that was all Kiera needed to hug him again. Then punch him, because he *swore* he would never utter that name again.

"How did you escape?" Evannah asked. "Oh, and I forget," she slapped him hard on the arm. "You are in so much trouble for pretending to betray us."

"I convinced Ihiria and a couple of others to unlock Jannary, Neyric, and I," Aaron explained, gesturing to a tall woman wearing armor. "Let's walk." They began to proceed the way Kiera and Evannah had come, back to the coast of the Isle. "A lot of the

Watcher's human army doesn't support him, or not anymore. They were on our side.

"I had to find a way out. The Watcher showed me the first source of water on the Island, it's at the top of Watcher Peak. He couldn't touch it, apparently it injured him. And there were no guards around it, I guess he thought I had no way of escaping. But Jannary told me of an Island legend about a hidden network of rivers that flow from the source, so I jumped in, figuring I had no other choice, and I didn't get hurt."

"The sacred water damaged the Watcher because it was so pure," Neyric said. "He's committed horrible crimes against the Isle, which makes him the destructor of the Island. The source of creation was like poison to him. But Aaron could touch it."

"It was true," Aaron continued. "There was a small cave underwater, and we followed it. It led to an underground tunnel. It was long, and dark, and we thought we'd never make it out. But finally we did. And we followed Crystal River after that. It took all night. There was a hidden escape route under the Watcher's nose the whole time, and he had no idea." Aaron grinned.

"Oh," he started again. "Oh, I just remembered something awful. Evannah, we're—"

"The Watcher's niece and nephew?" Evannah replied dryly. "We know."

Aaron gaped. "How?" Kiera explained the story about Aalliah's journal.

"There's one more thing," Aaron told them urgently. "The Watcher's planning a final attack tomorrow at dawn. Shadows, humans, creatures, everything. He's eliminating all obstacles before he can reach full power once and for all."

"You didn't think to tell us that first?" Kiera sputtered. "That the Watcher's going to wipe us out?"

"We have one last chance," Aaron said determinedly. "I have a plan. This is it, isn't it?" he asked Neyric. They had reached a split in the river, and Aaron pointed to the right.

"Yes," Neyric confirmed. "That will lead you straight to Cressiara."

"The ocean village?" Kiera remembered.

"Yup," Aaron responded. "We have one day to unite the villages. So let's go."

"We'll find the Fenlithrians and Vaharians," Jannary told them. "Keep going straight?"

"Straight, then cross Bluedawn Bay," Evannah instructed. "There's a little islet there. You'll see the Guardians."

"We'll come with you," Ihiria offered to Aaron. "For protection."

Aaron shook his head. "You'll be in danger. I think it has to be just us."

"We have Moss for protection!" Kiera interjected, and Moss bared his tiny teeth. The puppy *was* actually a gigantic wolf, after all.

"Guard Jannary and Neyric," Aaron instructed. Ihiria nodded.

"We'll send Night Star for transportation to Silverspire," Jannary promised. "They must have suffered when the mountains fell."

"Thanks," Aaron told her. "I guess we'll be off, then." They said goodbye, and the trio set off along the right route while the rest of the group took the left route.

"You're so energetic, Aaron," Kiera commented as they walked.

"I finally got it, Kiera!" Aaron turned to her with bright eyes. "The answer to your question. About the prophecy. Maybe we have a destiny, but *nothing* can control us," he grabbed her hand excitedly. "No prophecy controls us. Don't you see? We are our own people, and nobody can change that."

"Wow, I—" Kiera started.

"We're here to save the Isle because *we* want to. So forget the stupid prophecy. We'll make it come true on our *own* terms," Aaron grinned. "Starting now."

"Yes," Kiera was filled with enthusiasm. "When did you have this striking revelation?"

"Imprisoned," Aaron said casually. "I had an identity crisis when I saw the Watcher looked exactly like me. That got me thinking: what does all of this really mean?"

"I agree," Evannah added. "Let's do this our way. Why does anybody have to die?" Moss yapped in agreement.

"Exactly," Kiera smiled. Aaron had figured it out. This was *their* prophecy, and destiny or not, nobody could take away the choices that they made. It seemed that his typical self-doubt had been lessened after he had survived several encounters with the Watcher.

"So we're going to unite the villages," Aaron announced. "And give this one last shot. Here we come, Cressiara."

The river journey took a while, and Kiera kept expecting a Shadow ambush, even if the dark creatures couldn't touch them in the water.

Eventually, the river began to branch off into tiny streams, and the sound of the ocean became audible. "I think this is it," Aaron murmured. Just as he said it, houses came into view. Tan, white, and sand-colored, they lined the beach. Platforms extended into the sea, and more houses were attached to them, over the silvery water. It was definitely the biggest village yet, with people bustling around, carrying baskets of seashells or swimming in the sea. Larger structures rose from the shores and were made of stone, shaped in a natural, flowy way to mimic natural processes of being shaped by water.

They left the river, which flowed into the ocean, and ducked behind a cluster of plants. They could hear faint conversation fading in and out. "Not enough fish to feed everyone... out of time."

"Ready to go?" Evannah asked quietly. Kiera and Aaron nodded.

They stood up and stepped out into the village. "Hello? Excuse me?" Kiera asked. Her words set off a terrified reaction as people dropped baskets, screamed, or took off running.

"Intruders!" a scared kid yelled. "They're here to KILL US!"

"Wait!" Kiera tried again. "We're here to help! We're the Wanderer, Warrior, and Whisperer!"

The kid stopped screaming. "Oh."

"We can't trust that!" A man shouted. "Anyone could be the enemy! Tie them up!"

"Stop! Hey, let go!" Kiera shouted as she kicked at the large group of villagers converging on her. But there were too many of them, and strong arms held her down as she was tightly wrapped in fishing nets.

A woman gave her a sympathetic look. "I'm sorry. Just a precaution."

Wrapped up like mummies, the trio was carried toward one of the large, elegant structures in the center of the village. Besides the capture, the ocean village had a different atmosphere from the forest villages, more peaceful and easygoing. But nobody could ignore the tension and fearful whispers, the glances at Watcher Peak and at Aaron, Kiera and Evannah. They yelled for release, but their pleas were ignored.

Eventually, they were dumped at the feet of a woman wearing turquoise robes with many long braids. Her headpiece was decorated in sea glass and shells. "We've been waiting," she said in a lilting voice. "I'm the Everdawn, Sorelle."

"Nice to meet you," Kiera grumbled from the ground. "Can someone untie us?"

Sorelle sighed, then addressed the Cressiarians. "I appreciate the precaution, but these really are the Wanderer, Warrior, and Whisperer. I've heard the news. Release them."

Kiera scrambled up, free once more, and decided to skip the introductions. "The Watcher's attacking tomorrow at dawn. The Island needs help."

Chapter 23

The discussion didn't take more than ten minutes. Sorelle had apparently had her army prepared since the Watcher's declaration the previous day. "I will meet with the other Everdawns," she insisted. "The time for village divisions has ended. We are united once more."

The army had gathered, made even larger by regular village citizens who wanted to fight. Aaron was ready to let them out of the village using his power, when, to his surprise, a lone warrior tripped over a rock and ended up falling outside the village border.

Sorelle stepped easily through, blinking in confusion. "The border is down? Why?"

"I don't know," Kiera responded. "Just get everyone out as quickly as possible."

There was a rush as the large crowd stampeded out of the village, eager to be beyond its limits once more. Aaron escorted Sorelle to the river to keep her safe.

Less than a minute after they had entered Crystal River, a scared chattering began, and warriors pointed up. Aaron tilted his head to see a giant image floating in the sky, exactly the same as the one the Watcher had created the day before.

"*Hello, once again*," the Watcher announced. He stood in his same thorn covered cloak, on his ledge by Heart Falls. "*My people. It is nearly over. We shall be forever protected. I have more power than the Island itself. More life. Come to me and pledge your undying loyalty, and I may spare you. We can move together into this glorious future. And if you need any convincing, behold.*"

The Watcher made a grand, sweeping gesture toward Heart Falls. It sparkled in the sun, sacred in its pureness.

He bent down, reaching out toward the waterfall, until he brushed it with the tips of his fingers. "He didn't get hurt," Aaron murmured. But where the Watcher touched Heart Falls, it began to turn black. The dark color raced down the waterfall until the whole thing was the color of shadows.

Aaron realized what was happening with just seconds to spare. "Get out!" he yelled, scrambling to leave the river. There were splashes as people jumped out just in time. The shadowy black shot through the river moments later.

Then there was a shrill, high-pitched ringing in the air as the Isle quivered under his feet. Aaron's hands shot to his ears as people screamed. "What's that?" he called.

Kiera took a horrified step back, staring at what was once the last untouched part of the Island, but was now a flowing mass of darkness. "I think it's the Island... it's dying."

Aaron nervously reached toward the darkened river and cautiously brushed it. It was cold, and the instant his hand connected with the water, it felt like the coldness was shooting up into his soul, like the world was darkening. If the Isle once represented life, this was death. He yanked his hand back. "I think it's dangerous," he warned.

Evannah was still staring at what used to be Heart Falls. The picture in the sky had faded away. "That's why the village borders fell. He was saving up his power to corrupt the falls."

"We don't have safe transport anymore," Aaron said in agitation.

"You have us," remarked a familiar voice. Night Star touched down behind them, followed by both the tiger and wolf Guardians.

"The Guardians," Sorelle breathed dreamily. "Maybe we have hope after all."

"Jannary sent us," Night Star explained. "I will come with you to Silverspire, and Burning Bright will lead the Cressiarians out of here."

"Sounds like a solid plan," Kiera responded.

"Why is that *thing* still here?" Night Star asked grumpily, tilting his head toward Moss, who was snuggled in Kiera's arms.

"Moss is our protection!" Kiera cried indignantly.

"Goodbye, Sorelle," Aaron changed the subject quickly and bowed his head in respect toward the leader. "We'll meet you soon."

Burning Bright, the tiger Guardian, began to speak to the Cressarians and escort them away, while Night Star nodded to the silvery wolf Guardian. "Sterling will come with us." They mounted Night Star's back, and took off while Sterling leapt through the air beside them. "Aaron," Night Star rumbled after a few minutes. "Can we trust you?"

"Of course!" Aaron was a little thrown by this question, and tightened his grip around Night Star's neck to ground himself. "I was just pretending, to get information."

"I suspected," Night Star responded gruffly. "I'll admit that I hoped this was the case. The Watcher really told you his plan?"

"Well, even though I was acting like I was on his side, I don't think he actually expected me to go anywhere," Aaron admitted. "Because of the prison and everything. And I think he really did want a confidante. I'm sure it made him so happy that his enemy had joined him."

"Clever," Night Star remarked. "I would've thought the Watcher was smarter than that. I suppose he's missed making plans with his sister. Your mother, so I've heard."

"Yes."

"Is that it?" Kiera interrupted, pointing toward several metallic twisting spires rising high into the sky. They were near the mountains now, or what remained of them. The village seemed to be positioned around a smaller waterfall flowing from on top of a cliff.

"That is," Sterling confirmed. "I'll warn them that you're coming," he added, swooping down.

"I thought the Eyes of the Island had the blood curse on them," Aaron told Night Star. "People live here?"

"These are the Mistveil Mountains," Night Star corrected. "The smaller mountain range. We're technically just outside the Eyes of the Island here." He stopped in the air, standing as easily as he would on the ground. After a few minutes, he pricked his ears. "Sterling says they're ready."

"You can hear him?" Kiera questioned, but her query went unanswered as Night Star dove toward the mountainous terrain, and the village came into sight. The waterfall, the silver spires that the village was named after, and the rising peaks behind them all contributed to a kind of mysterious beauty.

"Oh," Evannah said softly. "Look, it's so damaged." As they got closer, it was clear what she was talking about. Several of the twisting silver spires had collapsed, many houses were broken, and rocks and rubble lay all over the ground.

"Yeah I guess it hurt them when the mountains fell," Aaron stared sadly at the damage. He had seen this kind of destruction all over the Isle, but this was different. Now that he knew that he was from here, it all felt different. He had cared about this before, but now it was like the emotion had filled him up and was all that he could feel. This could have been his home.

Night Star landed gently, and they got off easily. Kiera set Moss down, and he bounced next to them. It was colder here.

Then an older man with a bearded face marked with scars stepped toward them, spear in hand. "You must be the Warrior," he addressed Aaron. "Fight me."

Aaron took a step back. He hadn't expected this. He shook his head. "I'm not going to fight you."

"You must prove your worth," the man told Aaron in a gruff voice. "Fight."

"I'm not fighting," Aaron said, louder, in a clear voice. "I will not fight you when we are on the same side. The only one we should be fighting is the enemy."

The man tossed his spear to the side. "Well said. I am Ravel Everdawn."

"Aaron," he shook the man's hand as Kiera and Evannah introduced themselves. "Was that... a test or something?"

"A measure of your character, yes." Ravel said calmly. "Why should we join you? The Guardian informed me that you weren't a traitor, but in any case. Why should I risk the lives of my people again?"

"Why?" Aaron hesitated for a moment. "Well, because... look around you. The Isle is nearly destroyed, and the Watcher is behind it. Tomorrow at dawn, he's going to wipe us all out. He's sucking the life out of the Island. If we have a chance to stop it, why wouldn't we take it?"

Ravel stopped for a moment. "Well expressed, once again." He turned to the broken buildings in his village. "Do you know how long I've been Everdawn?"

"Um..."

"Thirty-five years. I helped lead the first uprising against the Watcher. My wife was a Whisperer. I lost her that day."

"I'm sorry," Aaron murmured. After a moment, added boldly, "Don't you want to avenge her? Make him pay for what he's done?" He didn't know why he admitted this, but he did it anyway. "The Watcher's my uncle. He's my family. But I still want him gone."

Ravel turned back to him, new interest in his eyes. "I see. Are you sure about this attack tomorrow?"

"The Guardians validate his claim," Night Star growled.

"Guardians don't lie to the people of the Island," Ravel mused. "Very well. I knew this was coming. Come with me." He gestured to the trio. He began to walk through the village. "This was once a great library," he pointed at a crumbled ruin, "that held knowledge from many generations. We have more of course, but so much was lost."

Ravel continued walking. "I knew your mother, you know."

"Oh?" Evannah remarked curiously.

"When our lake flooded, she came to Silverspire and created barriers to save our books. She was a great woman. By helping you, I honor her memory."

"Thank you," Aaron whispered, swallowing against the dryness in his throat.

"Here we are," Ravel stopped at a stone building. "I notice the Wanderer has a weapon, but you two do not." He went inside the building and came out a few minutes later. "Your mother left these when she visited." He handed Aaron a sword. "A weapon for a true warrior." He gave Evannah a bow.

"Um," Evannah interjected. "The thing is, I'm not very good a—"

"No matter," Ravel interrupted. "It's a Whisperer's weapon—no arrows are needed, just pull back, and an arrow will appear and shoot in the direction you want."

"Wow," Evannah looked at her new weapon approvingly.

Aaron turned the sword over. He had seen a lot of weapons these past few days, but the fact that this had belonged to Aalliah made it seem like this one was meant to be his. This sword in his hand... it was either going to be the end of the Watcher, or himself.

Ravel was now talking with Night Star. "Shouldn't be too long a journey," he finished. "I should stay with the Silverspirans. But we'll meet you there."

Night Star nodded. "Very well. Sterling will stay with you."

"As you wish," Ravel agreed. "We will meet again, Warrior." He bowed his head in respect, which surprised Aaron a little. They had so quickly risen to something like leaders in this war. Inspiration, perhaps. Something out of legend.

Night Star turned to them. "The Silverspire army will be joining us after they make their journey."

"We should head back now, then," Kiera proposed, picking up Moss. "And prepare."

"For tomorrow," Evannah continued, a little apprehensively. It felt like something was tugging in Aaron's stomach. Fear. Real fear, for this was a real life or death situation. A real war, like he had never been in before.

They boarded Night Star and he began to fly back. "How are you feeling?" Night Star asked gruffly, after a while. "You've gathered an army. You don't have to fight, you know."

"No," Aaron argued. "We're the children of the intruders who started this. We finish it, or die trying." He grasped his sword a little tighter. But he meant it. He had never felt this strongly about anything before. He had a purpose. He felt alive, really alive, for the first time in his life.

"Let's kill some Shadows!" Kiera cheered, and Moss woofed in agreement.

As they passed the beach at Bluedawn Bay, on the way to Desperation, Aaron saw crowds of people. "Hey, looks like they've moved onto the Island." So Night Star landed on the beach.

Jannary and Khalisse came to meet them, followed by Neyric, Sorelle, and a woman Aaron recognized as Aelra, Neyric's second-in-command. "You've moved?" Evannah asked.

"We were running out of room," Khalisse grinned. "Our forces are growing pretty quickly. Thanks to you."

"How long do we have?" Aaron asked.

"Not much time," Sorelle shook her many long braids. "We've got to come up with a plan before then."

"Why don't we take the first shot?" Aaron suggested boldly. "Attack the Watcher first. Do it on *our* terms, so we have the advantage."

Jannary and Neyric shared a look. "That might work," Neyric remarked. He squeezed Jannary's hand. "We've been thinking. We're all Everdawns, but we need one leader for this. That should be you, Aaron."

"Me?" Aaron's eyes widened. "But—I don't know anything about war!"

"You're the Warrior," Khalisse assured. "You're a natural. This is what you were made for."

After a second's hesitation, Aaron agreed. "Okay. We'll need a plan." He bent down to draw a map in the wet sand. "We'll need to get close to the Eyes of the Island, but we can't get too close. Do we have any healers here? Let's assemble them." They planned for the rest of the afternoon. After a little while, Ravel and the Silverspiran forces joined them.

"Look at this," Sorelle said fondly. "All the villages united, at last. It's been so long."

"What was that you said when you came to Vahari?" Neyric asked. "Oh! We rise together, or not at all."

"We rise together, or not at all," Evannah echoed, her eyes brightening. "It's perfect."

That line quickly became their new motto, and throughout the day, it could be heard murmured from person to person, shouted during training, echoing across the Island.

Even ordinary people had joined the fight. The young story-teller Liora awkwardly brandished a dagger, as the chef Barbenne kept the masses fed. Tovan could be seen with Kiera, working hard together. And a fierce determination could be felt throughout the villagers. A desire to reclaim the Island. One last chance.

The hours passed too soon, and it was getting dark now, and as the sun set, people stopped to admire it, all too aware that it might be the last sunset they ever saw. Aaron spent as much time as he could with Kiera and Evannah, firmly resolving that he would die before letting anything happen to them. They would be waking up early the next morning to mobilize their fighters.

This was real. It was happening.

The moon rose. Aaron finally fell into a light sleep as the countdown began.

It was still dark when they rose. Aaron awoke immediately as soft footsteps crunched on the sand. It was Khalisse, coming to shake them awake. He sat up. Evannah and Kiera woke too, no traces of sleepiness evident. They were ready, and alert. "We leave in an hour," Khalisse whispered.

Evannah reached out to squeeze Aaron's hand. "Ready?" The pale, weak light washed over her face.

Aaron squeezed back. "Of course."

The Guardians had lined up on the beach, enormous in both size and power. They would fight until the end, Aaron knew.

He looked over at Kiera, who was shaking sand out of her hair. He had to tell her, just in case. So she would know if the worst happened to either of them.

"Aaron," Sorelle called a little while later. "They're asking for you. I think we need a speech."

"Oh," Aaron responded. "Um...okay. I can do that." He walked toward the gathered crowd, and Ravel thumped him on the back in encouragement.

He stepped into the softly lapping waves. "Hello, everyone." His voice wavered a little, and he cleared his throat. "Um. I know that you must be scared, and this is a lot to take, but... look how far you've come. You must have thought you'd never see the villages united again." There was a murmur of agreement. Emboldened, Aaron went on.

"I'm supposed to be your Warrior. When I heard this, I thought, that isn't me, I'm not a fighter. But now I understand that it's not about fighting or hurting anyone. It's about protecting, leading, and saving this island. Because the Isle of Whispers is one of a kind, and we need to protect it."

There was a moment of silence. "GO AARON!" Kairen's high pitched voice rang out, followed by a bout of laughter. Auri tried unsuccessfully to quiet her little brother.

"So," Aaron finished. "Let's go out there and fight our hardest. We have each other, and that will be our advantage. The Watcher tried to keep us apart but we're united once more. And we will win, no matter the cost." Cheers rang out as the sky began to lighten, and Aaron found himself swarmed with people. He stepped back to Kiera and Evannah.

"This is real," he whispered. "This is war." The politics of the Neomerican court could never compare to the real stakes of the battlefield.

"We're here," Kiera murmured. "We'll always be here. *Always.*"

"Remember what you said about the prophecy?" Evannah reminded him. "Nothing can take away our choice. Nothing can decide what kind of people we are."

"Yes," Aaron breathed. No prophecy would control him. Nobody would be dying today. And his two favorite people in the world were here, right by his side.

"We should leave," Night Star rumbled. As the forces assembled, warriors and citizens alike, Aaron could see just how vast their army was. Thousands, from every village, with the four Everdawns in front. Leading it all was the trio: Warrior, of the people. Wanderer, of the wilderness. And Whisperer, of the Whispers.

Their walk to their designated battleground was quick and quiet. Aaron's heart beat faster with every step.

They reached a while later at the lake at the foot of Watcher Peak, the lake where Evannah had been brought when she was kidnapped. Rays of early morning sun could now be seen in the sky. But since the mountains had fallen, gigantic structures of stone covered the ground, cracked boulders and pebbles where a mountain once stood.

"Perfect," Khalisse commented quietly. "The fallen mountains mean there's lots of caves and hiding spots for the healers and the injured. And a spot for fighters to rest."

"How many times must I tell you that you can't keep a secret from me?" a voice rang out from above, and Aaron's blood went cold. "It's tiresome, really."

There were screams and gasps as the Watcher floated down. His hood was off today, and malice shone in his green eyes as his thorns twisted. "After all, I own the Island. The Island *is* me."

A massive army of Shadows, creatures turned dark, and humans forced to work for the Watcher swarmed out from behind him, rivaling the forces of the villagers.

"Aaron! Lovely to see you again!" The Watcher smirked at him as he landed lightly. "I was quite annoyed that you left. But several people were punished for that."

He walked up to Aaron until they were face to face. Shadows flanked the Watcher, and Evannah and Kiera stepped up to his side. Behind the Watcher, his army, and behind Aaron was his. Dividing them was only a few inches.

It was only then that Aaron really understood. He had thought he was not worthy of being the Warrior, but it wasn't about who was the biggest and strongest. It was about who was willing to look evil in the face, and take them on. He was the Warrior by choice, not because of a prophecy.

The air crackled with tension as everyone was unnaturally still. "It's too late," the Watcher said soothingly. "I've almost completely reached full power. *Nothing* can stop that."

Aaron's brown eyes met the Watcher's green ones, gazing defiantly. He raised his sword. "Then you haven't met us."

Chapter 24

Standing at Aaron's side, Evannah watched as he thrust the sword toward the Watcher. It was eerie how similar they looked, face to face like that. At the same time, she shot a bolt of light at the Watcher's stomach.

The Watcher scoffed as he raised his hand, and the light rebounded. Aaron's sword slipped off an invisible shield, and he staggered backward.

"Alright, if that's how you want to do it," the Watcher smiled. "Come, my Shadows."

And within seconds, the silence and stillness broke, as thousands of Shadows rushed forward to attack the village army, who raised weapons in defense. The world exploded into cacophony and chaos.

Evannah's senses were immediately overwhelmed as Kiera was swallowed by the crowd. She twisted around. "Aaron?" she shouted, but her words were barely heard over the din.

Three Shadows glided toward her at the same time, and she raised her hands. Spears of light were shot at two of them, and she flicked her hand toward the third. It flew backward, knocked away by an invisible force.

Huh. I didn't know I could do that.

All this time, she had been holding back her abilities, a little scared and apprehensive. But what could she really do?

Blazing with fury, she flicked her hands toward the other approaching Shadows, and they were knocked to the ground. A spear of light to their throats finished them off, and they disappeared into clouds of darkness.

As far as the eye could see, there was fighting, weapons clashing against weapons, creeping Shadows converging on groups of people around the lake, and Everdawns directing various groups where to strike, and when to hide.

The villages were all contributing, with the Fenlithrians as high-mobility fighters, the Vaharians and Silverspirans fighting on the terrain, and the Cressiarans around and in the lake. They each had a distinct role, and together, they pushed the battle forward.

During all this, the sun rose higher in the sky, until light washed over the battlefield. It was too beautiful a day for such a tragic event.

"Kiera!" Evannah tried to call again. She thought she caught a glimpse of Kiera's golden-brown locks, but she disappeared into the crowd again. More Shadows appeared, and she shot off another round of spells.

Maybe it was time to try her bow. She lifted it out of its strap, testing its weight. Moving back to the outskirts of the battle, she pulled the bowstring back, aimed at a random Shadow, and released. An arrow appeared, flew through the air, and stabbed the Shadow in the side of its dark neck. "Yes!" Evannah cheered. Finally, she could shoot a bow and arrow.

Perhaps she could be more useful from a distance. Clutching her bow, Evannah sprinted away from the lake, toward the series of stone structures, hiding spots, and caves, checking over her shoulder every few seconds to make sure she was not being pursued.

Evannah entered through a cave, and found herself in a series of dark tunnels. She chose a path at random and continued along it, lighting up her hand for visibility. The sound of footsteps echoed through the dark stone maze. "Hello?" she called, then immediately regretted it. In here, you would never know who could be an enemy.

Reaching another fork in the caves, she picked the right path at random. Oh no, What if she ended up stuck in these tunnels forever with no way out? She tried not to think about it.

There! Light! She followed the path that sloped up, and exited the tunnels, emerging on the top layer of the gigantic stone structure. Down below, she could see the fighting figures.

Evannah clambered over to a pillar of rock, and crouched behind it, bringing out her bow. Squinting her eyes, she could make out the dark shapes of Shadows, along with other corrupted creatures. Identifying Neyric fighting with a particularly large Shadow, she pulled the bowstring and let the arrow fly. To her delight, even from such a far distance, it pierced the Shadow, which collapsed to the ground. "You're welcome!" Evannah whispered as Neyric looked around in confusion.

Down below, the Guardians were making the most damage, with blazing fires burning the enemy, huge claws ripping them to shreds, and large bodies shielding throngs of fighters. But the Watcher's army was making even more damage. Evannah saw many villagers lying on the ground, pierced with darkness. Even humans clashed with humans, as the Watcher's followers went head to head with the villagers.

Evannah spent the next while like that, crouched behind the rocks, taking out one Shadow at a time and watching out for her Island friends. She was making progress, but it was slow, and she wished she could be doing more. She was their only Whisperer! She could be doing so much more.

You have so much power...

At this point, she couldn't tell if the voices in her head were her own thoughts, or the Whispers. But the voices were right—why was she hiding up here when she should be in the midst of the fighting, making a change? She had powers that nobody else had. She was a *Whisperer*. It was time to own it.

What if?...

An idea came to her, unexpected, but intriguing. The Whispers were a force to be reckoned with, and Evannah got all her power from them. The Shadows were fallen Whispers themselves. What if she somehow involved the Whispers in the fight?

She needed a better view. She climbed over the rocks, until she reached the highest peak on the stone structure. Standing on top of it, wind whipping her hair, she could see even more clearly that the battle was not going well. Shadows took down multiple human fighters at a time, and dark creatures like the weasels converged on the Guardians to prevent them from doing much. They needed help.

She took a deep breath. She had never seen the Whispers before, but maybe she could somehow make them come to her. She closed her eyes, and reached out to the voices. *Come to me.* The voices began to get louder, and she could feel the Whispers' energy. *Come to me.*

When Evannah opened her eyes, five translucent figures came into focus. They had a vaguely humanoid shape, and shimmered in different colors, unlike anything she had ever seen. "Whispers," she instructed. "Can you help the Island?" She pointed toward the battle below.

Of course. The Whispers swooped off to join the battle, where they began attacking Shadows with streaks of light.

I am the only Whisperer, Evannah thought again. *The only connection these ancient spirits have to the real world.*

So why don't I bring them into the real world?

She closed her eyes again, feeling the cool air on her skin. She could sense the Whispers, but if she really concentrated, she could sense them spread across the Island. *Come here, Whispers,* she called again mentally.

This would require the biggest spell she had ever cast. Could she do it? Evannah rubbed her arms nervously. Was she really ready to use the power she had never wanted?

No. She was done being controlled, first by the court, then by her own self-doubt. She was done with limits being set.

I am Evannah Farrah, Whisperer. "I am Evannah Farrah, Whisperer," she repeated it out loud in determination.

And nothing will stop me.

Evannah raised her arms to the sky and was immediately consumed in a rush of power and energy that she had never felt before. The world turned into a blaze of light as she felt her feet leave the ground.

Heads turned in her direction as a shock wave rippled over the Island. Then her feet touched the ground again, and she twisted her head from side to side. *Did it work?*

Slowly, the translucent, shimmering shapes began to appear across the lake and clearing, more and more until there were hundreds of the opalescent and ethereal beings Some were humanoid, but others were shaped like animals or creatures. Some didn't have a defined shape and drifted around as formless whisps.

There were murmurs of surprise and astonishment as the Whispers came into view. The people could see them. It had worked.

Now they had an advantage. Now, Evannah was a real Whisperer.

Twelve. That was Kiera's count so far of Shadows she had taken down. Not bad, considering that they were double her height and had exponentially more power. But she had the Blade of the Wild. And her own passion. It was very satisfying to flick the sword in their direction and watch them get bound by roots rising from the ground.

Then, to her astonishment, translucent spirit-like creatures started to appear, majestic and ethereal among the bloody battle. Were those Whispers? Kiera saw Evannah, on the top of the stone structure, radiating light with Whispers floating around her. "Yes, Evah!" she cheered, and was followed by many villagers. It was an amazing show of power, probably one of the biggest spells the Islanders had ever seen.

The battle had been going on for *so long* already, and she was exhausted. Even though it had only been an hour or two, it wasn't as if she could take breaks when she needed them.

There *were* no breaks in war.

The Watcher himself was nowhere to be seen. That coward was probably letting his army fight for him. But the appearance of the Whispers had given them the edge that they desperately needed. Whispers swarmed to protect villagers, aid Guardians, and fill the battlefield with their radiant magical glow.

"Help!" came a cry from further off. Kiera turned to see the chef Barbenne, along with Liora, cornered by two Shadows.

Nobody was killing Kiera's favorite chef on *her* watch. She bolted over immediately, sword in hand. "Hey!" she called at the two Shadows. They elegantly turned their heads around. Kiera spun the sword, whacking one in the head and stabbing another. "Run!" she instructed, and Barbenne and Liora obliged. With another flick of her sword, a nearby tree reached out with its branches, wrapped them around the Shadows, and snapped them back so that they went flying.

"Thanks!" Barbenne called.

Running further along, exhausted and panting, Kiera skidded to a stop near some bent-over Shadows. She stabbed them neatly through the stomachs, then bent to see what they were examining.

She took a step back. The grass and dirt were dark with spilled blood as three villagers lay on the ground, eyes wide and unblinking, gashes torn in their body. No. She didn't know them personally, but they had given their lives for the cause. Who else would, before the day was over?

"Kiera!" a familiar voice resounded. It was Tovan. A pack of dark wolves with silky fur and red eyes was creeping toward him, baring their sharp teeth.

"Tovan!" she cried back, springing into action to run toward him. But he was far, and the wolves were getting closer and closer. *Come on...*

Then the wolves sprang, covering Tovan with a mass of black fur and snapping teeth. The grass was stained red. "NO!" Kiera screamed. Finally, she reached, and with a surge of fury, hit a wolf hard with the sword and slashed at another. They snapped at her, but backed off. She crouched down next to Tovan.

He was still breathing, but barely. "Kiera," he shuddered softly.

"I'm sorry, I'm sorry," Kiera cried. Her eyes grew unfocused, she couldn't see anything.

"No. Don't worry about me. I'm an old man, I knew I would meet my end in this war. I'm not the warrior I used to be. I expected it. It's not your fault. Just...continue being yourself. You are such a special person." He reached up and grasped her hand weakly. "I will see you again someday."

Then his eyes closed and he went still. "No," Kiera sobbed. In just a few days, Tovan had quickly become the father figure that she had never truly had before. She had loved him. And now he was gone.

But he wouldn't have wanted her to waste her time in battle crying over him. He would have wanted her to put her all into fighting. So that was what she was going to do. It seemed that Tovan's final words had freed her from the suffocating grief she would have felt. She stood up, and dragged Tovan's body to a semi-sheltered spot so it wouldn't be ravaged.

She took a deep breath to stop the tears. "Goodbye, Tovan," she murmured. "You will be remembered." And that was all she had to say. She wasn't going to be held down with grief. Fueled by Tovan's memory, she was going to continue the fight.

The dark wolves who had backed away had grown in number, and began to approach her again. She wiped away her tears and picked up her sword again, which felt heavier than ever. Eight wolves now snarled at her, more than she could easily take on.

The first one leapt at her, springing through the air, red eyes fixed on her, and she swung her sword at it, sending it flying backwards. But its pack was on her, and the next one was ready, dragging its claws down Kiera's back. She bit her tongue to suppress a scream of pain as she shook it off.

Then the next one sprang, but a large mass of blue fur slid in the way, easily blocking the dark wolf. It was Moss, back to his gigantic wolf form, and one growl sent the wolf running away and whimpering. "Moss!" cried Kiera. "Thanks!" She patted his large golden antlers.

Then another arm was there, sword slicing through the air, and Kiera wasn't alone anymore. "There you are, Aaron! What took you so long?"

"Busy fighting Shadows," he retorted. "Get away, creepy wolf...things," he grunted while slashing at them. Between Moss, Kiera, and Aaron, the wolves quickly decided they had had enough and ran in the other direction. "Kiera, is that Tovan?" Kiera nodded, unable to find the words. "I'm so sorry."

"No, more Shadows," Kiera groaned, seeing three of the dark humanoid figures approach them, reaching out their spidery fingers. "Remember when we found them terrifying? Now they're the easiest opponent."

The Shadows creeped closer, but before they reached Aaron and Kiera, they glided closer to each other, until they merged into a single, gigantic Shadow, towering at least nine to ten feet into the sky. Aaron let out a yelp. "Shoot! It's huge!"

Nearby, more Shadows were combining, until three of the large Shadows stalked Kiera and Aaron. "Run?" Kiera asked.

"Run," Aaron confirmed. Hand in hand, they took off toward the stone structures. Heart beating fast, Kiera risked a quick look over her shoulder, and immediately regretted it when she caught a glimpse of the dark monster pursuing them.

"Faster," she urged. "Go to the tunnels, they're too tall to fit!"

"Over there," Aaron pointed to an entrance, literally pulling her in. The comforting darkness of the caves enveloped them. "I think we're safe." He peered out at the three giant Shadows.

"Oh no, they split back into normal Shadows. Now there's nine of them!"

"Are they coming for us?" Kiera tightened her grip on Aaron's hand.

"Yes."

"Then let's go!" Kiera yanked Aaron forward so fast she nearly tore his shoulder. "We can probably lose them somewhere here."

"I can't see anything!"

"I can't either, just pick a direction!" Kiera retorted. "Where's Evannah and her glowing hand when you need her? Ouch!" she complained as she ran straight into a wall.

"Whisper!" Aaron pointed to the glowing, opalescent wisp casting a faint light around the tunnels. "It has light, follow it. Are the Shadows still on us?"

Kiera looked backwards. In the complete darkness, she could sort of see moving figures, but it was hard to tell. "I think so. Let's keep going." They ran on, taking turns at random, guided by only the pale light of the Whisper, until they reached a path sloping up.

"I think this is the way out," Aaron panted in fatigue.

Kiera looked around. "Pretty sure we finally lost them." They climbed out on top of the stone structure, not very far from where they had last seen Evannah. Kiera squinted at the sudden brightness. And what she saw made her stomach drop. "Oh no. Aaron, look!"

In the middle of the lake, Shadows were combining at a rapid pace, growing bigger and bigger, dark bodies lengthening and increasing in power. Soon, the most colossal Shadow Kiera had ever seen stood in the lake, at least forty or fifty feet tall.

"It's a Shadow Giant," Aaron gaped, horrorstruck. "It's huge!"

The head of the Shadow Giant easily passed the top of the large stone structure. It took a step out of the lake, spilling large quantities of water over the ground and upheaving the lake.

The battle was now in even more chaos. The Shadow Giant easily swiped at groups of villagers and sent them flying. As Whispers pelted it with spells, it swatted them off as easily as insects, while it let out a roar that shook the earth. Two Guardians flew at its head, but the Shadow Giant swung at them with a ferocity that knocked them right out of the sky.

Then the Shadow Giant turned slowly to look at Aaron and Kiera, two tiny little figures compared to itself, and reached an arm the size of a large tree toward them.

Kiera gasped. "Go back down!" She grabbed Aaron's arm again and pulled him back into the narrow tunnels right as dark fingers would have knocked them off the remnants of the fallen mountain. "That was close."

"How are we supposed to defeat that thing?" Aaron groaned. "This is really bad."

"I guess it's our turn to go help," Kiera suggested. "Let's find a way out of here, and hope those Shadows aren't around."

They ran back into the caves, trying to find some bit of light to guide them. "I see light," Kiera said after a minute or two as the world grew a bit brighter. They reached some sort of nook in the caves that had a chunk of stone missing in the wall like a window, so they had a clear view outside. Kiera peered through it. "Yikes." The Shadow Giant was still rampaging around, roaring and stomping. "We need to go out there."

It was actually quite pretty in the nook. The rays of sun illuminated the walls and made them glimmer in the brightness, and specks of light drifted around. "Wait," Aaron said hesitantly. He had stopped by the window to the outside.

"What is it?" Kiera tilted her head in confusion.

Aaron paused for a few more seconds. "I don't know... if we're going to make it back from this. So I have to tell you now."

"Don't talk like that, Aaron!" Kiera scolded. Then curiosity got the better of her. "Wait... is this what you were hiding earlier?"

Aaron nodded, face paling. "Back in Neomerica, right before we left, my dad told me... he told me I would be engaged to Lady Janessa as soon as I returned. And we'd have to get married by summer."

It hit like a blow. Everything inside her went cold, and the only word she could force out her stiff lips was, "Oh." She didn't know what this feeling was: the feeling like something precious had been torn from her, but was painfully still there.

Aaron took a deep, shuddering breath, turning to look outside. "But I didn't want one of us to, well... I didn't want to leave this world without telling you."

Kiera swallowed, then eventually, quietly asked. "Why?"

"Because...," Aaron turned back to meet Kiera's gaze, his bright eyes raw and unguarded. "Because the only one I want to be with is you."

Kiera froze. But as quickly as the ice had spread over her body, it melted, leaving behind a tingling feeling of apprehension. She stepped closer to Aaron, and boldly uttered, "I... I've always felt the same way."

She brushed Aaron's hand gently in the silence. Kiera had felt for Aaron for a long time now, but had always ignored the feelings in order to preserve their close friendship.

A faint smile appeared on Aaron's face, soft in the glow. "I've wanted this for a long time now."

"Then if we survive this," Kiera leaned a little closer. "Let's make it happen."

Outside, the Shadow Giant roared and stomped in the lake, and Aaron took Kiera's hand in his, as a tidal wave of destruction swept across the battlefield.

Chapter 25

Hand in hand, Aaron and Kiera left the caves together. They had matching smiles, and despite being in the middle of the most dangerous fight of their lives, Aaron felt a warmth bubbling inside him. As long as he and Kiera were together, everything would be just fine.

"AARON!" Night Star roared, speeding through the air and dodging a swipe from the immense hand of the Shadow Giant. "QUIT SKIPPING AND START FIGHTING!"

Aaron quickly dropped Kiera's hand while they both began blushing furiously. Maybe now wasn't the time. "Coming!"

"WATCH OUT!" Kiera dived to the side, trying to pull Aaron with her but losing her grip. Aaron looked up to see the Shadow Giant's foot mere inches from his head, but a sudden force sent him flying to the side, landing on the wet grass and barely avoiding death by crushing.

Evannah held up her glowing hand and smirked. "What would you do without me keeping you alive?"

Aaron stumbled back up, brushing at his bruised knees. "How do we kill this thing?"

"We have to get it to break into the smaller Shadows again!" Kiera remarked. "Look, the Watcher's controlling it." They followed her look to where the Watcher was floating not too far from the Shadow Giant, influencing its movement with little flicks of his hands.

"If we could make it fall, somehow, that might work," Evannah suggested thoughtfully. "It's so big that a fall would either kill it or break it into little Shadows."

"That could work," Night Star growled, landing next to them. "How exactly are you going to knock it over without hurting anyone?"

Evannah addressed Aaron. "Aaron, you and Kiera could make it fall, and I'll stay on the ground to float anyone in the line of danger away."

"Yes," Aaron confirmed. "Night Star, do you think all the Guardians attacking at the same time would knock the Giant over?"

"Perhaps," Night Star rumbled, glancing at the rioting Shadow Giant. "But if it sees us coming, it can easily stop us."

"So we'll distract it," Kiera interjected confidently. "Right Aaron?"

"Right," he said unsurely.

"Alright," Night Star pronounced, lifting his head boldly. "I'll round up the Guardians. Evannah, you stay here. You two, cause a distraction. Got it?"

"Got it," Kiera gave him a thumbs-up that quickly died after another ground-shaking roar from the Giant. Night Star flew off.

"Evannah," Kiera looked at her friend. "Could we borrow your bow?"

"Why?" Evannah handed it over, brows knit together in confusion.

"If we shoot at the Watcher, that might distract him. And he's controlling the Shadow Giant," Kiera explained.

"That's brilliant!" Aaron exclaimed.

"Be careful," Evannah told them. "I'll meet you after."

"Watcher's over there," Aaron pointed out. "Come on." They ran over the grass, wet from the flooded lake, toward the shape of the Watcher in the sky, avoiding ongoing skirmishes between the army. The Guardians were beginning to gather in a cluster on the opposite side of the lake.

"Hiding spot," Kiera gestured to a little cluster of trees. From here, they could see the Watcher's eyes half-closed in concentration as he waved his arms like a conductor leading a grand symphony.

They hid behind the trees. Kiera handed him the bow. "All yours."

"Mine?" Aaron asked. "Shouldn't it be you?"

"You're the one who's supposed to be intuitive at fighting," Kiera argued. "Take it."

After a few moments, a Whisper shaped like a fox landed in front of them. "They're ready," it murmured in a soft, melodious voice, then disappeared.

"I guess that's our cue." Aaron pulled back the bowstring, aimed as best he could, and released. The magically guided arrow launched itself at the Watcher's arm, but rebounded in the air an inch away from hitting his skin. "Watch it!" Aaron ducked to the side as the arrow shot past them.

"Ugh," Kiera groaned. "He has some kind of protection spell. Of *course*." The Watcher, still concentrated, hadn't even realized anything had happened. Kiera gave him a sly look. "How many arrows can that bow shoot?"

Aaron began pulling the bow back and releasing at a rapid speed. The multitude of arrows that appeared flew at the Watcher and rebounded.

Then the Watcher's eyes opened completely.

"He noticed!" Kiera whisper-shouted. "Keep going!"

Aaron doubled the pace and shot a barrage of arrows. The Watcher dropped his hands in annoyance, sighed, and turned in their direction. With a casual flick of his hand, he sent a shockwave rippling toward them.

"Aar—" Kiera started, but the wave of energy threw them backwards. The world became a blur of color and Aaron's stomach dropped in a sickening way before he crashed to the ground, dazed.

Head spinning, he sat up to look for Kiera, who had landed next to him. "Come," he urged. "We should get away from him."

"Did the distraction work?" Kiera mumbled.

"Let's see." They got up, a little wobbly and unsteady, but mostly fine, running out of the trees into the large lake clearing.

In the one second the Watcher had been distracted, the Shadow Giant paused. Just one second. But it was enough.

Together, the Guardians, in blurs of gold and silver, indigo, and many more, blazing with fire, glimmering with ice, and dotted with stars flew at the Shadow Giant's chest. The ancient, powerful creatures blasted the Giant with everything they had.

There was a second's pause as the Giant teetered. Then it began to topple.

"IT WORKED!" Aaron cried as they ran back in the direction of the caves.

As the Shadow Giant fell, it swiped at the air, hitting a Guardian who just happened to be in the wrong place and sending it flying. A black blur studded with dots of light. Night Star was falling.

Night Star twisted slowly in the air, trying to regain his power of flight, but he had been hit with too much force. He couldn't do anything. Within seconds, he slammed into the ground with such force that Aaron felt a vibration, and a small crater was carved out into the ground.

"Oh no," Kiera gasped, the color draining from her cheeks.

The Shadow Giant continued falling, as battling humans screamed and attempted to outrun the fall of its gigantic body. But Evannah was there, to levitate the people in trouble away from the Giant. Eventually, it fell with such a thunderous impact that several trees fell over.

Upon falling, it broke down into hundreds of regular sized Shadows, many of which disappeared into darkness from the fall. Aaron and Kiera cheered, and jogged to reunite with Evannah.

She looked at them anxiously. "Did you see what happened to Night Star?"

Aaron nodded gravely. "Is he... alive?"

"Let's go check." They walked to the little crater that Night Star's impact had made. Inside, Night Star lay on his side, his dark pelt more of a shade of gray, completely still. Aaron touched a hand to his fur. No movement, and it was cold.

He met Evannah and Kiera's hopeful looks, and shook his head. Kiera blinked away tears, and Evannah's eyes became cloudy.

"I wish we could take his body from here," Evannah cried. "He deserves a proper burial. But he's too big."

"We'll come back," Kiera touched her arm in reassurance. "He'll get a hero's goodbye."

Aaron mentally recited a final goodbye to Night Star, the cat who had first brought them to Fenlithra, guided them, protected them. Now he had given up his life.

"Evannah! Aaron! Kiera!" It was Sorelle, calling them from a distance, near the entrance to the caves. "Come!"

"What happened?" Aaron asked when they reached.

"Nothing," Sorelle reassured them. "Jannary wanted you three in for a break. You look exhausted. The healers are set up inside, and there's nourishment as well."

"But—" Aaron began.

The dreamy leader shushed him. "I know you want to fight. But if you're going to do it properly, you need to rest. So go. *Now.*" They reluctantly stepped into the entrance to the caves. Sorelle smiled. "Take the first two right turns!"

Two turns right through the narrow tunnels led them to a large open cave space, big enough to fit several dozen people. Several of the wounded lay on the floor as they were tended to, and battered-looking fighters sat to rest, drink water, or eat something, their weapons thrown into a haphazard line against the walls.

Jannary caught their eye and beckoned them over. "Ah, you three came! Perfect." She was joined by Ihira and Aelra. "Come, take a break."

"I think we're fine," Evannah tried, but Jannary shook her head.

"The battle is slowing down for now anyway," Jannary argued. "A good amount of the Watcher's forces have retreated to regain their energy. So it's a good time for us too."

"Shadows need rest?" Kiera questioned.

"I think the Watcher is strategizing," Jannary explained. "His Shadow Giant idea didn't quite work out. But their main advantage is that we're human. They can easily tire us out. So we need to recharge while we still can. Come, we have food."

A man handed them wrapped leaves that contained water, which soothed Aaron's parched throat. They were each handed a few pieces of fruit by Barbenne.

"The healers will take care of you." Aelra led them to the line of pale-green robed villagers.

"You should save it for the people who need it," Aaron attempted to protest as one of the healers handed him a drink.

"You need to stay alive," Aelra narrowed her eyes sternly. "Quit being noble." Aaron gave up and drank the medicine, which tingled through him, clearing his head and making him feel rejuvenated. It did help.

"And you can see outside," Ihiria added, showing them a couple of stone chunks of the wall that had fallen out. Aaron peered out, seeing that the battle had actually slowed down, with only about half of the forces actively fighting.

"Are they okay?" Evannah asked in concern, looking at the wounded.

"Some of them," Jannary responded honestly. "The Whispers have been helping a lot. When Evannah summoned them, many came here and are helping to heal." For a moment, they all watched an opalescent, ghostly-shaped Whisper hovering above a wounded man, the gash in his leg slowly knitting itself back together.

"That was amazing, Evannah, by the way," Jannary added. "Spectacular magic. I've only heard of spells like that in the books."

Evannah blushed. "Thank you."

About an hour passed by. It was past noon now, and various fighters came inside to take breaks, including Khalisse and Ravel. They swapped out in groups to allow everyone to have the chance to rest. Aaron sat with Evannah and Kiera, resting his sore muscles.

"What happened to the Watcher?" Evannah murmured finally. "To make him like this. I know he lost his sister, but what else? He's gone mad."

"He was always ambitious, I think," Aaron explained. "Remember in that story, our mother was the one holding him back. And when she left, he lost it. Then when he kept taking power from the Isle it corrupted him."

"The vines he has," Kiera added. "Those are the ones that attacked us. And his eyes... it's like he's not human anymore."

"I think we have to kill him," Evannah remarked, and Aaron gave her an alarmed look. "I know," she continued. "I don't like it. He *is* our uncle. But he's past the point of return, and if we want the Isle restored, if that's even possible, doesn't he have to die?"

"Yes, I suppose," Aaron agreed reluctantly. "For the greater good."

"Who's that?" Khalisse asked suddenly, peering outside. "Why are they so small? Wait a minute. Is that..."

Aaron quickly looked outside too. Stolen weapon in hand, a tiny shape was running across the battlefield.

"Kairen," Aaron groaned.

"I need to get him." Khalisse immediately sprang to her feet.

"No." Evannah gently helped her sit again. "We've been here for a while. It's our turn."

"Yeah, we got this," Kiera insisted quickly. "Come on Aaron. This is your fault."

"What?" Aaron threw his hands up in protest. "How?"

"The kid worships you!" Kiera retorted. "Of course when he knew you were fighting he wanted to come join. So now we have to rescue him. Thanks a lot." She nudged his arm playfully.

Evannah shook her head at both of them. She had definitely missed *something* while summoning the Whispers.

They left the caves. "There's Auri," Aaron pointed out. Auri was frantically searching, looking around in distress.

"Thank goodness," she cried, when they approached. Her golden-streaked hair was in disarray and her normally cheerful face was flushed and upset. "I need help. It's Kairen, he—"

"Sneaked out into the war," Kiera finished. "Don't worry, we saw him."

"We're coming to get him right now," Evannah reassured her. "Did you see where he went?"

Auri shook her head miserably. "He escaped from our little camp when I went to help catch fish. I knew immediately where he'd gone. He'd been talking about fighting for the past three days." She rubbed her eyes. "It's my fault. I'm all he has." She pointed to a small crowd of fighters. "I tried to chase him but I was too far behind. I saw him last over there."

"We'll get him," Aaron told her. "You need to stay safe. Take two rights in that cave and you'll get to a safe area."

"Can't I help?" Auri pleaded.

Evannah shook her head. "It's better if you stay here. It's dangerous out there." That was obviously the wrong thing to say, because Auri burst into tears. Kiera gave her a look as Aaron ushered Auri toward the caves.

Evannah looked in the direction that Kairen had run. It was a crowd populated with human fighters, the Watcher's humans against their own. If Kairen was somewhere in there, he wouldn't last very long.

When Aaron rejoined them, they decided to split up. "I'll go there," Evannah pointed to the crowd. "Kiera you go to the opposite side of the lake and Aaron, the right shore."

"Send a message with a Whisper if you found him or need help," Aaron suggested.

"Good idea. Let's find this kid as fast as we can," Kiera responded. They ran in their directions.

"Kairen?" Evannah shouted, getting closer. "Come back! Auri is worried sick! Kai-aah!" Her calls were cut off by a swipe of a spear that she jumped back and missed by inches.

Two of the Watcher's human warriors were coming toward her with their weapons. But they were no match for Evannah, who shot a blast of fire at them that made them dive out of the way.

She caught a glimpse of a little shape further in the crowd. *Kairen!* If he didn't get killed in this mess, Auri and Evannah herself were going to kill him. "KAIREN!" she yelled again, but her shouts disappeared in the din.

She parted the crowd with a flick of her hand, and warriors went flying every which way, including some of their villagers. "Sorry!" she tried, but eventually just ran through her newfound space.

There was a flash of light on metal, a dagger raised, about to strike... *Kairen!* Putting on a burst of speed, Evannah tackled the child, the dagger just milliseconds from striking him.

The Watcher's warrior who had been about to stab Kairen advanced on them both. "Stop!" Evannah commanded. "He's just a child!"

"He's armed," the warrior growled, motioning to Kairen's little sword, undoubtedly stolen.

"Do you think he can use it?" Evannah fumed. "You disgust me." With a little help from the Whispers, the warrior was thrown into the trees.

"Evannah!" Kairen cried happily. "You saved me!"

Evannah bent down to check him. Apart from a few small cuts, he seemed unharmed. "Are you okay?" she asked. He nodded. "Good. Now I'm taking you back to Auri, and that's where you're going to say. What were you thinking?"

"I wanted to fight!" Kairen perked up. Then he hung his head. "But everyone's so much bigger and I'm not good at it."

"When you're older," Evannah said sternly, trying very hard to be patient. This was why she was never going to have kids. "Come on now." She sent a quick message through a Whisper to Kiera and Aaron, and began leading Kairen back.

Then Kairen stopped in his tracks. "WATCHER!" he screamed.

"We know he's here, come on," Evannah groaned while tugging his arm.

"No, he's *right there!*" Kairen insisted, pointing. A few yards away, the Watcher hovered in midair, his dark robes fluttering around him.

And he was looking right at them.

"Well START MOVING!" Evannah shouted at the child, dragging him along. The ground began to rumble. *Not good.*

"Yikes!" Kairen exclaimed.

A chasm began to open up, like at the battle at the Trail of Truth, shooting through the ground like a snake. And it was headed right for them. "RUN!" Evannah yelled, and a terrified Kairen started moving immediately. Evannah held his hand, pulling him as they picked up speed, hearts in their throats, trying to outrun the chasm rumbling toward them.

The Watcher smiled, gazing at two annoyances that would soon be no more.

No matter the distance they ran, the lengthening chasm caught up, eating away the ground in its path and leaving gaping holes so deep the bottom couldn't be seen.

Then Evannah felt a great weight on her left side that brought her to her knees. "HELP!" Kairen screamed, legs dangling. The cracks had caught up to him, and now Evannah was the only thing holding them up. There was less than a second to process this.

Then the chasm caught Evannah and they both began falling into the endless abyss.

The Watcher turned away, satisfied.

"AAAAH!" Kairen gave a bloodcurling shriek in Evannah's ear as they plummeted into darkness.

Evannah wrapped her arms around him in midair, and they fell together. Could she float them out? She had made objects levitate before, but never people. She closed her eyes, concentrating hard.

Then they stopped in midair.

"—AHHHH… oh," Kairen trailed off. "We're floating!"

Before Evannah could lose focus, she tightened her grip around Kairen, looked upward, and they shot out of the chasm, so fast that her eyes began to water. They rocketed through the sky until Evannah slowed them down, and they gradually came to a stop somewhere near where the mountain peaks used to be.

"We're so high!" Kairen exclaimed, looking down at the ant-sized warriors near the little lake. Wind blasted their cheeks. "Let's fly some more!"

"Time to go back," Evannah told him firmly, and they began to lower back to the ground, lightly touching down near the caverns. She led him to a panicked Auri.

"Here he is." Evannah handed off Kairen to Auri as Aaron and Kiera joined them.

"Thank you," Auri wrapped Evannah in a hug that she awkwardly received. "I thought you were both gone for sure when you fell! But you saved him! I can never repay you. As for you, Kai... you're grounded for the rest of eternity." Kairen began arguing as Auri took him inside the tunnels where they would be sheltering for however long the battle continued.

"Wow," Aaron breathed. "You can fly?"

Evannah shrugged shyly. "I didn't know either."

"That was amazing!" Kiera cheered. "We both saw the whole flight."

"You make an incredible Whisperer," Aaron told her.

Evannah smiled. In a way, she felt as though she was stepping into her mother's old role as the protector-Whisperer of the Isle.

"Oh no," Aaron remarked suddenly. He pointed to a dark mass on the far side of the lake. "It looks like they're gathering again."

"Is it just me, or are there even more?" Kiera groaned. It definitely looked like they had grown in number.

The Shadows, dark creatures, and human army began marching toward them. "Aaron." Evannah shoved him. "Go get backup."

Her eyes glanced toward Night Star's place of death. It seemed empty. No, who had destroyed his body?

"On it," Aaron dashed into the tunnels to bring the villagers back to the fight.

"Ready?" Evannah looked to her best friend, lighting up her hand in preparation.

"Always," Kiera grinned, pulling out her sword.

The first fighters, human ones, approached them. But Evannah and Kiera were prepared. With the power of the Blade of the Wild, vines burst from the ground and bound the warriors on the right side, while Evannah shot fire at the warriors on the left side, taking down the front lines in moments.

That was when Aaron arrived, and it seemed like he had brought the entirety of the Island army. The lull in the fight was quickly forgotten as it resumed with double the passion and fury than before.

As Evannah got into a rhythm, time passed in a blur of fighting and dodging and casting spells. She couldn't see the Watcher anymore, but knew he had to be around. They needed to get to him soon. Who knew how long this would go on otherwise? She had a last-ditch attempt plan to take the Watcher out of the picture, but it would be dangerous. So if she could avoid that, it would be better.

But there are things more important than yourself, her mind sang to her. *Saving the Isle, for one. And everyone and everything on it.*

Yes, if this just resulted in more death, she would need to use her plan soon. It was clear that they were losing. For every member of the Watcher's army taken down, many of the Island army were lost.

There was a tap on her shoulder, and she whirled around, ready to attack. But it was just Aaron. "Oh!" she gasped. "You scared me!"

"Have you seen Kiera?" Aaron questioned quickly.

"She was just here." Evannah looked around. "She can't be far."

"Evannah." Aaron looked at her seriously. "It's been an hour!"

"What?"

"Since we started fighting again!" Aaron explained. "And I haven't seen her since then. And we're getting beaten pretty badly."

He was right. Despite their best efforts, and the passion of the Island army, Shadows didn't tire. Humans did. And the Watcher was nearly at the peak of his power, occasionally deigning to enter the battle himself, kill a few dozen, and leave.

"Oh." Evannah turned to a point in the distance. "Found her."

Chapter 26

"ATTACK!" Kiera yelled as Moss galloped onto the battle-field. Kiera, on his back, clutched his golden antlers and leaned forward while releasing her battle cry.

Around Moss's racing paws, hundreds of the surviving Island creatures scurried, slithering scales and furry paws in colors of the rainbow, and bright feathers. They ranged in size from tiny purple mice to huge wild cats, growling and roaring as they heeded the call to protect their home.

After all, in all their battle planning, they had left out one very important part of the Isle of Whispers: the creatures. And once Kiera had sent out a summons through the Isle, they had listened. This was the reinforcement that the Island army desperately needed. Now, maybe they would have a chance.

"Going somewhere without me?" asked a melodious voice as a gigantic white snake head swooped into view.

"Serpent of Song?" Kiera remarked incredulously. "I thought you don't fight!"

"I don't," the great snake replied, slithering over the ground elegantly. "But there would be no music if the Isle were gone. And also I would likely be dead." He flicked his long tongue in annoyance. "So I suppose I will join my fellow Guardians, just this once."

"That's very much appreciated." Kiera smiled faintly. She turned back to her animal army. "GET THEM!"

Heading the animals were Kiera's top choice for attackers: the quangles. The mischievous feathered creatures were bouncing excitedly. At Kiera's command, they swarmed the Watcher's human army, baring their teeth, although that didn't really make them look any tougher. Warriors cried out as they disappeared under a mass of chubby bodies and feathers. Even Shadows recoiled a bit as the naughty animals snapped at their ankles.

Then came the rest of the army. The bigger animals pounced, ripping at Shadows with their teeth, while the smaller animals teamed up to bring down the human warriors. The Serpent of Song seemed to be enjoying himself, humming a tune while whacking around fighters with his large tail.

"Come on, Moss!" Kiera urged as Moss went on a rampage through the battlefield, trampling dark creatures and clawing at Shadows, while Kiera hung on tightly to his antlers. When Moss was satisfied, she steered him back around toward Evannah and Aaron, where he slowed to a stop.

Aaron's jaw dropped. "Where did all these animals come from?"

"They were hiding," Kiera explained as she dismounted Moss. "When I called, they all showed up to help."

Evannah gazed at the pack of animals viciously tearing through the Watcher's army. "That was brilliant. It definitely leveled the playing field."

"They're citizens of the Island too." Kiera murmured as her voice trembled. "At least they're holding their own." She watched as a group of quangles picked up a warrior, flew him into the sky, then dropped him. He flailed and screamed before landing as the quangles moved on to the next warrior.

"We have an edge now," Evannah continued tightly. "But this is going to keep going on if we don't get to the Watcher. We're doing exactly what he wants—he wants to wipe us all out so he can reach full power easily. All our efforts will be for nothing if the Isle falls—no matter how many we save right now."

"Aaron," Kiera asked, "what about binding his powers?"

"I've tried," Aaron admitted, breathless. "It—it didn't work. He's too strong and there's too many Shadows—"

Kiera's breath tightened. "Oh. It's okay, we'll figure out another way."

"What about just for a second?" Evannah interrupted. "If you took away his powers for only a second, I could try freezing him in place and Kiera, you would need to... well, end it."

Aaron thought about this. "Maybe one second would be possible," he responded shakily. "If I try."

Kiera swallowed. Even though the thought of killing someone like that made her feel cold inside, she steeled herself and tried to put on a determined mask. "I... I can do it." Her voice broke off, but she forced the words out—for the sake of the Isle. "Aaron, did you find out exactly when he was going to reach full power?"

Aaron shook his head. "I only know that it's by the end of today."

"I think they hold the fight for now." Kiera glanced at the rioting animals and fierce Island fighters. "But not for long." And although she could be imagining it, there was a faint metallic scent in the air. The smell of spilled blood.

"It's nearly dusk," Aaron added.

"So we're almost out of time," Evannah cut in urgently.

"So we have a plan?" Kiera asked. "The battle's taken away a lot of his protection, so—"

"Now or never," Aaron finished. "The animals are tearing down his defenses."

"He's distracted," Kiera added. She took a long breath as her stomach began to flutter. "So I guess that means it has to be *right now*." She mounted Moss once more.

"Good luck," Evannah said solemnly.

Kiera looked back at them. "I'll see you soon," she replied, hoping that it would be true. She swung Moss's antlers, and he began to gallop away.

Despite the uproarious din of the fight, the only thing she could hear that moment was the pounding of blood in her ears. This was it. Either the Watcher's final moments, or her own. The meaning of "do or die" was never as clear.

As she rode, a pack of the same dark wolves that had killed Tovan gathered in front of her, hungry. "Get away from me!" she shouted, but they just moved closer.

Then a huge dark shape landed between the wolves and Kiera. "Go!" a familiar voice urged.

"Night Star?" Kiera asked incredulously. "But you died!"

The panther winked. "Don't you know that cats have nine lives? Now, go on!"

Riding Moss allowed her to get through the crowds quickly, as the fighters jumped out of the way when they saw the huge wolf charging. Soon, they had reached the other side of the lake, where the Watcher was floating, watching the fight. He narrowed his eyes angrily whenever the animals brought down a member of his army, and occasionally used his powers to assist his fighters. He even seemed a little agitated. And his gaze never left the battle. He *was* distracted after all.

Kiera used the opportunity to steer Moss away from the lake, and cut through the forested area instead. They took a wide loop until they reached a cluster of boulders behind the Watcher. Kiera dismounted and looked Moss in the eye. "Hey, Moss," she told him. "I have to leave now to... do something important. So you have to go now. But I'll be back okay? And if I don't come back... maybe come get me? Otherwise, go straight back to Evannah and Aaron." Moss whimpered and nudged her arm with his big head. "I know buddy. But I have to. Bye."

It was clear Moss didn't want to leave her. Kiera had to give him a little shove and he ran off, wounded. But she wasn't going to bring anyone else into this, not even an animal.

As she crouched down, she felt something hard in her pocket. She fished it out. Seriously? The court pin had survived this long? As soon as her fingers brushed the object she knew what she had to do.

She pulled her arm back, and she chucked it as far as it could go. The court pin flew into the trees and was never seen again. It was all so clear now. Neomerica hadn't been her home. *This* was where she belonged, with people who loved her for who she was, and an island she would do anything for.

Kiera hadn't needed to wait for acceptance, not from the court, not from her family. She had found a family a long time ago, in Evannah and Aaron, even if she hadn't realized it at first, and now it had been extended to Khalisse, Jannary, Neyric, and so many others. Her home, the place she belonged, was here. She had found it, at last.

Even in the midst of a war, even before their final plan that might go horribly wrong, even while crouched behind the Watcher alone, Kiera didn't feel lonely. If these were her final moments, she would face it with her family. With the people and the place she loved.

Then she caught sight of Aaron running into the midst of the battle, and began to move closer to the Watcher. She would only have a moment. "It's time," she murmured to herself, getting her sword ready.

The tiny figure of Aaron threw his hands up, and for a second, everything went silent. Shadows froze in place, leaving confused villagers reeling. Dark creatures paused their attacks and looked at each other uncertainly. The Watcher held up his hands as a dark look crossed his face, ready to overpower Aaron and fix the problem.

Then the angry expression froze on his face as he stopped moving. His eyes were still and he hovered silently in the air. Evannah had succeeded in freezing him after all!

Without hesitation, Kiera ran, leapt, and aimed the sword at the Watcher's stomach. She had one moment of regret a second before the sword would have plunged into his chest, that the Watcher had turned her into a murderer. His vibrant green eyes stared off into space. He would not see anything else for the rest of time. Kiera would make sure of it.

The sword was barely a hair's length away from his skin. It was over.

Then the green eyes flicked back to life.

The battle erupted again in a riotous blur of color and motion as the sword went flying away from the Watcher's body, light as a toy, and Kiera began to fall back to the ground. The Watcher let out a laugh. "Did you actually think you could overpower me?"

He gestured with his hand, and Kiera's limbs went numb. She shot into the sky next to him and floated limply on her back, suspended by the Watcher's magic. She couldn't move any part of her body. Her heart dropped, pulse hammering. It was a horrible kind of helplessness, knowing she was seconds from death but unable to do anything about it.

The Watcher smiled, and as the light hit his face, he looked inhuman, close to deranged. Wild. "Let's see what happens to those who defy me."

They had failed. Aaron had actually managed to bind the Watcher's powers, Evannah's spell had succeeded, Kiera's sword had been an inch away from the Watcher, but they had failed.

Perhaps it was true. There was no way to beat the Watcher. He would win, every time. And now he had Kiera.

It had shocked Aaron as he was running through the battlefield. The deaths. Familiar faces, covered in blood, lying lifeless on the ground.

Liora, the bright young storyteller. She would never tell another tale.

Thalen, the jolly village guard, eyes forever open, staring off into nothingness. There had been deep claw marks across his chest.

Orrin, pale and blood-covered, but looking peaceful in death. He had joined Marra wherever she had gone. Reunited at last.

Then there was Tovan, Kiera's mentor. But the loss that hit Aaron the hardest was when he saw a scarred figure lying beside the lake. Ravel. In the short time Aaron had known the older man, he had made an impression as wise and brave. It was clear that Ravel had cared deeply about his people. And now Silverspire had lost its loyal leader forever.

Each loss, each recognizable body broke Aaron a little, until all that was left was a deep chasm of emptiness inside him.

"This is your Wanderer," the Watcher announced. Kiera floated beside him, limp as a rag doll, and Aaron's heart clutched. "She believes that she is saving the Isle. These are *lies*," he roared. His face twisted into a snarl. "I am the only one who can protect us now. I am the one who spent all these years looking for a solution, so that we could live the rest of our lives in peace." He gave Kiera a small smirk. "Goodbye, Wanderer."

Then Kiera's limbs began to shake, and her eyes widened in horror and pain. She screamed, a horrible, bloodcurling sound, full of agony. "NO!" Aaron cried. The din had quieted down to listen to the Watcher, so his voice was heard. "Leave her alone!"

"Oh, Warrior," the Watcher cooed. "Would you like to join?" And suddenly Aaron wasn't controlling his own body anymore, he was floating up to the Watcher, unable to move, lying on his back. Kiera's screams abruptly stopped as her eyes rolled back in her head and she fainted from the pain. She dropped back to the ground and landed hard in a crumpled heap.

The Watcher flicked his hand, and Aaron was knocked out of the sky, crashing beside her. He shook Kiera until her eyes fluttered open. "Come on," he whispered, taking her hand. They both stood up.

"Where are you going?" the Watcher asked threateningly. There was a blast and Aaron and Kiera were knocked back to the ground again. Aaron raised his head weakly, and was blasted back down again. "Stay down!"

They lay in a heap on the ground, too weak to move. "I wouldn't want you to miss this," the Watcher continued. "The last bit of life in the Island will soon be mine... and we will be safe forever. Watch," he commanded the people and creatures.

Then the trembling began. The ground quivered as the Watcher took a deep, satisfied breath. Cracks in the ground opened up, and streaks of color, blue and green and black and golden rose up from the earth and traveled to his hands. The life of the Isle. It was all going to him.

The Watcher seemed to glow as the power continued flowing. His green eyes grew even more vibrant as his vines shifted victoriously. As Guardians tried to attack him, he easily blasted them away.

Khalisse sprinted over to Aaron and Kiera to try to help them up, but the Watcher shot her down without even looking in her direction, and she collapsed to the ground as well. "You can't do this!" Aaron cried, trying one last time. "Don't you see that you're killing the Island?"

"If the Isle must suffer now so it never suffers again," the Watcher declared, "that is a mercy I'm willing to give."

And the last streaks of color, of life, flew into his hands. "The Isle chose me long ago. I am not its demise. I am its deliverance."

The trembling grew stronger as trees began to fall, and chasms grew deeper and started to eat the destroyed land. Further away, the edges of the Island crumbled into the ocean as the Isle fell.

It was over.

"STOP!" cried an angry voice. The Watcher gazed in a furious Evannah's direction. Her eyes were wide and angry as her chest heaved.

Evannah strode up to the Watcher and looked him in the eye. "Take all the power you want," she began calmly, then her voice rose to a shout. "But you'll *never* own the Isle. Not while we still stand!"

Then Evannah raised her arms in a beckoning gesture, as if she were calling someone for an embrace. The fighting Whispers turned in her direction, and swarmed toward her.

As the Whispers got near, they brushed Evannah's skin, and the second they did, they disappeared, as though they had somehow been absorbed by Evannah.

"What is she doing?" Kiera asked, alarmed.

The Whispers continued to sink into Evannah, and with every Whisper she took, the veins in her body began to glow in lines of gold and silver and blue. Her eyes lit up with a golden glow and she didn't look human anymore. She was pure power, energy personified.

Then Evannah rose up into the air, radiating light and power, colorful energy swirling around her hands and body. She was getting so bright that Aaron had to look away.

"No..." Khalisse murmured. "It's the Whisperer's final attack."

"Final? Evannah, stop!" Aaron yelled desperately, but the Watcher just blasted him again. He groaned, head throbbing painfully.

Now, Evannah was face-to-face with the Watcher. "You wanted power," she snarled. "So here it is."

Then she raised her arms, and light began blasting out of her hands and body toward the Watcher. Aaron could see indistinct shapes of Whispers swirling around the both of them, as Evannah struck the Watcher with all of her strength. The Watcher's protection spell was quickly failing, and as he repeatedly tried to reinforce it, it was penetrated rapidly.

There was a final blast of light that rippled across the battle-field, and the crowd had to shield their eyes. Both the Watcher and Evannah were thrown backwards through the air and landed, unmoving.

There was silence. Nothing had changed. The Isle was still crumbling.

A brave warrior went to examine the still Watcher closer. "He's alive!" she called. "But barely."

Aaron immediately scrambled up and bolted toward Evannah. Kiera followed, and they both collapsed at her side.

Evannah's eyes were closed, her skin pale and cold, her chest unmoving. Aaron put his ear to her chest. "I don't hear anything," he whispered in horror.

Kiera picked up Evannah's wrist to listen for a pulse. "Nothing," she murmured, her lashes wet with tears.

Aaron shook Evannah's shoulders. "Come on, wake up!" he muttered, just as he had when she had drowned. But she had woken up then, and now she wasn't responding. Aaron looked up, feeling chilled, and met Kiera's wet eyes. She nodded, hesitantly but solemnly.

The emptiness that Aaron had felt returned tenfold, a hundredfold. He wanted to disappear, to fall forever. His sister was gone, forever this time. There would be no waking up from this dream, no Evannah rising and breathing again.

The prophecy had come true after all. Evannah was dead.

Chapter 27

Something hurt—then nothing did at all. Evannah was float-ing, or at least that was what it felt like. Her eyes were closed, she couldn't see around her. She felt at peace.

"Evannah," a voice echoed, sounding fuzzy and distant. "Evan-nah, it's time to wake up. Open your eyes."

She obliged, and found herself lying in a blank white space. It was almost like a gigantic hall. The ceiling was so tall that it arched out of sight.

On one end, the wall was etched with symbols of mountains and the ocean that almost looked like the Island. On the other end of the hall, mysterious and seemingly random patterns that looked like clouds covered the wall.

But who had been talking to her?

"Hello, Evannah." She looked up to find out that it had been a man, young-looking, with kind eyes and dark blue robes that shifted slightly even though there was no wind. There were soft whispers around him. "Do you know who I am?"

Evannah blinked several times to clear the fuzziness from her head. The answer jumped into her mind instinctively. "The first Whisperer." The name felt ancient, legendary.

The man nodded. "Correct. My name is Asharin, and I was the first Whisperer."

Suddenly, the memories of the last few moments flew into Evannah's mind, and she pushed herself to her feet immediately, stumbling. "I left Kiera and Aaron! And the Watcher, is he..."

Asharin hesitated. "Not quite. The one you call the Watcher has become very weak, but he lives."

"*What?*" Evannah exclaimed. "I gave up my life to take him with me." In the moments after their plan had failed, she had known what she had to do. Make the same choice that her mother had. She paused. "Is this life after death?"

Asharin shook his head. "You are not there yet. *That* is where you came from," he pointed to the wall with the mountain symbols. "That is where you will go." He gestured to the door with the cloud symbols.

"So I'm really dead," Evannah confirmed, feeling cold, her voice small in the vast emptiness. It wasn't as terrifying as she had imagined, but it made her ache to think of what Aaron and Kiera were going through.

"Yes," Asharin said apologetically. "And I wish I could send you back. The Island needs help. But that is not in my power. It is up to your friends now."

"Is there a reason you're not sending me through there?" Evannah pointed at the wall with cloud patterns. "Isn't that where I should be now?"

"I wanted to talk first," Asharin explained. "I don't meet every Whisperer who comes through that door, but I came to you.

Come, I will show you someone who has been waiting for a long time." He took her hand and began leading her forward.

As they walked, the hall seemed to extend. They were moving, but not really going anywhere. The walls stayed the same distance away. "You have been tremendously courageous," Asharin told her. "Braver than perhaps any Whisperer I have ever known. The Whisperer's final attack... where did you learn that?"

"I read it," Evannah said quietly. "In one of the Fenlithrian books."

"Ah," Asharin gave a little laugh. "Quite brilliant. Have you heard my story, Evannah?"

"Yes. You visited the Pool of Glass for one hundred days, even when you were dying. You returned as the first Whisperer."

"What I saw on the Trail of Truth changed my life," Asharin explained poignantally. "As I reached the end, many Whispers appeared in front of me. They healed me, and gave me a message. The Island had decided to grant me the ability to connect with its most powerful, elusive inhabitants. The Whispers connect with the people, who connect to the wilderness of the Island, who return to the life of the Island when they pass on. It's a cycle. The Island was fully connected at last, and the people were empowered."

Asharin paused for a moment, then said in a voice full of emotion and weight, "At the end of everything, Evannah, the only truth is this: life and death are merely two breaths of the same Isle."

"You heard voices," Evannah murmured.

"I thought I was going insane," Asharin smiled faintly. "You heard the same voices. Every other Whisperer has had someone to guide them, except us. We... we didn't have anyone who understood."

They walked in silence for a few moments, then Asharin remarked, "Ah, there she is."

And standing there, familiar in her soft brown eyes, bronze skin and dark hair, was Aalliah. "My daughter," she breathed, holding out her hands.

Evannah froze. No, no, this couldn't be possible.

Then she ran toward, and was wrapped up in a warm embrace. She couldn't move, it wasn't real. She breathed in Aalliah's sweet scent of tropical flowers. "Mother," she whispered.

Aalliah took a step back, hands on Evannah's shoulders, and looked into her eyes. "I've been waiting here for many years, more than I can remember."

"Are you real?" Evannah asked, trying to memorize every inch of her mother's face, to sear it in her memory forever.

"Yes," Aalliah smiled. "My body returned to the Isle long ago, but my spirit lives. I must take my brother home with me."

"And me?" Evannah questioned.

Aalliah sighed. "You're so young... I wish it didn't have to end like this. It depends on the living now." Her eyes became glassy. "Evannah, the Island needs you. Like Asharin, your distant ancestor, you will be the first Whisperer again. The Isle waits for you. It always has."

She took Evannah's hand. "I'm so proud of you, my child. You faced what destroyed Naharan, and you chose differently."

"Power doesn't shape who we are, Evannah," Asharin told her. "Fate doesn't shape who we are. It is our actions and choices that reveal your true self. How you lived, and what you were willing to die for."

Evannah thought about this for a moment. Aaron had thought the same thing, but the prophecy had come true. She had died. Although, Asharin was right. The prophecy couldn't control what kind of person she was. It was a balance between power and control, fate and choice.

"We unlocked your journal," Evannah told Aalliah eventually. "I heard your message."

Aalliah squeezed Evannah's hand. "I'm glad. You deserved an explanation, and I needed closure. I wrote down many things in that journal before I left my final message. Spells, notes, and the like." She sighed. "Naharan and I wrote most entries together. Oh, how did we end up like this? I wish I knew what I could have changed. I would never wish death on my own twin, but the Isle is nearly destroyed."

Evannah stood for a minute, pressed against her mother's side, with Aalliah's arm wrapped around her, in a way that she had only dreamed of.

At once, both Aalliah and Asharin looked off into the distance at the same time, as if watching something that Evannah couldn't see. "I was waiting to guide you home," Aalliah started eventually.

Asharin jumped in to finish. "But the Isle is not finished with you quite yet."

Chapter 28

The Island's inhabitants were silent in mourning. Their Whisperer had fallen.

One shall fall.

The Watcher lived.

One shall fade. One shall see the darkness slayed.

But Evannah was dead.

Kiera and Aaron were huddled together, over Evannah's body. It was like Kiera was falling down into one of the Watcher's chasms, where darkness and loneliness engulfed her. Her best friend was gone. It was her fault, if only she'd been a second quicker with her sword.

She rested her head on Aaron's shoulder, who was shaking with sobs. She felt too heavy and was too exhausted to move.

"I'm sorry," Khalisse murmured, eyes wet with tears. Kiera couldn't bring herself to respond.

The life of the Island was nearly gone as well. All that remained was a weak pulse, a mere echo of the thriving life it used to have.

Wait a minute. The life of the Island...

Kiera sat up immediately. "Aaron," she implored, "I need help. But we have to do this quickly."

Aaron looked at her with a heartbreakingly hopeful voice. "What?"

"You need to bind Evannah's powers," Kiera explained urgently.

"*Evannah's*?" Aaron asked, taken aback. "You mean the Watcher's?"

"No." Kiera shook her head. "Evannah's."

Aaron looked startled, but nodded, not asking any more questions. He wrapped his fingers around Evannah's wrist and closed his eyes.

Almost immediately, Whispers began detaching themselves from Evannah and melting out of her skin, gliding away and disappearing from sight. "Oh!" Aaron breathed. "The Whispers are leaving her."

Yes, this was what Kiera had hoped for. Evannah had died because her final attack had been too strong, because the energy of so many Whispers had taken its toll. Now, there might be the tiniest bit of hope.

She took one of Evannah's hands, and placed the other on the ground, closing her eyes and *feeling* the life of the Island as Tovan had taught her. It was barely there, but some still existed.

Come on, Isle of Whispers, she pleaded. Evannah died for you. Can't you give her the tiniest bit of your own life?

For a few seconds, nothing happened. Then Kiera felt a tingling sensation in her fingertips that slowly spread up her arm, through her body, and to the hand that was gripping Evannah. And as it passed through her, Kiera felt what the Island felt, saw how ancient it was, how it was the foundation of everything. Old legends and stories passed before her eyes, too quickly to make sense of it. She was connected to something much bigger than herself. Then the feeling disappeared.

Kiera dropped Evannah's hand. Had it worked?

Aaron gasped and also dropped his hold on Evannah's hand. "She's moving!" he cried. Evannah was shifting, ever so slightly, until her eyes finally flew open.

Kiera and Aaron both tackled her at the same time. "Am... am I back?" Evannah asked softly.

"You *died*," Aaron exclaimed, tears streaming down his face. "Where were you?"

Evannah shook her head solemnly. They were interrupted by a cry of, "He's up!"

The Watcher pushed himself to his feet, blazing with fury. "That should be an example," he snarled. "I tried to tell you many times. It's *too late*. You can't kill what has already conquered you."

The memory of what she had seen during her death lingered in Evannah's mind. And she understood. Everything Aalliah and Asharin told her... it was about balance. The imbalance between power and control was what had created the Watcher. Whisperers maintained balance between the worlds. Life and death weren't two separate paths—they were the way the Island kept balance. And the Watcher had destroyed the balance, the harmony of the Island.

Evannah glanced at Aaron to her left and Kiera to her right. Aaron, the Warrior, represented the people of the Island. Kiera, the Wanderer, represented the wilderness. And Evannah, Whisperer, stood for the Whispers of the Island.

Together, they brought balance. It had always been so. She had just needed to die to see it.

"You broke the Isle when you broke the balance," Evannah told the Watcher fiercely, standing up. "But we are its balance: the people, the wilderness, and the Whispers. And together... we will end this. You forgot the Island's truth, Naharan. But we didn't."

Then she took Aaron and Kiera's hands in hers, and she felt it.

The connection, the different parts of the Isle snapping together into one.

This was the power they needed. It surged within her, as if the Isle itself had awakened in her veins, ancient and overwhelming.

For the first time, she was *complete*.

The Watcher's eyes narrowed. "No," he hissed. "It can't be."

The power exploded out of Evannah, and they slowly rose into the air as a vibrating ray of light shot out toward the Watcher, and within the light, life and death, destruction and creation. Every part of the balanced Island. Their unity, and their choice, would be strength.

The Watcher frantically created a shield that the beam easily passed through. In the heartbeat before it slammed into him, his eyes widened in shock and realization. Perhaps there was a moment of awareness, or even remorse there. A flicker of something crossed his face. Fear? Regret? Understanding.

He knew exactly why he was losing.

Time paused. The light swelled. Then there was a blast. The Watcher screamed as he was thrown backwards, shards of light penetrating his body.

Evannah, Aaron, and Kiera, lightly landed on the ground.

Suddenly, Evannah was back in the large white hall. A man stood a little ways off, nearly identical to an older version of Aaron, eyes returned to a normal brown.

"Naharan," Aalliah murmured. "I've been waiting."

"Aalliah," Naharan breathed. "What have I done? Will they even let me through the door?"

"I don't know," said Aalliah remorsefully. "But I will try my best to bring you with me. You don't belong here Evannah." She smiled. "I will see you much later." Then she took Naharan's hand, and the two of them walked into the distance as the white hall dissolved around them.

The moment the Watcher hit the ground, something changed. A shift in the air, perhaps. Upon impact, the Watcher's body started crumbling, until it dissolved into the ground upon which it had laid. The earth drank him in with a shuddering sigh. The life he had stolen had returned to the Island.

There was a minute of silence, while people stared and processed what they had seen. The Watcher was gone, returned to the Island he had stolen from.

Then Aaron was surrounded by cheers and shrieks of joy, and the warm feeling of thousands of bodies pressing in to congratulate him.

Kiera leaned in for a kiss, and every part of him melted as the crowd cheered for them. "We did it!" she cried.

"Look!" Evannah commanded.

The Island was rumbling again, but this time, the chasms in the ground sealed themselves up. The stones of the fallen mountains rolled and reconstructed again until the peaks stood as tall and proud as before.

"The Island is recovering," Kiera breathed. It was rebuilding, alive once more.

New life sprung up around them, green shoots and saplings where there had been stretches of withered, dead trees. The blackened Heart Falls and Crystal River brightened until they were a shining clear color once more.

"*Evannah. Kiera. Aaron.*" The soft voices seemed to echo all around them.

"Who is that?" Kiera wondered.

"I think it's the Island," Aaron smiled. "*If the wild they dare to claim, the isle shall whisper their true name.* We reclaimed the wild by saving the Island."

"And now the Isle whispers our name," Evannah finished.

The Shadows melted into light and disappeared from view. They were fallen Whispers, Aaron remembered. It seemed they had become Whispers once more. The dark creatures slowly returned to normal form, and trotted into the forests.

They stood there for a moment, taking in the newly thriving Island, the celebrating people, the joyful Guardians.

And at last, the Isle was whole again.

Epilogue

"Wait!" Evannah called, running through the crunchy wet sand. "You forgot half your food storage!" She stepped into the gently lapping ocean to hand Kiera the large basket.

"Oh whoops!" Kiera laughed. "It would have been pretty bad if I'd forgotten that. Thanks!" She turned over her shoulder. "Aaron! Where do these go?"

Aaron was zealously attaching two smaller canoes to the side of the larger boat. There would be no shipwrecks this time, he had told Evannah. "To the left in the storage!" he called back.

"You'll take care of Moss, right?" Kiera asked Evannah for the sixth time.

Evannah sighed. "Yes, of course I will! Where's Night Star? I thought he was going to see you off. Night Star? *Night Star?*" she finished incredulously. The huge panther was lying on the sand, bending his head to lick the fur of Moss, back in puppy form, who was happily squashed between Night Star's paws, enjoying the grooming.

Night Star jumped up. "Um," he cleared his throat gruffly. "There was something on his—I mean *its* pelt."

"Cats and dogs *can* get along," Kiera joked. "Aww, Night Star, I knew you were a big sweetie." The cat scowled.

"Hey!" a voice called. Khalisse strode out of the forest, followed by Jannary and Neyric. "Oh, good, you're still here. I thought we'd missed it!"

"Wow, a whole send-off party?" Aaron asked. He finally strapped the canoe to the boat. "Aha!" There was a creaking, and it fell off. "Oh no."

"Just leave the canoes, Aaron!" Kiera scolded. "They'll add too much weight. You can swim anyway!"

Aaron reluctantly pushed the canoes back to the beach. "Fine."

"How was Silverspire?" Evannah asked Khalisse. It had been a week since the battle, and Khalisse had been in Silverspire, helping settle things after the death of Ravel, their leader.

"Fine," Khalisse responded. "Getting better. They just picked a new Everdawn."

"Oh good." Evannah turned to Neyric. "And Vahari?"

"Still recovering, of course," Neyric answered. "But things are looking much better. After I make sure everything is taken care of, I think I'll spend a little while in Fenlithra." He squeezed Jannary's hand and she smiled.

"You got the weapons?" Khalisse double-checked.

Kiera shot her a thumbs-up. "All packed. Although I hope we won't need them in Neomerica."

"Just in case Father doesn't let us come back home," Aaron joked, but behind the joke lingered a look that said *we are the Warrior and Wanderer now. The court has no power over us. And* somewhere in the past few days, the Island had started to get referred to as *home.*

Which was why, without even discussing, the trio had unanimously agreed to stay on the Island.

Kiera and Aaron had decided to sail back to Neomerica to meet their parents one last time, explain things, and tie up some loose ends. They would tell a simplified version of the truth—that they had discovered an island that they'd like to live on, and they would be staying there. Some secrets deserved to be kept, and they had decided to protect the Island's secrets for the rest of their lives.

And if the court didn't let them come back or tried to send others with them, well, they always had their weapons. Whether Lord Cyrus deemed them "worthy" or not felt irrelevant after they had already chosen their places in life.

As for Evannah, she had already had her last say with Lord Cyrus in Neomerica. Someone needed to stay on the Island, to help them rebuild and recover. The people needed a Whisperer, after all. And Kiera and Aaron could use some time together.

Then when they returned, they would resume their roles on the Isle. Aaron would take his place among the leaders and warriors, not as an outsider this time, but as one of the Isle's people, mending and unifying the villages. Kiera would continue doing what she did best: exploring the Island and bridging the gap between the people and the wilderness, ensuring they thrived together.

"Last chance," Aaron warned Evannah. "Are you sure you don't want to come?"

"No, that's okay," Evannah answered. "I think they'll need me here."

"Have you decided where you're going to stay?" Khalisse asked. "A Whisperer needs a good home base. There's always the Watcher's old lair on Watcher Peak, once we clean it out."

Evannah shook her head quickly. "Oh, no, I don't think I could stay there."

"Understandable," Khalisse responded. "Well, you know, your mother and uncle, when they were sort-of leaders of the Isle, had a nice house built in the forest between the villages. Nobody lives there now. I can show you the way."

"Hmm." Evannah thought about that for a moment. "I think I'd quite like that."

Meanwhile, Aaron and Kiera had both boarded their boat. "What about Janessa?" Kiera murmured to Aaron.

Aaron put a hand around her shoulder. "Lady Janessa can find someone else to marry. I'm taken." Kiera shoved his arm off her shoulder with a laugh.

"You did the boat already, right Evannah?" Aaron checked.

Evannah sighed. Aaron would continue worrying until well after the boat set sail. "Yup, all finished." In Aalliah's journal, she had found a speed spell that she had cast on the boat to accelerate the journey a bit, hopefully from multiple weeks into one.

"I think we're ready, Aaron," Kiera observed. "If we don't leave now, you'll think of a hundred more things we need to do."

"But—all right," Aaron relented. He headed to the front of the boat to take the wheel.

"Bye!" Evannah cried, waving. Kiera waved back madly, the wind whipping her hair as the ocean carried them further and further away, until the boat became a tiny dot among the waves. The thick mist that had once suffocated the Isle had lightened into thin clouds of silvery-white, obscuring the Isle of Whispers from outside view.

Night Star, who had flown above the boat to ensure a safe start, now landed back on the beach. "They're gone," he rumbled, and Evannah was sure she could sense the tiniest bit of sadness in his voice.

Evannah let out a breath. "They'll be all right." Maybe *if the wild they dare to claim* had referred to choosing the Isle as their true home.

In the moments of silence, where the only sounds that could be heard were the rustling of leaves in the jungle and the swishing of waves, Evannah closed her eyes to listen, and smiled.

From the wind, faint and gentle, echoed a voice only she could hear.

Welcome home.

Acknowledgements

A word of thanks to everyone who made this book a possibility. I can't believe I actually managed to write a full-length novel after years of writing stories that I never finished.

First and foremost, I have to thank my family. Thank you to my mom and dad, Rachna and Karthik, for always supporting and encouraging me, and to my sister Sama for all your unwanted advice. I enjoyed our late-night talkathons about our stories and all the times we would write together when we were supposed to be doing something else.

A shout-out to all my friends. You always make my day brighter in so many ways: distracting me in chemistry class so I could write instead, playing heated rounds of Monopoly, eating lunch and carpooling with me, and even giving me plot ideas. I think I ended up promising at least three of you that you would be the first to read the book so I will just send it to everyone at the same time!

I am grateful to all my teachers, who guided me and equipped me with the necessary skills to write this book. This wouldn't have been possible without you.

Finally, to my readers, I hope you enjoyed reading! Be on the lookout; I hope this is just the first of many future books.

Sincerely,

Veda Raman, Author

About The Author

Veda Raman is a sixteen-year-old currently in tenth grade in the Bay Area, California. When she is not writing, she can be found reading or spending time with her dog Obi, her cat Fireheart, or her crew of foster kittens. She loves animals, traveling, and music. *The Isle of Whispers* is her debut novel.